BEFORE
THE
STORM

Praise for Leslie Tentler and Her Novels

"Taut, page-turning suspense and heart-stopping romance: Leslie Tentler is a rising star of romantic suspense."
- New York Times Bestselling Author
Allison Brennan

"A smooth prose style and an authentic Big Easy vibe distinguish Tentler's debut...the shivers are worthy of a Lisa Jackson."
- Publishers Weekly on *Midnight Caller*

"Suspenseful, intense and impossible to put down, Midnight Fear will thrill and seduce, as it leaves the reader begging for more."
- Examiner.com

"A compelling plot, thick suspense, a cunning villain, a shattered cop and a victim who wants answers at any cost place Tentler in the same category as bestselling authors Lisa Jackson and Beverly Barton."
- RT Book Reviews on
Edge of Midnight

"Fallen is a fast paced, energetic novel, full of suspense and action...A great read."
- Fresh Fiction

BEFORE
THE
STORM

a rarity cove novel

LESLIE TENTLER

To my brother, Michael. This one is for you.

PROLOGUE

Memphis, Tennessee

"YOU REALLY THOUGHT I'd let you leave here?" Devin Leary's harsh laughter echoed through the spacious loft apartment. "I didn't just fall off the turnip truck, darlin'."

Despite the air conditioning's chill, Trina Grissom felt a bead of perspiration roll down her back. She worked to keep her words even. "I-I was planning to talk to you, I *swear*."

With a cynical grunt, he roved through her open suitcase on the bed, extracting a pair of delicate panties from the hastily packed clothing. Trina glanced away, training her gaze on the hardwood floor as he lifted the lace to his nose and inhaled. "Talk, nothin'. You were gonna run out on me."

He loomed suddenly closer, and she found herself staring up into cold, dark eyes. A lock of longish, midnight hair fell into them. *Stay calm*, Trina implored herself. She knew all too well Devin got off on fear.

"Look, I can pay you! I've got some money saved up—"

"Now you want to *buy* your way free of me? That hurts." He placed a hand over his chest in feigned grief. His eyes narrowed. "I don't want your damn money, Trina."

"Twelve thousand dollars! I've been saving up tips minus cuts to the house. You can have all of it if you just—"

"Stupid bitch. You got any idea how much you're worth to me? You leave, it's like stealin' money right out of my pocket." His tone lowered and grew huskier, a threat wrapped in black velvet. "Besides, this thing between us goes back a long way…"

Her heart hammered as his fingers skimmed lazily over her upper arms, then bit punishingly into her flesh. Dread nearly choked her. He smoothed her platinum-blond hair back from her face as his hot breath played over her skin. Trina suppressed a whimper. She shouldn't have come back here to retrieve her things, but sentimentality—and the desperate need for money—had been too large a temptation. Besides, Devin was always at the club this time of night. She'd even called to check. How had he known? It had to be Cassandra. Trina had been a fool to trust her.

"Where you been hidin' these past few weeks, sugar? I figure with the nights you haven't shown up for work, you owe me most of that cash you're goin' on about, anyway. I've had men out all over town, lookin' for you. That cost me money."

"I'm sorry—"

"Sorry don't buy much," he snapped. Pushing her aside like a discarded toy, he began pawing again through her suitcase. With a snide shake of his head, he yanked out her mother's cameo locket and the worn teddy bear, tossing them onto the bed. He began pulling out her clothing next. Trina took a step forward, her hands clenched into fists at her sides. Behind him, floor-to-ceiling windows displayed the glittering Memphis cityscape.

Please, no. Hope leached from her as Devin jammed his

fingers into a side panel and discovered the thick stack of bills. Victoriously, he stuffed the wad into the pocket of his leather jacket. It was everything she had.

"If you take that money, I-I get to leave." Trembling, Trina tried to hang on to her control, fragile as it was. "And you don't try to find me."

"That's the deal?"

She swallowed with difficulty and found her voice. "Yes."

He gave another sharp laugh, his eyes glinting like knife blades. Trina flinched as he grabbed her again, this time shoving her back against the exposed-brick wall. She cried out as her skull met it with a sickening thud. Devin had the smile of a snake, and his lean, hard frame appeared ready to strike. Trina already knew the full extent of his bite. His poison.

She felt dizzy, ice-cold terror curling around her spine. Breathing in shallow gasps, she struggled to get away, but his right hand had closed around her throat, anchoring her in place. His other arm braced against the wall over her head.

"Know what I think?" Devin towered over her, his body pressing into hers. Lust and rage contorted his brutally handsome features. "I think you need to be taught a lesson."

CHAPTER ONE

Rarity Cove, South Carolina
Six Years Later

"EMILY?" MARK ST. Clair looked around crowded Main Street. *She had been right here,* watching as a clown with a painted face and red wig twisted balloons into barnyard animals.

He scanned the street vendors hawking pecan pralines and tourist souvenirs. But there was no sign of a blond, pigtailed almost-five-year-old. He had turned his back for what? Ten seconds? On the street in front of him, the parade continued. An open convertible rolled past, a smiling Miss Peach Blossom waving regally from its backseat. He tamped down a surge of panic.

"Mark St. Clair, as I live and breathe!" A heavyset woman wearing too much perfume stepped into his path. He recognized her as head of the Junior League. "Happy Founder's Day! I do believe your great-great-great-grandfather would be so proud of our little town."

"Thanks. Nice to see you, Mrs. Botwin."

"I was just at the hotel last weekend. Tell your chef the pork tenderloin was out of this world—"

"I'm glad to hear it." Mark smiled thinly, and with a polite excuse, he shouldered past, peering down the sidewalk for his daughter. As he searched, he tried not to think about the child-abduction stories that scared the *bejeesus* out of him, but he still couldn't keep his heart from racing. It was early August, the humidity high, and his Ralph Lauren sports shirt stuck to his back. In the balmy afternoon breeze, the cloying aroma of cotton candy mingled with the briny sea air.

Don't panic, he told himself. But if Emily...if anything happened to her...

He wouldn't survive another loss.

A break in the parade allowed him to catch a glimpse of the town square with its ancient live oaks and garlands of Spanish moss. A number of vendors had booths set up there, a banner overhead proclaiming *The Perfect Summer in Rarity Cove*.

Relief washed through him. Amid the throngs of people, he spotted a small red skirt and sandals, then flaxen pigtails reflecting sunlight. Emily stood at one of the cloth-covered tables. What had he told her about crossing the street? He waited until a squadron of Shriners from the Masonic Lodge marched past in their red fezzes, swords drawn, then went after her.

"Emily," he called, catching her attention. She turned, beaming as he approached, and Mark felt his anger evaporate. He knelt in front of her. "You scared me to death, sweetheart. You were supposed to be watching the clown make balloon animals. Didn't you want one?"

Instead, Emily pointed at the table, bouncing with excitement. An impressive assortment of pastries was enticingly arranged, and not of the Ladies Garden Club bake sale variety. Sophisticated tartlets held jewel-like curds, and an arrangement of buttery linzer cookies and shell-shaped madeleines filled a silver platter. Decadent lemon bars and rich cream puffs looked nearly too perfect to eat. But most notable were the cupcakes. Each was a work of art, with thick caps of buttercream frosting and edible flower decorations.

"I told her she could have one, but she needed to get her parents' permission first."

Mark looked up at the comment. A slender, dark-haired young woman in a sleeveless white blouse stood behind the table. Doe-like brown eyes complemented delicate features. She was attractive—beautiful, actually. As he stood, he caught a glimpse of her long, tanned legs in faded jean shorts.

"She doesn't say much, does she?" She smiled at Emily. "I asked her name, but she wouldn't tell me."

"She doesn't really…talk," Mark explained, his chest tightening. "Her name's Emily."

The woman nodded as a faint frown creased her forehead. "I see. Can she have a cupcake?"

"Sure. Which one do you want, baby?"

Emily pointed to a rich-looking confection, causing the young woman to laugh. "A girl after my own heart. That's the devil's food. It's chocolate-filled. The little purple flowers are lavender."

Mark noticed one with a deep red base and pristine white icing. A miniature rosebud sat on its top. Seeing that it had caught his attention, she said, "That's red velvet, of course. A Southern favorite."

"We'll take that one, too." Their eyes met briefly, until the woman lowered her thick lashes and busied herself with placing the two large cupcakes in a white cardboard box. She tied the package with a blue satin bow and presented it to Emily, who practically danced in delight.

Mark reached for his wallet. "How much?"

"No charge. I promised one to Emily."

"How about mine, then?"

"All right. That'll be three ninety-five."

He shook his head good-naturedly. "Four bucks? That must be one heck of a cupcake."

She grinned as he handed her the bills, his fingers briefly brushing hers in the process. Mark experienced a small thrill of attraction, followed nearly as quickly by a sharp stab of guilt that made it hard to breathe. His eyes fell to the printed sign in front of the table. Café Bella.

The place must be new; he'd never heard of it, and Mark could count the better restaurants in the small coastal town on one hand. He'd never seen the woman before, either. He realized that he should introduce himself, ask her name or at least the location of the eatery. But instead, he murmured a hoarse thank-you and took Emily's hand. They made their way across the street after several more parade floats sailed past.

Mark nearly choked on his hot coffee. "He's coming when?"

He'd been trying to get some paperwork done while he had a bite of food, but he now realized the hotel dining room probably wasn't the best location. The tall windows that provided a scenic view of the Atlantic Ocean also made him visible to anyone going past on the boardwalk. And this particular afternoon, that *anyone* was Olivia St. Clair. Spotting him, his mother had come inside and sat at his table, seemingly oblivious to his open laptop and stack of files.

"He'll be here next week," she said blithely, unfurling a sage linen napkin from the table and placing it on her lap. "They're filming a Lifetime movie in Charleston."

"And you're just now finding out about this?"

"Carter was a last-minute casting replacement." Olivia

requested a mimosa from one of the wait staff, then returned her clear blue eyes to her eldest son. "The first actor—the young man on that silly detective show—dropped out. The filming schedule fit perfectly with Carter's time off from the soap opera."

"He's not staying here, is he?"

"Why wouldn't he?" Brushing at a lock of hair in her well-maintained silver bob, Olivia shot him a look of censure. "He wants to be with family. The St. Clair belongs to him, too, you know."

"Why can't he just stay with you?"

"Well, he could. But the hotel has such fine amenities. He also needs wireless Internet, and you know I don't even own a computer." She made the latter admission with a note of pride. "He was adamant about taking a room here."

Mark rubbed his closed eyes with his fingers. "If Carter stays here, there's going to be a big to-do about it. We have *guests*, Mom. People who pay a lot of money for solitude and relaxation."

"Oh, pooh." She waved her hand in a Scarlett O'Hara-like gesture and took a sip from the crystal flute that had just been delivered. "You'll hardly know he's here. And we'll keep the reception very low-key."

"Reception?"

"Carter *is* Rarity Cove's only celebrity. He needs a proper welcome home. Of course, we *could* have the reception at the country club, but I'd prefer it here in the ballroom. So much more nostalgic to have it in our own hotel, don't you think? The place where he grew up."

Mark said nothing. Acting every bit the matriarch, Olivia leaned forward and covered his hand with her own. "For goodness sake, Mark. The two of you are brothers, not to mention grown men. You used to be so close. Can't you get along for a few days for your old Momma?"

He looked at her, slightly shocked to hear her refer to herself as *old*. Olivia's beauty in her youth was legendary, and even in her early sixties she was the picture of Southern grace and style. Mark released a breath and nodded. "Okay. Carter stays here, but he isn't getting the star treatment. He's a regular guest like anyone else."

"Of course, darling. He wouldn't want it any other way."

"And you can have the reception here, provided the ballroom is available. You'll have to check with Mercer on that."

"I already have, and it is." Olivia rose. She bent and kissed him on the cheek, probably leaving behind a stain of expensive coral lipstick. Then she located her designer handbag. "Now on to other things. I don't suppose you've thought some more about asking out Felicity Greene?"

"Don't push it, Mom."

Olivia ran her fingers through her son's hair, her voice softening. "She's interested, Mark. And she's quite a catch, in case you haven't noticed. Felicity was homecoming queen at the University of South Carolina, did you know that?"

"No."

"Well, she was. And it really *is* time you started living again." Her pretty, still-unlined face held concern. "If not for your sake, for Emily's. You're only thirty-three. You still have your whole life ahead of you."

When he failed to respond, she laid her hand on his shoulder, then tucked the handbag under her arm and exited the dining room, passing a young couple whom Mark knew to be on their honeymoon. He watched the man pull out a chair for his new wife, clearly doting on her. He couldn't help but think of how in love he and Shelley had been.

He'd been a widower for over two years now, and he supposed the passage of time had lessened his grief. At least made it less

9

raw. But Mark found himself grateful for the distraction of the sweeping antebellum-style hotel. It had fallen under his keeping when his father, Harrison, had died from a heart attack four years earlier on the seventeenth hole of the Rarity Cove Country Club golf course. Its management kept him more than occupied. The property the resort was on had been in his family for countless generations—first as a working Sea Island cotton plantation and then later, as a premier vacation destination on the Atlantic seacoast, some forty minutes outside of Charleston. The century-old hotel was built around the remains of the actual plantation home, the building a much larger replica of what had once stood there. The St. Clair was one of the few remaining independent toprated hotels in the Southeastern United States and was also on the National Register of Historic Places.

"Mom's trademark drink, I see. She must've come by to warn you about Carter."

Mark looked up as his sister slipped into the chair Olivia had vacated. Mercer St. Clair picked up the crystal flute and polished off the last of the champagne and orange juice. "Should we prepare for the paparazzi?"

"Soap actors have paparazzi?"

"If they don't, knowing Carter he'll go out and hire some."

Mercer's sardonic grin pulled Mark from his melancholy, and he was glad for her appearance. A graduate of the private Truesdale Women's College in Atlanta, she'd returned home and fallen into the role of marketing director at the St. Clair. Mercer was a blessing to him—not only because of her help with the family business, but also because she'd become something of a surrogate mother to Emily.

"Have you talked to Carter recently?" she asked.

"A few weeks ago. He was purchasing a penthouse apartment

in Manhattan and wanted the hotel to advance him part of the down payment." Knowing how he sounded, Mark added, "And I know—it's well within his rights. He *is* a co-owner, as Mom just reminded me. I gave him the money. But with the economy still recovering and renovations on the east wing, we haven't been nearly as profitable over the past year."

"I've seen the books. We're doing just fine. You worry too much, Mark."

"Maybe I have a lot to worry about."

She sighed in quiet acknowledgment, fiddling with the table's fine silverware. "So how did Emily's appointment with the new neurologist in Charleston go?"

"He basically said the same thing the others have. Physically, there's nothing wrong with her. We're starting with a new child therapist next week." He attempted a smile but couldn't quite pull it off, thinking back to when his daughter's voice had been a daily, welcome sound. A time before his wife had died. "This one works with puppets."

Mark saw sympathy reflected in Mercer's eyes. *It isn't your fault,* her gaze seemed to say. But most of the time, whose fault it was didn't really seem to matter. Shelley was gone, and his daughter's life had been profoundly altered because of it. He stared briefly at the crystal chandelier that hung from the dining room's high ceiling and grasped for a change of subject.

"Have you heard of a new restaurant in town?" he asked. "They had a booth at the Founder's Day celebration. It's called Café Bella."

"The eight-thousand-calorie cupcakes? Those created quite a buzz," Mercer commented. Although now curvaceously in shape, she'd had a bit of a weight problem in her teen years, something she now kept under control through diligent exercise and healthful eating. "I didn't have one, but I heard they taste like pure heaven."

"They do. I've got to admit they put the hotel pastries to shame."

"Café Bella's a great idea, if you ask me. Gourmet takeout aimed mostly at the daytime tourist crowd. The owner's a graduate of the New York Culinary Institute. Her name's Samantha Marsh." Mercer leaned forward and added conspiratorially, "She's new in town and a real looker, too. More than a few ladies had their claws out at the parade yesterday. Their husbands were making too many excuses to walk past the booth."

"Where's the place located?"

"Honestly, Mark. The hotel really does keep you busy." Pushing back her shoulder-length, honey-blond hair, Mercer opened her ever-present red leather organizer, which also held her smartphone. She handed him a business card for Café Bella. "It's been open for weeks now. Recognize the address?"

A member of the wait staff called her over, and she left the table. Mark stared at the card's elegant typeface and Café Bella logo in gold foil print. Sea Breeze Centre, Suite Three. The white brick building with wrought-iron accents was newly renovated and just a block off the Rarity Cove town square. It was also in the portfolio of commercial properties the St. Clair family owned.

Samantha Marsh—the woman with the *to-die-for* cupcakes and soft-brown eyes—was one of his tenants.

CHAPTER TWO

"I LOADED UP THE Hobart, Sam." Luther Banda wiped his large hands on his apron as he lumbered into the Café Bella storefront from the kitchen. "If it's all right, I'd like to get on over to the BI-LO now."

"Would you mind running by the farmer's market in Mount Pleasant, too?" Samantha walked to the butcher-block counter, retrieving a list of seasonal fruits and vegetables she'd put together, and handed it to him. "After you've dropped the groceries off, go ahead and call it a day."

"You sure? I mean, I don't mind—"

She waved off his protest. "I've already sent the rest of the lunch help home. We close at six today. I can manage by myself for the last few hours."

Luther cleared his throat and studied the floor. He was a hulking man in his late forties with rich cocoa skin, a shaved head and sad, timeworn features that looked as though he'd already lived several lifetimes. A faded vertical scar ran from just under his left eye down to his jaw. "I want you to know how much I appreciate the job, Sam."

She gave him a soft smile. Luther had been working with her for the last couple of months as she readied the café to open for business. "I should be thanking you, Luther. Getting this place up and running has been a challenge, and you're doing excellent work. Besides, who else other than you and me is willing to get here so early every morning to make red-skinned potato salad?"

"I *can* roast potatoes with the best of 'em." Grinning, he removed his apron and hung it on a peg behind the counter. Luther went out through the front door, nearly brushing shoulders with a customer entering at the same time. "Afternoon, Mr. St. Clair."

Samantha glanced up from where she knelt on the hardwood floor, placing jars of Café Bella pesto and olive tapenade on the shop's bottom shelves. Rising, she brushed off the knees of her jeans and was surprised to find herself face-to-face with the man from the Founder's Day parade last weekend. The man with the pretty little daughter who didn't speak. Luther had called him Mr. St. Clair, and Samantha only now realized who he must be.

St. Clair, as in the posh seaside resort on the other side of town. As in owner of this very building, among sundry other properties around Rarity Cove. In fact, the Founder's Day celebration had been in honor of Thaddeus St. Clair, the town's first mayor.

"I'm afraid we didn't meet formally the other day," he said. "I'm Mark St. Clair."

"You're my landlord. I recognize your name from the contract I signed at the Realtor's office."

He extended his hand to her. "You've been dealing with Jim Drummond, my commercial properties manager."

Mark St. Clair had soft-blue eyes and brown hair light enough that it neared a dark blond. He was even-featured and square-jawed, and he looked as comfortable in the crisp white button-down and khakis he wore now as the casual clothes she'd seen him in previously. He seemed rather young to be so successful, but Samantha figured his lineage had a lot to do with that.

Once he released her fingers, he placed his hands in his pockets and looked around. Samantha followed his gaze to the brick walls with shelving bearing Café Bella condiments and food gifts. A chest-high counter and refrigerated display case held cold salads and pre-made items and, of course, a variety of pastries and desserts. The place was small—only a half-dozen dining tables inside and a few more out on the sidewalk shaded by market umbrellas—but it was a good start. If she discounted the sizable bank loan and her rent payments for the building space, Café Bella was all hers. It had been a longtime dream.

"The structural changes are in accordance with the contract," Samantha assured him. "I have a copy of it in back, if we need to go over anything."

"Everything looks great, actually. It smells pretty good, too."

"Oh...I have a cheesecake in the convection oven."

Mark strolled to a display of bell-shaped jars filled with marinated peppers. Next to it, jars of preserved lemons bore the Café Bella logo. He picked up an elegant gift box of chocolate-dipped biscotti.

"I've contracted with a commercial food manufacturer in Greenville," Samantha told him. "Everything is made according to my recipes in small batches, and I go up there to supervise the preparation. Right now, I'm selling online and here in the store, but I hope to extend to upscale groceries and gift shops, eventually."

"My sister tells me you're a graduate of the New York Culinary Institute?"

Samantha nodded. She recalled meeting Mercer St. Clair at one of the Founder's Day events. She'd liked her immediately. "I worked at restaurants and bars in Manhattan while I was putting myself through cooking school, but decided to strike out on my own. I like doing things my way."

His eyes held curiosity. "And you chose Rarity Cove of all places?"

"New York's an expensive place to start a business, and I had fond memories about coming here once as a child," she admitted. "My mother brought me on vacation. It seemed so peaceful. It was the first time I saw the ocean."

"Did you stay at the St. Clair?"

Samantha shook her head, a bittersweet nostalgia filling her. "The St. Clair wasn't exactly in our budget. We stayed at a little fleabag motel a good six blocks from the water, but it was a wonderful time just the same. I remember burning my feet on the asphalt walking to the beach in the mornings. I searched for the place when I first moved to town, but I don't think it's here anymore."

Snapping herself from wistful memories, she asked, "So what can I do for you, Mr. St. Clair?"

"Please, call me Mark. My daughter's birthday is this Saturday. We're having a few of her playmates over, nothing lavish, and I was going to have the hotel chef make her a cake. But she got such a kick out of your cupcakes that I was thinking maybe I could order some?"

Samantha retrieved her notepad. "How many?"

"A dozen, maybe? Will I need to take out a mortgage on the St. Clair?"

She glanced up at him, saw the disarming levity in his blue eyes and felt her stomach flutter. But she reminded herself of the gold band she'd noticed on his left ring finger. Not that she was in the market for any man—even a charming, aristocratic one like Mark St. Clair.

"Do you and your wife have a theme for the party?" she inquired. "Something I should keep in mind when I design the cupcakes?"

"Oh. I'm not…" He looked down, his fingers absently grazing his wedding band. "My wife…she died. I'm a widower."

Samantha's throat tightened in sympathy. "I'm so sorry."

Mark simply nodded. He clasped the back of his neck. "As far as the cupcakes go, I'll let you decide. Emily loved the ones with the flowers, though. She's been drawing pictures of them for the past two days. She even picked some buds out of the hotel planters and put them on one of the cakes in our kitchen before anyone caught her. Our cook staff had to throw it out since the flowers weren't edible like yours."

Samantha tapped her ballpoint pen against her lips in thought. "I have an idea. If you can spare me an oven in the hotel kitchen, I think I can come up with something Emily and her guests will love."

"An oven?"

"What would you think about the party guests making their own cupcakes?" Samantha asked tentatively. She'd read about the concept in an entrepreneurial magazine. Cooking parties were all the rage, including ones geared toward children. It could be a profitable sideline. "If you're interested, I can provide the supervision and decorating supplies. Of course, if you have other activities planned or you'd rather not deal with the mess…"

"It sounds great," he said, looking pleased. "You can use our overflow kitchen. I'll pay you for your time."

She smiled. "Of course."

"Thank you, Ms. Marsh."

"It's Samantha." Their gazes held until the chime on the café's front door rang. A family of vacationers, judging by their flip-flops and sunburned faces, entered and sat down at one of the tables.

"I'll be right with you," Samantha called over to them.

"It was the Sand Dollar."

She again looked into Mark's eyes, a tingling in the pit of her stomach as he leaned his head closer to hers. "That was the motel's name. It was off the beach and away from the other places. They had these big fishing nets filled with seashells hanging from the lobby's ceiling. The swimming pool floor had a mermaid painted on it."

Samantha nodded. She could almost see her mother sitting by the pool with a beer and a magazine she'd bought at the drugstore. Her heart constricted at the memory. "That's right."

"It was on Clearwater Street, but it was razed a few years ago. The place was in pretty bad shape. The new library's there now." He cleared his throat. "I'll see you on Saturday, then? Things are starting at six o'clock. I know it's a little late for a kids' party, but Emily's grandmother has another engagement that afternoon and she wants to be there."

Once she agreed, he said good-bye and left the café. As his broad shoulders disappeared from view, Samantha thought of Emily. She wondered if losing her mother had anything to do with why the sweet little girl didn't talk. Samantha knew what it was like to lose your mother at a young age. She was grateful at least that Emily had a daddy who seemed to care for her deeply. Samantha had never even known her own father's identity.

"Miss?" A woman in the group waved at her, a fussy toddler straddling her lap.

Samantha grabbed the paper menus next to the cash register and went to take the family's order. Once they'd finished their meal and left, she began sweeping the floor where the toddler had dropped bits of cookie and pasta salad. A postcard lay under the table. She bent to pick it up, a jolt sweeping through her as she realized what was on its front.

It was a photo of Graceland Mansion, accompanied by the words *Greetings from Memphis* in bold, red letters.

The cheerful salutation cut off her breath. Trying to ignore the tremor in her hands, she slowly turned it over. Blank. There was no message or address scrawled on its back, no stamp or postmark. In all likelihood, it had fallen out of a tourist's purse or backpack. Some vacationers exploring the Southeastern United States had probably gone through Tennessee before making their way to South Carolina and the Atlantic shoreline.

It wasn't a threat, she chided herself—just a simple, harmless coincidence and certainly no cause for alarm. She dropped the postcard into the pocket of her apron.

Still, Samantha realized her mouth had gone dry, and her heart was beating too hard.

CHAPTER THREE

SAMANTHA SAT ON the concrete stoop outside her apartment, drinking a diet soda and watching kamikaze bugs incinerate themselves on the streetlight. But her thoughts were still with the Memphis postcard, which she had ended up tearing in two and throwing into the trash at the café.

If only her memories could be that easily discarded. Six years had gone by, but even now the slightest reminder of her past could still throw her into a tailspin.

In her nightmares, Devin Leary was coming for her, and he was going to make her pay.

But that's all they were—nightmares. Devin couldn't hurt her anymore. And Trina Grissom no longer existed.

My name is Samantha Marsh. Closing her eyes, she repeated the statement in her head like some desperate mantra, trying to erase her unease. She had taken careful steps to create a brand new identity, a new life for herself. She had to learn to relax and trust that she'd covered her tracks well. That no one would ever find her.

Samantha thought of the documents she'd paid ten thousand

dollars for when she had first arrived in New York. It had taken nearly everything she'd managed to save to obtain a new name, driver's license and social security number, pilfered from the deceased. The idea of it had disgusted her, but there hadn't been another choice. Her life had been on the line.

A full moon glowed in the dark night overhead, and the peace was broken by a pack of boisterous young men headed in the direction of the beach with coolers in hand. The boldest of them gave a wolf whistle and asked if she wanted to come along and have a cold beer. Samantha ignored them, just as she ignored most men, rising from her seat on the stoop and going back inside to the air conditioning.

The small apartment held only the essentials—a second-hand couch and television set, a single chair at the snack bar. It was almost completely bereft of personal items, partly because Samantha had pretty much invested her last dime in Café Bella, but also because she took comfort in the anonymity. No framed photos placed around the room or hanging on walls, no personal mementos. Nothing that told a life story, not that she had one worth telling. Her one prized possession was the high-end cookware she had bought after graduating from culinary school, copper pieces that now hung from a pot rack in the narrow galley-style kitchen. That one part of her background was genuine, at least, even if the high school diploma that had been a prerequisite for enrollment belonged to someone else. Cooking *meant* something to her.

It was getting late and six thirty a.m.—the time she met Luther six mornings a week to start food preparation—would come early. Samantha double-checked the lock on the door and went into the bedroom to prepare for bed. As she pulled a soft T-shirt and pair of pajama shorts from the top drawer of the bureau, she uncovered the white-painted jewelry box tucked among the clothing. On impulse, she opened the lid, lifting the inexpensive cameo from inside it.

The cameo had belonged to her mother. Along with Walton, a one-eyed, worn-out teddy bear that sat on the bed, it was the only remnant of her true past that Samantha still clung to. Proof that she had been someone's child. That she'd had an actual childhood, at least for a while, before her world had come apart.

Those sentimental items—along with the cash she'd been saving—were the things she had foolishly returned for that fateful night. Without warning, Devin's hard features filled her vision. Her stomach churned. She could still smell his musky aftershave and feel his bruising grip on her throat.

I'm gonna take what's mine, Trina. What's always been mine. And tonight, you're gonna be up on that stage shakin' that sweet little ass or I swear to God I'll beat you 'til no one's ever gonna want to look at you again.

Before closing the drawer, her fingers touched the small derringer she kept there. The postcard still had her rattled.

She went to sleep with the light on.

CHAPTER FOUR

"I HEARD SHE HAS Luther Banda working there, of all people. You *do* know that man spent fourteen years in Bennettsville Correctional Institute?" Olivia peered suspiciously into the St. Clair's auxiliary kitchen from the hallway. Normally used as a staging area for large events, the space was now inhabited by Samantha, Mercer and five little girls, including Emily, who were enthusiastically spreading buttercream frosting on oversize cupcakes. Pink balloons bobbed in the air, tied around the room with ribbons.

"At least the tourists don't know about him, working right there in town," Olivia added with a disdainful sniff.

Mark gazed over his mother's shoulder at the activity, aware of the happy look on his daughter's face. He also admitted to himself that Samantha's casual sundress—which bared her shoulders and set off her long, dark hair—hadn't escaped his notice, either.

"Luther did his time, Mom. And he's stayed out of trouble since. How long ago was that, anyway? Twenty years? I've been hearing about it since I was a kid."

"A leopard doesn't change its spots. You wouldn't hire him at the St. Clair, would you?"

"I don't know. He's never applied for a job here."

"If I didn't know better, I'd think you were turning into a liberal, Mark." Worriedly, Olivia toyed with the double strand of pearls around her neck. "And what do you know about this Samantha Marsh, exactly?"

"Not a lot," Mark replied truthfully. "I went to her shop to order some of those fancy cupcakes she makes for Emily's birthday, and she offered to come here and have a baking party with the girls. From what I can tell, it was a good idea."

"That was opportunistic of her."

"It was *capitalistic*. I'm paying her well for her time."

Olivia frowned. "Mercer said she was from New York. If you ask me, she doesn't sound much like a Yankee. She tries to hide it, but I detect a hint of a Southern drawl. Maybe northern Alabama?"

His mother prided herself on being able to identify someone's birthplace based on his or her accent. Usually, she was right on target.

"She moved here from New York, but I've no idea where she's from originally."

"Are you interested in her?"

He pressed his lips together and stared back into the kitchen. "No."

"That's a relief. Because I was just going to say that Felicity is a much better match for you. Her mother was just telling me the other day that—"

Pushing the door open the rest of the way, Mark left Olivia opining on the virtues of Felicity Greene and entered the kitchen. He was instantly greeted with a round of *Hi, Mr. St. Clair* from the young party guests and a sweet smile from Emily, who had a smear of frosting on her cheek. All the girls, Mercer and Samantha included, wore white aprons.

"How're things going in here?"

"Deliciously," Mercer declared, licking frosting from a spatula. "I think I've gained five pounds so far."

The stainless steel work island held all the items for mixing, baking and decorating. Frostings and sugars in dazzling colors filled small ceramic bowls, and a bounty of edible flowers, from roses to miniature carnations and nasturtiums, floated in a pan of water. Samantha stood behind Emily, her arms around the child as she helped her grip a pastry bag. Emily's small tongue darted out in concentration as Samantha guided her in squeezing frosting onto a cupcake in an artistic swirl.

Chatting with one another, the girls sat on tall stools borrowed from the hotel's bar so they had better access to the decorating supplies. Mark only wished Emily would join in their animated conversation. But at least she appeared to be having a good time.

Samantha looked at Mark. She gave him a soft smile before lowering her dark lashes again and helping Emily select a flower for the cupcake's top.

"Did you know Sam's a runner?" Mercer asked around a mouthful of cake. Apparently satisfied with her decorating skills, she'd begun eating the results of her work. "She's going jogging with me in the morning to make up for force-feeding me all these refined carbs. I swear I might as well be rubbing the frosting directly on my thighs."

"Why would you do that?" one of the young guests asked, wrinkling her nose. "That's gross!"

"The café's closed on Sunday, so we can go whenever you want tomorrow," Samantha said. "Weekdays and Saturdays, though—"

"But you *do* have help, right? Surely you can escape for an hour a few times a week." Mercer shot her brother a teasing glare. "Mark practically runs a sweatshop around here, and even *he* lets me outdoors on occasion."

"Let you out? I encourage it. I call it my *break from Mercer* hour."

Mercer flipped a spatula loaded with frosting in retaliation. The blob hit Mark's white dress shirt, splattering in the center of his chest.

"Uh-oh!" one of the girls exclaimed.

Mark stared down at his shirtfront in pretended dismay. Then, dragging his finger through the confection, he popped it into his mouth.

The group broke into giggles.

⟳

"I think you earned this." Mark held two glasses of wine, one for himself and the other for Samantha. The party over, she was in the kitchen cleaning and packing up the decorating supplies she'd brought with her from Café Bella.

"Where's Emily?" she asked. He waited as she removed her apron and wiped her hands on a dishtowel embroidered with the St. Clair logo, then hesitantly accepted the stemmed glass.

"Outside with her guests. They're still waiting on some of the parents. Mercer's going to take her home afterward and get her ready for bed."

"I hope she can sleep with the sugar buzz she's on." Apparently picking up on what he'd said, she added quizzically, "Home? I thought your home was here."

"It is. We live in one of the ocean-side bungalows farther down on the property. You can drive or take a golf cart to it from the hotel. I had to send someone there from the concierge desk earlier to get me a clean shirt."

"And Mercer?" She suppressed a smile, probably thinking of their earlier frosting war.

"She keeps a room here, which, according to my sister, is preferable to living with our mother. Olivia resides in what pretty much everyone calls the Big House," he said jokingly, referring to the stately white-columned estate home located just outside the resort.

"That must be the place I saw driving in. Is that where you grew up?"

He nodded. "There and here. I remember playing with Tonka trucks with my brother on the oriental carpet in the lobby. I think that's my earliest memory. That or the time Carter threw a croquet ball through a glass panel in the sunroom's atrium. We were both in some trouble that day."

"*Two* St. Clair men? I didn't know you have a brother."

"Carter lives in New York—in your old stomping grounds of Manhattan, actually." Mark decided to fish for information. "But you're not a native New Yorker, are you? My mother claims she can tell by your accent, as faint as it is. It's Southern, not Northern."

"Olivia and I already discussed it. I was raised in Alabama—in a small town that's not much more than a wide place in the road," she admitted. "But my family's all gone now. I don't have ties there anymore."

He watched as she pensively took a sip of wine, stopping short of saying anything more about herself. Instead, she commented, "Honestly? I can't imagine growing up around all this. I'm surprised you're not spoiled silly, Mark St. Clair."

"Who says I'm not?"

She laughed then, and Mark had that same awkward feeling he'd experienced before around her. She really did look gorgeous tonight. *It would take a dead man not to notice*, he thought, trying to ease his guilt. And it wasn't the made-up kind of gorgeous that took two hours in the hotel spa to achieve. As far as he could tell, she wore no makeup except for a touch of sheer color on her lips. Her dark hair appeared glossy and soft to the touch. Looking down, he glimpsed flat sandals and tan, bare toes painted a shell-like pearl.

"Would you like to take a walk on the beach?" he asked, surprising himself with the question. But the truth was, he wasn't ready for her to excuse herself and go home. "We can bring our wine with us."

She stared uncertainly into his eyes, and he noted again their color, which was like rich caramel. Samantha bit her lip. "I really shouldn't—"

"It would give us a chance to get to know one another. And I'd like to hear more about your business plans for Café Bella. I might be able to offer some ideas."

She hesitated, then nodded. "All right. But just a short walk. I can't stay long."

Mark escorted her from the kitchen into the hotel's large main dining room, where uniformed wait staff served guests. The lights on the tiered overhead chandelier had been lowered, and each linen-covered table had a centerpiece crystal bowl filled with floating gardenias and tea candles. The clink of silverware against fine china accompanied the low hum of conversation. Several employees greeted Mark as he and Samantha made their way toward the patio. He opened a set of wide French doors that led to a graceful outdoor bar area, proud to show her more of the St. Clair. To their right, the underwater lights of the Olympic-size pool glowed, making the chlorinated water appear a dazzling blue. A man swam laps, and several other guests were gathered at the pool's edge, lounging in wicker furniture and having drinks.

Mark halted. "I should've asked if you'd like something to eat."

"Thanks, but I killed my appetite with the cupcakes. Just a walk on the beach and the wine is good."

They went onto the boardwalk, passing guests in bathing suits who were headed back to their rooms for the evening. An outdoor showerhead allowed beachgoers to wash the sand from their bodies before coming into the pool area. He stood, waiting as Samantha stopped to watch a small child—her water wings flapping—squeal with delight as her mother rinsed her off under the spray. The warm breeze made the briny sea air especially pungent, and in front of them, the Atlantic spread out in a deep blue haze that melded into the darkening sky.

"Everything is so beautiful here," Samantha observed as they reached the end of the boardwalk.

He agreed, seeing the oceanfront resort through her eyes. Mark sat on the top of the stairs that led to the beach. He removed his dress shoes and socks and rolled up the bottoms of his suit pants. Samantha followed his lead, temporarily placing her wineglass on the railing as she slipped out of her sandals and put them next to his shoes. He reached for her hand and helped her down the wood-planked steps, experiencing a little jolt of electricity at the feel of her slender fingers in his. He let go once she reached the bottom. Mark walked with her across the beach until they reached the shoreline. Cool, wet sand squished between their toes, and foamy waves lapped at their feet as they traveled southward from the hotel.

"Emily's such a sweet child," Samantha said once they'd talked a little about the café. "Why doesn't she talk? Is there…something wrong?"

Mark gazed at the white caps of the crashing waves, feeling a familiar jab of pain at the question. "She stopped speaking after my wife, Shelley, was killed in a car accident a little over two years ago. I've taken her to specialist after specialist, but they all say there's nothing really wrong with her. At least not physically. They refer to it as trauma-induced muteness."

"Oh," Samantha said, growing silent. Then she asked, "Is there a chance she'll come out of it?"

"They hope so. But the longer it continues, it's seeming less likely."

They walked for a time, slowing to watch the ghostly silhouette of a large fishing vessel as it made its way into deeper waters. Its low horn blared a good-bye as it escaped into the horizon.

"I really am sorry, Mark. About your wife." Samantha gazed up at him. "For you as well as Emily."

He simply nodded and took a sip of wine, desiring a change of subject. "So what's your story, Samantha? You *are* single, right?"

She took her time in answering, looking out to sea. "I was in a relationship, but it didn't work out."

"So you left the big city behind for a return to small-town life?"

"Something like that." The wind whipped her dark hair. She pushed a strand of it from her face, then pulled the length off her shoulders, lifting it from her nape so that he caught a glimpse of her long, graceful neck. Mark swallowed hard. He should be back at the hotel. The dining room was in full swing, and since it was one of the last remaining weekends before schools were back in session, occupancy was full. But right now, all he knew was that he couldn't quite stop staring at her. He gathered his courage, in disbelief of what he was about to do.

"Samantha…I was wondering if—"

"Your mother tells me I'm not right for you."

He stopped in his tracks at her soft comment, astonished. Mark felt his face heat. "She said what?"

She smiled faintly, although he noticed the act didn't quite reach her eyes. "Well, not directly, of course. But she intimated as much. She was going on about your MBA from Emory University and all the Charleston socialites with their sights set on you. It was pretty impressive, actually. She also asked about *my* family— what line of business my father was in and whether I was related to the *Birmingham Marshes,* as she put it. I'm fairly sure I failed the screening process."

He sighed heavily, his irritation with his mother intense. "You really have to take her with a grain of salt."

"Don't be upset with her, Mark." She sounded sincere. "Her ways are a little bold, but she's just looking out for you, and I *am* the stranger in town. I think she wanted to set me straight about any designs I might have on you. I actually find her protectiveness admirable."

"I don't. She's meddling in my life," he grumbled. "It's one of her specialties."

They stood face-to-face now, mere inches apart. Samantha gazed up at him, her soft-brown eyes sympathetic. Mark felt his stomach flip-flop. The wind once again blew her hair into her face, and unable to help himself, he reached out and slowly slipped his fingers through it, settling it back into place. It was as silky as he'd imagined.

"My mother's pretty intuitive where her children are concerned," he conceded hoarsely, his heart beating hard. "The truth is, since my wife died, I haven't...there hasn't been anyone. I was on the verge of a lame attempt at asking you out, but I'm guessing you know that."

She bowed her head. Her voice when it finally came was gentle. "Your mother's *right*, Mark. I'm not right for you. I want to be up-front with you about that. We can be friends. I'd *like* to be friends, but it can't be anything more…"

They simply stared at one another. Mark felt his blush deepen. A line of sea gulls squawked high in the air above them, their calls sounding over the heavy ocean roar. A little farther down the beach, someone set off a firework, launching a red starburst into the eggplant colored sky.

Before he could form a response, she handed him her empty wineglass, pressing it to his chest until he took it. She appeared resolute, even sad. "In fact, I think it's best if I go back to the hotel now and go home."

She said a polite good night and retreated, not waiting for him. Mark didn't follow. Embarrassed and confused, he watched as her figure moved away, growing smaller in the distance until she reached the stairs and disappeared along the boardwalk.

CHAPTER FIVE

F*EEL THAT, CHILD? Hell's a thousand times hotter. Your Momma's burning in eternal damnation. If you don't get right with the Lord, you will, too.*

The day Trina Grissom went to live with her grandmother, the woman dragged her to the kitchen stove, still hot from baking cornbread. Trina begged and screamed as Mamaw Jean forced her hand onto the oven rack, holding it there long enough to give her a blistering burn. She claimed she'd taught her eight-year-old granddaughter an important lesson, which was to not turn out like the drug-addicted whore her mother had been, or else suffer the consequences.

There had been other lessons after that, usually involving a dog-eared bible and a leather belt.

Few of them had taken.

Pensively, Samantha gripped the steering wheel of her used Toyota Camry. She'd made so many mistakes, lived up to Mamaw Jean's worst predictions.

You got her looks, Trina. The boys will be sniffin' around soon enough. And just like her, you ain't got the sense or the morals to keep your legs together.

Boy crazy. Jezebel. Hot-tailed piece of trash.

When Trina turned seventeen, she'd run away from Mamaw Jean's abuse and religious fanaticism...and ended up in Memphis. Over a decade older than she was, handsome and with money to spare, Devin Leary had provided her with sanctuary from the streets. Foolishly believing herself in love, she'd done everything Devin asked her to do and then later, the things he'd forced her to. At first, she hadn't fully realized the fear his seedy connections should have induced. And by the time she recognized the danger she was in, it was too late. Devin already considered her his property.

Four years of her life had been lost to him. Time that had quickly morphed into hell. Samantha criticized herself for ruminating over a past she couldn't change. She was twenty-seven now, no longer a scared runaway teen. She shook her head in reflection.

Instead, she was something far worse.

Something that could get her prison time at best, or if Devin's brother ever caught up to her...

The thought tore at her insides.

One thing was for certain. The smartest thing, the best thing, she could do was to put a stop to whatever attraction seemed to be blooming between her and Mark St. Clair. Hopefully, she had done that tonight. He and his little daughter deserved so much better.

Samantha had told herself that her offer to do a baking party for Emily was based purely on business, a chance to moonlight and gain some extra, needed cash. But she admitted now that Mark had affected her in some way—something she hadn't expected or been prepared for. The temptation to spend time with him on the beach had been too great. And the truth was, she'd thought her ability to feel anything for a man had been snuffed out years ago. Whatever her original reasoning had been, she'd been wrong to go to the St. Clair tonight. Letting her guard down, letting herself be attracted to anyone and risking them finding out the truth about her…inviting in trouble…it just couldn't happen. She'd been able to keep her dark secret all these years precisely because she had kept to herself.

Samantha continued on the isolated, two-lane peninsula road that separated the elegant St. Clair resort from Rarity Cove proper. Her car beams illuminated the silhouettes of ancient live oaks on either side of the thoroughfare, their branches spread out in ghostly Medusa-like patterns. Overhead, an obsidian darkness had set in that not even the occasional streetlight could penetrate. Headlights appeared in her rearview mirror. Someone else was apparently leaving the resort, as well. She watched intermittently as the car moved closer, going faster than the posted forty miles per hour speed limit. Samantha accelerated a little, too. It was even closer now—directly behind her—but it still made no attempt to pass. All she could tell was that it was a large, older-model sedan, possibly a Crown Victoria. The only people who drove such cars were retirees…

And plainclothes police.

An arrow of worry darted through her. She'd had some wine at the St. Clair. What if she was pulled over? It didn't matter, she told herself. She had the proper ID and wasn't drunk. But another, less rational thought invaded her head. If it was the police trailing her…

What if she had somehow finally been found?

Get a grip. That isn't possible. That's what rehashing your past will do to you.

She half-expected to see the strobe-like flash of blue lights behind her, but it never appeared. Instead, the car backed off a bit but remained in her wake. Finally reaching the main road, Samantha put on her blinker and made a careful, right-hand turn toward town. The sedan followed—not too unusual, she conceded. But she noticed that it failed again to pass her, even when the lanes expanded and she deliberately slowed to a crawl. When the car followed her through several more turns in a residential section of small duplexes and two-story stucco apartment buildings just off the beach, she felt certain it was tailing her.

On impulse, she drove past her own apartment, heading toward the downtown square, which she hoped would still be populated despite the evening hour. She could see the sedan in her rearview mirror as she passed under the stoplight a full second after it turned red in front of McSwain's drugstore. A car horn on the intersecting street let out an angry blare. But her mission was accomplished—whoever was following her had been caught waiting for the light to change.

If it were a cop, he would have certainly come after her for running the light.

Relax. You've just spooked yourself tonight.

Samantha turned onto the picturesque square. But she was so busy looking for some sign of the Crown Victoria in her rearview that she didn't glimpse the vehicle in the next lane over making an improper lane change until it was nearly too late. She swerved to avoid a collision, causing the Camry's front-right tire to bump the curb. Samantha felt the tire wobble and go flat. Her stomach sank. She had no choice but to roll to a stop.

The car in front of her continued on, oblivious to the damage it had caused. Another vehicle passed. Apprehension tingled along her skin as the Crown Vic made the turn onto the square. Suddenly, they were the only two cars on the sleepy downtown street.

The vehicle pulled directly up alongside her, idling. But no one made a move to roll down the window or get out. Her heart jumping inside her chest, Samantha turned her head and looked. But the sedan's windows were tinted dark. She couldn't see the driver or any other passenger, for that matter. The Crown Vic sat there for another ten seconds, the deep bass of its stereo speakers vibrating the Camry. Then, strangely, it gunned the engine and drove away. Samantha watched in disbelief as its red taillights disappeared down the street. What had just happened?

She let go of the breath she'd been holding. But a knock on the window startled her and made her cry out.

Luther Banda peered at her. "Samantha? You all right in there?"

With shaking fingers, she lowered the glass. "Luther! What're you doing here?"

"Oh, just out walkin' around. I've been down at the Shamrock havin' a cold beer. My air conditioner's broke at home." A heavy crease appeared in his forehead. "Looks like you got yourself a flat. If you've got a spare in the trunk, I'll change it for you."

"Luther...did you see the car that stopped next to me?"

"Yeah. That a friend of yours?"

She shook her head. "I couldn't see who was inside. I think they might've been following me."

"Probably just some horny teenagers with nothing better to do, tryin' to get themselves a look at a pretty young woman. Had their music turned up like a bunch of fools." Despite his assurance, however, he frowned and glanced down the road in the direction the car had gone.

Samantha emerged from the Camry and handed him the key fob. But before he could move to the back of the car and open the trunk, another vehicle turned the corner onto the street. This time it *was* an actual police cruiser. It came up and halted beside them. There were two officers inside.

"Everything all right, miss?" the middle-aged one on the passenger side asked as his window came down. He peered at Luther. "This man giving you trouble?"

"Not at all," she assured him. "Mr. Banda is my employee, actually. I own the new café in Sea Breeze Centre. He's helping me change a flat."

The officer pressed his lips together, appearing unimpressed with the information. His eyes remained on Luther.

"Finish what you're doing and then get on home, Luther," he advised sternly. "Not to the bar or wherever the hell else you go."

The cruiser started off again. Incensed, Samantha stared after it. "I can't believe that. They can't tell you where to be—"

"Don't worry about it, Sam." Luther gave a weary sigh of resignation. He opened the trunk and began rummaging for her jack and spare tire. "I'm an ex-con. Comes with the territory."

Luther had revealed the information when she'd interviewed him for the position at Café Bella. To his credit, he had been upfront about his past. He'd hung out with a rough crowd as a young man and gotten involved in a car-theft ring in metro Charleston. While serving time in prison, he had also killed another inmate, something he'd received an extra sentence for, although he'd sworn he had been acting in self-defense.

Samantha shook her head. "You've proven yourself. You've stayed out of trouble for a long time."

Hauling the spare around to the front of the car, Luther knelt on the ground and fitted the jack into place behind the wheel well. "Don't matter. Folks around here stick to their beliefs, and I made my bed with 'em years ago."

Still, she didn't like it. Samantha believed in second chances.

She crossed her arms against her chest and looked around the town square as he worked, noticing the strands of small white lights decorating the trees and the tiered fountain that dripped water onto a bed of swamp lilies.

"Noticed you didn't say nothin' to the cops about that car you thought was following you." Luther's big, tattooed muscles bulged as he pumped the jack and began raising the car enough to remove the damaged tire.

"No," she said quietly. She hadn't wanted to involve the police. "It was probably nothing."

He grunted. "I doubt whoever was in that car meant you any harm, but you should still be careful, Sam. Even 'round here. This might not be New York City, but take it from someone who knows—trouble can be found most anyplace."

Samantha thought again of the mysterious Crown Victoria. Feeling foolish, she shoved down her faint paranoia that *she* had been found.

CHAPTER SIX

MARK STARED OUT his bedroom window at the darkened ocean. He had tossed and turned for most of the night, unable to stop thinking about Samantha Marsh. Until now, he had firmly believed he could never be drawn to another woman, that doing so would be some kind of betrayal to Shelley.

Then what had he done? He'd gone and invited Samantha for a walk on the beach. He had actually *touched* her. Openly admitted that he was attracted to her, and that he'd been trying to ask her out. Humiliated, frustrated with himself, he raked a hand through his hair. He'd never done anything so impulsive.

We can be friends. I'd like to be friends, but it can't be anything more…

The rejection had stung. Immersed in his thoughts and feeling guilty for his actions, he watched as pearlescent moonlight illuminated the peak of a cresting wave. It wouldn't be light for another solid hour. Restless, clad in pajama bottoms and a T-shirt, Mark crept down the hallway toward the kitchen. On the way, he checked in on his sleeping daughter in her bedroom.

Emily lay on her side. Her tousled blond hair was spread out on the pillow, and her cupid's-bow lips were slightly parted with her even breathing. She clutched a ballerina doll Olivia had given her for her birthday. Despite his current mood, Mark smiled ruefully, recalling that he'd once told Shelley that it looked like a fairy princess had thrown up in their daughter's room. It was entirely pink and awash with ruffles, from the bed to the window treatments. Emily loved it.

Returning to the hall and passing through the large living area, Mark looked around his home. It was casually appointed with whitewashed furniture, paneled pine and beadboard walls, and vintage checked and floral patterns on the curtains and upholstery. Everything in the sunny, cozy bungalow bore Shelley's stamp. *She's in every corner of this house*, he thought, throat tight.

Two years younger than he was, Shelley had been his high school sweetheart. Except for a temporary but volatile breakup after Mark had left for college, they'd been inseparable. Meant to be together forever. But sometimes fate had other plans.

He felt another pang of self-recrimination. The love of his life and mother of his child was dead, and he'd spent the night thinking about another woman. Maybe Mercer was right; the loneliness was getting to him.

Fully giving up on sleep, Mark went into the kitchen to start the coffeemaker. As he measured grounds, his cell phone on the countertop shrilled. He answered it quickly so it wouldn't wake Emily.

"Mark?" a male voice asked, sounding tinny through the phone's receiver. "I didn't wake you, did I?"

"Carter." Mark sighed and rubbed his forehead. "No, actually. I'm up already."

"I figured. Just like Dad—early bird gets the worm, right? Hey, I'm calling from one of those in-flight phones."

He frowned. "You're on your way here now? I thought you weren't coming until Monday."

"I wrapped filming on the soap early. I thought, why not come on home? I took a late flight with a layover in Raleigh. My plane lands at the Charleston airport in about an hour. Want to come get me?"

"I can send the hotel limo service."

"I want *you* to pick me up, Mark. I thought maybe we could have breakfast together, just you and me. Someplace besides the St. Clair. What do you say?"

Hesitating, Mark looked at the digital clock on the microwave face. "All right. I just need to arrange for someone to be here for Emily."

"Great. See you then."

The phone went dead. Carter hadn't been home in more than two years. Not since Shelley's funeral, although Olivia and Mercer had taken Emily to New York for a visit several months earlier. Mark hadn't gone on the trip, instead remaining behind to oversee the hotel. He went back to making coffee. He needed all the caffeine he could get to prepare himself for his brother.

"I told them I wanted a fifteen percent pay increase and ten weeks off a year." Carter took a bite of his lowcountry seafood omelet and chewed before speaking again. "The time off's standard in David Paul Mancier's contract, and it would give me time to explore other options. I'm ready to move on to something else."

Mark and Carter sat on the outdoor deck of Mila's Pancake House, which overlooked the Rarity Cove community beach. Instead of having breakfast in Charleston, Carter had insisted on driving back to town and dining at what Mark considered a way too public spot for his relatively famous brother. Carter's hair, normally a light brown like Mark's, was subtly streaked with highlights that set off his high cheekbones and chiseled jawline. His eyes, however, were obscured by the dark tint of his Ray-Bans. Concerned about the hotel, Mark checked his watch, something that apparently didn't miss Carter's notice.

"I'm trying to get your advice here. Are you even listening, Mark?"

"Of course I am."

"Then what did I just say?"

"*I heard you*," Mark said. "But you need to remember this Mancier guy's been on the show for two decades. You haven't. And I thought soaps were having it tough these days."

"That's not the case with *Friends and Lovers*. Our ratings are solid for daytime, and the network's sticking by us, especially since that talk show tanked in the afternoon time slot." Carter lowered his voice. "My agent's hinted to the producer that I'm considering not renewing my contract. And, well, it's kind of the truth—"

Two women in shorts and bikini tops appeared at the table, interrupting them.

"Are you Carter St. Clair?" one asked excitedly.

Carter exchanged pleasantries and signed his name on their paper menus. Once they'd left, he took a sip of his coffee. "Sorry."

"Like any of that hero worship bothers you."

He grinned, his dimples deepening. "Jealous?"

"Not especially. But I am curious as to why you wanted to have breakfast with me. Why not Mom? You know she'd love showing you off at the country club."

"I'll be seeing her soon. Besides, I've had Mila's on my mind for the past week, not that bland geezer food the club serves."

Looking at Mark, he laid his fork on the rim of his plate and paused contemplatively. His features grew serious. "The truth is, I also wanted to see how you're doing."

He didn't have to say more. Shelley had always been a sore spot between them, but he also knew Carter had been deeply saddened by her death. Vaguely, Mark recalled him flying in and being here, offering his help. But so much of those days following the accident seemed lost to him, as if he'd been living inside a black mist.

"I've talked to Mom," Carter continued carefully. "She says you're still not over…things. She worries about you."

"She doesn't need to. I'm fine."

"Maybe what you need is a break from the hotel. Have you ever even thought about that? What if the best thing for you and Em is to pack up and move from here? Start over someplace that doesn't hold all these memories. You always talked about living in Atlanta again. You liked going to school there."

"That was before Dad died," Mark pointed out. "Someone needs to run the hotel. You have your career. Mom doesn't have the interest or the business sense, and Mercer's still young and trying to figure out what she wants to do with her life."

"Mark." Carter removed his sunglasses, revealing piercing, midnight-blue eyes. "Have you even *considered* selling the St. Clair? The hospitality industry is tough these days, and it's getting harder to turn a profit. Independents are struggling, and we could be looking at a decreasing valuation over the next several years."

The pitch sounded familiar. Putting down his coffee mug, Mark shook his head, the realization rising up in front of him like an interstate billboard. He now understood the real reason why Carter had wanted to have breakfast with him alone, away from the hotel and on neutral ground. "They called you, didn't they? That big hotel chain that's interested in the St. Clair."

"Don't overreact like you always do. All I'm saying is that it's an option—"

"Nice, Carter. So this whole brotherly get-together was just a scam?" With a cynical release of breath, Mark pushed away his plate and got up from his chair. He reached into his back pocket for his wallet, then tossed enough money on the table to cover their bill and the tip. "I should've known as much. Meet me at the car when you're done."

"Mark—"

"The answer's *no*," he said, his tone hard. "Make that a *hell, no.*"

He started toward the parking lot, but instead ended up staring at the beach, his hands braced on the railing of the restaurant's deck as he tried to get control of his irritation. Below him, people were dressed in bathing suits, walking and playing at the shoreline or lying on brightly colored towels, soaking up the morning sun before the rays got too strong. He breathed in the salty sea air laced with the smell of coconut-scented tanning lotion. Mark turned his head as Carter called after him again before being stopped by another autograph-seeking fan.

He wasn't really all that surprised that Luxor Corporation had made an appeal to the other owners of the St. Clair. But it was unbelievable to him that Carter had attempted to parlay his grief over Shelley into a rationale for selling. It seemed that every time he thought Carter had hit a new level of selfishness, he somehow managed to outdo himself.

"Look, I know I didn't go about this the right way, but you should at least consider it," Carter urged as he caught up to him. "It's a good offer. A damn good one, actually. And the St. Clair doesn't just belong to *you*, Mark."

Mark's jaw tightened. "Dad made me majority owner for a reason."

"What about Mom and Mercer? Don't they even get a say in this? We're talking about a lot of money here. If we all go against you—"

"I'm not going to discuss this."

Carter shoved his hands into his pockets, frowning heavily. "Okay, I get it. No more talk about selling. But you need to understand something, Mark. This wasn't a *scam*, as you put it. Despite how everything just sounded, I care about you. You're my brother. I'm sorry about Shelley…*I am*. I want to see you get past this."

"I am past it."

Carter peered pointedly at the gold band Mark still wore on his left hand. "Really? I don't think you are. And neither is Emily. As long as you're still holding on to Shelley, she will, too."

"Let me worry about Emily—"

"*She's my niece*," Carter emphasized softly. "And as God is my witness, I asked you to breakfast because I really did want to spend time with just you. It's been too long, and I miss the way things used to be between us when we were kids. Besides, once I get to the hotel, you know Mom's going to be on me like shrimp and tasso gravy on grits."

Carter nudged his brother's shoulder, then nudged him again, this time a bit harder. "Don't stay mad, bro. What if your face freezes like that?"

Mark looked at him, thinking of the carefree, charismatic brother he'd grown up with. Carter had been an attention-getter even back then, catnip to the fairer sex and able to charm the hind legs off a donkey, as their father used to say. Mark suspected those qualities had only become more refined with age.

"We're not selling," he stated flatly.

"Message received. But could you do one thing for me?"

"What?"

"Introduce me to that long-legged vision jogging with our baby sister."

Mark followed the direction of Carter's gaze, feeling a spiraling disquiet. Sure enough, Mercer and Samantha ran along the shoreline. Samantha's long, dark hair was tied back in a ponytail, and she wore a tank top with running shorts.

"Mercer!" Carter yelled and began waving his arms like a maniac. Mercer stopped and touched Samantha's shoulder, pointing up to the deck where Mark and Carter stood. Mark ran a nervous hand through his hair as the two women began moving toward them.

Grinning, Mercer called Carter's name as she raced up the stairs. She threw her arms around his neck as he grabbed her by the waist and spun her around.

"I didn't think you'd be here until tomorrow!"

"I figured I'd slip in early. Mark picked me up at the airport this morning." He eyed Samantha, who'd also come up the steps.

"Sam, meet my other brother, Carter." Mercer made the introduction. "This is Samantha Marsh, culinary genius and my new running BFF."

"Nice to meet you." Carter smiled like a hungry wolf at a sheep as he took Samantha's hand.

"Thanks...you, too."

Samantha glanced at Mark, who stood slightly behind Carter. An image of her on the darkened beach and the way things had been left between them caused heat to rush to his face. He wanted to say something to her, but couldn't figure out exactly what, and it wouldn't be appropriate in front of the others anyway. Instead, he simply nodded in a silent greeting.

"We just finished breakfast, but if you ladies want something, I'm sure Mark has time to sit back down," Carter offered. "How about you, Sam? Some coffee or juice, at least?"

"No, thanks," she said, crossing her slender arms over her chest. "I've really got to finish this run and be going—"

"You look familiar. Did you go to school with Mercer?"

"You can stop fishing. She's not from around here," Mercer supplied. "She just moved here from New York City. Small world, right?"

Carter's eyebrows rose. "Really? That's where I live. Have you done any modeling or acting, because maybe we've crossed paths—"

He stopped speaking as a starry-eyed teenager approached, her mother encouraging her from behind.

"Are you...are you Carter St. Clair?" When he nodded, she shrieked and giggled. "It really is you! I don't believe this! Can my mom take a picture of us together? Please?"

"Excuse me for a second." With an apologetic look at Samantha, Carter walked to the other side of the deck with the teen and looped his arm around her shoulders. He flashed a smile as the girl's mother began taking shots with her cell phone.

"Is he someone famous?" Samantha asked.

"Don't let him hear you say that." Mark tried to conceal his smile. "You'll crush his ego."

"*Carter St. Clair*," Mercer emphasized. "He's a soap opera actor. He plays Jake Burton on *Friends and Lovers*? Don't tell me you've never watched it, Sam. Not even once? He was nominated for a Daytime Emmy last year. His character developed a split personality."

"I played *identical twins*," Carter corrected as he returned. He sounded a little peeved that even Mercer had gotten the details wrong. "It turned out my character has this evil brother—"

"I know the feeling," Mark muttered.

"Sam used to bartend in Manhattan," Mercer said. "While she was putting herself through culinary school."

"What clubs?" Carter asked.

Samantha fidgeted. "I moved around to different places. West Thirteenth, Hudson Street—"

"The Meatpacking District? That's a hot area. I bet you used to work at Sapphire, didn't you? It's known for having the best-looking wait staff in New York. They say if you don't make it as a Victoria's Secret model, Sapphire is the next best thing. I can totally see you there."

"I did work at Sapphire for a while. It was my last job in New York, actually," Samantha replied, sounding uneasy.

"I hear the tips are amazing."

"They weren't bad," she admitted.

They talked for a few more minutes, with Carter continuing to ask Samantha questions about her former life in New York until she reminded Mercer they still had another mile to go on their run. As Mercer gave Carter another tight hug, Samantha looked at Mark, her brown eyes uncertain.

"I still owe you a check for last night," Mark said. "You left before I could give it to you."

She tucked a loose strand of hair behind her ear, appearing as nervous as he felt. "You can drop it in the mail. Or give it to Mercer before she and I meet up again. We're going to try to run in the evenings during the week."

"Samantha," Mark said, his voice low. "I—"

"Okay, then. Let's go." Mercer tugged at Samantha's elbow. Before Mark could finish, his sister began dragging her away. They turned and headed back down the steps to the sand. Mark and Carter watched as the two women picked up their pace and soon disappeared into the throngs of beachgoers.

"Jesus, I think I'm in love," Carter murmured.

Mark pressed his lips together, his only consolation being that Samantha had seemed uninterested in Carter despite his best attempts to charm her. Still, he felt a knot in his stomach. It wasn't the first time he and his brother had been attracted to the same woman.

Shelley had been the first.

CHAPTER SEVEN

"MARK AND CARTER have one of those love-hate rela-
tionships," Mercer confided, slightly winded as she jogged
alongside Samantha. Their approach caused a trio of egrets fishing
at the shoreline to take flight. "They were close growing up, but
things got competitive in their teen years. I love Carter like crazy,
but he had classic middle-child syndrome, always wanting what
his big brother had."

"How much older is Mark?" Samantha asked.

"Two years. Of course, things went from good-natured
competition to knock-down, drag-out fighting where Shelley
was concerned."

They reached the beach parking lot area where Mercer had left
her car, a sleek Lexus convertible in cherry red. The women came
to a stop, catching their breath. Samantha wiped perspiration from
her face with her forearm. "Shelley...that was Mark's wife, right?"

Mercer nodded, bending forward with her hands on her
thighs before speaking again. "She and Mark were high school

sweethearts. But when Mark left for college in Atlanta, Shelley was still here in school. So was Carter."

"Oh," Samantha murmured, realizing where the story was headed.

"I don't know what upset Mark more—that Shelley cheated on him or that Carter would actually steal his girlfriend. Let's just say things were mighty tense for a while in the St. Clair household."

Mercer shrugged. "That was all a long time ago, but it changed Mark and Carter's relationship forever."

Samantha thought of the man she had just met. Carter *was* remarkably handsome, but a little too perfect for her liking. While there were definite physical similarities between the brothers, Carter appeared toned, highlighted and tanned within an inch of his life. She supposed all of it was necessary for his occupation, which in some ways wasn't unlike her previous life. She felt old remorse pass through her. When Devin had first pressured her to start dancing at his club, he'd told her to pretend she was an actress on stage. Trina Grissom wasn't taking off her clothes for money—it was simply a character she played. But that mental ploy never worked for her, not that Devin had cared. He'd had other ways to ensure her compliance.

Body makeup had sometimes been required to cover the bruises.

"Sam? You still in there somewhere?" Mercer touched her shoulder.

Realizing she'd zoned out, Samantha shook off the exhumed memory. She gave Mercer a small smile of apology and self-consciously tightened her ponytail. "Sorry, I guess the run tired me out."

"You're living at the Wayfarer Apartments, right? How about I drop you off at your place? You did run over here to meet me this morning. I think you've hit your quota on self-punishment for the day."

Samantha agreed, and they walked to the car.

As Mercer got in on the driver's side, she continued her story. "Things didn't last too long between Carter and Shelley. She broke it off with him after a few months. I think she was always meant for Mark. It took a little while, but he and Shelley eventually found their way back to each other. They were married for seven years."

She frowned as she backed the Lexus from the space. "Losing Shelley nearly destroyed Mark. It was hard on the whole family, actually. We all loved her."

"Mark told me she died in a car accident two years ago," Samantha acknowledged quietly.

"Is that all he told you?" Mercer stole a glance at her as she made a right turn from the parking lot. When Samantha nodded, she sighed softly. "They were hit by a drunk driver coming back from Spoleto in Charleston."

"They? Mark was with her?"

"And Emily. The driver crossed lanes and hit them head on. Emily was in the back in a car seat and wasn't hurt, thank goodness. Mark broke his collarbone and had some pretty bad cuts, but Shelley…" She shook her head, her fingers visibly tightening on the steering wheel. "She was pinned inside the wreckage. Mark tried to help her, but she died at the scene right in front of them. Before paramedics could even get there."

"That's when Emily stopped speaking, isn't it?"

"Yes."

Sympathy welled inside her. Samantha had an urge to go straight to the St. Clair and scoop the sweet little girl up in her arms.

"Emily wasn't even three at the time. They're not really sure how much she understood at that age, but…" Mercer pressed her lips together briefly. "Mark's taken her to specialists all over the country. For a long time, I think Emily was the only thing holding him together."

A minute later, they pulled into the crushed-shell parking lot in front of the Wayfarer Apartments. The pink, two-story stucco building was old but pleasant enough, with black shutters on the windows and stubby palmettos lining the walkway. Large red geraniums sat in concrete urns outside the office door of the building manager. Samantha made another date to go running with Mercer and then climbed from the vehicle. Their combined moods had turned somber with the discussion of the car accident, and Samantha wondered if Mercer's return to Rarity Cove had been of her choosing or whether she'd come home to look after her oldest brother and niece.

"I know you and Mark went for a walk on the beach last night." Mercer squinted up at her from behind the steering wheel. "That's a big step for him. For what it's worth, he really does seem to like you."

Fishing in the glove box, she slipped on a pair of designer sunglasses. With a wave, Mercer drove off down the road. Samantha waited until the car was out of sight, and then she walked to her first-floor apartment stoop, her heart heavy and mind full. Her own mother had died of a drug overdose, drowning in her own vomit on the bathroom floor while her daughter was away at school. She…Trina…had been the one to find her. Still, she couldn't imagine a child as young as Emily witnessing her mother's death in such a violent, heartrending way.

For what it's worth, he really does seem to like you.

Samantha picked up the Sunday edition of the *Post and Courier,* the Charleston newspaper, that had been left on her welcome mat, hugging it to her chest as she unlocked the door with her key. She thought of Mark, with his easy smile and soft-blue eyes, and wondered how he managed to appear so strong when his life had all but caved in around him.

※

"My darling, baby boy!" Olivia rushed to meet Carter as he exited the passenger side of Mark's Volvo station wagon. She had been outside, wearing a wide-brimmed sunhat and gardening gloves, when they'd pulled onto the circular driveway in front of the Big House. Mark had called her from the restaurant parking lot, letting her know of Carter's early arrival.

"Now just let me get a good look at you," she said, setting down her basket of freshly cut roses. She beamed up at him, then threw her arms around Carter's shoulders and kissed him on both cheeks. "I've missed you so. It's just not the same seeing you on television!"

"I've missed you, too, Mom," Carter said, voice husky.

Olivia's gaze moved between her sons, and Mark thought he saw a faint mist form in her eyes. She shook her head. "Both of you have so much of my Harrison in you."

"Yeah," Carter agreed jokingly. "But which one of us is better looking?"

Mark rolled his eyes.

Olivia withdrew her hands from the gardening gloves, then used them to give Carter a playful warning slap on the shoulder. "None of that. You know I never pick favorites. And it's not nice to tease your mother. Let's all go inside. I know it's early, but I had Marisol mix us up a pitcher of mimosas. I've got some of those tiny little ham biscuits you like, too, Carter."

"We just had breakfast," Mark reminded, following them

inside. Retrieving her basket, Olivia placed her other arm around Carter's waist.

"So we'll just fatten him up. Carter's gotten way too skinny."

They walked through the wide foyer with its polished hardwood floor and soaring curved staircase and into the large, formal parlor Olivia reserved for company. The room was tastefully decorated in shades of cream, coral and robin's-egg blue. A baby grand piano sat in front of the picture window, and on the far wall an enormous curio cabinet held Olivia's expansive collection of antique Limoges porcelain.

She drew Carter down on the sofa next to her. "Now I want you to tell me every little detail about this movie you're shooting in Charleston."

While they talked, Mark walked to the piano. He ran his fingers over its glossy top, experiencing a familiar tug inside him. No one in the St. Clair family had an ounce of musical talent, except for Shelley, who had been an accomplished classical pianist. She had even played with the Charleston Symphony for two of its summer seasons. The piano had belonged to her, but it had been too large for their ocean-side bungalow. Olivia had offered to keep it here and Shelley would come often to play. Mark looked at the sheets of music that still rested above the keyboard, untouched. It was Shelley's favorite arrangement of *Mozart's Sonata in C*. He released a tight breath and stared out the window across the wide, green lawn, watching as the underground sprinkler system watered the thick Bermuda grass.

"Oh, my! The *leading* role," Olivia enthused as Marisol came into the room carrying a white wicker tray loaded with refreshments. "Did you hear that, Marisol?"

"I sure did. That's really something, Carter."

Both Mark and Carter warmly greeted the housekeeper, who

had worked for the St. Clair family for years. Carter rose and hugged her as soon as she'd put down the tray. She poured drinks from a crystal pitcher and handed them out before leaving again.

"So who's your leading lady?" Olivia asked as Carter helped himself to one of the dainty ham biscuits.

"She's a model, Mom. It's her first acting job. You've probably never heard of her, but—"

"Not the movie, child. What I mean is who's your leading lady in *real life?* And don't go trying to tell me you don't have one." Olivia smiled and batted her eyelashes, pleased by her attempt at cleverness.

"The truth is, I don't," Carter said around a mouthful of biscuit. "There's no one special right now."

He looked at Mark, who'd turned back around but still stood with one hand on the piano. Mark felt himself tense, knowing the exact direction of his brother's thoughts.

Carter gave him a sly wink. "Who knows? Maybe that's something I can work on while I'm here."

*

CHAPTER EIGHT

Pain exploded in Trina's cheekbone. She fell against the night-stand, tipping over the Turkish lamp and shattering its cobalt glass. Gasping, she lifted her hand to her face. Devin towered over her, a cold smile planted on his lips.

"That's not going to look good on stage, now is it?"

She tasted blood in her mouth. Above the rising buzz in her ears, she heard her own unsteady voice. "I-I won't go back! I can't do it anymore!"

He jerked her upright, his fingers clamping on to her upper arms.

"You'll do what I want," he ground out in a low voice, nostrils flaring and eyes filled with dark meaning. "Haven't you learned that by now, little girl?"

TAKING A DEEP breath, Samantha tried to keep her thoughts from darkening further. She stood in the rising steam cloud inside the shower, hoping the pelting jets of hot water might somehow cleanse her mind along with her body. But at times the memories were so strong she couldn't shake them. An article in the Sunday newspaper—a profile on adult entertainment clubs in North Charleston—had been the trigger. The piece had talked about the seedier aspects of such establishments, including the women they exploited and often destroyed. It had sent her thoughts hurtling back to places she tried never to go.

She swayed slightly under the heavy, warm spray. Even now, she felt herself flinching at the recollection of Devin's husky drawl.

I own you, Trina. I own you, body and soul.

When she'd first met Devin, she...Trina...had been on the streets for two solid nights. She'd also run out of the petty sum of cash she had brought with her. She had been cold, hungry and utterly alone. There hadn't been money to buy a bus ticket back to Mamaw Jean, even if she had wanted to go. Devin had been sweet and protective. He'd taken her to an all-night diner and bought her the first actual meal she'd had in days. Then he had offered to let her sleep on his couch, help her find a job and get on her feet. Craving the love she'd never had at home, Trina had easily fallen under his spell. Before long, she started sleeping in his bed. He bought her clothes. Told her she was beautiful and made her feel special. A short time later, he'd also gotten her a fake driver's license that said she was four years older than she actually was. Soon, she was dancing at a club he ran—the smoky, dimly lit Blue Iris.

The other girls did favors for patrons, but Trina belonged only to Devin.

She had been his obsession. He loved the dark thrill of other men watching her, wanting her, but knowing she was his alone.

Samantha turned off the water and stood there for several moments, listening to the soft plunk-plunking of water dripping from her hair onto the molded plastic shower floor.

It's over. It has been for a long time. That's not my life now.

Wrapping a towel around herself, she forced her mind back to the present. She thought of the challenging run she'd had with Mercer that morning and tried to conjure up the calming sounds of ocean waves and cawing sea gulls along the shore. But eventually her wandering thoughts turned to Mark St. Clair and the things she'd learned about him. It had surprised her that such tragedy could touch a life like his—one that otherwise seemed so ideal.

Samantha couldn't help but wonder what Mark's wife had looked like. She imagined a classically pretty, sunny blonde with sky-blue eyes and a beauty queen smile. She could see Mark with someone like that. Samantha—Trina—had been a blonde at one time, at Devin's insistence. But nothing about it had been natural.

Don't go back there, she implored herself. But the haunting memory of that horrific, fateful night seemed to always be waiting to claim her.

Afterward, she had fled Memphis under cover of darkness, dyeing her hair back to its original color in a dingy bus station bathroom. Then she had headed northeast, hoping to get lost in the biggest city she knew of. Several months later, after getting a job at a high-profile Manhattan nightclub using her new identity, she'd saved enough money to have the breast implants removed. She'd had to wash the outward signs of Trina away. Her life had depended on it.

You got any idea what you're worth to me? All those men paying my cover charge and swilling twelve-dollar drinks for the privilege of putting cash between your titties?

Tits I paid for.

She shivered at the ghostlike feel of Devin's hands on her, squeezing. Pinching.

He had been possessive, volatile and sadistic—things he'd initially hidden from her behind a mask of charisma. Both Devin and his older brother, Red, were frightening and invincible, with their hands in a number of illicit dealings, much of it handled at the club while nude women danced. The Learys were the Southern equivalent of Mafia, and just as dangerous.

Irritated by the destructive direction of her thoughts, Samantha pulled the towel from her body and used it to blot her hair. She took a long, discerning look at her reflection in the vanity mirror. The woman before her was trim and fit, with dark hair and small, rounded breasts. Trina was gone.

Still, when she closed her eyes, she was back in that Memphis apartment again—shivering, shards of cobalt glass around her, her hands stained with blood.

Samantha went into the bedroom to dress. Sunday was her only full day off from the café, and she didn't want to waste it torturing herself with painful memories. Instead, she planned to go to the outlet mall outside Charleston and look for a new pair of running shoes. Then perhaps later she would catch an afternoon matinee by herself in a dark, air-conditioned theater. Maybe she'd even go by the mega-bookstore and pick up a few new culinary magazines and books. She read a lot, for enjoyment and to make up for her lack of a more formal education.

During their run, Mercer had invited Samantha to the St. Clair to sunbathe and have lunch by the pool. As enticing as the invitation had been, she hadn't thought it prudent. There was no point in putting herself in Mark's path.

She didn't really mind being alone—*she didn't*. Still, she felt a stab of loneliness.

It was an isolated life, but far better than the one she'd left behind.

CHAPTER NINE

I T WAS THE tenth of August and Monday, but as far as Mark was concerned, it might as well have been Friday the thirteenth. Murphy's Law had been in full effect all day, with everything from a double booking for the honeymoon suite to the hotel's industrial hygienist voicing concern about bacteria levels in one of the steam rooms. Mark had handled the former with a comped room and a magnum of Cristal champagne for one of the couples, the latter by shutting down the saunas until more testing could be done. Not to mention, the tiered marble fountain in the atrium had stopped working, due to a child's toy that had found its way into one of the main water lines.

The hotel business. Glamorous work.

He'd just sat down in the dining room for a badly needed cup of coffee when Carter entered, carrying a white box tied with a blue satin ribbon. Mark felt a pervading grayness. He didn't have to ask—he recognized the packaging and knew it had come from Café Bella. He regarded the box as Carter set it on the table in front of him. "I thought you didn't do carbs."

"I don't. Usually. These are for Mom or Emily," he said. "Want a cupcake? They're called *Homemade Sin*—chocolate covered with caramel filling on the inside."

"No, thanks. Aren't you supposed to be on location today?"

Carter dropped into the chair across from Mark. He wore jean shorts and a V-neck T-shirt, not suitable attire for the dining room, although Mark didn't mention it.

"I have been. We had a table reading this morning. It finished up at noon, so I thought I'd drive back here and drop by Samantha's place to try out her menu."

He patted his washboard abs. "The food's good. Great, actually. I'm going to have to put in an extra hour in the hotel gym."

"The place busy?"

"Packed. I went after the lunch hour, but there was still a line waiting to order. I'd hoped to get a chance to talk to Sam privately, but no dice."

Mark wasn't sure he wanted to know, but he took the plunge anyway. "Talk to her about what?"

"The reception Olivia's throwing on Saturday night." Carter casually scratched his cheek. "I'm going to ask her to go with me."

Mark felt his jaw clench. He set the delicate china cup in its saucer with a soft clatter. "Can't you just ask someone from the movie set? I'm sure there're plenty of actresses hanging around who'd die to go with you."

Carter shrugged. "I'd rather go with Samantha."

"You can't."

"Why not? She's single, right?"

Mark absently twisted the gold band on his ring finger. Not meeting Carter's eyes, he said, "Because she's already going with me."

Carter's mouth hung open for a full three seconds. "You're making that up."

"I'm not." Mark felt his face infuse with heat. "I asked her as soon as I heard about the reception, before you even got into town. Stop staring at me like that."

"*You* have a date. With Samantha."

"Why is that so hard for you to process?" But the truth was, Carter wasn't the only one caught off guard by the announcement. Mark couldn't believe the impulsive lie that had come out of his mouth. He tried not to think about Samantha's rejection of him the past weekend.

"So how come this didn't come up when we ran into her at Mila's?"

It was Mark's turn to shrug.

Carter studied him. "Well, I guess you really *are* doing all right. You're getting on with your life. It's time, Mark. Good for you."

"Yeah," he agreed in a tight voice. "Good for me."

"But you could've told me about this earlier. I feel like a jack-ass now for the way I've been going on about her." Carter frowned at him, a suspicious tone in his voice. "Were you planning to just spring her on everyone on Saturday?"

"No. I...just wasn't ready to talk about it yet."

Carter gave a slow shake of his head. "But you enjoyed watching me fawn over her, didn't you? Knowing full well—"

"Carter."

"Don't worry about it." He sounded nonchalant as he rose from the chair and glanced at Mercer as she entered the dining room with Emily in tow. Before he left the table, he reached over and tapped Mark's ring with his index finger. "One small piece of advice, though. You might want to consider ditching the wedding band. At least for Saturday night. From what I hear, that kind of thing tends to start dates off on the wrong foot."

Carter picked up his niece, nuzzling his nose playfully against her cheek, then returned her to the floor. To Mercer, he said, "Did you hear? Big brother has a D-A-T-E."

He spelled out the word so Emily wouldn't pick up on the meaning. Although Mark didn't look up, he could practically feel Mercer's surprised gaze burning a hole through his dress shirt.

"Really?" she asked.

Emily squeezed between the table and Mark's chair so she stood in front of him. She blinked her large blue eyes and smiled.

Shelley's smile.

Mark stroked her blond curls and pulled her onto his lap. He kissed the top of her head as she wriggled into a more comfortable spot.

He had a date, apparently. Now all he had to do was somehow break the news to Samantha that she had plans for Saturday night.

A light breeze traveling in from the bay ruffled the tops of the palm trees lining Market Street just off the town square. From inside the café, Samantha watched their sway as overhead, the evening sky faded closer to dusk. It was just before eight o'clock, and she and Luther were still there, cleaning up after an early evening rush. Luther had settled into the role of helping Samantha with the morning food preparation each day, but tonight he'd also come by to assist with closing since one of the other workers was out with a stomach bug. At the moment, he was busy moving cold food items from the front display into the larger refrigeration unit in the rear of the kitchen.

Samantha was standing at the door, turning over the sign from *open* to *closed*, when a silver Volvo station wagon pulled up at the curb out front. A moment later, Mark emerged from the driver's side. As his eyes met hers through the door's glass pane, she felt her heart do an involuntary somersault. Lifting her hand in a slight wave as he approached, she opened the door so he could enter.

Mark raised both palms in a reassuring manner. "Don't worry. I know you're closing. I promise I'm not here to order anything."

"That's a relief," she said, trying to keep her tone light. Samantha eyed him curiously, wondering why he was here.

He handed her a check, her payment for Emily's party. "I know I could've just given it to Mercer, but I had to come into town anyway."

"Thank you." She folded the paper in half and dropped it into her apron pocket.

He hesitated, releasing a breath. "The truth is, I also wanted to talk to you about something—"

"All finished up in back, Sam," Luther announced as he returned to the storefront through the swinging double doors. Seeing Mark, he nodded his head in polite greeting. "Evenin', Mr. St. Clair. Nice to see you again."

"You, too, Luther. But just call me Mark."

"Oh...all right." Luther's gaze shifted to Samantha. She wondered if he'd picked up on her unease, because he appeared reluctant to leave. Instead, he loitered by the cash register, taking extra care in erasing the daily specials from the chalkboard.

"You can go ahead, Luther," she said. "Thanks for helping out."

"Don't you want me to stick around and walk you to the bank to make the evenin' deposit?"

"I'll be fine." Samantha gave him a reassuring smile, although part of her wanted to ask him to stay. That way, she wouldn't be left alone with Mark and another brush with temptation. He looked handsome, as usual, still dressed for work in dark suit pants and a blue dress shirt that matched the color of his eyes. His tie, however, had been disposed of.

"Then I reckon I'll see you in the morning. Good night." Luther removed his apron and hung it on a wooden peg, then went back into the kitchen and left the shop through the rear service door.

Swallowing, Samantha returned her attention to Mark. "You wanted to talk to me?"

He shoved his hands into his pockets in what seemed like a nervous gesture. "I have a business proposition for you, actually. Café Bella is getting rave reviews around town, and I've been wondering if you'd be interested in the St. Clair gift shop carrying some of your food products." His gaze traveled to the shelving that held various jars of condiments, pestos and relishes, all with the café's logo on their labels. "If you're interested, I was also thinking we could feature some of your products in our food preparation at the hotel. Our head chef could collaborate with you on the recipes."

She stared at him, her lips parting in surprise. What he was offering would be an incredible boon for her business. "I…I'd love that. It sounds like a wonderful opportunity. Thank you."

He nodded. "We'll have to discuss pricing, of course. The gift shop will require a modest profit margin. Maybe around fifteen percent?"

"That would work."

They talked for a while about the products Mark thought might be most appropriate for the shop, including the possibility of Samantha creating gift baskets that would contain an assortment of items. Lowering the blinds on the storefront windows so no one got the impression the café was still open, Samantha went about creating a sampler platter of olive tapenade, parsley and sundried tomato pestos, spreading them on thin water biscuits for

Mark to sample. She felt a glow of pride when he declared them all delicious.

When it seemed that most of the initial decisions were nailed down, Mark glanced at his wristwatch. Outside, the streetlights were on, and the evening sky had transformed into a darkened canvas streaked with smoky purples and blues.

"Luther mentioned a nighttime deposit? I could walk you to the bank."

Samantha shook her head. "Thanks, but you really don't have to. I'm sure you need to get back to Emily."

"It's all right. My mother has her for the evening. She wanted a little *Nana* time." He frowned slightly, hesitating again. "I also need a favor from you, Samantha. There's a reception at the St. Clair this Saturday for my brother…I need you to be there."

She was puzzled. "Be there? Does it have something to do with the gift shop?"

"Not really. I need you to sort of be my…date." Mark rubbed his forehead. "I'm sorry. I'm not very good at this, am I?"

Samantha felt a wave of anxiety wash through her. Mark was light years away from Devin—from any other man she'd ever known. But she still couldn't control the feeling he'd just attempted to buy her. Old resentment squeezed her lungs.

"Is that why you offered me space at your gift shop?" she asked in a tight voice. "So I'd go out with you?"

"What? Of course not—"

With a small shake of her head, she took the check from her apron pocket and added it to the deposit bag on the counter. She didn't look at him. "I'm sure someone with your kind of money must be used to getting whatever they want. *Who* they want. But I need to make something clear—"

"Samantha." Mark stepped forward and gently touched her arm, causing her stomach to flutter. Her eyes returned to his face.

"I'm sorry. I swear to you I didn't mean it that way. But in retrospect, I guess that's probably how it sounded." He appeared genuinely distressed. With a sigh, he ran a hand through his hair before dropping it down to his side again. "Look, the offer about the gift shop stands regardless of whether you turn me down or not. You have good products. The guests at the St. Clair are the perfect demographic for your business. Going with me to the reception...that's a completely separate matter. I made a mistake rolling the conversations together. It's been a really long time since I've done anything like this."

She pressed her fingers briefly against her face. Clearly, she'd overreacted.

"I'm sorry I misunderstood," Samantha conceded. "But why me? Why can't you ask someone else?"

Clasping the back of his neck, he stared at the floor. "I know this is going to sound unbelievably immature, but it has to do with Carter. He told me he was planning to ask you. So I sort of freaked out and told him you were already going with me. It was an impulse move. I feel like an idiot."

"You're not wearing your wedding ring," she noted somberly.

His blush deepened. "I was advised it was bad form."

He seemed so off-balance that Samantha felt her resistance crumbling.

"I know what you said the other night about us only being friends. I haven't forgotten it," he added a little hoarsely. "Going with me to the reception...it doesn't have to change that. I don't... I wouldn't have any expectations. It would be completely platonic. And you could make some good business contacts."

"What would you tell Carter if I refuse?"

He lifted his shoulders in a helpless shrug. "I don't know. To be honest, I haven't thought that far ahead. Fess up that I lied and eat crow, I guess. Or maybe tell him you came down with the flu at the last minute. I hear there's something going around."

He added self-deprecatingly, "I'm feeling a little ill myself right now."

Samantha studied him. Then she took a deep breath, deciding against her better judgment. "So what would I need to wear for this *platonic* arrangement?"

A short time later, he escorted her to the bank on the town square, waiting as she made her deposit through the nighttime security slot. Then Mark walked her to the Camry that was parked in the alley behind the café and made sure she was safely on her way home. She studied him in her rearview mirror, still standing there, as she pulled onto the street. Driving to her apartment, Samantha allowed herself to think about the prospect of attending such a fancy reception. Mark had seemed so appreciative of her agreement to go with him. And despite her best effort, the idea of spending an evening with him caused a small knot of pleasure to form inside her.

She was playing with fire.

Don't fall for him, she cautioned herself again.

They could attend the reception together and simply come away as casual friends, couldn't they? He'd said as much himself. Mark was a civic leader. Going with him *was* a good business decision.

But he'd already told her once that he was interested in her— there was no getting around that. Even if he was too much of a gentleman to push the point. Samantha frowned. After losing the love of his life, he'd had the remarkable bad luck of her being the first woman who'd captured his attention.

Carter's arrival had prompted Mark to come out of his shell, apparently. If she'd turned him down, how far might she have set him back? She tried to cling to the belief that she'd done the right, decent thing.

It can't go anywhere. You can't allow anyone in like that. It would be too easy for him to see the missing spaces and start asking questions.

It wouldn't be safe for him, or you.

Hopefully, their outing would give Mark the nudge he needed to put his personal tragedy behind him and get on with his life. He would meet another, much more suitable woman, she rationalized. But as she parked her car in one of the vacant spaces outside her apartment building, Samantha relived the sensation she'd felt at his touch. She admitted again to herself that she felt a strong physical attraction to him, something she hadn't felt in a very long time.

It worried her.

CHAPTER TEN

CARTER SLOWED AS he drove past the town square, fairly certain it was Samantha he saw lounging on one of the wrought-iron benches under the shade of a century-old live oak. She sat absorbed in a magazine, a curtain of sleek, dark hair partially obscuring her features. He was headed to an old high school pal's beach house to hang out with some friends for the afternoon, but on impulse he wheeled his rental—a bright yellow, open-air Hummer—into an available parking spot.

"Samantha?" he called as he crossed the courtyard, heading toward her. She looked up from the magazine.

"I thought that was you." Carter smiled as he reached her. She had on a white, fitted T-shirt emblazoned with the Café Bella logo on its front pocket. Her long, tanned legs stretched out from a pair of khaki shorts. "Taking a break?"

"The lunch crowd's over, and there's a breeze, so I thought I'd sit out here for a little while and catch up on my reading. Aren't you filming today?"

"I'm not on set until tonight—I've got the day free." He

noticed the magazine's cover. It was a foodie publication with a photo of what looked like a rustic pizza with arugula and grilled shrimp on top. "Professional research?"

"I like to keep up with the trends."

Taking a seat on the bench beside her, he leaned back and pushed his sunglasses onto the top of his head. Carter wore swim trunks under his golf shirt and flip-flops.

"If you ask me, you don't need any tips. What I had at your place the other day was pretty amazing." He patted his stomach. "It's a good thing I'm just here for the movie, or I'd become a regular and eat myself right out of a job."

She arched an eyebrow at him. "Well, you could always go from leading-man status to character actor. A little paunch would work well for you."

He chuckled lightly. "I'm glad business is going well, Sam. Thank God for tourists, right? Most of the locals around here think a pork chop with a parsley sprig is haute cuisine."

Her caramel-brown eyes assessed him. "I doubt that. Charleston is known for its world-class restaurants, and it's only a short drive away. And from what I've heard, the St. Clair's restaurant is pretty top-notch. Mercer says it stays busy even in the off-season."

"It's good, but a little conventional. I've talked to Mark about jazzing up the menu, but he can be pretty conservative about changing things."

Samantha said pointedly, "All of this culinary sophistication is interesting, especially since Mercer claims your favorite food is Chef Boyardee."

Carter shook his head good-naturedly, feeling his face heat. "When I was ten." He stared across the courtyard, focusing on the large, blossoming magnolia and tiered fountain in the square's

center. Two children, their hands loaded with pennies, were tossing coins into the water and loudly announcing their wishes as a
gray-haired woman, probably their grandmother, supervised from
a nearby bench.

"So I'm busted, thanks to my motor-mouthed sister. I was trying to impress you," he admitted. He leaned forward, his elbows
on his knees as he squinted up at her. "The truth is, I do know
my chèvres from my Gruyères. I've been living in New York for a
while now, and despite what Mercer may have led you to believe,
I eat more than pizza and bagels up there. Talk about some great
restaurants, not to mention the street food."

Samantha gave a nod of agreement. "There was a Vietnamese
food truck that would set up near my apartment. I've never had
anything better, anywhere."

"Which leads me to something I've been wanting to ask..."
Carter *was* genuinely curious. "New York's the epicenter of the
culinary world, at least on this continent. After getting a big-time
chef's degree, why leave there to set up a little café in Podunk,
USA?"

She paused before answering.

"I was never really that happy in New York, I guess. As much as
I didn't want to admit it to myself, I'm still a small-town Southern
girl at heart. It's also way too expensive there to open a business. I
studied the demographics here, and it seemed like a good choice."
She brushed back a few strands of hair the sultry afternoon breeze
had blown into her eyes. "Besides, I hardly consider this place
Podunk. Trust me, I grew up in Podunk."

She peered out over the square. "I also visited here once as a
child and never forgot it. It's beautiful."

"Yeah, you're right," Carter conceded quietly. Sitting back
against the bench again, he took in the lush scenery, aware of the

twittering sound of birds and scent of gardenias wafting in the warm, heavy air. He had loved growing up here, and despite pretenses otherwise, he missed it. "Hey, I hear you've got a date with Mark on Saturday night."

Her hands fluttered nervously over the magazine, smoothing its glossy cover. "Well, sort of a date. Mark…he asked me to go with him to the reception."

"That *is* a date," he pointed out. "Isn't it?"

It was her turn to blush. "Yes, of course it is."

"Well, I won't hold this"—his grin widened as he drew quotation marks in the air with his fingers—"*date* with my brother against you."

She looked at him curiously.

"Relax, Sam. I'm just messing with you. It's great you're going with Mark. And it's good he's finally getting out again. He deserves some fun—he works way too much this time of year. We'll all have a good time together, despite Mom's attempts to turn it into something pretentious."

He focused briefly on a clump of Spanish moss overhead, dangling from a tree bough. "I just thought of something. I'm headed to a buddy's beach house out on Folly Island. He's having a little party this afternoon—some of the old gang. We're going to throw back a few beers, grill some steaks and float around on the water. Want to come along? I'll introduce you around, since you're new here. You can make some friends. Hell, bring some business cards and hand them out."

She shook her head. "I need to get back to work."

"C'mon. What's wrong with a little *toes in the sand, drinks in hand?*" he pressed easily. "You said yourself the lunch rush is over. Let someone else handle things. We can stop by your place for your swimsuit."

"Thanks, but I'll let the old gang reunite without a stranger showing up. Have a good time, Carter."

The refusal was polite but firm. Samantha stood, then bent to tighten the strap on one of her sandals. Picking up her straw tote bag that lay next to the bench, she took off in the direction of the café, giving him a small wave good-bye over her shoulder.

Carter studied her as he returned his sunglasses to the bridge of his nose. He felt a stab of guilt for testing the waters, unsure as to why exactly he'd done that, considering Mark had already staked a claim. Based on her awkwardness concerning their date, he'd thought maybe she wasn't all that interested. But she *had* accepted Mark's invitation, while she'd had no hesitation in turning *his* down. It wasn't often that a woman refused him, and he almost respected it.

Carter was also aware that despite several conversations with her now, Samantha still remained pretty much a mystery, demure and unwilling to divulge much about herself.

He had noticed something else about her, too. When she'd bent to fix her shoe strap, the raised hem of her tee had revealed the expanse of her slender lower back. He'd gotten a partial glimpse of a rather large, exotic tattoo. It was something he hadn't expected, not on someone who seemed so reserved. It intrigued him.

Carter watched as she disappeared from view. He had a sixth sense about women. Something told him there was more to Samantha Marsh than met the eye.

CHAPTER ELEVEN

THE NEW PSYCHIATRIST Emily had been referred to was African-American and younger than Mark expected, with a mass of curly hair and stylish, tortoise-shell glasses. He'd been watching through an observation window as she sat with Emily on the floor of her Charleston office, using finger puppets and an elaborate three-story dollhouse that vaguely reminded Mark of his mother's home. His cell phone rang, but instead of answering, he switched off the sound, intent on trying to discern some action in their play that might provide insight into Emily's emotional status.

In almost every way, she seemed like a normal child. Emily's motor skills and development levels—with the exception of verbal—were right on target, according to the specialists' assessments. Mark released a labored breath. Before the accident, Emily had been a talkative toddler who'd asked more questions than a wise parent should be willing to answer. Now he would give everything he had just to hear her utter a single word. Even when she cried, which wasn't often, tears would streak silently down her cheeks. Her voiceless sobs would cause Mark's heart to shatter.

He tensed as the psychiatrist finally stood. Through the glass, he could hear her praising Emily and thanking her for her time. Mark prepared himself to learn the results of this latest evaluation.

"I'd like to start seeing Emily twice a week," Dr. Richardson said once she had entered the area where Mark was waiting. He continued to watch his daughter, who remained in the office, still absorbed in the dollhouse and its miniature people and furniture.

"Do you have an initial assessment?"

The psychiatrist's curls bounced as she shook her head. "It's really too early, I'm afraid. But I've been through Emily's charts. She's a bright child, obviously. But her inability to communicate verbally makes it more difficult to elicit information from her, which is why it's important to engage her in play and make observations."

"Did you observe anything notable today?"

Dr. Richardson hesitated. "Both the puppets and dolls are used to represent family. There's a daddy doll, a mommy doll, and a couple of children. In both play situations, Emily took immediate ownership of the mommy doll. In fact, she refused to share it with me, even when I asked her twice. There was some obvious anxiety about relinquishing it."

Mark rubbed his forehead, a familiar ache inside his chest.

Her eyes were sympathetic. "Mr. St. Clair, I'm aware of the situation surrounding your wife's death and that it triggered Emily's muteness. These things—extremely traumatic events in a young child's life—can take time to work through."

"She's been in extended therapy before," Mark pointed out. "With two other child psychiatrists."

"I know, but I do things a little differently." She gave him a hopeful smile. "Maybe the third time will be the charm. The key is not to give up too early. Since today was our first session, I wanted to get to know Emily alone and get her to feel comfortable with me. The next time, I'd like to observe her interaction with you."

Mark nodded. "Of course."

Dr. Richardson looked over her shoulder at Emily, making sure she was still busy with the toys. "How does she react around others?"

"She seems fine."

"What about strangers?"

"She can be a little standoffish," Mark admitted, but then thought of Emily's easy interaction with Samantha. In fact, it was Emily who had initiated their meeting at the Founder's Day parade. There and at the baking party, she had seemed immediately comfortable, happy even, in Samantha's presence. Emily had been very much okay with Carter, too, but she saw him often since he and Mercer Skyped regularly, and she had been to visit him in New York. He was hardly a stranger. In fact, Carter always asked to speak to her whenever he called home.

"Well, shyness around people she doesn't know isn't unusual for a child her age. I'm looking for extremes in reactions."

"I think she behaves pretty normally." Mark hesitated before asking the question he'd been dreading. "Emily's supposed to be starting kindergarten—next month, actually. I've already gotten her registered, but…"

"We can talk more about it after we've had a few sessions, but right now I doubt that Emily would fare well in a classroom. Most teachers aren't trained to deal with children with…emotional difficulties. Holding her back a year might be advisable." She touched the bridge of her glasses, pushing them higher on her nose. "Ideally, we'll be able to make some progress over the next few months."

Dr. Richardson's statement wasn't entirely surprising since

Mark had already considered the possibility. Still, hearing it from a professional was harder than he had expected.

⌇

"I think a treat might help," Mercer noted from behind the wheel of her convertible. She'd accompanied Mark and Emily to Charleston and had gone to the open-air City Market to browse the vendor stalls while they were at the psychiatry office. They'd taken her convertible and put the top down to enjoy the gorgeous Wednesday afternoon.

Mark used the mirror on the sun visor to peer at Emily in her booster chair in the backseat. The wind whipped her golden curls.

"Emily seems fine," he said.

"I'm not talking about *Emily*." Mercer gave him a pointed glance. She'd tied her long, honey-blond hair into a ponytail, but it still flew around her face. "You've been gloomy since we left Charleston."

Mark didn't respond, although he sat up a little straighter, not wanting Emily to pick up on his mood. It was a forty-minute drive back to Rarity Cove, and they were traveling along the scenic highway that ran adjacent to the ocean. Private beach homes lined the road, a few visible from the car but most of them shielded by high wooden fences. Several of the residences had signage at their driveway entrances, bearing names like *A Shore Thing* and *The Crab Shack*. Mark had been on this stretch of road so many times he knew each of them by heart. As they went past, he caught occasional flashes of white sand and the green plane of ocean in between the beach properties.

"You missed the turn," he remarked a short time later when she failed to make the right onto the peninsula road that led to the St. Clair resort. Mercer continued to drive. If Mark weren't so preoccupied, he'd have put two and two together earlier. By *treat*, she hadn't been suggesting an ice cream sundae in the hotel restaurant.

"I don't have time," he protested quietly, frowning at the miniature disco ball that hung from the car's rearview mirror. It twirled in the breeze.

"The last time I checked, the St. Clair had an assistant manager. Richard is completely capable of handling things without you for another hour."

"I should get back. Why don't you and Emily drop me off there and—"

"Don't be ridiculous, Mark. She's your date to the reception on Saturday. Are you afraid to see her or something?"

"Of course not," he replied, voice tight. "I just don't want her to think I'm stalking her. She was skittish enough about accepting my invitation in the first place."

Mercer rolled her eyes. "She's not going to think you're a stalker. Besides, Samantha was asking about Emily when we met for our run last time. I'm sure she'd love to see her."

She looked at her niece in the mirror, then said loudly enough to be heard above the noise of the open air rushing past, "Hey, Em. You'd like to visit Samantha, wouldn't you?"

Emily bobbed her head enthusiastically.

"You're outnumbered." Mercer grinned, victorious.

His date. Even the terminology sounded awkward and somehow...wrong. Mark touched the ring finger of his left hand, feeling the bare patch of skin where his wedding band usually rested. He'd put it away in a drawer in the bureau of his bedroom before asking Samantha out and hadn't worn it since. Its absence was taking some getting used to, as was the idea that he would soon be out with a woman who wasn't Shelley or another female relative in more years than he could remember.

Reaching the quaint downtown, Mark grumbled, "This is the last time I'm letting you drive."

They entered the café as a group of teenagers slurping lemonade from plastic cups loped out, discussing their plans for the evening. Samantha stood at the cash register, counting bills.

"Hey, Sam," Mercer called. "We're looking for something sweet. Can you help us out?"

Samantha smiled, her brown eyes briefly meeting Mark's.

"Well, you came to the right place," she said, indicating the refrigerated display case with its shelves of bakery items as she walked from behind the counter.

"Hi, Emily." Samantha knelt to give her a hug. "Do you see something in there you like?"

Emily chewed her lip, rapt concentration on her face. Then she pointed to a golden cream puff drenched in dark chocolate.

"Make that two," Mark said.

"I shouldn't, but I'll have the raspberry cream cheese brownie." Mercer added, "With a diet soda. And Emily will have some milk."

"Coming right up."

"I hope you don't mind me coming by," Mark said to Samantha once Mercer had taken Emily to settle her at one of the tables while he paid for their food and drinks.

"No, of course not."

He returned his wallet to his back pocket. "Mercer and I took Emily to her therapy appointment in Charleston this afternoon. We were already out, so…"

Samantha slid her gaze toward Emily. "How'd it go?"

"The psychiatrist doesn't think she should start kindergarten in the fall."

"Oh." Samantha frowned and lightly touched the sleeve of Mark's dress shirt, apparently sensing his upset. "Does Emily know?"

He shook his head. "It's going to be a disappointment. All her friends will be going without her."

"How are you?"

Mark sighed. "I was sort of expecting it."

They talked for a few more moments, then Mark went to join Mercer and Emily at the table while Samantha went about plating their desserts. He watched her discreetly as she worked, her dark hair appearing glossy under the café's recessed lighting. Maybe Mercer was right, he conceded. He *did* need a distraction. But he couldn't stop focusing on the session at Dr. Richardson's office and what she'd told him about Emily's anxiety over the mommy doll. Despite her sweet and generally happy demeanor, it was clear she still felt Shelley's absence profoundly. He felt responsible. He toyed with his daughter's hair, curling it around his index finger and looking up as Samantha approached the table, carrying a tray with their orders.

"I have a special treat for Emily," she revealed, setting one of the cream puffs in front of her. The chocolate ganache on top had been decorated with dainty purple violets and gold, edible beads. Emily's small face lit up.

"Why don't you sit with us, Sam?" Mercer suggested as Samantha handed out the other desserts and placed their drinks on the table. She indicated the space next to Mark, then began tucking a paper napkin into the neck of Emily's top. "It looks like the place has slowed down for the day."

Samantha hesitated, glancing around the otherwise empty interior before laying the tray on an adjacent table and complying. The bistro table was small, and her bare thigh accidentally brushed

Mark's as she sat down. *She's nervous around me, too,* he realized, noticing the way she smoothed her hands over her khaki shorts.

"How's business?" he asked.

"Don't let the momentary lull fool you," Samantha replied. "They were packed in like sardines at lunch."

"So have you settled on an outfit for the reception yet?" Mercer dug her fork into the rich brownie.

"Not yet."

"We just got back from Charleston, and I saw this really pretty cocktail dress in the window at Serendipity on King Street—it's one of my favorite boutiques. It would look amazing on you."

Samantha tucked her hair behind her ear. She'd appeared to blush a little at the reference to the upcoming event. "I'm planning to do some shopping late tomorrow afternoon. In Charleston. Luther's going to close up for me."

"Great." Mercer chewed and swallowed. "This brownie is heaven, by the way. Hey, want me to go with you? I can point out the best shops."

"That'd be great."

"Or better yet, Mark could take you."

Mark had just taken a large bite of his cream puff. At Mercer's surprise offer, he felt his throat close around the flaky pastry and custard filling. He reached for his glass of water to keep from coughing.

"I'm sure Mark's too busy," Samantha backpedaled, a slight strain in her voice as she looked at him. "You really don't have to. Carter told me how hectic things are at the hotel this time of year—"

"Carter?" Mark managed to ask.

She nodded. "I ran into him on the square earlier today. He was on his way to a beach barbecue or something."

"That thing at Tommy Houghton's place. He has it every year." Mercer took a sip of her soda. "If I know Carter, I just bet he asked you to go with him."

Samantha's blush deepened. Although she didn't reply, Mark already suspected the answer. He was also fully aware that Mercer was pushing his buttons. But her strategy had worked—his competitive hackles were raised. Since Samantha was here, she had turned down Carter's invitation at least.

Mark lifted the paper napkin from his lap and wiped his mouth. He directed his gaze to Samantha and tried to sound casual. "So what time should I pick you up?"

CHAPTER TWELVE

"I SPLURGED AND TOOK a private carriage tour when I first moved here," Samantha said to Mark as they strolled on the cobblestone path along the Battery in Charleston Harbor. "But this has been so much better. Thank you."

Mark carried her garment bag slung over one shoulder. The shopping completed, they were killing time prior to the dinner reservations he'd made for them on East Bay Street. He had been showing her around the Historic District, pointing out the centuries-old buildings and regaling her with some of the more colorful folklore. Samantha couldn't remember when she'd had such a pleasant time. She had discovered that in addition to being an astute businessman, Mark also had a witty, self-deprecating sense of humor. Around them, the summer day had faded into a balmy evening, and the streetlamps in White Point Garden had begun to glow. To their right, the harbor's blue waters stretched out like endless, smooth sea glass.

"I'm happy to serve as tour guide," he said as they passed by graceful live oaks and cast-iron benches facing the waterfront. "It reminds me that I take living so close to here for granted."

She followed his gaze to the row of well-maintained, antebellum mansions on the edge of the Battery. Soaring church steeples and spires punctured the hazy sky, giving credence to Charleston's nickname of The Holy City.

"I'm sorry about Mercer yesterday," Mark said. "She means well, but she can be a little pushy. I know going on *two* dates with me isn't exactly what you had in mind."

Samantha guiltily lowered her gaze, an ache in the back of her throat. She didn't want Mark thinking she didn't want to be with him. In reality, the opposite was true, if only her situation was different. "Please understand, it's not that I don't *want* to be here…"

But she fell silent, unsure of what to say. He gave her an inquisitive, slightly pained smile as they continued walking. "Then what *is it*, exactly?"

There were times when she wanted to confide in someone about her past and the serious trouble she'd left behind. But unable to answer and afraid, she felt self-loathing creep in on her.

"I've made you uncomfortable."

"I *don't* feel forced to be here," she stressed. "And I think Mercer did us a favor, actually. We're both a little nervous. Tonight's helping break the ice before the reception on Saturday. I really am having a lot of fun."

He appeared relieved by her assurance. "I just wish you would've let me pay for your dress. If it wasn't for me, you wouldn't be needing it in the first place."

She shook her head. "I couldn't let you do that."

The designer cocktail dress had taken a serious bite out of Samantha's budget, but she knew it was a prerequisite for fitting in at the fancy event. She had never owned anything quite like it before. It was elegant and understated, dipping just a little in front and subtly clinging to her curves. At the boutique, she'd also purchased a pair of sling-back heels and matching clutch purse, items she now carried in a shopping bag with ribbon handles. When she'd tried on the black silk dress for Mark in the upscale boutique, she'd felt a little like Julia Roberts in *Pretty Woman*. But that had been a movie, she reminded herself wistfully. There were rarely such fairy-tale endings in real life.

"Besides," she said, forcing lightness into her voice, "I've heard every woman needs a little black dress. My wardrobe consists mostly of jeans and running clothes."

Mark took her arm, gently guiding her to the left to avoid a gaggle of adolescents tossing a Frisbee on the park's wide expanse of lawn. "Well, I've had the sneak preview. I'm afraid to let Carter see you in that. He's going to want to wrestle me for you on the spot."

She stopped walking and peered at him. "You *do* realize I have absolutely no interest in Carter, don't you?"

"I was joking."

"Carter *did* invite me to the barbecue, but I really think he was just asking me to tag along as a friend, nothing more."

Mark frowned. "Sort of like you and I are just friends?"

"I…just don't want to be the source of any more conflict."

Realization traveled over his features. He clasped the back of his neck. "Mercer told you about Carter and Shelley."

Samantha sighed. "She said it was a long time ago, when all of you were barely even adults—"

"What else did she tell you?"

She regretted the turn of conversation but didn't want to lie to him.

"She told me the details about the accident," she admitted

softly. The wind coming off the harbor whipped her simple cotton skirt and pushed her dark hair into her face. "I'm so sorry for all you and Emily have gone through, Mark."

He fell quiet, and Samantha could see the wash of pain in his blue eyes. Her fingers slid up his forearm in a comforting gesture. His shirtsleeves were rolled up, and she could feel the firm sinews under his warm skin. For a moment, he appeared as though he wanted to say something, but instead he looked off across the water, his profile somber in the dwindling sunlight.

"We should probably get to the restaurant," he mentioned finally, checking his wristwatch and closing the subject between them. "We're still a few blocks away."

≈

They sat in the outdoor courtyard of a new restaurant that had just received a glowing write-up in *Bon Appétit*. The setting was romantic, with candlelit lanterns on the wrought-iron tables and night-blooming jasmine forming a lush veil over the building's aged brick walls. Behind them, the graceful silhouette of another ancient church stretched up into the now-black sky.

"So what do you think?" Mark asked once Samantha had tasted her entrée, a spicy, lowcountry-style shrimp scampi.

"It's delicious. I'm just wondering how you managed to get reservations. I've read about this place, and it's booked weeks in advance."

"I called in a favor with the owner. He's a business acquaintance. I thought with your culinary interests, you'd appreciate the place."

"I do." Samantha smiled softly at him, touched by his thoughtfulness. From spending an entire late afternoon and evening with her during the busy vacation season, to finagling last-minute seating at the most popular restaurant in the city, Mark had gone to a good deal of trouble. Not to mention, most men's idea of a good time wasn't sitting in a ladies clothing boutique, sipping punch from china cups and waiting while their date tried on outfits. Samantha was glad their earlier conversation hadn't ruined their time together.

"How's your meal?" She looked at Mark's roasted trout with brown butter.

"Fantastic. Want to try it?"

When she agreed, he scooped a generous amount onto the tines of his fork and reached across the small table with it. Samantha leaned forward, curling her fingers around his wrist to help guide the food to her mouth. The trout melted on her tongue, competing with the warmth that spread through her body at the intimacy of Mark feeding her.

"Good?"

She nodded, swallowing. Their eyes met and held in the candlelight for an endless moment.

"What?" she asked finally, after she'd touched her linen napkin to her lips.

"I'm just wondering," Mark said in a low voice. "The St. Clair resort. Shelley, my issues with Carter. Why is it you seem to know so much about me when I still feel like I know next to nothing about you?"

Samantha lowered her gaze. She took a sip from her goblet of iced mint tea before speaking.

"*Your family's here*, Mark. And I go running with your very talkative sister. Not to mention, the St. Clair name is legendary in these parts. Of course I know more about you." She attempted a carefree shrug. "Besides, there's really not that much to know about me."

She felt her heartbeat quicken. Mark seemed to be evaluating her response, and she did her best to appear unaffected. But he reached across the table again, this time lightly covering her hand with his.

"I doubt that," he said quietly. "I do want to get to know you, Samantha, if you'll ever consider giving me the chance."

She must have lost herself in his gaze and the courtyard's amorous atmosphere, because it took several seconds before she realized her fingers had become intertwined with his. An electrical current had built in the air around them, the quiet conversations of the other diners receding until Mark slowly withdrew his fingers and lifted his fork from the edge of his dinner plate again. Samantha took another bite in silence. As much as she fought it, her entire body had thrilled at his touch. She felt relief when Mark redirected their conversation to a topic she was more comfortable with—the business venture they had discussed earlier.

"I'm considering the infused oils and several of the pestos as individual products for the St. Clair gift shop," Samantha told him. "Maybe also the preserved lemons? They look great in the vintage-style jars. I can see them being purchased as decoration for customers' kitchens even if they don't plan to cook with them."

Mark nodded his agreement. "What about the gift baskets?"

"Traditional sweetgrass baskets handmade here make the most sense. Luther put me in touch with a woman who's an artisan weaver. She's bringing some samples by the café."

They continued talking about Samantha's ideas for the baskets as they finished their entrées and shared a rum-laced cake with two espressos for dessert. But as they were polishing off the last few delectable bites, a waiter arrived with a single drink and a long-stemmed, blood-red rose on a silver tray.

"A cocktail for the lady," he announced, placing the glass and rose on the table in front of Samantha.

She looked up at him, confused. "I didn't order that."

"No, ma'am. It was sent to you with compliments." He turned to indicate the restaurant's large bar area, visible through a set of wide French doors. "Enjoy."

Before Samantha had a chance to ask anything more, the waiter moved to another table of diners. A plump maraschino cherry sat submerged in the drink's amber liquor. She knew the drink's name from her bartending days. *A Manhattan.* But it was the rose that caused apprehension to prickle her skin.

"It looks like I'm not your only admirer," Mark said.

"Is Carter here?" she asked.

"I doubt it. He's supposed to be on set until morning. They're doing another nighttime shoot. It's a suspense-horror movie, so there're a lot of them."

Her pulse had begun to pick up. She needed to see for herself who had sent her the cocktail and rose.

"Samantha?"

Standing and tossing the cloth napkin that had been in her lap onto her seat, she walked briskly into the restaurant's interior. Stomach clenched tight, she scanned the length of the antique, dark wood bar, searching anxiously. Dozens of patrons filled the space, talking and laughing with one another. But she saw no one she recognized. The domed lighting fixtures illuminated no familiar faces from her past or her nightmares. Still, she felt an unease that rivaled what she had felt the night she'd believed a car had followed her from the resort.

The unwanted memory tore at her.

Devin would send her a red rose at the club after she left the stage, his signal that he wanted her in his office for a *private session.* He got aroused watching her dance in front of other men. Even now, she felt his hot breath on her skin as he bent her over his desk, his hand fisting roughly in the hair at her nape. She heard his husky drawl against her ear. He would hurt her.

Do it the way Daddy likes.

Fingers grazed her upper arms from behind. Startled, she choked back a cry, whirling and stumbling a step back.

"Samantha." Mark stood close. "I'm sorry. I didn't mean to scare you."

Heart pumping, she stared at him for a half second before glancing again around the bar. She had to be sure.

"What's going on?"

She shook her head and tried to tamp down the strain in her voice. "I…I thought someone I knew was here."

"Who?"

"Just…someone," Samantha said unevenly.

Mark continued studying her, his eyebrows knitted together. It was clear he wanted to press her as to who she thought it was. But instead he handed her the shoulder bag she'd left hanging on the back of her chair at the table. "I asked the waiter. The restaurant's owner sent the drink and rose. When we spoke this morning, I told him you were a graduate of culinary school in New York. He wanted to welcome you to the area as a fellow restaurateur."

She was perspiring, she realized. Embarrassed by her erratic behavior, Samantha put a hand to her face. The disquiet inside her began to ease. *It was nothing. Just like the Crown Victoria last week.* Her own version of post-traumatic stress disorder, triggered without warning by the smallest things. She had to stop being so jumpy and control her irrational fears. Her overreaction humiliated her.

"We should go thank him," she managed to say.

"I'll call him tomorrow. Things are pretty busy, and you're looking a little pale." Mark's eyes held concern. "I already paid the check, so we can go ahead and leave if you want. I just need to get your shopping bags we checked with the hostess."

She nodded mutely.

A pianist started up from the far corner of the bar, playing a sedate version of a song Samantha recognized as being on the playlist at the Blue Iris. She felt goose bumps rise on her skin at the eerie coincidence. Mark looked around the upscale bar and dining room a final time, as if trying to find whomever Samantha had been searching for. Then, placing his hand protectively on the small of her back, he guided her to the vestibule.

CHAPTER THIRTEEN

"YOU'RE AS CLOSED-MOUTHED as Mark," Mercer huffed as she jogged on the beach alongside Samantha. "All I want to know is if you had a good time—"

"We had a good time."

She grinned. "How good?"

Giving her a stern look, Samantha increased her pace. If Mercer was breathless, it would be harder for her to keep asking questions.

"Hey, I was kidding! Slow down—are you training for the Olympics or something?"

Samantha heard Mercer's soft curse behind her, but didn't let up. Instead, she focused on her own hard breathing, trying to out-distance the memory of her near freak-out at the restaurant. In the car with Mark on the drive back, she'd waved the incident off with a laugh and a sheepish apology, claiming the caffeine-fueled espresso had put her on edge.

Although she suspected Mark didn't believe her, he hadn't pushed, instead engaging her in pleasant small talk until they reached her apartment building. But after walking her to the door of her unit, Mark had touched her arm and asked if she was really okay. Samantha assured him she was, then thanked him again for a lovely night. She could see in his eyes that he wanted to kiss her, but instead he had taken a gentlemanly step off her stoop and waited until she was safely inside before leaving.

She had wanted to kiss *him*, as well. Self-recrimination twisted her insides.

"Just so you know, Mark gave me hell," Mercer managed to say between gasps as she caught up with Samantha.

"For what?"

"For telling you about Carter and Shelley. And about the accident. He says he feels like a pity date."

Samantha slowed, then stopped running altogether, reaching for Mercer's arm to bring her to a halt, too.

"That's ridiculous." Panting, she wiped at the perspiration beading her forehead. "Mark's a decent, wonderful man."

"So you *do* like him? Because I get the feeling he isn't sure…"

Staring at the crashing ocean waves, Samantha watched as a small white bird with stork-like legs waded into the surf seeking dinner. The early evening sky appeared dusky, and the lowering sun looked like a muted orange globe over the grayish-green water. She was giving Mark mixed signals, she knew that, but she hadn't been able to hide the attraction she felt to him. Her mind involuntarily conjured up one of the intimate, outdoor *garden rooms* in the Charleston waterfront park. They'd passed through several of them during their stroll, and she imagined Mark kissing her there, hidden behind tall boxwoods and ornamental trees. It had been years since she'd felt a man's mouth on hers, years since a male touch didn't send revulsion rushing through her. The truth was, she felt safe and protected with him, things she'd never felt before with a member of the opposite sex. Not in her entire life.

"I do like him," she said quietly. "But you have to understand that things are…complicated."

Mercer tugged her damp T-shirt away from her skin as she gazed at Samantha with serious eyes. "Anything worth it usually *is* complicated, Sam. I know Mark comes with a lot of baggage. He's widowed and he has a young child. Emily has problems—"

"Emily stole my heart from the moment I met her," Samantha assured her. She hesitated. "The complications I'm talking about… they aren't Mark's. They're mine."

Mercer appeared surprised. "Do you want to talk about it?"

"No." She shook her head, wishing desperately for a change of subject. Wishing she could get Mark off her mind. "Let's just go, okay? We're almost done."

They took off again, this time at a more manageable pace. Not too far off in the distance, Samantha could see the public parking lot where they had left Mercer's convertible. Their beachside runs were becoming a regular thing. But Samantha had missed last night's due to her trip into Charleston, and she and Mercer would both be skipping tomorrow because of the reception at the St. Clair. She hoped once the event was over, Mercer would find something else to discuss. Even more, if Mark asked her out again and she declined, she hoped Mercer wouldn't be angry with her.

"I heard you bought the dress at Serendipity."

She nodded. "Thanks for recommending the place."

"Mark's wearing his gray suit. You'll look gorgeous together."

Samantha felt a tug of sadness but remained resolute that her future with Mark was a very finite one. She would go to the reception with him, they'd have a good time and that would be that. It had to be.

"Are you feeling all right?" Mercer asked as they climbed the sun-bleached, wooden stairs that led to the parking lot. "Because you haven't had much to say."

"I'm sorry. I think I'm just tired. We were out late last night, at least late for me. And I had a long day at the café that started at six thirty this morning."

"Hey, want to stop at Fiorini's before I drop you at home?" Mercer suggested, referring to the town's one Italian restaurant as they climbed into her car. The place was a cliché with its red and white-checkered tablecloths and candles made from old Chianti bottles, but the food was good. "I'm really not in the mood for the hotel dining room, let alone room service. We can get a side salad and a slice of pizza, or pasta if you prefer. Wouldn't that be better than eating dinner alone in your apartment?"

"I don't know—"

"C'mon, Sam. I know I've been going at you like Homeland Security, but I've been feeling a little worried since I sort of manipulated the whole date thing last night." Mercer raised her right hand as if she were being sworn in to testify in a courtroom. "I'll make you a solemn vow. If you go to Fiorini's with me, no more nosy questions about you and Mark. Just red sauce, simple carbohydrates and maybe a light beer."

Samantha pressed her lips together, trying not to smile. "How can I refuse that?"

He had never considered himself an artist, but Lenny Cook admitted the weight of the camera in his hands felt, well...*right*. He loved the clicking sound the shutter made with each press of his finger. The way the new telephoto lens he'd purchased brought his subject up close and personal.

Click.

The images captured on the digital screen were clear as daylight, even though it was dark now and he was on the other side of the street from the apartment building, hidden by the glossy foliage of a flowering camellia bush. The tips on flashless nighttime photography the clerk at the camera shop in Charleston had given him were like money in the bank. Lenny peered at the backlit screen and grinned in satisfaction at the image. He had raw talent, even if he did say so himself. In another life, he might have been one of those high-fashion photographers shooting supermodels for a living. Those guys could get a lot of grade-A pussy, except for one problem: Most of them were fags.

He'd already taken a dozen photos of her face and profile. Now she had her back to him as she said good night to her cute girlfriend in the pricey red convertible. He allowed his lens to linger on the well-defined shape of her ass in the blue running shorts.

Click. Click. Click.

Those last shots were solely for him. Something he planned to jerk off to later that night in his hotel room. But the others had another purpose.

If he played his cards right, they were going to make him a whole lot wealthier.

The photos he'd taken through the car windshield that night had been too dark and grainy to prove much of anything. But these were going to turn out just fine. Lenny patted the long scope of the lens and congratulated himself again on his wise investment, even if he'd had to wait a week for the special order to arrive.

He watched as the convertible drove off, its red taillights glowing. Trina went into the first-floor apartment.

She had changed, sure. Gotten older, no longer practically jailbait. Her tits were smaller, too—a disappointment since he liked them nice and big. *Tig Bitties,* he thought, chuckling lewdly to himself. But he had to admit he was partial to the long, dark hair. It was more natural looking than her previous platinum blond.

But, damn. *It really was her.* The close-ups the telescopic lens provided confirmed it. And Lenny should know better than anyone. How much time had he spent at the Blue Iris, nursing his whiskey and staring up at Trina as she took it all off on stage? How many nights had he nearly come in his pants, fantasizing about the things he wanted to do to her while she practically had sex with herself right in front of him? Nobody worked a pole like Trina. Six years later and the thought of it could still give him a hard-on.

He had wanted to get to know her. But unlike the other girls, Trina had been aloof, unwilling to give a lap dance for fifty bucks or even sit with a customer for a drink. In fact, she rarely smiled or made eye contact with anyone in the crowd. She didn't have to, since she was Devin Leary's exclusive property and everyone knew it.

Lucky man. Except for one small detail.

Devin was stone-cold dead.

But look at this—he'd actually found her after all this time, living it up in this little ocean resort town. Lenny figured *he* was the lucky one now.

Finding her had become his hobby, something he'd dabbled in over the years whenever paying work was slow. She'd been careful and smart, but eventually Trina had slipped up.

They always did.

He praised her sentimentality and the roses that had arrived on her mother's headstone nearly a year ago. The marker's engraved date indicated they'd been sent on what would have been Liza Grissom's fiftieth birthday. After being tipped off by the cemetery's maintenance chief, Lenny had tracked the wired order to a florist in Manhattan. The arrangement had been paid for in cash, the sender unnamed, but it had given him a geographic starting point, albeit a large one. Tenacity had been his friend. It had taken months to home in on her new identity, and by the time he'd located her address and her workplace, she was already gone. But armed with her new name, he'd picked up the scent again and trailed her to here fairly quickly. His previous career as a skip tracer had come in handy. In his day, he had been one of the best.

Eventually, he would turn her over to Red, the scary son of a bitch. But first he was going to whet his appetite. See how much that ginger-haired gangster was really willing to pay for her after all this time. He'd overnight the photos to a friend who owed him a favor. His pal would make the anonymous delivery—that way, there would be no postmark to divulge the location.

Meanwhile, he'd let Trina think he was open to bargaining and squeeze her for some cash, too. Everyone knew she'd stolen big from the Learys before disappearing.

Lenny's lips thinned into a smile. Maybe she'd be willing to do *anything* to keep out of Red's hairy-knuckled grip. He could finally fulfill his X-rated fantasies about her. He imagined her on her back, him on top of her, pumping into her tight snatch.

Once he'd had his fill, he would tell Red where to find her. Maybe he'd even kidnap her and deliver her himself.

He thought of her nude, lithe body swaying on stage. His sadistic side wanted to make this last. He was due for a vacation anyhow, and the southeastern seacoast was nice. Lenny sniffed the pleasant ocean air. One thing was for goddamn sure.

Trina wouldn't snub him again.

CHAPTER FOURTEEN

MINGLING WITH THE well-heeled guests in the St. Clair ballroom, Samantha felt as though she'd stepped into a more elegant, genteel time. Arched windows soared to a twenty-foot-high ceiling, and a massive, sparkling chandelier hung from the ballroom's center over a polished wood floor. The hotel's antebellum ambience made it seem as though the female guests should be wearing corsets and hoopskirts instead of modern-day cocktail attire.

Mark had kept by her side, handsome in a gray suit with an ice-blue silk tie. They had danced and nibbled on hors d'oeuvres being passed around by wait staff on silver trays, and she'd also been introduced to many of Mark's friends and business associates. Observing him as he so easily conversed with guests, Samantha wondered what it must be like to have been born into such Southern aristocracy as the St. Clair family. Mark seemed to accept his birthright with a natural grace.

"I was right about the dress," he commented in a low voice once they were alone again. "Everyone's staring at you."

"They're staring at *us*, actually," Samantha replied, trying to keep the mood light despite the small thrill she felt each time her eyes met his. "I think we've created a bit of a scandal…"

Mark's gaze followed hers to the reception line, where Carter stood after a late arrival, greeting guests. Olivia hovered nearby, along with an attractive, petite redhead in a plum-colored sheath dress. The two women had their eyes fastened like laser points on Mark and Samantha.

"Great," Mark grumbled.

"Is that Carter's date?"

"Unfortunately, no. He came alone. That's Felicity Greene. She's a friend of my mother's from the country club."

A heavyset African-American male whom Samantha knew to be president of the Rarity Cove Chamber of Commerce interrupted them. Mark introduced her, and she listened politely as the businessmen talked about a redistricting proposal that would allow fast-food chains inside the town limits. As he theorized with Mark on the best method for blocking the initiative, Samantha looked across the ballroom again. Carter had escaped from the reception line but hadn't gotten far. A small throng of women of varying ages surrounded him.

"Sorry about that," Mark said once the man had left.

"It's fine. I want to keep the town's atmosphere, too. The fast-food restaurants would only be competition for Café Bella."

"I doubt it." Mark kept his hand low on her back as they reached the bar. "Mercer hasn't stopped talking about the fresh crab salad she had for lunch there. That's not something you get at a drive-through."

"Where *is* Mercer, by the way?"

"She went to take a phone call in her room. I haven't seen her in a while."

At the bar, Mark ordered a soda for himself and a sparkling water for Samantha, who had declined another glass of the bubbly champagne. As he handed her the goblet, Olivia approached with Felicity Greene in tow.

"Look who I found wandering around all by herself," Olivia announced brightly as she nudged Felicity forward.

"Mark, how nice to see you again," the redhead enthused in a heavy Southern belle accent, pressing a kiss against his cheek. "Everything just looks exquisite tonight—you've outdone yourself. And where is little Emily?"

"She's in the children's playroom. They're showing a movie."

"Well, you *have* to bring her out here." She laid her hand on Mark's arm and smiled up at him through thick lashes. "But I warn you, if that child's gotten any sweeter I might have to eat her with a spoon!"

"Felicity, this is Samantha Marsh," Mark said. "She owns Café Bella. You may have seen it. It's just off the town square."

Felicity gave her a cool glance, as if only now realizing her presence. "Nice to meet you."

"You as well," Samantha replied.

Music started up again through the ballroom's sound system. Felicity clasped her manicured hands together. "Oh, Michael Bublé! This is such a romantic song."

"Mark, did you know Felicity studied ballroom dance in Europe during her post-college sojourn?" Olivia remarked. "She was *semi-professional.*"

"Now, Olivia, don't you go overselling me. I was only on the circuit for a year."

"I'd just love to see her skills on the dance floor." Olivia touched her son's coat sleeve. "Would you mind taking her out for a spin, darling? I remember cotillion and what an excellent dancer you were."

Felicity looked at him hopefully.

Mark nearly flinched. "I really can't—"

"Please go ahead, Mark," Samantha offered, realizing the awkward situation he was in. She gave an understanding smile.

"Don't worry about Samantha," Olivia assured him. "Carter will keep her company."

Samantha became aware of Carter's presence. He'd joined their group and seemed just as surprised by Olivia's offer. Still, he shrugged and smiled. "I'd be honored. Should we hit the floor, too?"

Before Samantha could form a response, Carter took her goblet and handed it to Olivia. Then he swept her gracefully into the crowd of dancing couples. Overhead, the chandelier's lights had dimmed, adding to the romantic tone. Mark looked apologetically at Samantha from a distance away. Felicity already had her arms looped around his neck.

"Sorry about the substitution." Carter sounded sincere as they swayed to the music. "I hope you're having a good time, though?"

He was tall, like Mark, and Samantha looked up at him. "I should be asking you that, Carter. The reception's in your honor."

With a nod he indicated Olivia, who still stood at the edge of the floor. "This is Mom's shindig, not mine."

Executing a graceful turn, he dipped Samantha so that she had no choice but to cling to his broad shoulders. She released a small gasp at the unexpected but smooth maneuver.

"Mark's not the only St. Clair who had to suffer through cotillion," he noted once she was upright again.

"I can see that," she said a little breathlessly.

He gave a sexy grin. "Tell me that wasn't fun."

"It was," she admitted, unable to suppress her own smile. There was no denying Carter had a charming magnetism all his own.

"At least the dance classes Mom forced us into turned out to be useful. *Friends and Lovers* has a fire-and-ice ball every year during February sweeps. I'm the only guy on the show who can waltz worth a damn."

"Do you like being on a soap opera?"

"The hours are insane," he said on a sigh. "We cover thirty pages of script a day, six days a week. No re-shoots, either, unless it's a real screw-up, so you have to be on your game. But it's good training. A lot of big names started on daytime. Kevin Bacon, Brad Pitt, Julianne Moore—"

"But, like them, you'd rather be doing something else?"

"I'm appreciative to be working anywhere. It's a competitive business," he said thoughtfully. "But I have bigger goals—prime-time television, maybe movies, if I'm lucky. I shot a network pilot last season, but it wasn't picked up."

Samantha recalled what Mercer had told her. Carter had been athletic like Mark, involved in sports, but the acting bug had hit him in high school, and he'd also become immersed in theater. In fact, he'd moved to New York right after graduating high school, appeasing his parents by taking courses at NYU while he auditioned. He'd landed a modeling contract, eventually getting some national commercials and television guest spots, and then finally the role on the soap. He'd also done several off-Broadway plays. Samantha once again appraised Carter's features—the strong jaw and high cheekbones, his flawless complexion and smoldering eyes. They were several shades darker than Mark's, a deep sapphire blue.

"So how's the *date* going so far?" he asked, reminding her of their conversation a few days earlier on the town square. He added, "No air quotes this time."

"It's been pretty great," she said honestly.

"Good. I meant what I said. I'm glad Mark's started dating again. It's time." He paused, his full lips pressed together. "But I've got to admit I'm still a little bowled over that he asked *you*."

"Why's that?"

Carter's gaze moved to his brother and Felicity. "There's something to be said for working your way up, is all. Mark's been out of the game a long time. He surprised me. I didn't think he was ready to take the training wheels off the Schwinn yet, and here he is driving around in a Porsche."

Samantha nearly laughed. "And you're thinking I'm the Porsche in this scenario?"

The sexy grin reappeared, revealing white, straight teeth. "I'm just wondering if Mark is ready to handle such a high-performance machine."

Although his tone was light and teasing, Samantha felt a small stab of defensiveness. Her voice remained casual, however. "Oh, I'm sure Mark can *handle* anyone he wants. From what I've heard, Shelley was a very beautiful woman. A very beautiful and *sought-after* woman..."

He apparently caught her implication. His expression sobered, and he shook his head faintly. "That was all a long time ago. We were kids. But even now I see Mark's still painting me as the villain."

"He never mentioned it, actually. Mercer told me. Mark wasn't happy she did."

He didn't speak for several heartbeats. This seriousness was a side of Carter she hadn't seen before.

"May I tell you something? No matter what you've heard or

who you heard it from, I *loved* Shelley, too. From the very minute I saw her," he rasped, his handsome features earnest. "She might've belonged to Mark first, but that doesn't mean my feelings for her weren't real. Mark left her here when he could've gone to a closer school, like the University of Charleston. It was his choice. Shelley's parents had just gone through a bad divorce, and she was confused and alone."

"Carter," Samantha murmured, surprised by his emotion.

"I tried to keep my distance, but she needed a friend, and *she* sought me out. What happened between us…happened. It wasn't meant to hurt Mark."

"But it did."

"Yeah," he agreed tightly.

And asking me to the barbecue reopened the same old wound. But instead of saying it, Samantha lowered her gaze and they continued dancing in silence. It was clear the relationship between the brothers was complicated, the tension long-running. Whatever rift Shelley had caused between them was still a sensitive spot, even after all the time that had passed. Samantha couldn't help but wonder if the blowup had actually been the catalyst that sent Carter to New York to chase his dream.

The recorded song faded and another began. Samantha glanced around for Mark, but he was no longer on the dance floor. Instead, he had been pulled into conversation with guests on the far side of the ballroom. He and Felicity had their backs turned to her, and Felicity's hand rested possessively on Mark's shoulder.

"Your date still looks occupied," Carter pointed out. His usual smooth persona appeared back in place. "If you want, we can keep dancing…"

Samantha gently disentangled herself. "Thank you, Carter. But if you'll excuse me, I need to visit the powder room."

He smiled at the old-fashioned euphemism. "I haven't heard that term from anyone younger than Mom. You're a paradox, Sam."

"I'm not even sure what that is—"

"I just think there's more to you than what's on the surface, that's all. What's the saying? Still waters run deep." He hesitated, actually having the grace to blush a bit. "Take that tattoo on your lower back, for instance. I saw it the other day when you bent to fix your shoe. Don't get me wrong. What I saw of it was sexy as hell, but it wasn't something I expected on someone so reserved. I bet there's a real story behind that."

Samantha's stomach knotted. The amethyst butterfly tattoo served as a painful reminder of the past she'd left behind. The inquisitive way Carter was looking at her made her nervous. It was almost as if he was peering inside her and could see Trina Grissom staring right back out at him.

"The secret life of Samantha Marsh," she said lightly, trying to hide how close his observation had hit to home. Self-conscious, she sought a change of subject.

"May I give you some advice, Carter?" she asked tentatively. "You're fortunate to have such a wonderful family. Don't take any of them for granted, especially Mark. Stop trying to one-up him, and do what you can to mend fences." She thought of her mother, could still smell her sweet perfume, even now. "You already know what it's like to suddenly lose someone you care about. You can't fix things when it's too late."

Carter remained silent at her words. Samantha held his gaze for several moments, then indicated the stunning, slightly mature blonde in a low-cut dress slinking toward them. She gave him a soft, parting smile. "Don't look now, but I think someone's ready for her turn."

He didn't get a chance to respond before the woman whispered something in his ear, pressing herself to his side and placing her hand on his chest as her hips swayed suggestively to the music. Samantha turned to see Mark still with Felicity, now ringed by an even larger group of guests. She couldn't help it—her chest squeezed. Walking from the ballroom, she went past the restrooms and headed toward one of the outdoor patios, needing a breath of fresh air. She had absolutely no right to feel possessive. Mark didn't belong to her.

He never could, she reminded herself.

Don't long for something you can't have.

Olivia St. Clair could see what her eldest son could not—even with all of her syrupy, fake charm, Felicity was a thousand times a better match for Mark than she was. The butterfly on her lower back had been a *gift* from Devin. He'd taken her to a Memphis tattoo parlor and picked it out. Samantha hadn't wanted it, but he'd given her no choice in the matter. *It shows you're mine, babe. My forever mark on you.*

Devin said he'd picked the butterfly because he knew she wanted to fly away from him. She closed her eyes, recalling how he'd supervised as she lay half-naked on her stomach on the tattoo artist's table. It had taken hours. The needles used on her skin had stung, and her submission to his demand had excited Devin.

He'd also reminded her that butterflies had remarkably short life-spans.

After settling in New York, she'd had the breast implants removed but had left the tattoo since clothing hid it and a specialist had advised that the painful, costly laser treatments probably wouldn't remove it fully due to the ink's deep-purple color. For not the first time, she wished she'd at least tried to have it erased, no matter the price. Even now, she picked beachwear and running clothes that hid it.

In the hotel's rear, French doors opened onto a granite terrace rimmed by a graceful wrought-iron railing. Cushioned rattan chairs were placed in groups. But Samantha instead went to sit on the first step that led onto a stone-and-grass courtyard flanked by palm trees. She was thankfully alone out here, with only the balmy ocean breeze to keep her company.

Trina Grissom, you've sure come a long way. Taking a deep breath, Samantha absorbed the courtyard's serene beauty, from its outdoor lamplight and well-tended gardenia bushes to the black plane of sea visible just beyond them. She noted again how far she was from rural Alabama and the hole-in-the-wall town, the doublewide trailer where she'd lived with Mamaw Jean. She was farther still from the smoke-filled Memphis strip club where she'd danced nude on a darkened stage, accepting cash from drunken men, the likes of whom made her skin crawl. She had no right to wish for more than the distance she'd achieved from all that... did she?

Lost in thought, she startled at the touch on her shoulder. Samantha turned to meet Emily's questioning blue eyes. A doll in a pink ballerina outfit dangled from one small hand.

"Hi there, peanut. What're you doing out here all by yourself?" Samantha smoothed the little girl's flowered T-shirt that matched her pink shorts and sandals. "I thought you were watching a movie with the other kids."

Emily gazed at her with a worried expression, as if she could sense Samantha's melancholy. Then she sat beside her on the step and leaned against her side. Her heart tugging, Samantha placed her arm around the child, who snuggled closer. She closed her eyes as she breathed in the fresh shampoo scent of Emily's hair.

Samantha had accepted a life that might be devoid of any real intimacy, but it was also without the fear and humiliation that Devin had used to keep her bound to him. She had managed to escape. To survive.

She sighed and told herself that what she had would simply have to be enough.

CHAPTER FIFTEEN

MARK LOOKED AROUND the crowded ballroom for Samantha. He had gotten pulled into conversation with guests, and he realized she'd been left alone for too long. But where was she? His first suspect in her disappearance would have been Carter, but his brother was still on the dance floor, only now with a curvaceous blonde whom Mark knew to be a high-end real estate agent. In his peripheral vision, he could see Felicity waving, trying to recapture his attention. He pretended not to notice and walked from the ballroom.

"Have you seen Samantha?" he asked Mercer when she rounded the corner in the lobby, nearly running into him. Seeing her face, he placed his hands on her shoulders to halt her. "Mercer. What's wrong?"

"Nothing," she said, sounding embarrassed. But her eyes were red, as if she'd been crying. "Just a silly argument I had with a… friend in Atlanta."

"Oh." Mark was reminded that Mercer had had a separate existence away from the St. Clair before she'd returned home to help him piece his own shattered life back together. "If you want to talk about it, we can go into the lounge. I'll get you a drink."

She shook her head and mustered a halfhearted smile. "I'm fine. But if you've lost your date, you really should go find her."

Giving his arm an affectionate squeeze, she headed into the ballroom. Mark stared after her, wondering what had upset her, and then continued along the hallway. He halted at the French doors that opened onto the first-floor veranda. Samantha sat on the top step leading out to the courtyard. Her back was to him, her sleek, dark hair lifting in the balmy breeze.

As Mark moved closer, he realized Samantha held Emily in her lap. His daughter had fallen asleep next to her, and she slumped across Samantha's thighs, one cheek pressed into the silk of her cocktail dress. Samantha ran her fingers through Emily's curls, softly humming a tune he didn't recognize.

She didn't look up until Mark practically stood over them. She placed a finger to her lips. "We have an escapee from the playroom."

"I didn't mean to leave you for so long."

"It's all right. I've been in good company. But you should probably get this little one off to bed."

Mark moved lower on the steps and gently scooped Emily up in his arms. She stirred briefly before falling back asleep.

"I should be calling it a night, too," Samantha mentioned, rising. She had met Mark at the hotel prior to the reception. He'd had the St. Clair's limousine service pick her up since he had been involved in the staff preparations. "Could you have the car brought around for me?"

Mark was unwilling to let their date end. "Go with me to the bungalow while I get Emily settled? I'll arrange for one of the au pairs from the hotel to come and stay with her while I drive you home."

"That isn't necessary—"

"It is to me. It's something I'd like to do, especially since I wasn't able to come to your place earlier to get you like a proper date. We can have a glass of wine or some coffee after Emily's tucked in. Maybe we can finally have some quiet and time to talk."

Still holding Emily's doll, Samantha gave a faint nod of agreement. Cradling his daughter, her head on his shoulder, Mark carried her from the patio and onto flagstone steps that led to a neat, white-painted storage shed where golf carts were kept. Once Samantha climbed into the passenger side of one of the carts, he settled Emily into her arms. Then Mark got in on the driver's side and started them on their way. They took a scenic route through the seaside gardens, with Mark pointing out some of the flowering trees and shrubs. To their right, a silvery lagoon reflected moonlight. It wasn't long before they came to the end of the cart path, and Mark steered the vehicle onto a walkway in front of a stacked-stone and shingle bungalow facing the sea.

He heard Samantha's soft intake of breath as she glimpsed the inviting front porch that held wicker rocking chairs and a double swing. A veil of climbing vines dotted with tiny white flowers wound around the porch railing, while baskets dripping with green ferns hung from the eaves. Wisteria entwined in the branches of bordering trees. The house's interior glowed with a golden warmth that came from the pair of Tiffany lamps Mark had left on in the front room.

"It looks like it's out of a storybook," she marveled as Mark parked the golf cart beside his Volvo in the driveway. Getting out, he reclaimed Emily, who yawned silently before settling her head back onto his shoulder and closing her eyes. As he disarmed the security system and led Samantha inside, she seemed equally enthralled with the home's interior. Through her eyes, Mark noticed again its casual mix of stripes and florals, the overstuffed chairs and whimsical paintings that had all been Shelley's doing.

"There's an open bottle of red wine in the kitchen and goblets in the overhead cabinet. I'm going to have coffee since I'm driving you home, but feel free to help yourself," Mark said as he headed down the hallway with Emily. "I'll be right back."

He left Samantha in the living area admiring a bookcase filled with leather-bound books, knickknacks and family photos, while he went to change Emily into her nightgown and put her to bed. Once she was tucked in, he went into his own bedroom and removed his suit jacket and tie, undoing the top two buttons of his dress shirt so he was more comfortable. When Mark returned, Samantha held a silver-framed photo. Seeing him, she replaced it on the bookshelf.

"Your wife...Shelley. Mercer told me how pretty she was."

He nodded faintly.

"Emily looks so much like her."

They stared at one another in the room's soft lighting, until Mark cleared his throat and remarked that she hadn't helped herself to any wine.

"I was thinking I'd have coffee, too. Decaffeinated if you have it? It's such a nice night. Maybe we can sit outside on the porch."

Samantha went with him into the granite and stainless steel kitchen. They engaged in small talk while he prepared coffee. Once they had their mugs filled, Mark led her onto the covered porch. They settled beside one another on the swing's soft pin-striped cushions, rocking slowly back and forth as the warm sea air brought in the scent of sea grass and brine. Along the shore, Mark could make out the images of two people—probably teenagers—holding hands and stopping briefly to kiss as the ocean water lapped around their ankles. He gazed at Samantha's profile in the filmy porch light. She watched the young couple, too.

"Do you miss him?" he asked carefully.

"Who?"

"The guy you left in New York."

"Oh." She shook her head, avoiding his eyes. "No. It wasn't a...good situation."

Mark digested the information, wondering what had happened. "How long were you together?"

"Since I was very young. Just a teen, actually."

"Like Shelley and me."

She looked at him then, her caramel-brown eyes somber. "No, nothing like you and Shelley."

Instead of saying more, she stood from the swing and placed the earthenware mug on the porch railing. Her shoulders lifted in a sigh as she stared out at the ocean. The teenagers they'd been watching moments earlier were out of view now, having traveled farther down the beach. Mark rose as well. Placing his mug next to hers, he stood behind her. His fingers ached to trace her bare upper arms, but instead he simply stood with his hands in the pockets of his pants.

"When you agreed to attend the reception with me...I know I said I didn't have any expectations." Swallowing, he felt his face flush with the admission. "But it's been a long time since I've felt like this. Since I felt hope."

Samantha turned to look at him, her eyes soft and lips slightly parted.

"We really just met, Mark. And you don't know anything about me—"

"Then *tell me* about you." When she remained silent, he said,

"The night we went for a walk on the beach, you said you weren't right for me. May I ask why?"

"It's…complicated."

He frowned. "Then explain it to me?"

She looked away, but Mark gently turned her gaze back to him, cupping her delicate jawline with his hand, his thumb stroking over her cheek. He was surprised by the physical desire that flooded through him at the mere act of touching her. His breath grew shallower as her fingers grazed his raised wrist in a caress. The romantic setting and their closeness emboldened him.

"Tell me you're not interested…" His voice was low and rasping. "Tell me you don't feel something between us, and I'll drive you home right now."

He searched her eyes, aware of the rising sadness in them.

"I do feel it," she whispered finally. She appeared both sincere and vulnerable. "But it's just not possible for us—"

Mark bent his head and pressed his mouth to hers, stopping her words. He savored the taste of her—his first taste of anyone since Shelley. Samantha didn't resist. Their kiss became slowly deeper, their mouths melding as she responded and relaxed into him. Her palms lay against his shirtfront, then slowly slid upward until her arms were around his neck. Mark felt nearly dizzy with the sensation of holding her. As their lips and tongues continued to mingle, he drew her even closer. He nearly came undone at the sweet scent of her, the little mewling sounds she made as he passionately kissed her neck. When she pulled away, he stared at her in the porch's deep shadows, his breathing hard and unsteady. Samantha appeared disconcerted, her face holding a mixture of desire and regret that Mark couldn't understand.

She bowed her head, eyes shielded by the dark veil of her lashes. Her voice was strained and barely audible. "Please take me home."

"Samantha," he whispered. "We can take this slow—"

"I'd really like you to take me home now," she repeated. "Please."

He heaved a quiet, defeated sigh. Leaving her on the porch, Mark went inside to call the hotel's concierge desk, requesting that one of the on-staff au pairs come to the bungalow.

Except for the occasional wash of light from the streetlights overhead, the Volvo's interior was shrouded in darkness. Already clutching her apartment keys, Samantha shrank into the soft leather of the passenger seat, her mind reeling. Mark's kiss had stirred feelings inside her she couldn't deny, and she was remorseful for having let things go as far as she did. But some selfish part of her had wanted to know what it felt like to have his mouth on hers, to experience his solid male body pressed against her.

And she'd been right. It was like nothing she had ever experienced. Maybe she would've been better off not knowing.

There had never been a breathless moment like that with Devin, not even in the early days when she'd been so young and naïve, so stupidly blind to his evil.

"I'm sorry if I offended you," Mark said as he pulled the vehicle into the parking lot of the Wayfarer Apartments. He parked and turned off the engine. "I broke my promise. I shouldn't have kissed you."

"It's not your fault," Samantha answered in a near whisper. "And it took two of us."

Mark looked at her in the shadows, his face pained. "What is it? Do you have a secret husband stashed somewhere?"

She shook her head. "No."

"Then what? You said you felt something between us, too—"

She opened her door and got out.

With a soft curse, Mark climbed from the car's other side. "Let me get the door for you, at least."

He caught up to her halfway up the walk. She stopped when he gently took hold of her arm, turning her to face him. She released an unsteady breath.

"Hey. Stop running from me, okay?"

A strand of hair blew across her face. Mark tucked it behind her ear, his fingertip brushing the delicate drop-pearl earring at her lobe. A small shiver ran through her at his touch.

Samantha took a step back from him. "Thank you for everything. But I…I don't think we should do this again."

He looked briefly at the concrete under his feet, his lips pressed together in a firm line. When he lifted his eyes to hers again, what she saw wasn't anger but a deep confusion that made her heart twist. She had to remind herself it was for the best.

"Good night, Mark."

Hands trembling, Samantha managed to open the door to her apartment using her key. She went inside and closed the door without looking back, although she waited unseen at the darkened window until Mark returned to his car. She watched as the station wagon pulled from the parking lot, its taillights fading into darkness. *I'm sorry.* A heavy sadness settled over her.

Turning from the window, Samantha sought out the lamp next to the sofa. Pale light flooded the room, bringing into view the grinning troll of a man who leaned against her bedroom doorway. She felt the blood drain from her face.

"Hey there, Trina, honey. Long time no see."

CHAPTER SIXTEEN

"I BROUGHT YOU A gift." The intruder indicated the coffee table, where sky-high stilettos made of clear plastic and a black G-string sat. "Don't you want to try 'em on?"

He'd called her Trina.

An electric current of panic jolted through her. Samantha glanced quickly around her normally tidy apartment. Sofa cushions were upended, and the foyer closet stood open, its contents tossed onto the floor. Books and DVDs had been pulled from the entertainment center in what looked like an all-out search.

"You're lookin' damn fine, babe."

He impaled her with his leering gaze. Heart pounding, Samantha's flesh pebbled as he came closer. He was short and thick-shouldered, with a stomach paunch and an oily comb-over that barely concealed his balding head. A dime-sized birthmark marred his right temple. She took a wobbly step backward. "I-I don't know who you are—"

"You don't remember me." He made a tsking sound. Samantha fled to the door. She got it open a few inches before the man put his full body weight against it, slamming it closed. He was quicker than he appeared. A slicing fear weakened her knees.

"You *could* scream, but my guess is you don't want to attract attention. Can't call the police about an intruder, either. I'm bettin' they'd like to hear what I have to tell 'em about you." He reeked of whiskey and sweat. "'Course, the cops are probably the least of your worries. Red's still lookin' for you, too. Let me tell you, that psychotic bastard holds a grudge."

She went cold at Red's name. Breath bottled up inside her, Samantha stared into the man's bloated face, trying to rise above her choking terror and think. She saw the same features looking up at her from a barstool. An image of thick, stubby fingers tucking bills into the elastic of her G-string caused bile to nearly rise in her throat.

"You...you're from the Blue Iris," she said shakily.

"The name's Lenny Cook. Not that you ever bothered to find out."

"What do you want?"

"Oh, *lots* of things. Including a little piece of the action."

What was he talking about? Confusion mingled with her fright, making her heart slam harder.

"You covered your tracks real good—I'll hand you that. Even bought yourself a new name and social security number. Pretty smart." He tapped his broad forehead. "But ol' Lenny here's smarter. 'Course, by the time I tracked you to Manhattan, you'd taken off again. Picking up your trail the second time was easier, though, since I had your new name. I worked a long time for a collection agency—skills that come in handy now that I'm strictly freelance. You've been my *hobby*, Trina. It took me six fucking years, but I finally found you."

She recoiled as he touched her hair. His closeness felt like a knife pressed to her throat.

"Samantha Marsh. Classy name."

"Look, I-I don't want any trouble—"

"I bet you don't. You've got a nice little setup here. I've seen your fancy café. Not to mention your rich friends. That man you were with tonight looks like money. You giving that sweet stuff up for him, baby?"

He groped her breast. When she shoved his hand away, he grabbed her arm and twisted it roughly behind her, causing her to cry out. He moved her away from the potential escape route the door provided.

"Where are they, Trina?"

"Where's *what*?" she gasped in pain.

"Don't play stupid! The diamonds! You still got some around or did you fence 'em? Even with that café you bought yourself, I'm sure you've got *something* left."

"I don't know anything about diamonds," she stammered. Her arm ached as he tightened his hold. "Please, you're hurting me!"

He pushed her into the bedroom, which was in the same disarray as the living area. The window's screen had been pried off, its glass broken so the inside latch could be lifted. Samantha thought of the derringer, but his tight hold on her kept her away from the bureau. Its drawers stood open and appeared rifled through.

"I oughta call Red right now and tell him I found his brother's runaway whore."

"Please," Samantha begged. Tears filled her eyes as he twisted her arm harder. "Don't."

"Then here's the deal. From now on, you're going to do what I say."

He let go, and she bolted toward the bureau.

"If you're looking for that cute little gun, you're not going to find it."

She whirled to face him, panting. His greasy smile made

Samantha's stomach churn. She'd seen that same hungry look in too many men's eyes.

"You *can* buy my silence with some of that money. But we'll talk about a business arrangement later. Right now, I'm more interested in pleasure." He licked his lips, his eyes roaming over her body. "How about you get undressed for me? Maybe dance a little like you used to on stage. A private show just for me."

In disbelief, she shook her head. "No, I-I won't do that!"

"Too good for that now, huh? Have it your way. Devin always bragged you liked it rough." Lurching forward, Lenny grabbed a handful of her hair, dragging her face to his. He made a sloppy attempt to kiss her mouth. Repulsed, Samantha jerked her head away.

"Take off those fancy clothes," he ordered in her ear. "Or I'll take them off for you."

He fisted his hand in the neckline of her dress and tugged hard. She made a strangled sound as the fragile silk tore, exposing her bra.

"I liked the big ones better, but these are still nice." His hands on her made a sickness wash through her. A fresh wave of terror prickled her scalp.

"Get off me!" Struggling, nearly hysterical, she heard her own voice rise. An image of Devin pinning her down, his fingers biting into her skin, filled her head. She wouldn't submit to this vile creature, even to keep her secret. She struck out, hitting Lenny in the mouth with a closed fist. He yowled, cursing and striking back at her with a thick arm. The blow dropped Samantha to the floor, her forehead bouncing off the bed's footboard on the way down. Starbursts danced in front of her eyes. She tried dizzily to get up. When she couldn't, she began crawling toward the living room. Lenny followed. He grabbed her hair again and yanked her painfully to her knees.

"Fine, *bitch*. I've got an idea what you can do from right there."

Sobbing, she tried to wrench free of his hold but fell silent at a sound from the front of the apartment.

"Samantha?" Mark's muffled voice came from outside. He pounded on the door. "Samantha! What's going on? Open up!"

Lenny cursed, frozen in place. He deliberated for a tense second. "We'll finish this later—tell him you'll be right there."

She worked to gain control over her voice. "Mark? I-I'm coming."

"Are you all right?"

"Yes. Just give me a minute, okay?"

Lenny's voice was a low growl against her ear as he bent over her. "I'll be watching you *real close*, Trina. My eyes are on you twenty-four/seven. You even think about running from me and it's over. I know your alias and your car license plate. You step one foot outside this town, and I'll call the police and tell 'em who you really are. How far do you think you'll get then? But it doesn't have to be that way. I'm a reasonable man. We can make a *financial* deal to keep your secret."

He kissed the top of her head. "Sweet dreams, babe. We'll talk again real soon. Give me a minute before you let in your boyfriend. Bet *he'd* like to know who you are, too."

Samantha covered her face with her hands as Mark continued pounding on the door, sounding more panicked by the second. In the bedroom, she heard Lenny's grunt as he hoisted his girth through the window.

"Samantha!"

She struggled to stand, knees wobbly, drowning in her new reality. The fears that had haunted her had finally come true. She'd been found—not by Red or the police, but by someone who would still hurt her if she didn't give him what he wanted. And what *did* this man want from her? She didn't know anything about diamonds! But the Learys had been involved in multiple shady dealings. There had to be some mistake. She tried to think about what to do.

She unlocked the front door and met Mark's worried gaze as he pushed past her and inside. He held her small black clutch purse. She must have left it in his car, and he'd returned to give it to her.

"I heard arguing and crying. What the hell?" He looked around the ransacked apartment. Samantha closed her eyes as he strode into the bedroom. Returning, he pulled her into his arms. She sank into him, letting him hold her as the weight of what had just happened crashed into her. Her body shook with a tremor she couldn't control.

"Who was here?"

"A burglar, I think," she managed to say.

"God. You're bleeding."

She became aware of wetness at her right temple. He gently tilted her head back, trying to get a better look at the injury.

"I'm okay," she mumbled. "I-I just need to sit down."

Taking her to a chair, Mark withdrew a clean cotton handkerchief from his pants pocket. He dabbed carefully at the cut, then held it against her forehead. "You need to go to a hospital. I'm calling the police."

"No." Samantha grabbed his forearm as he dug into his pocket again for his cell phone. She shook her head. "You can't... Please, Mark. Don't."

CHAPTER SEVENTEEN

"D ON'T? YOU WERE *attacked*." Mark knelt in front of her, his features hard.

"It was a break-in." Despite her best effort, her voice shook. "I surprised him, that's all."

"*That's all?* Look at your forehead."

"I panicked and fell trying to get away." She knew how ridiculous the explanation sounded. Samantha glanced down at her neckline. Seeing her lace bra, she pulled the torn edges of her dress together. "Whoever it was…he left through the bedroom window. We don't have to report this."

"Yes, *we do*." Frowning, Mark looked into her eyes. "What are you afraid of?"

She was tempted to tell him everything, confess who she really was and what she'd done. Besides, now that Lenny had found her, how long would it be before the truth was out? The new life she'd worked so carefully to build was starting to crumble. Fresh panic bubbled up inside her.

"Samantha," Mark urged in a low voice. "Whatever's going on, we've got to bring in the police. They can help you."

Closing her eyes, she sighed in weary resignation. "Call them, then. But there's nothing going on. It was just a burglary."

He appeared incredulous, even a little angry. "You're actually sticking to that story?"

Samantha didn't respond. Instead, she said softly, "I'm not going to the hospital. I hate hospitals."

"Your dress…the guy didn't…I was only gone a few minutes—"

"Nothing happened." She couldn't help it. Hot tears slipped down her cheeks. Wordlessly, Mark took her into his arms, his hand rubbing comforting circles on her back as he held her. Samantha felt the wetness on her face soaking into the polished cotton of his dress shirt. She tried hard not to make any sound as she cried.

"You're okay," he murmured. "I've got you. You're safe now."

Samantha clung to him, overwhelmed, wondering how long his words would hold true. The realization that someone had found her, that someone knew her secret—it made her heart race and stomach clench.

It had been Lenny in the Crown Vic following her that night.

I oughta call Red right now and tell him I found his brother's runaway whore.

She'd known Red was looking for her, seeking retribution, as well as the Memphis Police. But diamonds? Confusion swept over her again. She searched her memory for anything she'd seen, any conversation of Devin's she had overheard that could make some sense of Lenny's claim. But that had all been so long ago.

"I need to make the call, Samantha. This guy could still be in the area."

With a small sniffle, she released her hold on Mark. He stood and, withdrawing his cell phone, placed a call to 911.

Samantha got up shakily, only half-listening as he went into the kitchen to speak to the emergency dispatcher. Looking around the apartment, she felt a tingling in her chest as she spotted Lenny's gift. The high heels and raunchy G-string lay on a stack of culinary magazines on the coffee table. There was also a box of condoms—something she hadn't noticed before. Her stomach turned as she thought of what Lenny had been planning. Samantha picked the items up, opening the closet and hastily stuffing the G-string and condoms into the pocket of her windbreaker that hung on the back of the door. She hid the shoes under a mound of fallen clothes. When she turned around, Mark was disconnecting the phone.

"What're you doing?"

"I'm just making sure nothing was taken."

"Are you missing anything?"

"No." She shook her head. "Not that I can tell."

"They're on the way. They're sending paramedics, too. I won't force you to go to the ER, but you should still be looked at."

Already, Samantha could hear the faint wail of sirens in the distance. Rarity Cove was a small community. When one of its civic leaders called requesting police help, apparently they didn't waste time in responding.

"I'm going to go change," she said quietly.

Mark nodded. The worry she saw on his face caused tears to threaten all over again. She hadn't wanted to drag him into this.

She hadn't wanted to be found, either.

Where had she gone wrong? Samantha mentally retraced her steps, starting with the new identity she'd bought on the black market in New York. There had been only one time she had risked any interaction with her former life, and that was a year ago. Closing her eyes, she berated herself, wondering if that one foolish, sentimental move had been her downfall.

Regardless of how he had found her, how long would Lenny keep her secret? He'd talked about a financial arrangement. The only problem was that she had little to give in exchange for his silence. Nearly everything she had was tied up in Café Bella.

Head pounding, Samantha closed the door to the bedroom behind her. She checked the bureau drawer where she kept the derringer. Gone. Blue flashes of light reflected on the broken window glass as a patrol car pulled into the lot outside, the town's lone ambulance following behind it. Shell fragments crunched under the vehicles' tires as she watched them roll to a stop. Clutching her stomach, she sat on the edge of the bed and listened as Mark let the officers inside.

⸻

Driving back to the resort, Mark stole a glance at Samantha. She sat huddled in the passenger seat, wearing a sleeveless top and khaki shorts. Her overnight bag had been placed in the backseat. The small bandage on her forehead appeared to be only a shade or two whiter than her face. Other than seeming to check the road behind them in the visor's mirror every few minutes, she had barely moved since getting into his car. He suspected she was in shock.

Mark kept his eye on the rearview mirror, too, but saw no one following them.

She had brooked no argument when he'd told her she was coming back with him, at least until her broken window could be repaired. In fact, she had said little beyond what she'd recounted to the police: A man had been burglarizing her apartment, and she'd had the misfortune of walking in on him. In her panic, she had fallen, torn her dress and hit her head.

She hadn't gotten a good look at his face. But he'd been white, average height, average build.

Whatever had happened tonight, Mark believed it was no random burglary. Samantha had been roughed up, and he didn't like to think about what might have happened if he hadn't shown back up when he did. Even more suspicious, her car tires had been slashed, something the police had made note of. He shook his head, wondering what kind of trouble she was really in.

"You're not taking me to the hotel?" Samantha asked, finally speaking as they drove past the glowing lights of the St. Clair's main property. Guests were milling about under the hotel's awning as valet staff orchestrated the retrieval of cars.

"I called earlier. The reception's winding down, but people are still there. I didn't think you'd want anyone to see you…like this." Mark turned the Volvo onto the road that ran adjacent to the hotel grounds. "The bungalow has a guest room."

She bit her lip. "I don't want to put you out."

"You're not." He looked at her in the darkness. "I don't think you should be alone tonight."

A short time later, after passing through automated security gates that kept non-guests off the private lane, they arrived at the house. Mark took Samantha's bag from the backseat. As they reached the door, the au pair he'd called earlier to stay with Emily greeted them. Benita Santos was a gray-haired, motherly looking woman who had worked at the St. Clair for years.

"Miss Emily is still fast asleep."

"Thank you for staying, Benita. Should I take you back to the hotel?"

She waved a hand. "No, thank you. I enjoy driving the golf cart."

Her eyes, however, hadn't missed Samantha, whom she'd met earlier. "*Ay Dios mio!* What happened to you, *mija*?"

"I took a little fall. It's nothing." Appearing self-conscious, Samantha averted her gaze from the woman's curious stare.

Mark escorted Benita outside, then returned to find Samantha staring out through the large bay window at the darkened ocean. Her long, slender legs appeared golden in the soft lamplight, and her dark hair was lustrous and smooth as it fell around her narrow shoulders. She turned to face Mark as he made his presence known.

"Since the café's closed tomorrow, you can sleep as late as you want," he mentioned. "I'm sending one of the hotel's maintenance staff to your place tomorrow to repair the window. I don't want you to have to wait until the apartment superintendent gets around to it."

"Thank you, Mark," she said, swallowing hard.

He approached slowly, until he stood in front of her. "You can trust me, you know. Whatever you're dealing with…"

She didn't reply, although her fingers briefly touched the front of his dress shirt. A few drops of her blood marred the white cotton from where he had held her.

"Samantha. I *want* to help you."

"You are helping me. You're giving me somewhere to stay tonight."

Mark sighed inwardly, frustrated that she wasn't willing to share the truth about whatever had happened. He wondered again at the possibilities, including a violent ex-husband or boyfriend. But why then would she be unwilling to accept help, or place a complaint with the police? Whatever the reason, he was pretty damn sure she was withholding a more detailed description of her assailant. He'd heard too much standing on the outside of the apartment to think otherwise.

"The wine you offered earlier?" she brought up, her features tense. "I'd like to take you up on that now."

Mark went into the kitchen to pour a generous glass for them both. The evening had been unsettling for him, too.

"How's your head?" he asked when he returned, handing her the goblet.

Absently, she touched the bandage. "I have a small headache, is all. I forget what a klutz I can be."

She was still trying to play down what had happened, chalking her injury up to her own clumsiness. He gave her a stern look, trying to understand. "If I hadn't come back with your purse, do you realize what might've happened?"

"Whoever it was, I scared him as much as he scared me. He went out through the window when I—"

"I'm not an idiot, Samantha," Mark cut in, voice low. "I heard you crying and I heard a man talking. I couldn't make out the words, but I could tell he was threatening you."

She fell silent, bowing her head.

Defeated, Mark moved to the foyer, setting the security system. He wouldn't push, but this also wasn't over. At least she was here tonight, on the resort grounds where he knew she was safe. "I'm sure you're exhausted. The guest room is the first one on the right. There's pretty much everything you need in the hall bathroom."

"Thank you," she whispered, appearing on the verge of tears.

He gazed at her, his heart constricting at how alone she seemed. "I meant what I said. If there's anything I can do…"

Mark let his words hang in the air between them. Then, taking his wine with him, he said a soft good night and retreated to his bedroom. He wondered why she wouldn't tell him the truth. Worried, he went into his own bathroom to prepare for bed, his mind weighed down with questions.

CHAPTER EIGHTEEN

The hard punch imploded her stomach. Trina sagged to the floor, but Devin hauled her back up, the open suitcase toppling as he shoved her onto the mattress. She curled up protectively, trying to find her breath.

"You think you can just run out on me?" Scowling, he shrugged out of his leather jacket and let it fall, a volcano on the verge of erupting. "You think you're done with me, bitch?"

The metallic rasp of his pants zipper sent her back into flight mode, but another vicious blow—this time to her face—stunned her and stopped her struggling. Pinning her to the bed, Devin wedged his knee between her legs, forcing them apart. He shoved her skirt up her hips and tore away her panties, then forced himself roughly inside her. Pain exploded in her body as an anguished sob escaped her lips.

God, please! No more.

Tears leaked from Trina's eyes as he held her down and raped her, his right hand clamped to her throat. A twisted game he liked to play. He would decide when she could breathe. She bucked, coming out of her stupor, panic seizing her as her lungs began to burn for air. Glass from the shattered lamp lay under her, cutting into her back. Her frantic heartbeat roared in her ears as Devin rutted into her, grunting, eyes squeezed closed in brutal ecstasy.

She couldn't breathe! Trina's trembling fingers closed around something sharp on the duvet. Desperate for oxygen, her vision blurring, she raised it blindly and plunged.

Devin stilled above her. Trina coughed and greedily sucked in air as his fingers went lax on her throat. But as her world came back into focus, a knife-edge of terror cut through her. She gaped in horror at the cobalt-blue shard protruding from the base of Devin's neck.

Jesus...Oh, Jesus...

He slid out of her and backed off the bed.

"What the fuck did you do?" he croaked, panting as he shakily touched the lodged shard. His ashen face mottled with rage. "You're dead this time, Trina. You hear me? Dead."

Grimacing, he pulled out the long shard. A heavy line of crimson ran down his shirtfront. Trina scrambled to the other side of the bed. There was no escape. She cowered, whimpering, her palm bleeding from where she'd gripped the broken glass.

He'll kill me.

A prayer from childhood echoed inside her as Devin advanced on her with clumsy steps. Blood leaked from between the fingers he pressed to his neck, his other hand drawn back and curled into a fist. Then he stopped. His eyeballs rolled slowly to the back of his head. He swayed.

Collapsed.

SAMANTHA WOKE TO silence, the only sound in the unfamiliar room her own labored breathing. Outside, it was still dark, deep night. The bed linens were damp and twisted around her body. Her heart pounded as if it might burst. Her head hurt, too, from the amount of wine she'd drunk in order to fall asleep, the remainder of the bottle. She ran a hand over her face, trying to stop the gruesome images playing like a horror movie in her brain.

Even in death, Devin still had the ability to torture her.

Rising from the bed and going into the hall bathroom, she ruminated on what she had done. Had she meant to kill him, or had she only been defending herself?

Sometimes she didn't know.

There had been so much blood. Inching closer to Devin's motionless body, she had felt for a pulse with shaking fingers but found none. Then she'd dug through his jacket pocket and extracted the money he had taken from her. Weeping quietly, wrapping her bleeding palm with a strip of cloth she had torn from a T-shirt, she'd hastily repacked her belongings, snapped the suitcase closed and, holding her injured stomach, lugged it to the door.

Then Trina Grissom had disappeared forever.

Or so she'd thought.

Feeling queasy, Samantha ran cool water into the sink and splashed it onto her cheeks. When she looked again at her reflection in the framed mirror, what she saw was a young woman with sleep-mussed hair and too-large, haunted dark eyes. The bandage on her forehead stood out against her pale skin, the bluish bruise around it the only wash of color in her face.

You've got her looks, Trina. The boys'll be sniffing around soon enough.

Her mother had taken her own life with an overdose of pills, quite possibly intentionally. If she had access to the same drugs right now, would she?

No.

She squeezed her eyes closed. Nothing was worse than death, was it? But if the truth came out...

She thought of going to prison if she couldn't prove she had killed Devin in self-defense. And that was the least of two evils. She didn't want to imagine what Red Leary would do to her—his brother's murderess—if he got his hands on her. Red's taste for brutality was legendary. He wouldn't care why she had stabbed Devin. He would exact his revenge in pain and blood.

A small voice told her to run. But if Lenny was watching her like he had claimed...

I know your alias and your car license plate. You step one foot outside this town, and I'll call the police and tell 'em who you really are.

With an all-points bulletin out on her, she wouldn't get far. Regardless, Lenny had slashed her car tires, ensuring she wouldn't be leaving tonight.

For all she knew, he was here on the resort property, keeping watch. Samantha berated herself, knowing she shouldn't have let Mark bring her here tonight, shouldn't have drawn him further into her mess. She hadn't been thinking clearly. Wrapping her arms around the modest cotton nightgown she wore, she wandered aimlessly down the hall. She couldn't slip out of the house even if she wanted to, she realized—she didn't know the code to disarm the security system. Fighting back panic, she weighed the possibility of staying in town, waiting to find out how much Lenny wanted for his silence.

But in her rational mind, she knew blackmailers couldn't be trusted.

She padded slowly to the half-open bedroom door, drawn by

moonlight spilling from its threshold. Magnetized, shivering violently, she inched closer to the only source of comfort she knew. Mark lay sleeping in a large four-poster bed, one arm draped across his T-shirt-clad chest and the other over a plump goose-down pillow. In the dim light she could make out the elegant planes of his face, his thick eyelashes creating half moons against his skin. Her heart ached. He really was a beautiful man, and far too good at heart.

She wasn't certain how long she stood there just watching his slow breathing, but he finally spoke her name in the darkness. Pushing himself up, he squinted at her, his voice husky and sleep-roughened. "What is it?"

"You said…" She halted, her words tremulous and uncertain. The need to feel some measure of security, however temporary, overwhelmed her. "You said if I…needed anything…"

She rubbed her fingers over her chilled upper arms. Somehow, he knew exactly what to do. Wordlessly, Mark shifted in bed and opened the covers to her. Samantha slipped in beside him and felt the warm strength of him fold around her. But he didn't try to kiss or fondle her. Instead, Mark simply held her against him, his gentle breath playing over her hair. They lay silently together in the darkness. Slowly, her trembling began to subside as fatigue shuttered her mind.

She drifted into a troubled sleep in Mark's arms.

Shallow morning light entered through the bedroom window. Mark looked at the clock on his nightstand. It was still relatively early in the morning.

He was alone in bed. His first thought was that Samantha had slipped away during the night, until he remembered that he had deliberately set the security system to keep her there.

He became aware of the delicious aroma wafting from the kitchen. The scent of coffee mingled with something that smelled bread-like and sweet. Wearing his T-shirt and pajama bottoms, Mark went down the hallway. Samantha stood in the kitchen, sipping coffee from one of his mugs. A waffle iron that hadn't seen use in years was on the counter, and Emily sat perched on one of the barstools, clad in her nightgown. Samantha had changed back into the shorts and tank top she'd had on last night, and her dark hair was twisted into a messy bun. She attempted a soft smile over the rim of her mug, although he noticed there were deep hollows under her eyes.

"We're making waffles with fruit compote," she said, obviously putting up a bright front for Emily. "You had frozen raspberries in the freezer, so I improvised. I hope that's all right?"

A saucepan on the gas range held the simmering sauce.

"Sure. Homemade waffles are an improvement over the frozen ones we typically have, unless we go to the hotel restaurant. Right, Emily?"

His daughter nodded enthusiastically, her eyes glued to the kitchen activity. Samantha opened the iron and took out the first golden square, which she dusted with powdered sugar and covered with several spoonfuls of sauce. Looking at Emily, she said, "Okay, sweetie. We'll let you try the first one. Why don't you sit at the table and I'll pour you some milk?"

Helping Emily climb from the stool, Mark settled her into one of the rush-seat dining chairs at the breakfast table. She clutched a worn-looking teddy bear with just one black-button eye and a bow tie.

"Who's your new friend?"

"That's Walton." Samantha came over with the milk and set it in front of Emily. She sounded a little embarrassed. "I can't believe

I brought him with me from the apartment last night. I don't even remember packing him. He's sort of my security blanket—I've had him since I was a little girl. Emily found him in my overnight case."

Mark looked at Emily, who had a large mouthful of waffle. "You were going through Samantha's things, Em?"

"It's okay," Samantha assured him. She went back to the kitchen to prepare another waffle for Mark. He followed her and helped himself to coffee from the carafe she'd already made.

"I woke up and you weren't there," he said in a low voice, out of Emily's hearing.

"I got up early and went back to the guest room. I didn't want Emily to see us…like that."

Mark again noticed Samantha's withdrawn, tense features, her façade temporarily dropped. He thought of last night and the way she'd come to his bed, her arms wrapped around herself. She'd trembled against him before exhaustion had finally claimed her. Mark had lain in bed awake for a long time afterward, aware of the way her body fit perfectly against his. He'd breathed in the scent of her hair and felt the soft, rounded curves of her bottom as she spooned against him. But what he'd felt hadn't been sexual, at least not at that point in time. He had wanted to protect her.

He touched her shoulder. "Are you feeling better this morning?"

"I am," Samantha replied softly, but she didn't look it. Although she had removed the small bandage, her forehead was bruised, and an angry scab had begun to form over the cut. Mark had also seen the faint bluish circles on her upper arms where the intruder had grabbed her. Anger percolated inside him. Samantha busied herself with preparing his food.

He started to say something, but the phone's ringing halted him. Mark went to answer it.

"Mercer," he said upon hearing his sister's voice. "She's right here. Hold on."

"I left her a message earlier," Samantha said. "We were supposed to meet for a run this morning." She took the phone, tucking it between her shoulder and ear as she poured batter into the iron and closed its top. Mark looked over at Emily, who was pretending to feed the stuffed animal breakfast. The bear had sticky raspberry sauce on its nose. Although he'd walked from the kitchen, he caught bits of Samantha's conversation. She was giving Mercer the same story about a faceless burglar she'd surprised.

"Mercer's on her way over," she said once she ended the call and came into the breakfast area, carrying a plate with Mark's food. She set it on the table, sounding resigned. "Since I'm not up to running, she wants to spend the morning with me. She's insisting."

Mark nodded. "I think it's a good idea."

"It isn't necessary. I'm fine," she murmured, appearing distracted as she stared out the window at a trio of sailboats—racing sloops—gliding past on the greenish-blue water. Their brightly colored sails fluttered in the breeze.

You're not fine. But he bit back his disagreement since his daughter was there.

"Mercer said we could take Emily to the beach, but I'd really like to just get back to my apartment."

"Stay with Mercer and Emily, all right? I don't want you going back there until the window's been repaired. You also need a security system. I can have the hotel's technician put one in this afternoon."

"Thank you, Mark. But I can't let you—"

He touched her arm. "You *can.* Although what I'd prefer is that you take a room at the hotel for a while."

"No. I can't afford that."

"I'm not asking you to pay for it," he said softly. "I'll comp you a room. Or you can stay here with Emily and me, for as long as you want."

Eyes pained, she shook her head in polite refusal and retreated to the kitchen. "Your breakfast is getting cold. Go sit with your daughter and eat."

Mark sat across from Emily, positioning himself so he could keep an eye on Samantha. She leaned casually against the granite countertop near the sink as she nursed her coffee. But there was no doubt about it. Although the morning sunlight had strengthened her composure, Samantha was still rattled, no matter how hard she tried to pretend otherwise.

An hour later, Mark prepared to leave for the hotel. At the least, he needed to make morning rounds and ensure operations were running smoothly. Mercer had arrived a short time earlier, carrying a beach bag and one of her bathing suits for Samantha. It was a sleek black maillot, and as Mark passed by them on the bungalow's porch, he couldn't help but notice the way it showcased Samantha's trim figure even with the cover-up she wore over it. She and Mercer were busy coating the fair-skinned Emily with sunscreen.

"We'll keep her under the umbrella most of the time," Mercer assured him. "And we won't let her go into the surf without one of us. Even with those little water wing things on."

Mark nodded, knowing his sister was conscientious when it came to Emily. He noticed that the upset she'd displayed the previous evening appeared to have receded, and she seemed back to her usual cheerful self.

"We're planning to have lunch at The Palms," Mercer said, referring to the hotel's casual poolside eatery. "Want to join us? Maybe around twelve thirty?"

BEFORE THE STORM

"I'll try, but I doubt I can make it. I have a lot to do." His gaze moved to Samantha. She looked up at him briefly, then continued rubbing lotion on Emily's shoulders. He walked out to his car.

Mark hadn't lied, exactly. He *was* busy today, although he didn't plan to be at the St. Clair for more than an hour or so. Samantha's apartment key, which she'd given him for the hotel's maintenance crew, was in his pocket. He wasn't sending his staff over alone. Mark was going, too. He planned to search for something that might provide him with some answers into Samantha's past and who the hell wanted to hurt her.

143

CHAPTER NINETEEN

"WHAT WERE YOU thinking, darling?" Olivia's expression was reproachful as she sat in one of the leather armchairs in Mark's office. Her stylish bob swung as she shook her head. "Have you even considered the kind of impression you're making on Emily?"

Mark squeezed the bridge of his nose. "Samantha's a *friend*, Mom." He didn't bother keeping the annoyance from his voice. "Someone broke into her apartment last night—I was there right after it happened. I didn't think it would be a good idea for her to be alone."

She gave an incredulous laugh. "You have an entire hotel full of rooms. Yet you took her to your home for the evening? Please tell me she slept in the guest room."

Gossip traveled fast among the hotel staff, but Mark hadn't realized the grapevine ran all the way to Olivia's white-columned estate. He should have remembered that Benita, the au pair who had helped him with Emily last night, was the cousin of Olivia's housekeeper, Marisol.

"According to Marisol, this *Samantha Marsh* looked as though she'd been manhandled."

"She surprised the burglar," Mark said, his patience wearing thin. "She got a little banged up, but she's okay. The police are looking into it. Besides, I don't see how any of this is your business. Or Marisol's."

"A physical assault," Olivia fretted, her fingers worrying her ever-present pearls. "We don't have that kind of thing happen in Rarity Cove. You don't suppose Luther Banda did it?"

"No, I don't. Luther is a trusted employee of Samantha's, so why would he do anything to hurt her? Besides, she said the intruder was white." He busied himself with the papers on his desk, hoping she might take the hint that he had things to do. "Is there something I can help you with? Why are you here, exactly? Other than to stick your nose in my personal life."

Olivia rose and crossed the oriental carpet so she stood in front of his desk. "I just don't understand you, Mark. Felicity came to the reception last night at my invitation—"

"At *your* invitation, not mine," he emphasized. "And in case you didn't notice, I was there with a date of my own choosing. I was under no obligation to fawn over Felicity just because you invited her. It's bad enough you finagled me into dancing with her."

Olivia's tone was petulant. "You ran off in the middle of Carter's reception. With that woman."

"I thought you wanted me to date. *To get on with my life*, is how you put it. Or is that only if I'm dating someone you pick out for me from your inventory of Junior League socialites?"

"Shelley belonged to the Rarity Cove Junior League," she reminded softly, appearing hurt.

Mark blew out a quiet breath and checked his wristwatch. It

was almost noon already, and he was still mired in his duties at the hotel. He had the maintenance crew scheduled to go to Samantha's apartment at twelve thirty, and he was determined to make the trip with them. He'd also sent one of the workers ahead to meet the tow truck so the Camry could be taken to the garage and have its tires replaced when the shop opened on Monday. Samantha would want to repay him, but he didn't care about the cost. As the eldest of the St. Clair brood, he was used to taking charge.

"I love you, darling, that's all," Olivia said, earnest. "I won't apologize for wanting what's best for you."

"You don't even know Samantha."

Olivia frowned. "So you *are* interested in her."

Mark shrugged, not wanting to engage further in the topic. He received a text on his phone so he unclipped it from his belt to check the message.

"First you say she's just a friend, and now you've repeatedly referred to her as your date. You were awfully attentive to her last night—"

"I've got to go. There's a situation in the lobby." Mark walked around his desk, and placing his hands on Olivia's shoulders, he gently but firmly guided her toward the door.

"I'm not blind, you know. Samantha Marsh is an extremely attractive woman. I can see how she might turn your head. But what do you really know about her?"

When he failed to answer, Olivia sighed and picked up her purse, placing its strap over her shoulder. "Just tell me you'll think about slowing things down."

"There's nothing to slow down."

"You may be a grown man, but you're still my son, Mark Harrison St. Clair. And as sure as I'm standing here, there's something about that woman that sets off alarm bells. A mother's intuition is never wrong."

"What about Carter and the real estate agent climbing all over him last night?" Mark inquired pointedly. "From what I hear, Mitzi Ackerman's a bona fide cougar—she's bedded half of Charleston. Why aren't you concerned about that?"

Olivia's gaze was unflinching. "I love Carter every bit as much as I love you, but I have no illusions. He travels in a different world, and he gives as good as he gets. What would the young people call him? A *player*. But *you*, Mark. You're old-fashioned and one of the last true Southern gentlemen. Just like your daddy."

Her blue eyes were sincere. "You've been hurt too much already with Shelley's passing. I just can't bear to see you in any more pain."

Kissing him good-bye on the cheek, she turned to find her other son leaning against the doorframe.

"Carter," she exclaimed with an air of surprise.

"Did I really just hear my own momma calling me a player? You've been watching too much of *The Bachelor*."

Carter kissed her warmly despite the slight he had overheard. Once she'd exited, he came into the office, seating himself on the edge of Mark's desk. He picked up a Montblanc fountain pen, absently twisting its top.

"Don't you have a movie set to be at?" Mark asked.

"Not on Sunday. I'm footloose and fancy-free—"

"Well, I'm not. I just got texted. I'm needed at the front desk."

"I'll say," Carter agreed with a grin. "I just walked through. There's a lady—and calling her big-boned would be courteous—in a muumuu raising holy hell about the minibar in her room. Apparently someone *else* ate everything inside it, and she wants it all off her bill."

"Great. So what're you doing here?"

"I don't know, I thought we could do something together. Maybe take your boat out." Awkwardly, Carter cleared his throat. "The truth is, I wanted to talk to you."

"About selling the hotel again?"

He pressed his lips together. "No, Mark. I got the message on that."

"Either way, you'll have to take a number and get in line, right behind the guest in the muumuu. And after I put out that fire, I have an errand to run."

"Yeah? Where?" Carter appeared interested, and Mark wondered if he was really that bored hanging around the hotel. Despite her obvious assets, it appeared even Mitzi Ackerman hadn't been able to hold his interest for long. Mark sighed inwardly, trying to decide how much to reveal.

"I figured you'd already heard since everyone else has. Samantha's apartment was broken into last night. The guy was still there when she went inside. She had a close call."

Carter sobered. "Is she okay?"

"She's fine, I think. She's down at the beach with Mercer and Emily right now. I'm having hotel maintenance go to her place and repair the window. Our tech is also installing a security system since they aren't standard at the Wayfarer. It's an old building, and the wiring's tricky. I'm going with them to supervise."

"I'll go, too."

"There's no need."

Carter crossed his arms over his chest. "Then maybe I'll just head down to the beach with Mercer and Sam. I don't suppose Sam's wearing one of those thong bikinis?"

Mark glared at his brother, who raised his palms in self-defense.

"It was a *joke*." Carter slid off the desk. He went to stand in front of Mark, blocking his exit. "What's really going on, Mark? You're wound as tight as the inside of a golf ball."

"It's nothing. And how am I supposed to know you're joking? Word is, you asked Samantha to Tommy Houghton's barbecue."

Carter colored a bit. "Relax. She turned me down cold."

"But you *asked* her, Carter. When you clearly knew I was taking her out." Mark shook his head, deciding to speak his mind. What had happened with Samantha last night had his emotions running high, and Carter seemed the perfect target for his frustration. "It's like you can't let things go. You always want to keep some kind of competition going between us."

Carter briefly dropped his head, appearing repentant. "You're right, and I'll own up to it. I'm sorry, Mark. Asking Samantha to go to the barbecue was a jackass move—"

"*You bet it was,*" Mark ground out, barely keeping his anger on simmer. "Isn't it enough that you've got legions of female fans drooling over you? It's like you're still trying to prove that Shelley made the wrong choice."

Carter looked as though he'd been slapped, his eyes pained. He said hoarsely, "We used to be close growing up, remember? Before things went to hell between us."

Mark ran a hand over his mouth. He often recalled the closeness they'd shared, too, before Carter and Shelley's indiscretion caused the rift that had never fully mended between them. In truth, he hated that his relationship with Carter remained defined by what had happened years earlier—when neither of them was even fully an adult. Still, it was something they both seemed incapable of getting past. He was stuck in the role of the responsible, put-upon older brother while Carter was the perpetual bad boy and prodigal son. At one time they had simply been siblings, bonded by friendship and blood.

It had also occurred to him that he'd been willing to eventually forgive Shelley and let her back into his life, but he had never been so generous with Carter. Hurt, feeling betrayed, Mark had vilified him to their family and mutual friends, widening the chasm between them. Carter had headed north after high school and had rarely come back home except for the obligatory family occasion—a marriage, a birth, a burial.

"I know I'm the one who screwed everything up," Carter said roughly. "That's sort of what I wanted to talk to you about. Samantha said some things about you and me last night that hit home... I was hoping we could work on things. Try to start over."

Mark felt a stab of guilt. For the sake of family, he conceded it was time they both tried a little harder to let things go.

He also needed to confide in someone. Releasing a breath, he clasped the back of his neck. "Sorry if I'm irritable. There's just something going on with Samantha. Last night was more than just some random burglary. It seemed personal. Her car tires were slashed, too. She won't talk about it, and I need to find out what kind of trouble she's in."

Mark watched as the burly maintenance man known as Big Cal slid a new glass panel into the window frame in the apartment's single bedroom. In the small foyer, the hotel's security tech worked at installing a state-of-the-art alarm system. If it came to it, Mark realized he would be willing to have one of his staff keep guard in the parking lot.

Was he overreacting? Thinking back to the previous evening, he didn't believe so.

"I've got to go to the truck to get some tools," Big Cal said as he passed Mark in the doorway. "Be right back, Mr. St. Clair."

Mark nodded. Alone now, he placed his hands inside his

pockets and looked around the bedroom. It was sparse and unremarkable in decor, with a basic striped comforter on the bed that could have been purchased at any discount department store. There was also a rather worn bureau. Its drawers remained open, and the intruder had dumped some of its contents—T-shirts and shorts, underwear—onto the floor. Mark noted that on its top, there were no photos or knickknacks on display, things he might have expected in a woman's bedroom.

Stepping closer, he picked up the dropped clothing and then peered inside the open drawers. A small jewelry box was located in the top one amid the remaining garments. Brushing aside the guilt he felt about snooping, Mark extracted the box and opened it. But it held only a couple of pairs of earrings and a cracked, conch-shell cameo on a tarnished chain. The locket looked old and inexpensive.

A check under the bed and inside the closet registered nothing else of interest. He closed the closet door just as Big Cal returned with a toolbox and sealant gun.

"I'll have this taken care of in no time," the large man said. "I talked to Eli in the foyer. He wants to wire the system into the windows, too. Anyone tries coming in that way again, they won't get far. Give us another forty-five minutes, and this place'll be locked up tighter than a clam with lockjaw."

"Thanks, Cal." Mark went into the living room. Disregarding the mess, it appeared as sterile and impersonal as Samantha's bedroom. In fact, the apartment reminded him of one of the town's beachside rental condos that were furnished with only the bare necessities. He bent to pick up the items dumped from the entertainment center, but halted when he noticed Carter backing from the hall closet between the living area and kitchen.

"What're you doing?"

"Just looking around," Carter replied casually.

"Well, don't."

Carter lowered his voice, although it was unlikely anyone could hear him over the high-pitched whine of the tech's drill coming from the foyer. "I *thought* that was what we were here for. Don't tell me you weren't making out like one of those *CSI* shows in the bedroom."

The truth was, Carter had beaten him to the closet. It was where he had been headed next.

"Did you find anything?"

"Not so far." Carter went back to sifting through the fallen clothing and other items that had apparently been dumped onto the floor from the upper shelf. Mark walked into the kitchen and flipped through a stack of mail on the counter, but all he found were bills for electricity, water, cable and car insurance. There wasn't so much as a personal letter or postcard in the stack. Unlike his own home, the front of the refrigerator was a blank slate—no magnets holding photographs, no reminders of dental appointments or Emily's therapy sessions.

Mark sighed as he studied the nice-looking, copper cookware hanging from an overhead rack. He'd been trying to rationalize that he was rummaging through Samantha's things for her own good. How could he protect her if she wouldn't reveal the source of the threat? But deep down, he knew this invasion of privacy was way out of line.

"Well, I *did* find something."

He turned at Carter's voice. His brother held a risqué pair of women's shoes. Made of some kind of clear plastic, their stiletto heels appeared about six inches high. They were completely out of place with Samantha's wardrobe.

Carter waggled his eyebrows suggestively. "If I were you, I'd ask her to wear *these* on your next date."

The surprising find made Mark feel even guiltier, as did the image of Samantha wearing them that popped into his head. Everyone had his or her little kinks and accoutrements when it came to their sexual behavior. He recalled an X-rated, black satin teddy Shelley wore that had *done things* for him, as well as a silk blindfold and vanilla-scented massage oil they'd kept hidden in a drawer. Mark felt his face heat.

"That's not the kind of thing we're looking for, and you know it. Put those back."

Samantha and Mercer lounged on the bungalow's covered porch, out of the intense heat of the afternoon sun. After a poolside lunch, they'd returned to put Emily to bed for a nap. Mercer sat in one of the rocking chairs while Samantha swayed gently in the swing that just last night she had shared with Mark. She thought of their passionate kiss. If she'd only known that a short time afterward, her life would begin a death spiral.

She'd done her best to hide her anxiety from Mercer, to act normally, but her insides were churning and her mind spinning for some solution to grab on to. If she ended up attempting an escape, going on the run again, there was no choice—she'd simply have to leave everything behind. Her business, her few belongings, even her car. *Samantha Marsh* would also have to end, since that cover had been blown. Without a social security number or even a driver's license, finding legitimate work would be impossible. Twisting her hands in her lap, her throat tight, she wondered again how much Lenny would want in exchange for his silence. There was some cash in her bank account, but not much. And after financing the café, she doubted a financial institution would make her another loan.

Besides, in the glaring light of day, she again faced the likelihood that paying him would only kick off a vicious pattern. He would come back repeatedly, wanting more.

"What're you thinking about, Sam?" Mercer broke the silence. "You're so quiet, and you barely touched your food at lunch. Your head isn't still hurting, is it?"

"I'm fine," she lied. "Just tired."

"I'm not surprised. I still can't believe what happened to you last night." Mercer took a sip from a sweating can of diet soda. "You're holding up much better than I would. Of course, *I* can't seem to handle much of anything these days."

Samantha looked at her. Last night, Mark had mentioned Mercer was upset about something. But whatever was wrong, she wouldn't discuss it with him.

"Mark said he ran into you outside the reception," she mentioned carefully. "He said he thought you'd been crying."

For several long moments, Mercer gazed out toward the band of sea grass that whipped in the ocean breeze. "There's a guy. A man, actually. He's in Atlanta. We were seeing each other while I was living there. He wants me to come back."

Mercer had never mentioned a relationship before. Talking about Mercer's problem was preferable to thinking about her own, infinitely more dire, situation, so she asked, "What do you want to do?"

"It's not that simple." Her eyebrows gathered in pensively. "It isn't just about me. There's Mark and Emily to consider. I quit my job and moved back here after the accident. They needed my help."

"You've been here for two years. I'm sure Mark would want you to do what's best for you."

"The truth is, I don't think Mark or anyone in my family would be thrilled about Jonathan. No one knows about him. Mom would probably have a good old-fashioned conniption fit." Mercer smiled faintly at her own remark, then swung her long hair back behind her.

"It's sort of a May-December romance," she confided.

"*How* May-December?"

"Jonathan was my college professor. He's forty-five."

"Oh," Samantha said, surprised by the substantial age difference. She knew Mercer was twenty-six.

"You don't approve, either."

"I'm not judging," she assured her. "Believe me, I'd be the last one to do that. Mercer, do you love him? Because if you do, that's all that should matter."

Mercer appeared pensive. Pulling her tanned legs up into the chair, she wrapped her arms around her shins.

"I do care for him," she admitted. "At first, we kept telling ourselves it was just a fling. I felt so rebellious, even naughty, being with an older man. And the sex...I'm not...I mean, I wasn't that experienced. But it was really good."

She continued despite the attractive flush that crept onto her cheeks. "Jonathan's smart, obviously, and charming. He's also one of the kindest men I've ever known. By the way, he didn't ask me out until after I'd graduated. I contacted *him* for a job reference, and it sort of started from there."

"He sounds wonderful, actually."

"Things started getting more serious right before Mark and Shelley's car accident. Jonathan asked me to move in with him. But I was having trouble taking that step." She shrugged thoughtfully. "Maybe it *was* the age difference. That and worrying about what my family would think. His first wife died, and he's been a widower for a long time now. He also has a son who's only a year younger than me and who clearly doesn't approve. God, I'm going on and on, aren't I?"

"Not at all," Samantha said. Mercer had been a friend to her, and she wanted to help her, even if it was only lending an ear.

"I was trying to decide what to do when the accident happened. Shelley's death made the decision for me. It also made it easy to run away. Since coming back home, I've been to Atlanta a half-dozen times to see him—long weekends where we stay in bed the whole time. I tell my family I'm going to visit friends from college."

She rubbed her hands over her bare thighs, a wistfulness in her eyes. "Jonathan called me last night. We argued about what I should do. He says he can't get over me, and he wants me to tell my family about him. He wants to come here to meet them properly instead of sneaking around behind their backs."

"What do *you* want?"

She chewed her lip. "I honestly don't know. To be with him, I guess. Maybe I just have cold feet."

The phone rang inside the house. Excusing herself, Mercer went inside to answer it. Samantha leaned her head against the swing's back and closed her eyes. The afternoon's warmth soaked into her bones. She needed to remember this place, absorb it into her memory so she had something to hold on to if she made the decision to run. Samantha thought of the way she'd felt falling asleep in Mark's arms, in his bed. He represented a security she'd never had, an ideal of what her life might have been like if she hadn't been born Trina Grissom and ended up where she did.

She'd slept poorly last night and must have dozed off, because she woke to the squawking of gulls. Samantha glimpsed the portly man who stood on one of the sand dunes nearest the bungalow's property. He wore baggy bathing trunks and a flowered Hawaiian shirt unbuttoned to reveal his bulging, hairy belly. A pair of binoculars hung around his thick neck. Although the floppy sunhat put his face in shadow, Samantha felt her heart beat harder inside her chest. Lenny. He smiled, more of a grinning leer, and he used two fingers of his right hand to point at his own eyes. Then he pointed back to her.

I'm watching you.

Lenny traveled down the dune and out of sight. The swing rocked as Samantha stood, her knees wobbly. He *was* shadowing her, just like he'd said. Her eyes scoured the tourists who walked past, but Lenny had disappeared into the crowd.

CHAPTER TWENTY

"I FOUND IT SLIPPED under the rear gate this morning. Hand delivered, no postmark and no return address. Someone knew what they were doing. They threw a towel over the security camera." Cyril O'Keefe laid the manila envelope on the desk in front of his boss. He stood with beefy arms folded over his barrel chest like a sentinel awaiting instructions.

Blowing a stream of smoke through his nostrils, Red Leary balanced his cigarette on the ashtray's edge, then opened the package's clasp. A thin stack of photos slid out. He looked them over, one by one. A little older, different hair, different body even—but he had to admit their subject bore a striking resemblance to Trina Grissom. A handwritten note had also been tucked inside the envelope.

How much is she worth?

Based on the building in the photos' background—a pink stucco two-story bordered by stubby palmettos—he figured they had been taken somewhere along the coastal Southeast, or possibly even Southern California. Whoever had sent them made sure nothing captured by the lens gave away the location. Care had been used in avoiding any signage or license plates on the cars in the parking lot.

Red picked up the top photo in the stack for a closer look. In it, the dark-haired *maybe* Trina stood next to a convertible sports car. She was talking to the female driver—an attractive, busty, honey-blonde who looked as though she would be at home in an Ivy League sorority house. He flipped the photo over, searching for the mark of a camera shop where the film might have been processed. There was none. They were probably printed off a computer. He hated technology.

"You really think it's her after all this time?" Cyril asked.

"I don't know. Maybe."

"So what do we do?"

"What do you think, moron?" Red snapped. "We wait for whoever left these to contact us. Right now, he's fishing. He's seeing how bad we still want her."

"You *do* still want her? The money still stands?"

"You can bet this asshole's going to want more."

With an irritable release of breath, Red shoved the photos back into the envelope and tossed it onto the credenza. He retrieved the still-burning cigarette, flicked the ashes from its end and took another deep drag, thinking of his baby brother. *Devin, with his pretty-boy face and head full of rocks.* He could almost see his chiseled features and shock of Black Irish hair. Even from the grave, Devin was giving Red an ulcer. The kid had been nothing but a pain in the ass since the day he was born. Red had handed him the Blue Iris to run, but instead of showing his appreciation, Devin still hadn't been able to keep out of trouble. Too much greed, too much booze and cocaine. Their mother had spoiled him, made him soft, God rest her soul.

"Go to Starbucks and get me a venti double latte," he ordered. He peeled off a twenty from the bills in his wallet and handed it to Cyril. "And tell them this time no goddamn foam."

"You got it, boss."

Once the office door closed, Red unfolded his long legs from behind the desk and went to stare out the window. He consulted the Rolex on his broad wrist and then watched as a semi-tractor pulled from the parking lot below, passing through the gates that led into and out of the compound. Cyril's black Cadillac Escalade left the lot behind it. The afternoon Memphis sky appeared gray and promised rain before the evening rush hour. Red shoved his ginger-hued hair, threaded with silver now, from his eyes.

He'd nearly forgotten about Trina, had almost given up on ever finding her or recouping his substantial loss. She had to be the answer. God knew Boklov's men had turned Devin's place upside down looking for those rocks.

Red had paid off the debt to keep his name intact. Because in *his* business, reputation was everything. Whoever said there was no honor among thieves didn't know what the fuck they were talking about. But the Learys weren't *thieves,* exactly. They were more like *entrepreneurs* you didn't ever want to cross.

And Trina had crossed him mightily.

A train rumbled past on the nearby tracks, hauling freight to some unknown destination. Red wondered how long it would take their mystery jerk-off to spell out what he wanted in exchange for her whereabouts, if it really *was* her.

Patience.

He had waited six years. He could wait a little more.

CHAPTER TWENTY-ONE

S HE HADN'T FLED, at least not yet. But Samantha had
returned to her apartment, not wanting to put Mark or his
family any closer to danger. Spotting Lenny on the beach yesterday
had confirmed he was indeed hovering nearby, watching her every
move.

For now she was heeding his warning, staying in town and
waiting for him to tell her how much he wanted for his silence.
But late last night, unable to sleep, Samantha had packed a single
suitcase in case she made the snap decision to attempt an escape.
Without her car, however, it wasn't as if she could just hop a bus
or plane, since both would require traveling to Charleston. And
both would also require her driver's license as an ID. If Lenny
noticed her departure and told the police about her, chances were
she wouldn't be allowed to board.

It seemed any choice she made had the potential to be the
wrong one. Nerves frayed, she felt like a rubber band stretched to
the breaking point.

"Sam, you shouldn't be moving that," Luther fussed as she

trudged from the stockroom with a boxful of jars of preserved lemons. Samantha planned to pair them with recipe cards for lemon pound cake and stack them in the front window. Despite the looming peril, she tried to focus on business, her only way to keep from going insane.

"I have a few bumps and bruises. I'm not an invalid," she argued as Luther pried the box from her arms.

"Could've fooled me. You're as pale as your cake flour. Now go on and work the cash register. I'll take care of this."

"You were supposed to go home after setup—"

"I'll stay for a while. What else do I have to do?"

Luther had been sticking to her like glue since Samantha arrived at the café. He'd been informed of the break-in at her apartment, although he wouldn't say who had told him. She suspected Mark had contacted Luther and asked him to keep an eye on things. Mark had come to her apartment and driven her to work that morning. He'd said her car would be delivered to her around noon, and as she'd figured, he had refused payment for the new tires.

With her car back, at least she would have a means to *try* to leave, if she made that choice.

The door to the café opened, and another group of vacationers strolled inside, bringing with them the scent of sun and sand. Already, the place had begun to fill. Samantha stood behind the register, ringing up totals as two other lunchtime workers filled orders, mostly to-go items so diners could enjoy the beach or picnic tables on the square under the shade of moss-draped live oaks.

She made change for a twenty, handing it back to a sociable young couple who had purchased two sandwiches and a cupcake to share. The glint from the café door as it opened again caught her eye. Her heart turned over as Lenny ambled inside. He fit in perfectly with the hungry crowd, wearing a T-shirt that proclaimed *Historic Summerville*, his balding head sunburned. Samantha stole a look at Luther, but he was busy stacking the preserved lemons in the window.

"Business is good," Lenny commented as he came up to the register.

"What're you doing here?" she asked angrily, her voice low.

"I came for lunch." He made a show of casually scanning the paper menu. "How's the Greek panini with tomato jam and roasted peppers?"

Despite the innocuous question, he had a look in his eyes that told her he had come for more than food. Samantha rang up the order, feeling nauseated in his presence.

"What else?" she asked wearily.

"A brownie. And a large peach iced tea, extra sweet. What do I owe you?"

"That's…thirteen ninety-five."

Lenny tossed a one-dollar bill onto the counter, along with a piece of paper folded in half. Hands trembling, Samantha took the note and shoved it into her apron pocket. He leaned toward her, his words meant for her alone. "I'll be seeing you real soon, Trina. And don't do anything stupid like tryin' to slip out on me. You won't get far once I give the police your license plate number. Besides, why would you want to leave? You've made friends here."

He gave her a greasy smile. "Speaking of, that was a real cute little girl with you at the beach yesterday."

At the mention of Emily, Samantha's eyes crashed into his, her throat going dry.

Lenny shrugged. "I'd hate for anything to happen to her, that's all. The world's a bad place these days…"

She felt the threat in her veins. "Stay away from her—"

"Then you stay put," he ordered. "Look, I'm a reasonable man, sweetheart. I don't want to mess up your nice situation. I just want a little piece of the pie, and then I'll be on my way like a bird with wings."

He waggled his fingers to demonstrate. Samantha glared at him. Waiting until he had gotten his food and exited, she asked one of the workers to take over her duties at the cash register. Heart pounding, she went to the storeroom, locking the door behind her. She unfolded the paper he'd given her.

Sea King Motor Court, room six. One hour before midnight. Twenty thousand dollars and wear the gifts I gave you.

The air inside the storeroom felt stagnant. She sank to the floor against the wall. Tears of anger and helplessness brimmed in her eyes. Most of all, she couldn't believe he had threatened Emily. The thought of Lenny going anywhere near Mark's daughter caused perspiration to break out on her skin. She felt like a frantic, trapped animal—if she did attempt to run now, what if he took Emily to flush her out? If anything happened to that sweet child because of her...

She closed her eyes, sickened. If she made the ultimate decision to flee, she would make sure Mark knew to protect Emily. She rebuked herself yet again for having gotten them involved.

Twenty thousand dollars.

Where was she supposed to get money like that? Her car was eight years old and had well over a hundred thousand miles on it. She doubted she could get more than a couple thousand dollars for it, not that she could sell it between now and their meeting tonight anyway. Samantha tried to think. She had a couple of credit cards, and she might be able to get some kind of cash advance with them. But would it be enough? And despite what he claimed, how long would it be before he was back, wanting more?

Wear the gifts I gave you.

And Lenny *did* want more. When she delivered the black-mail money, he also expected sex as part of the package. Samantha pressed shaking fingers against her lips, swallowing down her disgust. No matter what, she wouldn't let it come to that. She thought of the way Devin had used her.

Not again. Never again.

If she could pull the money together, she would make it clear it was a one-time payoff. She'd have to convince him she had nothing more. Perhaps he'd leave town for a while, leave her alone long enough for her to make a more organized disappearance.

Emily. Her heart squeezed. He'd actually threatened Emily...

She jumped as the doorknob twisted and she heard Luther's deep voice.

"Sam, you in there? Ed from the repair shop's here with your car."

"I...I'll be right out. Can you just get the keys from him?"

"Why's the door locked?" The knob rattled again.

Rising, Samantha grabbed several packages of paper napkins and opened the door. She tried to appear in a rush to get back out front. "We're running low on napkins. We need to reorder—"

Luther placed his large hands on her shoulders, halting her. "What's goin' on?"

"Nothing, I..." Samantha avoided his stare. She gave a weak shrug. "You were right. I'm not feeling up to work today. Maybe I'll go home after the lunch crowd is gone."

She left him standing in the hallway.

≋

The Camry idled near the entrance to the St. Clair. Samantha slumped behind the steering wheel, feeling ill as she stared at its graceful front. Uniformed bellmen bustled about, unloading luggage from luxury cars as guests passed through revolving glass doors that were flanked by massive ferns in ornate pots. The beautiful weather and bright blue afternoon sky contradicted the bleak darkness inside her. *I don't want to do this.* But she had no other ideas, and she was running out of time.

When she'd left her apartment, she had glimpsed Lenny's Crown Victoria in her rearview mirror, tailing her from a distance, although it had dropped off once she reached the peninsula road.

Steeling herself, she rolled the Camry forward, coming to a stop under the hotel's black awning. A parking attendant opened the door so she could exit the car.

"Do you have any luggage, ma'am?" the slim-faced young man asked.

"No." Samantha smoothed her skirt and handed him the keys. "Just something in the backseat."

He helped her extract the large gift basket adorned with a blue satin bow. Numerous Café Bella food items were artfully arranged inside it.

"Do you need help carrying this inside?"

"I can take it from here. Thank you." Lugging the basket, Samantha navigated the revolving door, butterflies fluttering in her stomach as she traveled across the lobby's marble floor. She had tried desperately to find another way. But using both her credit cards, she'd been able to get an advance of only twelve thousand dollars. Resigned, Samantha walked up to the concierge desk. An attractive blond woman stood behind it, wearing a navy jacket bearing the St. Clair crest.

"I'd like to see Mr. St. Clair. My name's Samantha Marsh."

"Do you have an appointment, Miss Marsh?"

"No. But please ask if he has time for me."

Balancing the cumbersome basket on the desk's edge, she

waited as the concierge called Mark's office. Hanging up the phone, she smiled. "Mr. St. Clair will see you now. He's just down the hall to the left."

Samantha went down the richly appointed corridor. An oriental carpet runner covered the polished hardwood floor, and brass wall sconces illuminated tasteful wallpaper and a series of oil paintings in gilded frames. Mark met her outside his office, dressed in dark suit pants, a cream-colored shirt and silk tie.

"Samantha," he said. His soft-blue eyes reflected concern, causing her heart to constrict. "Is everything all right?"

She nodded.

"Did the shop return your car?"

"It's how I got here. I can't thank you enough."

"That looks heavy. Here, let me help you." Mark took the basket from her.

"It's for you, actually. It's a prototype of the baskets I'm designing for the gift shop." Samantha followed him into his office. It was spacious and decorated with masculine accents, including a barrister's bookcase and fine leather upholstery. Near the desk, a large picture window encased in teal silk curtains offered a view of the hotel swimming pool and, beyond it, the ocean.

Mark set the basket on the desk, studying its contents.

"This is the deluxe basket," she explained. "I'm planning several smaller ones as well so there will be a range of prices."

"It's nice." He returned his gaze to Samantha, his eyes saying all the things she guessed he could not. Then he moved to stand in front of her, taking her hands in his. They'd grown closer in the short space of time since Lenny's intrusion into her apartment. Despite her edict the night of the reception, she had leaned on Mark, accepting his kindness and becoming more familiar with him. Longing welled within her to be held by him, just as he'd held her in his bed, and she blinked to stop the tears that threat-ened to come to her eyes.

I'll get through this. Somehow, she would manage to survive this day and the night that lay ahead.

"This is a professional visit, Mark," Samantha clarified softly, slipping her fingers from his. "I was wondering if I could…"

She floundered, losing her words. She rubbed her bruised tem-ple, almost dizzy with dread and hating herself for what she was about to do.

"What I meant to say is…I need an advance on the sales from the gift shop in order to finish the baskets." The lie tasted bitter in her mouth. "Web site sales are coming along, too, and this time my order is so large the food manufacturer wants prepayment. I have most of the money, but I'm a little short and…"

He studied her. "How much?"

"Eight thousand dollars."

After a beat, Mark nodded. "All right. I'll send them a check—"

"I need it today, actually." She felt her face heat. "They're bumping me up in the production line, but I have to pay them today to hold my spot. If you could make the check out to me, I'll have the money wired out before the close of business. I would really appreciate it, Mark. I'll even reduce my profit margin on the baskets to make up for the inconvenience."

His eyes bore into hers for several long moments, as if he were evaluating what she had just told him. Samantha fought the urge to drop her gaze. But then, releasing a breath, Mark went to the other side of the desk and extracted a small leather booklet. Gripping a pen in his right hand, he made out a check.

"I'll pay you back if the sales don't cover the advance," she promised as he walked back to her. She took the voucher with trembling fingers. "If you can just give me ninety days—"

"I don't care about the money, Samantha." Deep concern tightened his features. "I care about *you.*"

She looked at the check and saw that it was from Mark's personal account, not from the hotel's. She knew in that moment that he had seen through her ruse, but he was giving her the money anyway.

"Thank you," she whispered. On weak legs, she walked out of the office.

Outside, Samantha waited for the valet to deliver her car. She half-expected Mark to follow her out and demand the truth. But instead she stood alone until the Camry was brought around. Feeling an ache inside her chest, she tipped the valet and slid inside. As she drove away from the hotel, Samantha finally allowed hot tears to slip down her cheeks. She had used Mark and his attraction to her, as much as any dancer at the Blue Iris had ever used any patron to gain cash or expensive gifts. The fact that her life depended on her lie was little comfort to her.

Bile burned in the back of her throat, but she forced herself to postpone her self-loathing. She had exactly one hour before the bank closed. Samantha would cash Mark's check, and then tonight, she'd go to Lenny's motel and give him the money. But that was all he would take from her, she vowed. She would tell him that was the last of it, and she wouldn't allow him to touch her.

She would defend herself if she had to.

CHAPTER TWENTY-TWO

T HE SEA KING Motor Court sat off the two-lane highway heading inland out of Rarity Cove. A good four miles from the beach, the one-story, painted cinderblock structure was outdated and somewhat run-down, with a small swimming pool surrounded by a chain-link fence next to the parking lot. Samantha walked past the unoccupied, darkened pool, clutching her purse that contained Lenny's payoff.

Room six. She stood outside it and reminded herself to breathe. But her courage felt shattered, like so many broken shell fragments washed up along the shore. The porch light beside the door had either burned out or been purposely extinguished. If not for the moon overhead and the iridescent, droning orange of the motel signage, she would be in eerie darkness.

Nearly choking on dread, Samantha knocked. As she waited, her fingers roamed inside her purse until she felt the handle of the kitchen knife she'd brought with her from Café Bella. If Lenny tried to take more than the money, if he grabbed her and tried to force her...

She had already stabbed a man to death. Could she do it again? On purpose this time? She didn't know and hoped the mere threat would be enough to curtail Lenny's advances. Samantha shivered despite the evening's humidity. Jittery, she knocked again, louder this time.

The muffled blare of a television came from another of the guest rooms. But the one in front of her remained silent. Samantha glanced at her wristwatch, checking the time again. Five minutes past eleven. An eighteen-wheeler pulled into the parking lot, its big tires crunching over gravel. It came to a stop at the far side of the motel. A driver wearing cowboy boots, jeans and a baseball cap climbed down from the cab. The man approached and nodded politely at her as he traveled past, then disappeared inside one of the rooms.

Samantha knocked again on Lenny's door, this time with the flat of her hand. Her palm smarted with the effort. But again there was no response. What kind of game was he playing?

Weak with pent-up fear and growing frustration, Samantha moved to the window and tried to peer between the slit in the closed curtains. But the room's interior appeared dark. She sagged onto the white plastic lawn chair next to the air conditioner vent. A thin trail of water leaked from the unit across the grimy concrete stoop, reaching her leather thong sandals. She hadn't worn the requested stripper heels.

She wondered what to do. Keep waiting? For how long? She squinted at a line of plastic flamingos planted in the motel's patchy Bermuda grass. They called attention to a sign urging passersby to inquire about weekly rent specials.

Lenny wasn't home, apparently. Samantha rubbed her hands over her upper arms, confused. Had he forgotten it was his payday? That didn't seem possible.

Despite the cold blast of the Volvo's air conditioner, Mark felt as if he were about fifteen seconds from suffocating. He ran his hand over his face and did his best to stay calm.

His vehicle sat in the parking lot of a fast-food restaurant adjacent to the Sea King on the outskirts of town. Only the feathery plumes of tall pampas grass separated the two properties, but at least the blanket of darkness provided some cover.

Unable to think about anything but Samantha, he'd finally called one of the hotel au pairs to his house and then headed to her apartment, only to see her car drive past him on the road. Mark had taken a U-turn and followed.

Who the hell was she meeting here so late and why?

He watched as she alternately fidgeted on the cheap plastic chair and paced in front of the door to room six. The term *no-tell motel* awakened his jealous streak, but the panic he had seen in her eyes earlier that day negated the thought that she was here for some kind of tryst. When she had asked for such a large advance on the gift-shop sales to pay the food manufacturer, Mark had known she was lying. And yet he had given her the money without question. Her need and the gravity of her situation—whatever it was—had been achingly apparent.

A group of teenagers sauntered from the restaurant, engaging in horseplay as they made their way to an oversize pickup. Mark slunk down in the leather seat, hoping the rowdy kids wouldn't attract Samantha's attention. Eventually, the one who was driving started up the truck's powerful engine, and it roared from the lot. But if Samantha had noticed, she gave no indication. Instead, she rapped on the motel door again. Mark sat up, alert, as another car pulled into a space near her car, its headlights briefly illuminating the stoop where she waited. She appeared to relax only when an elderly man and woman exited the sedan and tottered off into one of the other rooms.

Mark dragged his lower lip between two fingers, observing as Samantha passed her hand wearily over her face. She looked as out of place at the Sea King as fine porcelain among paper plates.

More than a half hour later, she returned to her car. Whoever she planned to meet there had stood her up, apparently. Someone she hoped to get rid of with cash. The thought that she had been meeting the man who had hurt her in her apartment both angered and frightened him. Starting the engine and pulling from the lot, Mark trailed at a discreet distance as she headed back toward town, unsure of what he should do. What he really wanted was to confront her and demand the truth, to crush her against him and hold her until she finally revealed it to him. But she had made it clear in his office that, beyond his money, she didn't need or want his help.

There's something about that woman that sets off alarm bells...

As she pulled into the lot in front of the Wayfarer Apartments, Mark remained on the main road, parking the Volvo outside the murky glow of a streetlight. He extracted his cell phone and called her number. Emerging from her car, Samantha fished her phone from her purse. She stared at its screen but didn't answer, confirming again that she didn't want to talk to him.

Instead, Mark got her voice mail. *You've reached Samantha Marsh. I'm unable to answer my phone right now...*

He disconnected the call, feeling worse.

Still, he waited until she was safely inside before turning back toward home. Despite what his heart wanted, he reminded himself that he had a troubled young daughter to care for and a large hotel to run. The rational part of his mind told him he was better off without Samantha, considering her ambivalence and secrets.

Maybe he should follow her lead and shove aside any attraction, any feelings he had for her.

Maybe this one time, his mother was right. He didn't need the complication of another heartbreak.

But as he made his way back to the St. Clair, it was all he could do not to call her again.

CHAPTER TWENTY-THREE

"WHAT'S THE BEST swag you ever got?" The pretty bartender leaned over the chrome-and-glass counter at Sapphire in New York's renovated, upscale Meatpacking District. Her chin rested in her palm. "You know, in gift bags at one of those award shows?"

"A TAG Heuer watch maybe." Carter sipped his scotch. "I also got a certificate for a weekend at a chalet in Vale once."

"I'm sure you took someone with you, too. Lucky girl, snowed in with you and a big, roaring fire. How *did* you pass the time?"

Carter merely smiled. What he didn't tell the bartender—he'd already learned her name was Leilani—was that soap actors didn't go to all that many awards shows, with the exception of the Daytime Emmys.

Filming on the made-for-television movie he was shooting in Charleston had taken a short break while the director handled another obligation. Carter had used the time to fly back to New York to meet with his agent and to audition for a guest spot on a prime-time television drama being shot on location in the city. The small but important role had come open at the last minute—they were seeking a prep-school-educated-type male in his early thirties to play an assistant district attorney. If he got the part, he'd be able to shoot it and be back in time to continue filming for the movie.

"So what's Amber Montrose *really* like?" Leilani asked, referring to one of Carter's co-stars on *Friends and Lovers*. Waiting for an answer, she ran her hand through her raven hair and batted almond-shaped eyes. "C'mon, dish. Is she as big a bitch in real life as she is on the show?"

"Actually, she's a sweetheart. She's from a small town in Montana. Her father's a minister, and she's engaged to her boyfriend from high school." At her expression, he added, "You look disappointed."

"I guess I expect actors to be like the characters they play." She gave him a seductive once-over. "Jake Burton's gorgeous and sexy. So are you."

He smiled again and stared into her eyes, going into full flirt mode.

She beamed. "You want a refill?"

"Absolutely." Carter watched as she turned to the shelf of liquor bottles and selected the Glenlivet. She had a fantastic ass, as did every woman who worked here. In fact, the establishment's proclivity for hiring beautiful women—and one woman in particular—was the reason he'd dropped by the popular nightspot on impulse.

"Could you give my headshot to the casting director at your soap?" Leilani refreshed his drink. "I just started acting classes, so I don't really have much on my résumé…"

"I'll give it to him and put in a good word."

"Thanks." Her fingers grazed Carter's hand that held his

scotch, sliding around to caress the underside of his wrist. "That would mean a *lot* to me."

She stepped away to serve a couple who had approached the bar, leaving him to nurse his drink. He glanced around the high-end establishment. The bar area was bathed in subdued lighting and played to a chic crowd of mostly young professionals and well-to-do Manhattanites. When Leilani returned, she brought him a small plate of sashimi, thinly sliced raw tuna that was one of the house specialties.

"They sent it over," she said, nodding toward two women seated at a nearby table. Carter tipped his glass to them.

Leilani raised an eyebrow. "I bet you get that a lot. Women offering to give you their *sashimi*."

Carter caught her innuendo. "What about you, Leilani? You offering?"

She nearly purred. "We'll see."

Deciding to move from the sexual banter, he asked, "So how long have you worked here?"

"Oh, for a while now. I started after college, working my way up from hostess to waitress, and just now to the bar. I had to do some training, but bartending's where the really good money is. Wealthy, drunk men are excellent tippers."

"I'm sure." Carter used his best acting skills to sound as if his next statement hadn't been premeditated. "Hey, I met a girl who used to work here. I think she was a bartender, too. Her name was Samantha something…"

"I remember her," Leilani said. "Samantha Marsh."

"That's right."

"She was tending bar when I was still waiting tables. That was about five months ago."

"What was she like? Nice?"

She shrugged. "I didn't really know her that well. There's kind of a caste system around here. Hostesses don't fraternize with the wait staff, and bartenders are higher on the totem pole, right under management. Besides, Samantha pretty much kept to herself. She'd turn it on for the customers, then put her shield right back up as soon as she was off-shift."

That sounded like her. Carter sipped his scotch, uncertain of exactly what he had been expecting to discover. But Samantha had been on his mind ever since he'd learned about the mysterious break-in and assault at her apartment. The exotic tattoo, the ultra-sexy shoes he'd found in her closet—none of it was a match with the reserved, serious businesswoman she appeared to be. Which normally wouldn't matter to him. Hell, with any other woman, the contradiction would only add to the allure...except that Samantha was finding her way into Mark's heart. It had become clear to Carter she hadn't just been a date for the reception as he'd first thought; his brother was developing a real thing for her. And, he admitted, his own damn curiosity was eating at him. He was in town anyway, so why not just drop by her past place of employment to see what he could find out? At least he had confirmation she'd worked here.

He chastised himself, figuring he'd been listening too much to his mother, who didn't like Samantha based on the simple fact that she wasn't Felicity Greene.

"It's funny you should ask about her, because there was a man here a month or two ago asking about her, too," Leilani said. "Weird-looking guy. Short and fat, with a spot on his forehead. He was trying to find out where she'd gone."

Carter looked at her, his interest piqued. "Do you know who he was?"

"Are you into this *Samantha* or something?" She appeared a little jealous.

He shook his head. "I barely know her. A friend of mine's going out with her, is all."

"Well, you might want to tell your friend to watch his wallet." Leilani wiped the bar's glass top. "This guy said he was looking for her to collect on some bad debt. Apparently, a lot of it. He wanted her forwarding address, but she didn't leave one. He said she'd moved out of New York."

"Do you remember this guy's name? I mean, for my friend," he added casually, despite the fluttering in his stomach. "He might want to know what he's getting into."

"I can do one better." Turning, Leilani opened a drawer underneath the liquor shelf. She squatted as she rifled through its contents, giving Carter a view of the lace thong underwear she wore under low-rise black slacks. When she stood back up, she handed him a business card.

"He left this. He said if any of us remembered anything about her to give him a call."

Carter took the card, which was printed on no-frills white cardstock with plain black ink. Wrinkled, with an oily smudge on one corner, it read *Leonard Cook, Private Investigator,* and gave his contact information. According to the card, the private investigator license had been issued in Tennessee.

≈

Carter lay next to Leilani, who was sprawled facedown on her bed, nude and snoring softly. Being careful not to wake her, he got up and picked his way through the darkness in the unfamiliar apartment, reaching its tiny kitchen. He opened the refrigerator to shed some light and look for something *non-alcoholic* to drink. Finding a bottled water, he rolled its cool plastic against his forehead before twisting off the cap and drinking greedily.

He wondered what time it was.

His mouth felt like cotton, and the dull beat of a headache played inside his skull. After taking a cab with Leilani to her walk-up third-floor efficiency, they had split a couple of bottles of red wine. Not a great match with the high-end scotch he'd been drinking earlier.

Carter closed the refrigerator door, frowning in puzzlement at the Hello Kitty magnet staring back at him.

Looking around, cursing as he bumped his shin, he spotted a shell-shaped floor lamp near the couch and turned it on, then attempted to find his wallet in the pale glow it provided. Finally locating it on the floor alongside his trousers, cell phone and Leilani's panties and bra, he picked it up and checked to make sure the PI's business card was still tucked inside. Carter had called both Leonard Cook's office and cell phone while he'd been at Sapphire. He had left voice-mail messages at both numbers, saying only that his name was *Mr. Carter* and that he wanted to talk to him about his recent visit to a nightclub. With a low grunt, Carter bent again to retrieve his phone. No messages.

Damn, his head hurt. He hoped the hangover was gone by his audition.

He wouldn't try again in the middle of the night. The guy was bound to call him back, especially if he was as interested in Samantha as Leilani had indicated. But even if he *was* looking for her, Carter didn't necessarily plan to tell him where to find her. He just hoped to maintain the conversation long enough to find out a little more about her, including how much she owed and to whom, and whether there was anything else in her background to be worried about. It wasn't a good sign that a private investigator had come all the way here looking for her. The debt must be substantial. And Samantha had never said anything about Tennessee, or Memphis, which was the area code listed on the card.

Uncertainty over what he was doing spread in his gut. Carter scrubbed a hand over his face.

You're fortunate to have such a wonderful family. Don't take any of them for granted, especially Mark. Stop trying to one-up him, and do what you can to mend fences.

Samantha's scolding the night of the reception had hit home. She had made him look beyond his own wounded ego and see his behavior for what it was. He'd been sincere when he'd told Mark that he hated how things were between them. Carter knew a lot of it—*hell, most of it*—was his fault.

He also knew Mark wouldn't approve of him going to Sapphire, and Carter wondered again if he should just let it go. But he saw what he was doing as being protective of Mark, as well as Emily. Perhaps New York and the entertainment industry had jaded him, but the St. Clair family had money, and he now wondered if Samantha's arrival in their lives had really been coincidence.

"I thought you'd left."

Leilani stood at the bedroom's threshold. She pouted prettily, her nude body on full display.

"Were you sneaking out?" she asked, moving closer. She ran her hand over Carter's bare chest. "I haven't even given you my headshot."

"Not a chance," he rasped. "Just getting some water."

"You look like one of those brooding leading men right now—like Heathcliff in that movie."

"*Wuthering Heights.*" Carter wondered a little meanly if she'd ever read a book.

She took the bottle he held and sipped. "Sex makes *me* thirsty, too."

Lifting on her toes, she kissed his mouth, her arms looping around his neck, and her pert, round breasts pressing against him. Still conflicted about his dilemma regarding Samantha, Carter had been contemplating the old saying about curiosity killing the cat. But his thoughts scattered as he felt his body respond.

"It's still early," Leilani whispered. "Come back to bed."

CHAPTER TWENTY-FOUR

FOUR DAYS HAD inched by, and Samantha still hadn't heard from Lenny. She'd been tense and on edge, expecting every phone call or customer entering the café to be him.

What had happened? She seriously doubted he'd had a change of heart about blackmailing her, but it didn't make sense that he had failed to meet her at the appointed place and time. Nor had he made any attempt to contact her since. Dicing onions in the café's kitchen, she wondered nervously if he was playing some kind of mind game designed to prolong her torture.

She was afraid to try to leave town, convinced that if he *were* still watching her, he'd make good on his vile threats. Queasy, Samantha could barely eat or sleep.

She hadn't talked to Mark in four days, either, not since he'd handed her a check for eight thousand dollars and she'd walked out of his hotel. He had called her once late at night, but she hadn't answered, and he had left no message. Samantha had been too ashamed to speak to him, as well as fearful of what questions he might ask. She felt herself missing him even though she knew his absence from her life was for the best. For now, she'd deposited the money in her bank account, tensely awaiting Lenny's next move.

It was still early, and a small television on the counter blared a national morning news show. Luther pushed through the kitchen's back door, hauling a box of potatoes that required peeling. Samantha laid her knife on the butcher-block counter and took a sip of her coffee. *Keep going. Keep it business as usual.* It was the only way not to go insane.

"Quentin at the farmer's market says the *mâche* you were looking for will be in early next week." Luther dumped the potatoes into a tub of water. "Got to admit I don't see what's wrong with plain, old-fashioned lettuce."

"It's for a salad with goat cheese I want to add to the menu," she explained, grateful for the distraction he provided. "It has a sweet, nutty flavor."

"Sweet and nutty, huh? Sounds like you're talkin' about dessert. Not rabbit food."

They conversed as they worked companionably together, with Luther once again bringing up his desire to see the world. She'd learned he visited the town's library often to read books on exotic places like Trinidad, Tobago and the Ivory Coast.

"Got family in Haiti where my momma was born. Never met 'em, but I'd sure like to," he mused as he scrubbed potatoes. "An aunt and two cousins. Only kin I have left."

"Maybe you should plan a trip."

He gave a sad chuckle. "Soon as I win the lottery, maybe."

Eventually, their conversation lapsed into silence. Needing to focus her thoughts somewhere, Samantha picked up the remote and switched the television channel to the local news on a broadcast station in Charleston. She'd finished chopping onions and had just moved her attention to a pile of celery stalks when a reporter's words caused her to look up at the television.

…body of a white male found last night here in a canal near the James Island Expressway. Drowning is suspected as the cause of death. An autopsy will be completed at the Medical University of South Carolina…

Clutching a microphone, the reporter stood at the canal's edge, a weathered strip mall in view some distance behind him.

Charleston Police are looking for anyone who might have known the victim, described as being in his late forties, heavyset, about five-feet-eight inches tall with what may have been a birthmark on his right temple, although decomposition due to saltwater and warm temperatures was advanced. If you recognize this description, you're asked to contact police…

"Sam, you're bleeding!"

Crimson dripped from her index finger onto the counter, but she barely felt the sting. Samantha had gone numb. Taking charge, Luther reached for the knife and guided her to the basin. Holding her hand under the stream, he scolded her about not being careful.

The birthmark. It *had* to be Lenny, didn't it? Samantha's stomach flip-flopped at the possibility that her blackmailer might be dead.

"It doesn't look too bad." Luther studied the cut. "It'll bleed for a while, but I don't think you're gonna need stitches."

"I'm fine," Samantha mumbled, still staring over her shoulder at the television.

"You better sit down." He dragged a chair across the floor and eased her onto it. "You look like you're gonna faint on me."

"I…I don't like seeing my own blood, I guess." Samantha held the dishtowel in place that Luther had wrapped around her now-throbbing finger. The news show had switched to the weather, and a blond woman in a silk blouse and tailored skirt began talking about a tropical depression forming in the Atlantic.

Questions about the possibility of Lenny's demise raced through her head. Not that she would wish anyone...dead, but had she just gotten the luckiest break of her life? She tried to shake off the worry that her troubles all seemed too neatly resolved.

"Sure you're okay?" Luther asked, looking at her curiously as he cleaned up the blood on the counter. He discarded the contaminated celery in a trash receptacle.

In disbelief, Samantha blinked and gave a small nod. She wanted to believe that maybe, just maybe, she really was.

It was early the next week before the Charleston County Coroner's Office released the official cause of death of the still-unidentified man in the canal. Glued to the television in the café's kitchen, Samantha swallowed past the lump in her throat as the field reporter confirmed it had been an accidental drowning. According to the toxicology report, the victim's blood-alcohol level had been more than three times the legal limit, the reporter revealed as he stood with one shiny dress shoe planted on the canal edge. After a reminder about the danger of intoxication around bodies of water, he segued back to the newsroom. The story had come on late in the newscast, as if it were already nearly forgotten, second-tier news.

Samantha wiped the already clean prep counter a second time, needing to focus her nervous energy before she burst into tears of relief.

I'll be seeing you, Trina. And don't do anything stupid like tryin' to slip out on me.

But in the end, it was *Lenny* who had slipped away. It still seemed impossible that just like that, he and his threats were gone. By all appearances, Samantha had won the proverbial lottery at the same time her adversary had run out of luck. She wondered if his body would ever be identified. She'd been keeping an ear out for mention of the incident, her heartbeat quickening at any little fragment of news. It had been reported a day ago that police had checked the victim's fingerprints against the FBI's national database, but hadn't gotten any hits. The canal had also been dragged, but no wallet—nothing, in fact—had been recovered. Although it could have been swept away by the current, the lack of identification had created speculation that the victim was a homeless person who'd been camping out under the nearby expressway.

And, at least based on the news reports, no one from the Sea King had come forward to say that someone fitting the dead man's description had been staying there. Perhaps no one there had taken much notice, especially if Lenny had been keeping a low profile? Not to mention, if police were checking hotels in case the deceased was a vacationer, chances were they were focusing on Charleston, where the body had been found, and not the much farther away Rarity Cove township.

Samantha also wondered where Lenny's Crown Victoria was, since there had been no mention of an unclaimed car being found near the canal. Nor had she seen it in the motel parking lot that night. She wondered about the possibility of a drunken Lenny simply falling into the brackish water somewhere, his body drifting until it got hung up in the canal and was spotted.

The night he'd broken into her apartment, he had reeked of liquor.

Straightening, she let the dishrag fall to the countertop with a wet plop, then massaged her neck muscles in an attempt to ease the ever-present tension. As she did, she heard the bell on the café's front door chime.

"Want me to see about that?" Denise, one of the workers who was also in the kitchen, asked.

"That's okay. I'll take care of it."

Samantha went into the storefront. It was early evening, and a family—parents with two children—had arrived with an insulated picnic basket they planned to fill with the trimmings for dinner on the beach. She recommended a variety of cold salads and sweet cornbread, as well as lemon bars for dessert. Throwing in paper plates, plastic utensils and a gallon of complimentary iced tea, Samantha rang up their order. Then she waved good-bye and watched through the window as they loaded the basket into the back of their minivan. On the other side of the street, Samantha noticed a silver Volvo station wagon parked in front of the palm trees. Her heart lifted involuntarily as she wondered if Mark was nearby.

Busying herself with tidying up, Samantha kept an eye on the Volvo, hoping for a chance to glimpse his broad shoulders and sun-kissed hair when he returned to his car. But a mother with an infant on her hip and another small child in tow arrived at the vehicle instead. It wasn't his, after all.

Deflated, she stepped forward to lower the blinds on the window. She reminded herself to be grateful for the miraculous gift she had been given. Despite Lenny's horrifying arrival in town, by some stroke of fate she still had her freedom, her life.

But it was Mark and the way things had been left between them—including the money she'd taken from him—that Samantha couldn't get out of her mind.

CHAPTER TWENTY-FIVE

I *SHOULDN'T BE HERE*. Samantha bit her lip as she stood on the bungalow's porch. The lights were on inside, and she could hear the faint sound of music playing. She knocked uncertainly, then considered just shoving the check under the doormat and leaving. But that thought evaporated as the door opened and she found herself staring into Mark's surprised blue eyes.

He appeared tired and somewhat disheveled. It was Tuesday night, the sun just beginning to set over the dark plane of ocean, yet he was still dressed in suit pants and a dress shirt that had been tugged loose at the waist. He frowned slightly at her. "How'd you get past the gate?"

"I followed another car in," she explained, aware the question wasn't a greeting. "One of the resort guests. If I came at a bad time…"

"No." Dragging a hand through his hair, he opened the door wider and took a step back to allow her to enter. A glass of red wine sat on the end table next to the sofa, and on the television, CNN showed a computer-predicted path of the slow-moving depression in the Atlantic that had recently been upgraded to a tropical storm. The sound was muted, however, so as not to compete with the music.

"You look exhausted, Mark," she said in concern.

He laced his fingers behind his neck. "There's a physician conference at the hotel all week, and Emily had another therapist appointment this afternoon. There's also Tropical Storm Gina to consider. They named it today."

She'd been keeping up with the reports from the National Hurricane Center, but it was still much too early to gauge the real threat of the storm or where it might make landfall, if at all. For now, it remained basically stalled hundreds of miles away, over a landless stretch of the Atlantic. When she looked at Mark again, he had reclaimed his wineglass and taken a sip, his features impassive.

"Where's Emily?" she asked, noticing her absence and missing her sweet face. She hadn't seen her since their beach outing more than a week ago.

"She's out with my mother and Mercer. The Charleston Symphony's doing a children's production tonight." His eyes were somber as he regarded her. "Why are you here, Samantha?"

"I...wanted to give you this." She reached inside her shoulder bag and nervously withdrew a folded check made out in the amount she had borrowed. She held it out to him. "It turned out I didn't need the money, after all. The café's doing better than I realized."

"That's good news."

She nodded. He took the paper and, without looking at it, placed it in his shirt pocket. "But I don't understand. You went to the trouble of asking me for a loan, then realized you don't need it?"

"I miscalculated," she said, feeling her face heat.

Mark peered at her. Then he took another long sip of wine,

draining the glass and replacing it on the coffee table. He shrugged, his shoulders appearing tense under his dress shirt. "I'm surprised, is all. I'd figured you for someone who knows her business much better than that."

The brooding challenge in his voice—the bare hint of harshness—was disconcerting, something Samantha hadn't expected, despite her recent behavior. Her initial instinct had been right; she shouldn't have come here. But with Lenny now out of the picture, she had been anxious to repay Mark. The other truth, the one she had been fighting for some time now, was that she'd also wanted to see him.

"I should go," she said, not acknowledging his probing comment. Despite her scrambled nerves, she forced lightness into her voice. "I just came by to return the money and thank you again. The gift baskets for the shop will be delivered next week—"

"Why not just mail me the check or give it to Mercer?" he asked. "You could've saved yourself the trip and avoided me altogether."

Samantha felt a pang. "I-I don't want to avoid you, Mark."

He moved closer, his features strained. "Who were you meeting at the Sea King last week?"

A coldness fell over her skin. "You followed me?"

"What did you expect? You came into my office looking like you were about to shatter into a million pieces. Then you give me some lame excuse for needing eight thousand dollars, right away, and you walk back out. I was worried."

She closed her eyes, embarrassed he'd followed her there. "You had no right."

"Who were you going there to see?" he pressed. "Did it have to do with why you really needed the money?"

She bowed her head, unable to speak. Once again, she said a prayer of gratitude that despite the mention of the birthmark, no one from the motel had identified the drowned man in the canal as one of its guests. If Mark had heard any of the newscasts, he would likely make a connection.

"You're angry with me. I understand, and I don't blame you." Holding her purse against her chest, throat tight, she turned for the door. She could only imagine what ideas were running through his head about her. "I'm sorry for the intrusion, Mark. Good night."

"Sam," he whispered into the air, still sounding irritated. He spoke louder as she walked out. "Samantha."

She had nearly reached the Camry when Mark caught up to her. He took hold of her arm and whirled her around to face him, causing her to gasp.

"I'm not letting you walk out on me again without giving me answers."

"Please. Just let me go. It doesn't concern you—"

"Like hell it doesn't," he ground out, his jaw hard. His hoarse words washed over her. "I *care* about you, Samantha. I might even be falling in love with you, if you'd give me half a chance."

Her heart squeezed at his admission. Staring at him in the graying twilight, the roar of the ocean behind them, Samantha saw sincerity, as well as the pain she'd inflicted, in his eyes. She felt something break loose inside her. She was so tired of running. Of keeping herself closed off from everyone. The terrible thing she'd always worried about had finally happened, but somehow, she'd managed to come out of it relatively unscathed.

"I went to see someone I used to know," she confessed in a frayed voice. "But he's gone now. It's over. He won't be back."

"That's the truth?"

"Yes. Please...don't ask me anything else."

He appeared frustrated and doubtful. Their eyes held for several long moments, until her vision slowly began to blur with tears. She couldn't help it. In Mark, she saw everything that was missing in her life. Things she could never have as long as she kept the walls up around herself. The unfairness of it constricted her breathing and made her chest hurt.

Before she knew it, she'd put her arms around him, her face pressing into the warm curve of his neck, seeking forgiveness for the things she could never tell him. Mark stood rigid and motionless until, finally, she felt him relax against her. He released a weary sigh of resignation. Then he gently cupped her jaw with his fingers and, tipping her head back, crushed his lips onto hers. His kiss was forceful, seeking. Samantha clung to him, her fingers curling into his shirt. She molded her body to his and felt her last defense against him scatter into the salty ocean breeze.

For a time, they simply kissed, made out like two teenagers, trying to satiate the shared hunger that had been building in them both for weeks now. Then Mark took a labored breath and briefly leaned his forehead against hers.

"I want you. No matter what. I've wanted you since the first moment I saw you. God help me, but I can't stop the way I feel about you."

She touched his face, her fingers stroking his jaw.

"You can tell me everything or nothing," he uttered. "But you can't tell me we shouldn't give this a chance."

She closed her eyes, leaning into him.

"Don't go. Come back inside," he whispered huskily.

They walked hand in hand into the privacy of the house, their mouths joining again once Mark had pushed the door closed behind them. Samantha let her purse drop to the floor. His masculine hands on her banished the lingering fears she held and the bad memories that for too long had controlled her. *She wanted him, too.* She reveled in the miracle of it. Sexual desire was something Samantha had believed Devin's abuse had extinguished inside her forever. But Mark managed to rekindle a flame. With him, she felt protected. There were no threats or coercions.

Lenny was gone. Samantha had managed to dodge that bullet. Didn't she deserve to feel love like a normal human being, at least for a little while? But at the same time, she knew if they consummated their feelings, she might never be able to let him go.

His tongue parted her lips, his mouth tasting hers more deeply. With trembling fingers, Samantha began unbuttoning his shirt. Her lips grazed the horizontal line of his collarbone as her fingers splayed through the light sprinkling of chest hair, making him release a shaky breath.

"What you do to me," Mark murmured. Already, his hands were pulling at the hem of her top, and he drew it over her head. His gaze traveled over her simple satin bra, his face flushed with need. His lean fingers trailed down the side of her throat, between her breasts. Breathing shallowly at his touch, Samantha felt an acute awareness of her body, her female core.

Despite the things she had done in the past, this all felt new and pure.

Leading her down the hallway and into his bedroom, Mark slowly caressed the remainder of her clothes away, until she was naked in his arms. Soon, his clothes joined hers on the carpet, and they found themselves entangled on the bed. His mouth traced a hot path down her skin, giving careful attention to the hardened peaks of her breasts. He sucked them, his teeth gently abrading her sensitive nipples as his fingers expertly stroked the wetness between her legs. Samantha undulated under him, suddenly desperate to feel him inside her. To give herself over to him.

He left her only long enough to remove a condom from the drawer of his nightstand.

It had been years since Samantha had experienced sex, and

the first time in a very long time that she truly wanted it. Through heavy-lidded eyes, she studied Mark's face as he concentrated on preparing himself. Then he gently held her hips as he guided into her. She wrapped her legs around him, feeling him bury his hard length inside her. Her body—unused for so long—stretched to accommodate him. The sensation of him filling her made her moan, sending thoughts of anything but their lovemaking from her mind.

Slowly, they found their rhythm, taking their time, their bodies moving together as their mouths and tongues mingled again. The friction of his thrusting felt like liquid heat. Samantha memorized the elegant planes of his face and the thick, slightly rough texture of his hair. Some time later, Mark caught her hands on the pillow above her head as he began to drive harder, deeper, his urgency increasing.

The orgasm that hit her sent waves of pleasure crashing through her body. Mark soon followed with a throaty cry, his eyes squeezing closed as he came. His forehead dipped, and his lips pressed against her shoulder as he murmured his adoration against her damp skin.

She'd never imagined it could be like this.

⚊⚊⚊

"That was Mercer. They're on their way back." Mark disconnected the phone and replaced it on the nightstand. Samantha's head rested on his chest.

She rolled over slightly to look up at him. "I should leave—"

"No. I want you to stay. It's late, and Mercer offered to keep Emily at the hotel for the night. It'll be like a sleepover for her."

"What about Olivia?" Samantha bit her lip worriedly. "She was with them in the car, Mark. She probably overheard you telling Mercer I'm here—"

"I don't care. I'm an adult and so are you. We have no one to answer to but ourselves." He paused, aware it was high time he started considering his own happiness, too. "The hotel's having an oyster roast for the guests this Saturday. It's a late-summer tradition. I'd like you to go with Emily and me."

The sheets barely concealing her curves, Samantha sat up and gazed at him. "I don't think that's a good idea—"

"I *do*. You have a date Saturday night." He brushed her hair from her soft-brown eyes. "And if we do some time management, maybe a few more between now and then."

They stared at one another until she pressed her mouth sweetly against his. The light weight of her breasts against his chest and the feel of her long, cool hair spilling over his heated skin caused him to instantly harden. He surprised himself by being ready to make love again so soon. Aware of his aroused state, Samantha smiled shyly. Her lips returned to his for another long kiss and then left them again to trail leisurely down his chest and lower still. Mark felt his heart beat harder.

"Samantha," he half-groaned in a mix of protest and ecstasy. Throat dry, he gripped a fistful of bed linens as every nerve in his body responded to what she was doing. She took him into her mouth, her dark eyelashes forming sooty half moons as her tongue did incredible things that threatened to send him over the edge. He let himself enjoy it for a while, then, shakily whispering her name, Mark reached for her, bringing her back up beside him.

"You keep doing that and I won't last long," he confessed. His thumb stroked over her cheekbone as he gazed into her eyes. "I want to be inside you again, Samantha. *To make love to you.*"

He prepared himself for her again, glad for the condoms that had remained in his bedside table all this time, but a little worried about their expiration date.

It had been a long time for him.

Slowly, he filled her. She closed her eyes, her lips parting in pleasure as she wrapped her legs higher around him. Outside, the night had grown dark, although a perfect white moon poured light through the window, casting a pearly glow over their shared bed. Thrusting into her, Mark kept his eyes fastened on her face, unable to look away from her sensual beauty.

Secrets remained between them, he thought a short time later as Samantha slept like a boneless rag doll in his arms. Too many troubling things he still didn't understand or know about her. He had also seen the surprising, intricate tattoo on her lower back. He hadn't asked about it, not wanting to ruin the mood or make her self-conscious, but at some point he would.

Mark sighed softly. They both came with their emotional baggage, he understood that. His was out in the open, while Samantha kept hers closed off and hidden, as if it were too painful to deal with. But she'd sworn to him that whoever had been holding power over her life was gone. For now, that had to be enough.

Maybe someday she'd come to fully trust him with the truth.

His lips brushing her forehead, he stared into the shadows of the bedroom that for seven years he'd shared with another woman, the love of his life and mother of his child. When Shelley died, Mark had been certain his life was over. At times he had even wanted it to be, if it hadn't been for Emily. But right now, with the softness of Samantha's body pressed into him and her warm, gentle breath fanning his neck, he felt more alive than he had in a very long time.

CHAPTER TWENTY-SIX

CARTER SAT ON a futon inside the air-conditioned trailer, memorizing the script changes delivered early that morning. He'd returned from New York without landing the part on the television show. It was a disappointment, but he'd gotten used to the rejection that came with the business, and he still had the Lifetime movie. The director had been especially pleased with the dailies—the raw, unedited footage shot so far—and he'd told Carter all he needed was the right part to break through. The praise offered some consolation.

Taking a sip from the coffee he'd gleaned from the craft service table, he looked up at the tentative knock on the door. A young production assistant stepped inside, her arms full.

"A few more rewrites, Mr. St. Clair. I'm just taking these around to the cast," she said, sounding nervous as she handed him several sheets from the collated stack she carried. Carter recalled her asking for his autograph on the first day of production.

He sighed at the additional pages. "Thanks, Amanda."

She tittered and smiled. "Oh! One more thing. The early

promo shots are in. If you want to see them, they're in the director's office. They're really amazing."

He nodded. "I'll try to get by."

Smile still in place, she backed from the trailer. Carter tucked the additional pages into his binder. But a short time later, he set down the foam coffee cup, leaned his head back and closed his eyes. Today's shoot was going to be a long one. It had started in makeup at five thirty that morning and probably wouldn't wrap until well after dark. They were in production now full-tilt, and the schedule these last several days had been intense.

Ghosts on the Ashley River was being filmed at an authentic plantation manor outside Charleston. The script told the story of newlyweds who had purchased the old house, unaware it was haunted. In the movie, one of the ghosts sets out to seduce the bride and take her with him to the underworld. Carter played the young husband bravely determined to save her. The made-for-television movie wouldn't be an Emmy contender, but it was a decent check and a way to broaden his exposure.

He had picked up the rewrites again when his cell phone rang. Recognizing the number and Memphis area code, Carter's stomach tensed. He'd pretty much given up after not hearing back from the private investigator, had even begun to think that maybe Leilani had gotten her lines crossed somewhere. He had seen Mark only a few times in passing since getting back from New York, and he was still contemplating what to tell him, especially if that *what* was based only on hearsay from a bartender at a place where Samantha used to work.

He stared indecisively at the ringing phone before answering.

"*Well, if it isn't Mr. Carter,*" a rough, female voice said.

Surprised, he nearly laughed. "Excuse me? Who's this?"

"Lenny's ex-wife. Who are you?" the woman demanded. "You left a message on his voice mail."

Suppressing a sigh, Carter pinched the bridge of his nose. "I've been trying to reach Mr. Cook—"

"Get in line, honey," she retorted. "He's good at disappearing, which is why I kept a key to the place when I moved out. Bastard hasn't paid alimony for the last two months, so any cash I find here's fair game. You hire him for a job?"

"No, ma'am—"

"Figures. Thought you might know where he is."

"He was in New York City not long ago," Carter offered carefully, thinking she might be able to tell him something. "He was looking for a woman—"

"Noticed your area code was NYC." Her tone sounded resigned, even bitter. "He was looking for Trina Grissom again, no doubt. Got a tip a year ago that little whore was up there."

Carter sat up a bit straighter at the comment. "Excuse me?"

"Strippers, whores—you ask me, they're one and the same. Lenny's been obsessed with her ever since he saw her shakin' her tits at the Blue Iris. Tries to pick up her trail every chance he gets, hoping to strike gold. Even ditches payin' work for it. Between that and his love of keno, it's no wonder he's behind on payments..." She yammered on, complaining about her ex-husband.

Carter interrupted. "I'm sorry—this woman, you said her name was what?"

"You slow? *Trina Grissom,*" she repeated with irritation. Suspicion seeped into her raspy drawl. "Now wait just a damn minute. Is that why you're calling him? If you found her, half that money Leary's offering belongs to Lenny, you hear me?"

Carter ran a hand over his mouth, glad his cell phone revealed only his New York-based number. He suspected the less this woman knew about anything, the better.

"I haven't found anyone...*yet*," he said quickly, hoping to throw her off. "It's just that I'm doing some investigative work, too. I'm new, just putting out my shingle, and I was thinking Mr. Cook and I could talk about pooling resources. Maybe he needs some local help—"

"Another PI, huh? Be prepared to make shit for a living. And Lenny works *solo*," she snapped. "Take it from me, he makes a lousy partner."

The connection went dead.

Still gripping the phone, Carter's thoughts raced. What were the odds that a Tennessee PI would be tracking *two* women to New York at the exact same time? He knew from Leilani that Cook had been looking for Samantha for some bad debt. But he was also up there looking for a Trina Grissom? His unease grew. Was it possible that Samantha and Trina Grissom were the same person? That Samantha Marsh was some kind of...alias?

Cook's ex-wife had mentioned stripping. Carter thought of the shoes he'd found in Samantha's closet. Tension arcing along his shoulders, he got up and paced the narrow width of the trailer. *Now just hold on. Don't get ahead of yourself.* Carter had been around his share of adult entertainers, and Samantha just didn't give off that hard kind of vibe. The opposite, actually. He grasped hard on to the possibility that he was way off base. New York was a huge city, and people relocated there all the time. Maybe Leonard Cook had indeed tracked two different women there.

Carter clung to that reasoning, tried to shut out the image of Samantha dancing nude on some stage. Of her living under an assumed name and what else that might mean about her...

He suddenly wished like hell he hadn't nosed around at

Sapphire that night. That he hadn't put himself into the middle of this. But the fact remained that he had, and he still had Mark and Emily's best interests at heart.

Carter realized he should have asked the ex-Mrs. Cook what Trina Grissom looked like, but he didn't dare call her back.

If you found her, half that money Leary's offering belongs to Lenny…

That sounded like there was some kind of bounty out on Trina Grissom—whoever she was. Carter nervously scrubbed a hand over his face. For the sake of family, maybe it was time *he* hired an investigator of his own. Someone who could sort all of this out before he ever had to divulge any of it to Mark. He felt a pain in his throat just thinking of it. And if it all turned out to be nothing, it would look as though he'd deliberately set out to cause trouble.

Maybe a PI would be able to tell him this was all just some epic, screwed-up misunderstanding. God, he hoped so. Dropping his head, Carter massaged his closed eyes with his fingers and tried to figure out what to do.

He startled as his cell sprang to life again. But this time it was only a text message letting him know he was wanted on set. The sick feeling he had worsened as an ominous line from the movie script popped into his head, whispered to his character by one of the ghosts.

Be careful what you look for. You might find it.

Thank you for sharing
your collection with us.
MDB

CHAPTER TWENTY-SEVEN

U NLIKE THE RECEPTION that had been held in the St. Clair ballroom, the beachside oyster roast was a more casual affair. Chefs manned a large bonfire, shoveling piles of oysters onto an enormous, griddle-like trestle. The delicious aroma wafted in the air as the fire's embers flew upward, swirling into the dark blanket of night. Glowing paper lanterns strung on wire lit the beach, and a live band played music to which couples were shag dancing. Even more hotel guests lounged at tables, enjoying the food and swigging from bottles of ice-cold beer.

Samantha walked barefoot in a fitted, sarong-style skirt next to Mark. Holding Emily's hand, she smiled down at her.

"This is my first oyster roast, Emily. What do you think I should have to eat? A hot dog or a hamburger?"

Emily grinned, catching on to her joke.

"If you don't like shellfish, I'm afraid you're out of luck." Mark indicated a long table laden with roasted oysters and the traditional trimmings of cocktail sauce, Tabasco and saltines. There were also hush puppies and deep pots of lowcountry boil teeming with chunks of potato, sausage, corn on the cob, crab and shrimp.

Samantha helped Emily fill a plate while Mark stopped to converse with a group of guests. As she was seating the child at one of the tables, he returned behind her, caressing her bare arms and creating a stir of pleasure. When she turned to him, he sweetly kissed her. Samantha's eyes closed at the feel of his lips against hers. The affection was quick, nearly chaste, but it drove deep into her heart. Despite both their busy schedules, they'd had a wonderful week, carving out spaces of time to see one another alone. To make love again.

When she opened her eyes, Mark was smiling at her, handsome, his short hair lifting in the sultry ocean breeze.

"Aren't you hungry?" he asked.

She touched his shirtfront. "Starving. I was just getting a plate and some lemonade for Emily first. Now I'm planning to help myself."

"Stay here—let me get some for both of us. I'll be right back." His hand lingered at her waist before he went off in the direction of the buffet. As Samantha sat next to Emily, she glimpsed Carter and Olivia coming down the wooden stairs from the boardwalk onto the sand. She hadn't seen Carter since before his trip to New York.

"How's my favorite niece?" he asked when he reached the table, dropping a kiss on top of Emily's head. She beamed as he pretended to gobble the side of her neck. But Olivia hung back, feigning interest in the chefs' activities and surrounding celebration.

Straightening, Carter peered at Samantha from under the brim of a baseball cap. It was pulled low over his midnight-blue eyes, and his dark blond hair curled in wisps underneath its band. She returned his gaze, noticing the levity he had shared with Emily had disappeared, his chiseled jaw set. He studied her with a somber air completely out of character for him.

"Is something wrong, Carter?" she asked finally.

He shrugged impassively. "Not that I know of. How've you been, Samantha?"

She pushed a strand of windblown hair from her face. "Fine, thanks."

"How's business?"

"Better than ever," she said. "The café's packed, and I start selling products in the St. Clair gift shop next week. I'm just waiting on the delivery from the manufacturer in Greenville."

He didn't look happy. "Mark's giving you space in the shop?"

"It's something we've been working on for a while."

With a nod, he indicated Mark, who was on his way back, balancing their plates and bottles of beer. Then he squinted at her for several long seconds, unsmiling. "It looks like you have just about everything you need, then."

Samantha didn't respond to the odd comment, unsure of whether he was talking about the food Mark was carrying or Mark himself, but it was clear something was bothering him.

"Carter. Have a seat with us," Mark invited when he reached them, handing Samantha a plate as he took the spot at the table beside her.

"I think I'll get a cold one first. Maybe a few of them." Broad shoulders stooped, he wandered off toward the large tin buckets that held iced beer.

"Is he all right?" Samantha asked, her voice competing with the live music and the breeze roaring in from the water. "He seems a little...intense."

Mark stared after him. "He's been on set twenty-four/seven lately, filming in the heat. Maybe it's gotten to him."

Samantha had just taken a bite from her plate when Olivia appeared at their table. "Mark, you need to send the staff up to the hotel for *cloth* napkins. Those flimsy paper things just won't do."

"It's an oyster roast. You're lucky I didn't put out rolls of paper towels." Mark wiped his mouth with one of the offending napkins. "Mom, you remember Samantha."

Olivia gave her a wan smile. "Of course. Are you helping with the catering tonight, dear?"

Mark's fingers entwined with Samantha's under the table. Still, she felt her face heat, suspecting Olivia knew she and Mark had become intimate. After all, she'd been in the car the night Mercer had offered to keep Emily at the hotel.

"Samantha's with *me*," Mark clarified, his tone making it clear he wasn't buying his mother's act of innocent confusion.

"This is becoming a regular thing, isn't it?" Carter had reappeared, sliding into a spot at the table. He took a long pull from his beer bottle, his eyes shadowed beneath the ball cap's brim as he divided a look between them.

"Maybe it is," Mark said, voice low. "What's your point?"

He lifted his shoulders. "Just that you're getting pretty hot and heavy, pretty fast. What's the rush?"

Mark glowered. "Sure that's your first beer?"

Samantha stiffened at the words being exchanged.

"Hush. Little pitchers have big ears," Olivia admonished, although she appeared to be more upset by the content of Carter's comment than Emily, who leaned against Samantha's side as she munched on a hush puppy.

"Are you planning to join us?" Mark asked his mother, who hovered at the table but hadn't sat.

"I don't think so. I'm not very hungry." With a petulant air, she crossed her arms over her chest and looked off across the water.

"Then sit down anyway and be with your family. There's a bar set up on the other side of the band. I'll get you a mimosa." Rising, he placed a hand on her shoulder before leaving. "I'll make it heavy on the champagne."

With the bearing of a queen, Olivia eased herself down at the head of the table while Mark went to get her beverage. The remaining group sat in a rather awkward silence, with Carter focused on his beer and Samantha helping Emily peel the shrimp on her plate. Although she did her best to ignore it, Samantha couldn't help but feel Olivia's discerning gaze. She was about to make an attempt at small talk when Mercer's voice caused her to look up.

"Everyone, there's someone I'd like you to meet." Her bright smile did little to hide the nervous tremor in her voice. She held hands with a tall, handsome man with stylish steel-rimmed eyeglasses and a head of wavy, salt-and-pepper hair. Like Mercer, he wore Bermuda shorts and a linen, short-sleeved shirt.

"St. Clair clan, this is Jonathan Leighton." Mercer looked up at him. "He's a friend of mine from Atlanta."

"Leighton?" Recognition dawned in Olivia's eyes. Her hands fidgeted with the pearls she wore even with her casual knit top. "As in *Dr. Leighton* from the university?"

"I believe we met once before, Mrs. St. Clair." Jonathan stepped forward. "At Mercer's graduation. I was her advising professor."

Carter downed the rest of his beer in a single gulp before rising and politely shaking Jonathan's hand. Samantha wondered if someone should get behind Olivia in case she decided to faint—or worse, tried to climb over the table and throttle her daughter's companion. It was obvious she was playing a mental game of connect the dots, and she'd gone as pale as beach sand.

"I suspected there was a…*boyfriend* in Atlanta," Olivia stammered. "But surely this isn't who…you're not actually…"

"Would you like to dance?" Jonathan asked Mercer, indicating the bobbing couples near the stage. Clearly, he wanted to save her from Olivia's impending outburst. "I used to be a champion shagger."

"I bet," Carter muttered under his breath.

"Save us a seat," Mercer called to Samantha as Jonathan whisked her from the group. Laughing, she nearly bumped into Mark as he returned with Olivia's mimosa.

"Who's that?" he asked the table at large.

Carter took the opportunity to escape, making a beeline for a group of women hanging around the beer stand. Olivia extracted her drink from Mark's hand and took a large gulp. Then she got up and stomped off in the direction of the boardwalk.

"Did I miss something?" Mark asked, reclaiming his seat next to Samantha. The confusion on his face made him even more endearing, and she supposed it was up to her to let him in on Mercer's revelation. Releasing a soft sigh, she ran her hand down his forearm.

"Look at it this way, Mark. You and I are no longer the only couple your mother isn't happy about."

As the evening wore on, the lively beach music gave way to something softer and slower. Mark held Samantha in his arms as they swayed together at the edge of the crowd. She stole a glance at Mercer and Jonathan, who were huddled at one of the tables, engaged in intimate conversation. Carter had disappeared an hour earlier, while Olivia had been absorbed into a gaggle of Rarity Cove residents who'd shown up to partake in the beach festivities.

"You took the news about Mercer's boyfriend better than I thought you would," Samantha said against Mark's ear. "She's been worried about telling you."

He looked at her. "You already knew?"

"For a little while."

"Did you know she was bringing him tonight?"

She shook her head. "I'm not sure Mercer knew in advance. She said he'd been wanting to come here to meet everyone, but she'd been putting him off. They were arguing about it the night of Carter's reception, which is why she was upset. She didn't mention him coming when we went running last night, so my guess is he surprised her."

"I can't believe she's been sneaking around with her college professor." With a stern expression, Mark studied the couple. "I don't want to think about when all this started. How old was she?"

"She was *twenty-two*," Samantha assured him.

"She's my little sister, and he's too damn old for her." But he sighed softly, watching as Mercer laughed at something Jonathan had said. "Do you think they're serious?"

"He's told her he's in love with her. I think maybe she feels the same way."

"Is he divorced?"

"He's a widower, like you," she said softly. "Although his wife died a long time ago."

Mark didn't say anything for a while, and Samantha wished she could banish his sad memories.

"Thank you," he murmured finally.

She looked up at him quizzically. "For what?"

"For the past week. For coming into my life." Mark swallowed. When he spoke again, his voice had roughened. "When Shelley died...when Emily and I lost her...I sort of gave up."

Samantha laid her palm against his chest, her heart hurting at just how bad things had been for him.

"I always believed my one chance was her," Mark admitted. "I missed her so much I didn't even want to try again. But now..."

He gazed into Samantha's eyes. Her blood pulsed harder as he toyed with a strand of her long hair. With some difficulty, she broke eye contact, staring down at the flaxen sand. But he gently put a finger under her chin and lifted her face back to his.

"Hey. I don't care about my mother and her social caste, or Carter's unsolicited opinions. *Or how much time we've known each other.* I already know how I feel about you."

"Mark…"

But he silenced her with his kiss. Samantha couldn't help but slide her arms around his neck, clinging to him as their mouths joined. Once their lips parted, Samantha caressed his face. A fragile happiness swelled inside her.

Their embrace ended as Emily broke from the nearby table where children were digging into wedges of juicy watermelon and making a mess. She ran to them, and Mark pressed her against his hip, uncaring of her sticky fingers that clutched the pocket of his khaki pants.

"Want to dance, Em?"

Samantha took a step back, smiling as Mark lifted Emily and twirled with her in time to the music, her pink cotton skirt floating around her like a ballerina's gown.

This place, this glorious night, was like a dream from which Samantha never wanted to wake. But fireworks exploded in the pitch-black sky, signaling the evening's conclusion. She strolled down to the ocean with Mark, Emily and the others, hearing the excited exclamations of the children at each new pinwheel burst of colorful light. Shallow waves lapped at her ankles, and the cool, wet sand pulled between her toes with the ocean's ebb and flow. Mark wrapped his arm around her. Samantha laid her head against his chest, thinking that even in her wildest imagination, no moment could be more perfect than this.

CHAPTER TWENTY-EIGHT

THE ST. CLAIR gift shop was more like an elegant boutique. Egyptian-cotton bathrobes and clothing bearing the resort's crest were interspersed with antiques, fine stationery, scented candles and luxury bath items, as well as handmade pottery by artists native to the lowcountry.

"So what do you think?" Sandra Johnson, who ran the shop, asked as Samantha viewed the display of Café Bella items with wonderment. Gratitude filled her.

"It's…lovely. I can't thank you enough."

Sandra smiled. She was a middle-aged, African-American woman with an attractive face and silver hair. "You should thank Mr. St. Clair. He decided on the placement himself."

Her products had been given a prime position inside the shop. Jars of preserved lemons and condiments lined the shelves of a massive, antique cupboard across from the cash register. Gift baskets with food items arranged inside them also sat on the massive hearth of a brick fireplace that Samantha had been told was part of the original plantation home where the hotel now stood.

"Mr. St. Clair's planning a tasting," Sandra revealed. "The hotel has a wine and cheese hour on the south veranda nightly at seven. He's asked the kitchen staff to feature your products. We'll use them for the first time tonight, with some lovely placards stating that the items are available for purchase here and at your location off the downtown square. The items will also be in the VIP packages for guests staying in the private bungalows. If I were you, Miss Marsh, I'd consider increasing production."

"I should," Samantha murmured, a lump in her throat, touched by all Mark had done. Tamping down her emotion, she feigned interest in a cashmere throw draped over the back of a chintz-covered chair.

"I shouldn't tell you this, because it's supposed to be a surprise, but I thought you should know. A writer from *Southern Living* will be at the tasting tonight. He's also planning to drop by your café."

It looks like you have just about everything you need.

Carter's words from the past weekend came back to Samantha. It didn't seem possible her life had taken such a fortuitous turn.

"That's wonderful," she managed to say. "Do you know where Mr. St. Clair is right now?"

"I believe he was going to the pool house with one of the technicians. Something about a problem with one of the spa motors."

Thanking her again, Samantha picked up her shoulder bag and headed in the direction of the hotel's beachfront plaza. Outside, the balmy breeze tossed her hair as she walked past vacationers enjoying the Olympic-size swimming pool. Sea gulls cawed overhead. Her heart lifted when she glimpsed Mark, who was talking with a jump-suited repairman outside one of the discreetly camouflaged utility buildings. When he saw her, he smiled and began striding back toward the pool area.

"What're you doing here?"

"The lunch rush's over at the café, and I couldn't wait to see the display," she confessed. "Mark, it's beautiful."

"So are you," he said in a low voice.

The tenderness in his eyes made Samantha yearn for his touch. The sleeves of Mark's dress shirt were rolled up, his tie loosened at his throat and gently flapping in the ocean breeze. He reached out, his fingers tangling with hers. Seeking a safer course for their conversation, she glanced at the television that hung over the covered, poolside bar. Although its volume wasn't loud enough to be heard above the outdoor conversation, its screen showed the now-familiar satellite image of the storm system swirling in the Atlantic Ocean. A graphic depicted several potential paths the storm, recently upgraded to Hurricane Gina, might take. It was a sobering sight.

"Should we be doing something to prepare?" Samantha asked.

Mark had followed her gaze. "It's still too early, unfortunately. It could hit anywhere between Savannah and south of Virginia Beach, and there's no telling at this point if it's going to continue to gain steam or fizzle. Regardless, we're going to get some bad weather. Heavy rain, at the least."

Samantha's nerves tingled. "I never really thought about something like this before moving here."

"It's just part of coastal living. August through October is the height of hurricane season. But don't worry—we're keeping an eye on things," Mark said reassuringly, although she could see the concern on his features. "If we end up in its path, we'll mobilize."

They went into the hotel. Mark held the door for her, his hand low against her back as the cool blast of air conditioning met them.

"Are you in a hurry to get back to the café?" he asked.

"I can probably spare some time. Why?"

He didn't answer. Instead, slipping his arm around her waist,

Mark guided her down a corridor to their right, taking them off course from the lobby. They passed the closed doors of guest rooms. Samantha had begun to ask where they were going, but fell silent as he walked her backward into an alcove, pressing her against the wall with his body. His mouth on hers was hot and firm. Samantha closed her eyes, her hands running over his strong shoulders before cupping his neck, her fingers threading through the hair at his nape as they kissed. When he finally broke contact, she glanced around breathlessly, making sure they were still alone.

She smiled softly as she looked into his eyes. "What if one of the hotel guests came through here? Or your staff?"

His fingers slid through her hair. "You're absolutely right. Come with me."

She laughed as he took her hand and led her farther down the hall. They stopped in front of one of the last rooms.

"It's vacant." He pulled a plastic card from his pocket. "And I have the master key."

Once they were behind closed doors, however, all levity disappeared between them. Instead, the air grew instantly charged as Mark's eyes darkened with passion. Samantha felt a flush of heat at what they were about to do. She went into his embrace, her arms around his neck. For a time, their mouths and tongues simply mingled, until their hands began working at one another's clothing—his tie and dress shirt, her blouse and khaki capris. The room's large window overlooking the beach was curtained and closed, creating a dark and intimate spot for their coupling. She sighed against Mark's mouth as his fingers undid her bra clasp, his hands cupping her breasts, his head lowering to them as the garment fell to the floor. He suckled her, his teeth gently rasping over one hardened, sensitive nipple and then the other.

Pulling away the luxury, goose-down duvet with a hard tug, he guided Samantha onto the bed. She lay on her back on the cool, crisp sheets, waiting for Mark to join her. She was fully nude now and unashamed as his heated gaze moved leisurely over every inch of her tanned skin, over her breasts and between her thighs. She spread herself for him wantonly, her heart beating hard and her rib cage rising and falling in anticipation. Mark removed the remainder of his clothing, prepared himself with a condom from his wallet and levered over her on the bed.

His fingers traveled over her cheekbone, and his blue eyes, intense with want, held hers.

Samantha's fingers brushed over his lips before sliding through his hair.

He entered her with a groan, and she gasped at being filled by him. At Mark being buried deep inside her once more.

"God," he murmured, his forehead pressing against hers.

They moved together, his slow, deliberate thrusts sending spiraling sensations through her. The heat building between them— the frictionless slide of their bodies, his mouth on her throat—all of it was maddening, overwhelming. For a long time, the room was filled only with the sounds of their ragged breathing and the air conditioner's muffled roar. Mark's fingers stroked her expertly in intimate places as he continued his sweet assault.

"Mark…" she begged against his fevered skin as he began to drive deeper into her, sending her up. "Mark, please, I can't wait anymore…"

Mouth gasping, her neck arching on the pillow, his lips hushed her cry as Samantha came hard a short time later, her body clenching and shuddering underneath him. Her surrender was Mark's undoing. Samantha could feel him tensing, being dragged under in the riptide of their union. His thrusts intensified. Mark buried his face in the dip of her neck as he finally expended himself with his own hoarse grunt, nearly causing her to orgasm again.

Their passion left her weak and limp-boned, and she clung to Mark as he rolled with her onto his side, keeping her cradled in the protective circle of his arms.

"You okay?" he asked once their heart rates had begun a slow descent. She nodded, and he gently kissed her forehead, her closed eyelids, her lips.

Samantha looked at him in the shadowed room, still a little dazed. "That was unexpected."

"What was? That I would want to make love to you? Because that shouldn't be a surprise by now."

He'd said make love. Not have sex, or screw, or any of the other, baser words for it. Words she had known with Devin. Words that were no longer a part of her life.

"Not so much *that*," she whispered, wanting to keep things light despite the rush of emotion she felt lying next to him. Her hand brushed over his chest. "But that you'd want to do it *here* in the middle of the afternoon."

"I feel like a different person since I met you. More spontaneous." Features somber, he played with her long hair, winding dark strands around his finger. "More alive."

Silent, Samantha pressed her lips against his shoulder. That night she'd gone to his place to return the borrowed money, Mark had told her that he *might* be falling in love with her. At the oyster roast, he'd also said she could be his second chance. Since then they had been mostly talking *around* their feelings, and she hoped it would remain that way. She wanted only to live in the moment, to not think about anything but the pleasure they were giving each other in the here and now. She was too afraid of wanting more.

But in the private chambers of her heart, she had already confessed her love to him a hundred times.

"Are you ever going to tell me about this?" he inquired when she rolled away from him onto her other side. He traced the small of her back with a fingertip. Devin's butterfly. He'd asked about it before.

"I *have* told you…" Samantha shrugged casually despite the dull pain inside her. "It was a mistake in my youth. I hate it."

"I don't," he said quietly. "I could never hate anything that's part of you."

Samantha turned to him, her throat tight as she studied his face. Then she softly pressed her mouth to his.

"I suppose there *are* a few benefits to running a hotel," he mused once her lips left his. "Like having access to vacant rooms. Even if I'll have to come up with a reason for maid service to revisit in here."

She caressed his jaw. "We might have to try this again, then."

"I'd like nothing more," he murmured.

Mark waited for Samantha to exit the guest room and then closed the door behind them. What he hadn't anticipated was running into Carter, who had just turned into the corridor. He felt an involuntary flush rise on his skin. Samantha must have also become aware of Carter's presence, because she averted her gaze, fiddling with the contents of her shoulder bag as he approached. There was little doubt he had seen them coming out of the guest room, but Mark refused to act like a child who had been caught breaking a rule. He placed a hand at Samantha's waist as they greeted Carter. He seemed downbeat, if anything, although Mark noticed his eyes trailing to the now-closed door.

"What're you doing here?" Mark asked. "I thought you were on location all day."

"They suspended shooting until tomorrow." Carter dragged a hand through his hair, sounding sheepish. "We had an...incident."

"What happened?" Mark knew the film crew was shooting an outdoor scene on the Ashley River all week.

"I was off my game and missed my mark. I got hit in the head by the boom and knocked off the boat. I might've passed out for a few seconds."

"*You might have?*" Mark echoed, genuinely concerned.

Carter shrugged. Mark was taken aback by such a rookie error, since both of them had practically grown up on the water and were expert sailors. The boom—the large, mobile post that hung horizontally from the mast—could pose a real danger to the uninitiated.

"You could've drowned, Carter," Samantha said worriedly.

"The paramedics checked me out. I'm fine."

Mark noticed Carter seemed tense, and there were faint smudges under his eyes, as if he hadn't been sleeping well. "You don't look fine. Think you should see a doctor?"

"You sound like the paramedics," Carter muttered. "I just want a shower, a bottle of scotch sent up to my room and some sleep."

"I should go," Samantha said. "Mark, try to talk some sense into him and get him to see someone."

She touched Mark's arm in a farewell gesture. The two men watched as Samantha made her way down the hall. Once she was gone, Mark placed his hands inside his pockets. "How about it? Head injuries aren't something to mess around with. I've got some things to take care of, but I can have the limo service drive you to the urgent care center in town."

Carter didn't answer. He was still frowning, staring hard at the corner Samantha had disappeared around.

"Carter, did you hear what—"

Carter lowered his voice. "I can practically *smell* the sex on you, for God's sake. You're the head of this hotel, Mark. Having a quickie in one of the rooms isn't like you. None of this is."

Mark rubbed the back of his neck, his anger percolating. He wasn't going to stand here and let Carter, of all people, lecture him about inappropriate behavior.

His brother moved restlessly, his features drawn. "We...need to talk in private. About Samantha. It's important."

The earnestness on his face created a tingling in Mark's stomach. But the cell phone clipped to his waist beeped, indicating he had received a text. He took it from his belt and glanced at the screen. "I've got to go."

He backed away, re-clipping the phone.

"Mark—"

"I'm happy," he snapped. "Can't you see that? Just leave it alone, all right?"

They stared at one another until Mark said, "Do you want the limo or not?"

Carter shook his head, subdued. "No."

"Get some rest, then." His heart beating hard in his ears, Mark went toward his office, leaving Carter standing alone.

CHAPTER TWENTY-NINE

T HE SCOTCH HADN'T helped with his headache, not that Carter had expected it to. He'd wanted it to try to stop his reeling thoughts. He had played it down with Mark that afternoon, but the truth was, his preoccupation with this whole situation had nearly gotten him killed.

They'd told him on the set that he'd been underwater for about twenty seconds while the film's key grip and several others who had gone in after him searched the river. Carter had come to on the boat's deck, coughing and disoriented, with the director and a half-dozen white-faced crewmembers standing over him. Amanda, the PA who'd been in his trailer a few days before, had rolled him over to drain the water from his lungs and given him a puff of air from her mouth before he'd started breathing again. He recalled seeing her afterward, red-eyed and sniffling, having kept herself together only until the crisis was over.

Embarrassed, he'd been an asshole, refusing to let the paramedics take him to the ER. A dangerous move, he now admitted to himself. His chest still burned from the water he'd taken in. He made a mental note to send Amanda a dozen roses.

Sitting on the bed in his hotel suite, Carter looked at the bottle he'd been putting a serious dent into all night as he awaited a call from the PI he had hired over the weekend. He'd received a text from him hours ago, promising an update. Tension knotting his shoulders, he finally got up and went onto the balcony. Hands braced on the railing, Carter stared out over the darkened ocean.

The investigator was local to Memphis. Carter had asked him to keep a low profile as he tried to find out more about Trina Grissom. He said a fervent prayer he might learn something to rule out the possibility that she and Samantha were one and the same.

I'm happy. Can't you see that? Just leave it alone, all right?

Carter bowed his head. He had been on the verge of telling Mark what he knew so far—about the bad debt, as well as the chance that Samantha wasn't at all who she claimed to be. But the desperation in his brother's voice had stopped him cold.

Mark *knew* something was off about Samantha. He and Carter had both known it since the mysterious break-in she wouldn't talk about. But Mark was in some serious denial, and each day he seemed to be falling harder.

He sighed heavily. If the worst were true about her and he had to be the one to tell him, he just didn't know how Mark would react.

It was getting late, and the waiting was driving him insane. As he watched the tumble of white-capped waves, Carter considered confronting Samantha. Just going over to her place and laying the whole goddamn mess at her feet to see what she would say. And if Mark was with her, he could hear it, too. He was weighing the pros and cons of that course when his cell phone rang from inside the room. He went in and picked it up to peer at the screen, his heart dropping into his stomach.

It was the PI. Carter tried to quell the sudden dryness in his throat.

He answered, reaching for the scotch again as he listened to what the man had to say.

CHAPTER THIRTY

T HE LATE SUMMER weather appeared idyllic. A cloudless azure sky reigned overhead, and the gray-green ocean was docile. Mark stood at the window in his office, absently observing tourists around the pool. He felt a weight pressing down on him, aware that in a matter of days, the scene in front of him could change drastically.

The latest bulletin from the National Hurricane Center had not contained good news. Gina was gathering power and had been reclassified as a category two. It now appeared to be headed for the Carolinas' coast, although its ultimate strength and exact point of landfall were still unknown. Depending on the storm's path, it was possible an evacuation could be enacted within the next forty-eight to seventy-two hours. Already, Mark's maintenance staff had begun double-checking the sturdiness of the hotel's storm shutters and bolts.

He made a silent plea for a weakening storm front and all-out miss to the area. But statistically, they were due. Charleston and its surrounding communities were hit about once a decade, and the last time, aside from tropical storms, had been in 2004 when

Hurricane Charley had done only minimal damage. Mark was just old enough to recall Hurricane Hugo in 1989 and its devastating effects.

He didn't want to think about the possibility of another catastrophe.

He turned as the door to his office opened. Carter entered, his physical appearance catching Mark off guard. If possible, he looked worse than the day before, the hollows deeper under his eyes.

"You look like hell," Mark pointed out. "You didn't make it to the set today?"

"I was there since before sunup." Carter appeared tense. In a troubled voice, he added, "We're on a break, so I drove back. We start shooting again at dark."

Mark glanced at his wristwatch, noting the late afternoon hour. "You ask me, you should've just stayed in your trailer and caught a nap."

Although he tried to sound casual, Carter's unexpected, somber presence gave him an unsettling sense of déjà vu. He hadn't forgotten their exchange in the corridor the day before. Carter closed the door behind him and came farther inside, his posture slumped and hands shoved deeply into his pockets.

"I'm here because we need to *talk*, Mark. This is the only chance I have today, and I'm not leaving until we do."

The weight pressing down on him grew worse. Seating himself, Mark averted his gaze and began searching the stack of papers on his desk. "In case you haven't been paying attention to the weather reports, I'm a little busy—"

"It's about Sam."

"Of course it is," he muttered under his breath and continued roaming through the papers.

Carter took a step closer. "Just stop what you're doing and look at me, all right? This…it can't wait any longer."

Mark took a slow breath and then met Carter's gaze. His tone held a quiet warning. "I asked you to leave it alone. I'm a grown man. I don't need you telling me how to behave or that I'm getting serious too fast—"

"It's not what you think." Carter's words were strained. "There're… some things you need to know. About her. Things I found out."

Mark felt the sluggish beat of his heart. The missing pieces of Samantha's past loomed up at him again.

Carter rocked slightly on his feet, looking uncomfortable. "I'd been waiting to find out for sure, to have some proof before I came to you—"

"Proof?" Mark repeated roughly.

"When I went up to New York, I went to Sapphire, the place Samantha worked before she moved here." He quickly held up his palms to hold off a reprimand. "I know you're going to tell me it's none of my business. But I was there anyway, and I thought I was helping. After the break-in at her apartment, you were so worried about what was really going on with her. I thought maybe I could learn something."

Dread knotted Mark's stomach. "So what did you find out?"

Carter shook his head softly. "Things I wish I hadn't."

Mark felt anxiety coil inside him. He couldn't help it—he also tamped down resentment that Carter had interloped in his personal life. But whatever he believed he had learned, Mark needed to know, too. Rising from behind the desk, he walked to where Carter stood.

"Just *tell me*, Carter," he urged, his voice clipped and sounding calmer than he felt.

Carter's stare was pained. Then, withdrawing his cell phone

from his pocket, he fiddled with it for a second before handing it over. Mark glanced at him, then looked at the screen. On it was a grainy image.

"What's this?"

"Just look at the photo," Carter said quietly.

Mark took in the girl's face—the delicate features, the full mouth and doe-brown eyes. She was young, probably no more than twenty, and scantily dressed. Nearly naked. Platinum hair spilled over her shoulders as she lay back suggestively. He felt embarrassed looking at the image, as if he were viewing some kind of porn. But the resemblance dawned on him, making his stomach harden.

He shrugged to hide his confusion, a slow numbness creeping over him. "So what do you want me to think, exactly? That this girl is Samantha?"

Carter dragged his palms along his thighs. "The things I found out in New York led me to Memphis. Samantha Marsh isn't even her real name, Mark. It's Trina Grissom. She worked at a place there called the Blue Iris—"

"Where'd you get this?" Still looking at the phone's screen, Mark tried to swallow past the dryness in his throat.

"I'm trying to tell you. I…hired a private investigator. He went to the Blue Iris and did some asking around. One of the dancers took him to a room with posters of past performers on the walls. He took a photo of it with his phone and sent it to me."

Mark tried to process what he was hearing. But it was hard to see past how far Carter had gone. He'd actually *hired* a private investigator, without his knowledge or consent? He continued staring at the image, his heart beating hard.

"It's a *strip* club," Carter emphasized carefully.

It wasn't her. Mark shook his head, his muscles tightening with the realization. There was a resemblance, but the body was wrong.

He had *been* with Samantha, had memorized every inch of her soft skin, every curve. She was slender and supple. But this girl's ample bust was barely contained in the black lace bustier she wore, her areolas clearly visible through the meshing.

He looked at Carter angrily. "What did you do? Photoshop this?" Carter's face reddened. "I didn't Photoshop *anything*."

Backing away, heat flushing through him, Mark tossed the phone dismissively onto the desk. Carter flinched as it sailed over its mahogany top and landed on the floor. Still, he took a tentative step closer. "Do you think it was easy for me to come to you about this? I'm telling you because I *care* about you. I know you have feelings for her, and you need to know who she really is before this goes too far. She hasn't been up-front with you, or any of us, not by a long shot. She's living a complete *lie*."

Mark looked away, his lungs squeezing.

"*Listen to me.* The stripping isn't even the half of it. I wish to God it was." Carter hesitated. "Trina Grissom *disappeared* from that club six years ago. She's in some real trouble— the Memphis Police want her for questioning in a murder. She stole a lot of money from the club's owner, too."

Mark felt nearly lightheaded. He went to stare out the window. "You should leave."

"I…know you're upset. But you needed to know this before she digs her claws in any deeper, before she damages your life and Emily's. You've been sheltered here, Mark…"

Mark winced. His vision clouded as his brother continued talking. He didn't want Carter here for another second, didn't want to hear another word coming out of his self-centered mouth. He had never cared about anyone but himself. Mark had been *sheltered*? His pulse pounded as he thought of how he'd taken over the hotel single-handedly after their father's fatal heart attack, not even thirty years old at the time. How he had helplessly watched as his wife lay dying in front of him, their sweet little girl witnessing all of it.

Carter laid a hand on his shoulder, his voice hollow. "I'm sorry, Mark. But it's better to learn this now than—"

Mark ignited at the touch, whirling and striking Carter hard with his fist. Carter staggered back, nearly tipping over the lamp on the desk. He held a hand to his eye, surprise and pain etched on his features.

"Mark," he pleaded shakily.

"I want you out of here," Mark ordered, breathing hard. He gripped his stinging knuckles with his left hand, a dam of long-held umbrage giving way inside him. Emotion made his voice shake. "And not just my office. The hotel. Today."

"You're not thinking clearly—"

"You want your share? Fine, I'll find a way to buy you out." He pointed a finger. "But we're done."

Carter's expression was bleak. The skin around his left eye had already begun to discolor. Several beats passed as the two men stared at one another, the only sound the muffled laughter of children coming from the pool outside the window.

"I'm sorry I had to be the one to tell you." Carter swallowed heavily, "But you had to know."

He left the room, softly closing the door behind him.

Mark bent his head and rubbed his eyes, still reeling over his brother's claims. He attempted to reason them away, to convince himself that Carter had made all of it up for some twisted reason only he understood.

But in his heart, he *knew*.

The things he'd already known about her crowded in with what Carter had told him. Mark tugged his tie loose at his throat and undid the top button of his dress shirt. Then he ripped the tie off completely and threw it over the back of his chair.

From almost the moment they'd met, it had been clear that Samantha was trying to distance herself—from others, from him. He wondered again whom she had gone to see at the Sea King that night, why she had been so desperate for money. He had called the motel and asked who had been staying in room six, but was told the information was confidential, which hadn't surprised him. Mark squeezed his eyes closed, thinking of the butterfly tattoo. He had been trying to prepare for any number of possibilities—that she had an ex who was trouble, maybe even a family she had left behind somewhere. He had hoped one day she would confide in him.

But he'd never expected anything like this.

He'd struck Carter. God. Mark ran a shaky hand over his mouth. He had never hit anyone before in his life, never had anger spill out of him like that. Remorse fell over him for his violent, irrational outburst.

Carter's cell phone still lay on the floor. Mark walked over and picked it up. He forced himself to look again at the image of this too-young girl with the wrong hair, the wrong body. But the eyes were unmistakable—caramel brown and nearly too large for her face.

She's in some real trouble—the Memphis Police want her for questioning in a murder. She stole a lot of money from the club's owner, too.

Mark felt sick.

He sent the cell phone's image to his printer.

The meal was right on schedule. Samantha had left Luther in charge of closing up at the café so she could go to Mark's to prepare dinner, a thank-you for all he had done for her at the St.

229

Clair. An herb-encrusted rack of lamb and potatoes roasted in one side of the kitchen's Viking double oven, while golden macaroni and cheese bubbled in the other. She'd made that for Emily since Mark had said it was her favorite.

They were going to watch a movie after Emily was put to bed.

Nearly everything was ready—the salad waiting to be dressed, the dessert of individual flans chilling in the fridge. Samantha wanted everything to be perfect yet casual and unfussy. Mark had been receptive to her plans to make dinner, giving her his security code and telling her she could find a key to the front door under a terra cotta urn on the porch steps.

A grandfather clock in the foyer chimed the hour. It was seven, and Mark had said he'd be home half an hour ago. She wondered if he had been held up by news of the threatening hurricane. The entire town was on its toes, waiting for the latest weather report, Samantha included. Mercer was also supposed to drop Emily off, but hadn't arrived yet, either.

As she pulled the lamb from the oven and covered it with foil to rest, she heard the front door open. Footsteps sounded in the foyer. Wiping her hands on a dishtowel and replacing it on the granite countertop, Samantha turned. But the bright smile she wore faded as she saw Mark's face.

Worry bloomed inside her. The hurricane. Emily. "What's wrong?"

He stared at her with pained eyes.

"I know your name's Trina," he said hoarsely.

CHAPTER THIRTY-ONE

T HE AIR DISAPPEARED from the room. Samantha tried to bring breath back into her lungs, but could not. The way he was looking at her felt like a knife plunged into her heart.

"Mark," she whispered, but could think of nothing else to say.

Her eyes fell to the image on the printed sheet of paper in his hand. It was wrinkled, his knuckles bruised. She didn't have to see it up close to know which photo it was. Recognition weakened her knees. She pressed her hand to her stomach, fighting the urge to flee. Instead, Samantha forced herself to speak. "Where..." Her voice faltered. "Where did you get that?"

"Does it matter?" His haunted eyes, the absence of color in his face—it was nearly more than she could bear. Mark stared at her for several long seconds. Then he laid the paper on the table between them.

Adrenaline spiked her pulse. That photo had been taken not long after she'd started performing. Her memory of the photo session itself was fuzzy due to the pill Devin had pressed on her, insisting it would relax her for the camera. She also knew the photo—used for a poster and put on flyers handed out to draw male passersby into the club—had been the most innocent of the ones taken that night, by far. Her face burned with humiliation.

"It came from a private investigator," Mark said finally. Samantha felt a wave of betrayal, but knew she had no right. She was the one hiding things, keeping secrets. Her only question was whether Mark had hired the investigator, or if Olivia had been the one.

"How old are you in that photo?"

"Seventeen," she admitted softly. "Almost eighteen."

He didn't reply, instead rubbing his hand over his mouth. Lines of tension appeared around his eyes.

"How long did you do it?" He swallowed before speaking again. "Taking off your clothes in front of—"

"Four years." She closed her eyes briefly. She didn't want to hear him describe it.

She shrank from him then, but he blocked her exit from the kitchen.

"You're not leaving," he rasped. The confusion she saw on his features tore at her. "*Talk to me*, Samantha. Make me understand why you'd—"

"His name was Devin Leary," she managed to get out. "I was a runaway and flat broke. Devin…took me in."

"He made you work for him?"

"It was his club. I-I thought I was in love with him. But then things changed…" Her breath hitched. "He told me I had to earn money for him, to pay him back for everything he'd done for me."

Mark winced at what her words implied.

"You could've just left," he reasoned.

"I tried." She felt a chill sweep through her. "Devin was dangerous. No one crossed him."

Her throat convulsed at the recollection, cutting off her words.

She was unable to say more, to tell him about Devin's possessiveness and need for control. About the mental abuse, or the times he had beaten her so badly she had to be hospitalized. Mark had been born into a loving family with social standing and wealth. She wondered if he fully realized that men like Devin or his brother, Red, even existed. He would think she was lying, making herself into a victim.

"Is he who you went to see at the Sea King?"

Samantha shook her head. "No."

She thought he might press her further, but Mark took a step away. He picked up the wine bottle on the counter as if he intended to pour himself a drink, but then set it back down on the chopping block she had used to make their salad. For a time, he simply stared at the tiled backsplash, his shoulders slumped.

"I don't even know what to call you," he murmured.

"Samantha." She heard the desperation in her voice as she inched closer to him. "It's who I am. It's who I've been for six years. I'm *not* Trina—"

He turned to face her again. "The Memphis Police are looking for you. They want to question you about a murder."

Samantha felt the floor fall away underneath her. Mark's gaze weighed heavily on her, his face ravaged as he waited for her to respond. How much did he already know? Had he been giving her a chance to come clean about all of it and she had failed him again? Her heart thudded hard. She'd never said the words aloud. "I-I killed Devin."

Mark's face went paler.

"I...stabbed him to death."

The confession unleashed rapid-fire images of that fateful night. Devin punching her. Choking her as he raped her. Nausea inched up her throat as she thought of the jagged glass she'd shoved into his neck and the bright spill of his blood. Panicked, Samantha

233

pulled at the hands that held her in place, until she became aware that it was Mark, grasping her forearms to bring her back from where her mind had gone.

"Samantha," Mark urged. "Tell me what happened."

His face swam in her vision, her lungs cramping with the memory. "He was...hurting me."

"If it was self-defense, then you didn't have to run—"

"I was an adult entertainer, and his lover!" Emotion thickened her voice. She looked at him, grief and shame welling inside her. "Do you think the police would've believed me?"

"You could've tried."

"It wouldn't have mattered. Devin's brother is looking for me, too." Her insides twisted at the thought of Red Leary. "Even if the police hadn't pressed charges, Red wouldn't have been so forgiving. He's involved in bad things—he makes Devin look like a choirboy. If he finds me, he'll kill me for what I did."

The weight of it seemed to crash down on him all at once. Mark's eyes roamed her face, as if searching for some sign of the truth. For the woman he thought he knew. Releasing her, he walked to the counter, holding on to it as if it were the only thing keeping him upright. Samantha said a silent prayer for forgiveness. She hadn't wanted to hurt him. But by letting him into her life, letting him fall for her, that was exactly what she had done. She'd been uncompromisingly selfish by letting him in. Slowly, she walked up to him, hesitantly touching his back. Her heart sank at the way his body tensed under her fingers.

"I know this is a lot to deal with. Too much—"

"I have a little girl, Samantha," he said hoarsely. "I knew you had secrets...but I can't drag her into something like *this*."

Samantha didn't move at all, her body absorbing the impact of his words.

"I understand," she managed to whisper. Numb, she asked haltingly, "Are you going to turn me in?"

He made a soft sound at her question, his eyes filled with anguish when he turned to her. "If I say *yes*, are you going to run?"

She shook her head faintly. "I'm tired of running, Mark."

He no longer appeared angry, just sad. She wished he would curse at her, shake her. Hurt her physically for the way she had hurt him. Anything would be better than the devastation written on his features. Her hands trembled as she moved to one of the barstools and reached for her car keys and purse. Tears clogged her throat.

"When you were working...did you sleep with the men?"

He meant the club's patrons. He was asking if she was a whore. Fresh self-hatred bubbled up inside her.

"No," she whispered, her back rigid. She felt a hard chill.

"Samantha, I..." But he just looked at her. She saw him swallow. He clearly didn't know what to say.

She filled the space left between them. "I'm so sorry, Mark. For letting things go this far. You deserve better."

Placing her purse strap over her shoulder, she stumbled blindly to the foyer only to come face-to-face with Mercer and Emily, who had just entered the house. Emily stared up at Samantha with questioning blue eyes.

Wiping the tears from her face, she pushed past them and rushed down the porch stairs. Behind her, she could hear Mark telling Mercer that he'd left her a message asking her not to bring Emily home yet.

"...Mantha."

Samantha froze. *Was that?* She turned. Emily had followed her onto the porch. Her little voice was rusty from disuse, but it caused what was left of Samantha's heart to crumple like old paper. She went back up to her. Dropping to her knees, she caught Emily in a hug, amazed by what she'd just heard. "It's okay, sweetheart. Everything's fine."

"Why you...cry?"

Emily concentrated hard to get some semblance of the words out, her forehead furrowed. She had a strong lisp. The sweet sound of it made Samantha's eyes mist all over again, genuine joy mixing with her pain. She didn't draw attention to the fact that Emily had spoken, fearing she might spook her.

"I'm just tired. You know how you feel when you miss your nap?" Still kneeling, she held Emily's small fingers in hers. "I'm going to go home and rest now."

"Don't...go." Emily's lower lip trembled, her eyes afraid.

"I'll be right in town. And I'll see you soon."

"Prom...ise?"

"I promise, Emily." Despite her best effort, her voice trembled. "I made dinner for you. Let Mercer get you a plate, all right? There's macaroni and cheese."

She peered up at Mercer and Mark, who were frozen in place in the doorway. They'd obviously heard Emily speak. Mercer's fingers covered her mouth in astonishment. Mark stood slightly behind her. He scrubbed a hand over his reddened eyes.

Weak-kneed, Samantha rose as Mercer called to Emily. She held out her hand and, with a questioning look at Samantha, took Emily into the house. Mark's gaze remained fastened on her. He appeared shattered. Her heart felt equally broken.

There was nothing left to be said. Whether Mark turned her over to the police or took her secret with him to the grave, Samantha realized she no longer cared. She was actually surprised she was still managing to breathe. Pivoting shakily on her heel, she forced herself to walk to her car in the driveway. Samantha started the engine and drove away, sobbing, leaving Mark behind.

"Emily's in bed now. She had a big day. I think she'll be asleep soon."

Mark looked up as Mercer entered the living area. He sat on the couch, gripping a tumbler of scotch.

"Thanks for staying for dinner, Merce." He briefly caught her fingers as she walked past. He and Mercer had done their best to keep Emily talking during the meal, managing to draw out a few more precious words from her. Afterward, Mercer had taken over. Having witnessed Samantha's flight from the house, she'd obviously wanted to give Mark some time.

"You've been a lifeline to Emily and me since Shelley died," he said quietly. "I want you to know how much I appreciate it."

"I think the scotch is making you maudlin." Her tone was light, although he could see the concern in her eyes. Mercer eased down on the couch beside him. "I still can't believe Emily spoke tonight."

"Yeah," he agreed, smiling faintly and releasing a breath of heartfelt relief. Hearing his daughter's voice after so long had brought tears to his eyes. But his joy that Emily had talked also mingled with a fear that she might stop again...especially if Samantha disappeared from her life. Clearly, what had happened tonight between Samantha and him had been the inciting incident that had led to her speaking. Mark felt overwhelmed by the revelation of who Samantha really was. He hadn't even asked her about the money she'd supposedly stolen, he realized.

"What happened with Samantha?" Mercer asked.

"I think it's over," he managed, believing it the most discreet answer. Mark took a sip of scotch and then leaned forward to place the empty glass on the coffee table.

Her shoulder rubbed his. "So you two had a fight. Whatever it's about, I'm sure it's something that can be worked out—"

"Mercer..." Wearily, he bowed his head. He'd been keeping up a strong front for Emily but felt emotionally exhausted. "I'm really not up to talking about it."

She waited for several heartbeats. "You're upset, Mark. I don't want to leave you like this. I could sleep in the guest room and help with Emily—"

"We'll be fine." He wasn't so sure, though. But he had leaned on Mercer far too much over the last two years. "Besides, don't you have someone at the hotel to get back to?"

"Jonathan has plenty to do. He's working on a paper for some academic journal. And he's going back to Atlanta tomorrow afternoon. The fall session at the university is starting soon."

"Then all the more reason to go be with him now." Mark pressed his lips together as he looked at her, only half-joking. "Although, we haven't had time to talk about your cradle-robbing professor. I feel obligated to give you some kind of *older brother* lecture."

Mercer frowned. "I'm not going to let you distract me, Mark. We're talking about *you*. You don't have to tell me what happened tonight, but Samantha's been good for you, and Emily is obviously crazy about her."

She added carefully, "I know things have been moving fast, but I think maybe you've fallen a little *in love* with her, too."

Mark's throat tightened. Mercer laid her hand on his forearm and squeezed softly. "It's like you've come back to life since you met her. You've been happy lately. Something you haven't been in a long time."

He remained silent, both unwilling and unable to open up about all the unsettling things he'd learned. He wondered what Mercer would think if he laid out the story for her. But he didn't want to expose Samantha further, and he was still trying to process the whole of it himself. Right now, his mind was stuck on an endless loop of their confrontation. He'd had every right to question her, but the torment he'd seen on her face was something that not even the numbing effects of the scotch could scour away.

"Okay then…" Mercer gently slapped her hands on her thighs and stood, apparently accepting that Mark wasn't going to talk to her. "I'm going. But I'm just a phone call away. If you need anything, I can be here in ten minutes."

Mark closed his eyes as his sister reached back down and hugged him.

"Thanks, Merce," he whispered.

A minute later, she had gathered her purse and was gone. Mark waited until he heard her convertible pull from the driveway, then rose from the couch and splashed another measure of scotch into his glass. As he sipped, he stared out at the white blanket of beach and dark night above it.

He'd wanted the truth, hadn't he?

Samantha had warned him from the start that she was wrong for him and Emily. She'd fought their involvement until Mark and fate had worn her down. He had believed he wanted to know her secrets, but now…

He hadn't been prepared for anything remotely like this.

Her time spent working at a strip club, dancing nude, was a shock to him. But her involvement in a man's death, theft, living under an assumed identity…Mark felt a choking disquiet. The revelation that Samantha was a wanted woman, on the run, rocked him to his core. And he did have Emily's welfare to consider.

Feeling hollowed out, he dropped his head into his palm and massaged his forehead.

There was still too much he didn't know. Who had she gone to the Sea King to meet that night, and why had she needed money? It sounded like an obvious blackmail attempt, and it worried him that someone knew her real identity other than him and Carter. He thought of the man Samantha had mentioned. Red Leary.

He makes Devin look like a choirboy. If he finds me, he'll kill me for what I did.

Even if they weren't together, Mark didn't want a life of fear for Samantha, which was what she had been living all this time, apparently. Or a life behind bars. Especially if she'd told the truth that she had killed only to defend herself. Unsure, he tried to bring his racing thoughts under control.

Walking down the hallway, he stopped in the doorway to Emily's bedroom. A pink seashell nightlight provided a soft glow that made his daughter's curls look like a golden halo around her head. Upon seeing Mark, she raised up a bit and blinked at him.

"Hey, pumpkin," Mark said, coming into the room. The mattress dipped under his weight as he sat on the bed's edge. He stroked her hair, his heart filling with love for her. "I thought you'd be asleep."

"You...sad, Daddy."

Mark's chest ached at the sweet sound of his daughter's rusty, lisping words. He looked at the stuffed bear tucked under the covers next to her. One of its button eyes was missing, and its synthetic fur had been worn to a fuzz. Emily had shelves full of toys, yet this one seemed to go to bed with her every night, maybe because it had been Samantha's. He sighed. "No. I'm just tired, baby."

"Like 'Mantha?"

For a bare moment, Mark's throat closed up. He nodded softly, stealing time to regain his composure. "Yeah. Like Samantha."

Emily yawned, and he bent to kiss her forehead. "I love you to pieces. Go to sleep now, okay?"

Mark got up and waited, his shoulder leaned against the doorframe as he watched Emily turn onto her side, her small hands tucked between her cheek and the pillow. After a short while, her eyelashes fluttered closed.

Making a noiseless departure from Emily's bedroom, Mark wandered into the small study that adjoined the master suite. He picked up his cell phone from where he'd left it on the Queen Anne-style desk, found the number on it he needed and made the call.

"Todd? It's Mark St. Clair. I know it's a little late to be calling, but—"

His former college roommate greeted him with obvious delight. The two had shared an off-campus apartment while Mark was getting his master's degree in business and Todd Hamilton had been enrolled at Emory University School of Law. Mark hadn't seen him since Shelley's funeral. But they still kept in touch by e-mail and occasional phone calls. After school, Todd had returned to his hometown of Germantown, Tennessee, an upscale suburb outside of Memphis, to join his father's law practice.

"Todd, there's something I need you to check into for me," Mark said, growing serious once they'd engaged in a few minutes of conversational catch-up. He hesitated, running a hand through his hair. "A murder, actually. It happened about six years ago in your neck of the woods. I'm happy to pay for your time."

"As much as I would enjoy taking your money, it's no fun unless it's over a game of poker," Todd bantered, his usual good-natured self. "Just give me the details, starting with the name of the deceased."

"Devin Leary."

Mark heard Todd's low whistle. "Holy hell. The infamous Leary brothers."

"You know them?"

"I'm a defense lawyer, so yeah. Think Sopranos, only Irish."

Mark's stomach clenched. "They're Mafia?"

"Something like that, although they front their illegal activities with a string of barely respectable businesses around Memphis. I vaguely recall Devin Leary taking the big dirt nap some years back." There was a brief pause. "What's your interest in all this, Mark?"

"Can we go ahead and assume client-attorney privilege?"

"Jesus. Not for you, I hope."

"No," Mark said. "A friend of mine."

He trusted Todd, deeply, and he told him everything he had learned about Samantha. Once he'd hung up, Mark stood lost in his thoughts, listening for a time to the deep croak of a bullfrog somewhere outside the bedroom window. Then he went back into the living room to catch the latest weather bulletin on the television. The news unsettled him more, if that was possible.

He woke sometime later sprawled on the couch, still wearing the rumpled clothes he had worked in that day. Perspiration made his white dress shirt stick to his skin, and his heart raced like a greyhound at the Myrtle Beach dog tracks. The television's glow offered the only light in the room. Mark sat up and rubbed a shaky hand over his face.

He'd had a nightmare about the car wreck. Not an unusual occurrence, unfortunately. Even awake his mind clung to the stomach-churning images, beginning with the twin beams of the car that crossed the center line and hit them head on. But in his dream, it had been Samantha, not Shelley, who was lying in the twisted metal next to him.

Mark feared it was an omen.

CHAPTER THIRTY-TWO

IF MARK INTENDED to turn her over to the police, Samantha realized she would have been in handcuffs by now. But nearly two days had passed, and no detectives or uniformed officers had shown up at her door. During that time, she had lived a numbed existence, with Café Bella and her promise to Emily the only things tethering her to the quiet beach town.

Keeping that promise would soon be out of her control, however. Hurricane Gina was now a category three. Previously, it had been headed north of them—closer to Wilmington, North Carolina, some one hundred and fifty miles away—but it had shifted course that morning and now appeared to be making a bee-line for the South Carolina coast. Charleston and its surrounding communities had been issued a warning. A direct hit to the area was predicted, and unless the storm weakened or again went off its trajectory, it would make landfall sometime the following night.

A mandatory evacuation had been put into place.

Everything Samantha had in this world was tied up in the café.

Fortunately, the Sea Breeze Centre had storm shutters as both a preventive measure and architectural complement. From the shop's kitchen, she could hear the heavy wham of the shutters being secured into place by workers trying to make good use of the last remaining hour of daylight.

"I put the patio tables in the alley and chained 'em to the Dumpster out back," Luther said as he came into the kitchen. "That'll have to do since they're too big to bring inside."

"What about the umbrellas?"

"Those fit in the utility room."

Between serving customers, they'd been making preparations for the better part of the day. Exhausted, Samantha pushed a strand of hair from her eyes. "I think we've done about all we can for tonight. But can we start again early in the morning? I was thinking we should try to get some of the appliances off the floor, in case of flooding. We can put two-by-fours underneath them."

Luther nodded. "I'll head on out and stop by Gimbell's Hardware for the planks on my way home. They've got the place open 'til midnight. If they're sold out, I might have to go into Mount Pleasant."

He made a move toward the exit, then turned back. "Sam... tourists are already leavin'. When do you plan on going?"

"I could ask the same of you."

He chuckled lowly. "Don't worry about me. I was born for this kind of weather. Probably ride the whole thing out at the Shamrock with a beer keg if the police don't run me off."

He eyed Samantha warily, though. "Skinny little thing like you is likely to blow away if you don't get inland before the winds kick up."

She forced a faint smile. "I'm not leaving until the shop's ready, but your message's received. I'll be out by tomorrow afternoon— in plenty of time."

Luther picked up a box to haul out to his truck. "I'm probably worried for nothin', anyhow. Mr. St. Clair's a good man. He'll take care of you."

As he went out the door, his words made her heart ache. She missed Mark, and she felt sick over her deceit and the way things had ended between them. But she deserved the pain and humiliation that clung to her like a shadow.

A few moments later, she heard Luther's ancient pickup spring to life. Once its low rumble faded into the distance, she wandered into the closed storefront, her arms wrapped around her midriff. Her eyes took in the hardwood floors and wrought-iron shelving, the domed refrigerated display counters rimmed with brass. Samantha sighed, a tightness in her throat as she looked at the now-shuttered windows. If Gina managed to do her worst, the shop she had so lovingly designed might look very different once the rain and winds subsided. She might have nothing left. Frowning, she thought of the elegant St. Clair and wondered how Mark was dealing with the approaching storm. She knew the hotel's main structure was more than a century old and had no doubt seen its share of hurricanes, but she could only imagine the responsibility and worry he carried.

And I've added to that worry. All she could do now was try to remove herself as a source of his problems.

Needing a distraction, Samantha took some of the jars from the shelves to move them to the windowless storeroom in back. She had already made arrangements to donate the café's perishables to one of the hurricane shelters inland. If she stuck to her schedule, she would be able to drop the items off on her way out of town tomorrow.

Filling a cardboard box with bottles of herb-infused olive oil, she began hauling it to the back when a knock sounded at the service door in the kitchen. Samantha set the heavy load on the counter. She wiped her hands on her jeans and went to see who it was.

To her surprise, Emily grinned up at her. Mercer stood uncertainly behind Emily. She lifted her hand in a tentative greeting.

"We thought we'd come by and see how you're faring. I mean, with the storm and all."

Mercer's tone was light, but her blue eyes, so much like Mark's, appeared solemn and questioning.

"I'm fine, thanks." Samantha bent to give Emily a hug. She wondered how much Mercer knew by now, what Mark might have told her. If she *did* know, then Samantha was truly shocked to see her. Flustered and uncertain, shame heating her face, she focused on Emily.

"It's good to see you, sweetie. Are you getting packed for a trip somewhere?"

"'Gusta," she replied, stumbling over the name of Augusta, Georgia, which was farther inland. Mark had mentioned he had an aunt there who lived in the city's Historic District.

Emily looked hopeful. "You…come, too?"

Samantha's heart pinched, but she did her best not to show it. "I'm afraid I can't. But I'm sure you're going to have a wonderful time."

"You know what?" Mercer spoke up. "I bet Sam's got a treat for you in the store somewhere."

Samantha straightened. "There're some crayons out front. I think there might be a cookie for you, too."

They went into the café. As soon as they'd gotten Emily settled with a treat and glass of milk, Mercer and Samantha went to stand near the cash register.

"I still can't believe she's talking," Samantha marveled in a low voice, observing as Emily scribbled on one of the drawing pads she kept for restless children. The little girl held a crayon in one hand and a heart-shaped sugar cookie in the other, and Samantha said a silent prayer of gratitude for her progress.

"Mark took her to the psychiatrist the morning after her breakthrough—Dr. Richardson seemed very pleased. They're going to assign her a speech therapist in addition to her regular sessions," Mercer confided. "Samantha...she's been asking about you. Emily's perceptive, and she's been worried about what she saw the other night. I wanted to bring her by and let her see for herself that you're all right."

Samantha nodded her agreement, looking at Emily so she wouldn't have to meet Mercer's eyes.

"You *are* all right, aren't you?"

Releasing a breath, she asked what her heart wanted to know. "How's Mark?"

"Not good," Mercer admitted with a soft shake of her head. "He won't say much to me, or anyone else, for that matter. He's tied up with the hurricane preparations, but beyond that, he's pretty much shut down."

Samantha made no reply. Mercer bit her lip pensively.

"You...need to know something. I found the photo at Mark's house. I took it with me so Emily would never see it. Then I ran it through the shredder in my office at the hotel."

"Thanks," Samantha whispered. She bowed her head, upset.

"Mark can be a bit straitlaced, but *he'll get over this*. You looked so young in that photo. I know the statistics, how many young girls get pulled into those...kinds of things. What you did years ago has nothing to do with who you are now," she reasoned, touching Samantha's arm. "It doesn't have to define your life."

It was clear Mercer was trying to piece together exactly what had transpired between her and Mark, and it sounded as though he had told her nothing. She had only tapped the surface with the photo from the Blue Iris. Samantha recalled Mark's face when she had confessed to killing Devin.

I have a little girl, Samantha. I knew you had secrets, but I can't drag her into something like this.

Her heart ached all over again.

"Does Olivia know?" Samantha asked, not wanting Mark's mother to make it any worse for him. Unless it was *she* who hired the private investigator. In some ways, Samantha hoped Olivia was the one. She wanted to hold on to the belief that Mark had trusted her—that he hadn't been having her investigated even as they'd been lovers.

"I'm sure Mark didn't tell her. She seems pretty oblivious." Mercer pressed her lips together before speaking again. "Carter's the one who told Mark about all this, I'm certain of it. He's been moping around the hotel with a black eye, looking like a depressed raccoon. I asked him what happened, but he said he ran into some filming equipment on set. I...noticed Mark's knuckles were bruised."

Her stomach twisted uneasily. Carter. That would explain his recent strange behavior toward her. Samantha felt terrible, knowing she may have been the final crack in Mark and Carter's already strained relationship.

"We shouldn't talk about this," Samantha insisted quietly.

Mercer looked at her, emphatic. "If you and Mark won't talk about it, someone has to."

Samantha stared at the storefront's shuttered windows. Only a weak stream of light filtered in around the edges, telling her it was pushing closer to twilight. She no longer heard the pounding of the workers outside. Samantha forced herself to look into Mercer's eyes, willing her to understand.

"Mercer...there's more to the story than you know. It's bad. I'm sure Carter will fill you in if you press him. But it's over between Mark and me, and it really is for the best."

She shook her head. "I can't accept that."

"You have to. You've been such a help to Mark. He's going to need your support."

Sudden awareness appeared in Mercer's eyes. "You're not staying after the storm, are you?"

At Mercer's question, Samantha felt a lump form in her throat. She hadn't told anyone of her decision yet, not even Luther. She raised her shoulders in a faint shrug. "I guess small-town life isn't right for me, after all. If the hurricane doesn't cause too much destruction, I'm going to list the business with a commercial broker. The café isn't very established yet, so I won't get much for it, but if I'm lucky, it might be enough to cover a decent portion of my bank loan."

She touched Mercer's arm. "You've been a good friend to me, Mercer. One of the few I've ever had. And it's good that you brought Emily by so she can see that I'm okay."

"Your mind's made up?"

Samantha gave a small nod. "I'll keep in touch with Emily for a while. If you wouldn't mind, I'd like to send some letters and cards to you, so that you can read them to her? I...think that would be easier than me just disappearing from her life all at once."

Frowning deeply, Mercer studied Samantha's face. Then she stepped forward and embraced her. She pulled away only at the sound of Emily's chair scraping backward. The little girl skipped over to them.

"For 'Mantha." Proudly, she held out a crayon drawing of

something that resembled a cupcake, a mound of pink icing and a candle burning on top. As Emily looked up at her, the pure adoration on her face caused tears to threaten behind Samantha's eyes. It took every ounce of strength she could muster to offer a tremulous smile.

"*Thank you*, Emily." She felt her hands shake as she accepted the drawing. "I'll cherish this forever."

"We should get going—we're leaving in the morning. Take care, Sam, all right?" With sad eyes, Mercer gave Samantha a last heartfelt look. Samantha hugged Emily one more time, then watched as the two of them went back into the kitchen, disappearing out the back door.

Just like that, they were gone.

Samantha rubbed her hands over her upper arms, hearing only her own heartbeat in the deafening echo of silence. Her life had not been an easy one so far. But right now, in an empty café with shuttered windows, she had never felt more alone.

CHAPTER THIRTY-THREE

THE NORMALLY SUN-DRENCHED lobby of the St. Clair had been featured in *Architectural Digest*. Its high, arched windows and sweeping adjacent veranda provided a breathtaking view of the Atlantic. But on this particular morning, the waters appeared choppy, the ocean and sky dark. A dreary mist prevailed. Not even the stained-glass skylight several stories above could dispel the monochrome grayness that was a harbinger of the approaching storm.

It might be the start of any other rainy beach day, if not for the sense of dread Mark felt and the sight of vacationers scurrying to remove themselves from Gina's path. Around him, desk clerks efficiently checked out guests while uniformed valets roamed the marble floor, pushing brass carts piled with luggage.

Twenty-six years ago, the lobby had looked vastly different, with paneled walls, rich tapestries and dark hardwood floors. But that was before Hurricane Hugo, which had completely destroyed the front portion of the hotel and a full wing of guest rooms. Mark had been only a child at the time, but he recalled what his father had told them as he tried to remain dutifully upbeat: *Nature has given us the opportunity for a redesign.*

Uncertain whether he had Harrison St. Clair's fortitude, Mark fervently hoped he wouldn't see a repeat of such devastation.

He headed down the hallway only to notice Carter leaning against the wall outside his office. Despite his demand that he leave the hotel, his brother had steadfastly remained, giving Mark the chance to offer an apology for his behavior. Carter had quickly accepted, again voicing concern only about Mark. To himself, Mark conceded that his brother wasn't responsible for Samantha's past, only his enlightenment of it. They had reached a fragile truce.

Carter pushed off from the wall as Mark approached.

"What's up?" Mark asked as he checked e-mails on his cell phone, mentally calculating how much time he had to take care of a number of outstanding issues.

"Mercer clued me in. I came to talk to you. Tell me she misunderstood, and you're not actually planning to ride this thing out."

Even in the hall's subdued lighting, Mark could see the bruise that still shadowed Carter's right eye. He flinched inwardly at what he had done. He'd heard—also from Mercer—that the injury had gotten Carter into hot water with the movie's director. His only saving grace was that filming had to be temporarily halted anyway, due to the approaching storm. Otherwise, his altered appearance could have caused serious production delays.

"The evacuation's mandatory," Carter reminded tensely. "That means *everyone.* They make anyone who stays sign a waiver that includes contact information for next of kin. That's for a reason."

"That's for a cat four or five. This is a three—it's not predicted to be catastrophic."

Carter threw up his hands. "Jesus, Mark."

Mark couldn't expect Carter to understand. He didn't share his mind-set or his obligation. The truth was, Mark hadn't fully made up his mind. The hurricane's recent change of course had left them all scrambling.

"Just because Dad stayed doesn't mean it was a smart thing to do."

"I have a *responsibility*," Mark stressed, his voice low. He felt a rise of nostalgia. "Dad entrusted me with running this place. If the damage is bad, it could be days before they let us back in. I'm not going to just leave it open to looters or whatever the hell else—"

"You're also the father of a little girl who doesn't have a mother," Carter said, his voice tight. "Don't be an idiot."

Releasing a breath, Mark conceded that Carter was right. He'd thought of Emily's safety and had already made preparations for it. But she needed *him*, as well. He had been so intent on doing whatever he could to protect the St. Clair that he hadn't given a lot of thought to his own preservation.

"People *die* in category threes. They drown or get electrocuted. Roofs cave in," Carter pointed out. "And if there *are* looters, what're you going to do? Hold them off with Grandpa Aiden's antique shotgun?"

"You're right, all right?" Mark clasped the back of his neck. Considering the hell of the past several days, maybe his judgment was more screwed up than he realized. "I'll be out well before nightfall. It's going to take some time to get things locked down here, and to make sure all the guests and employees are out. Mercer and Mom are going to Aunt Lucinda's in Augusta. They're leaving soon and taking Emily with them. I'll join them there later after the traffic has thinned out."

Carter narrowed his eyes. "Then I'll stay with you."

"You think I won't leave?"

"Yeah, I'm worried about it."

"I *said* I'd go, and I will." Mark looked at him. "What about you? They're still letting planes out of the airport until four. I thought you had some meeting in New York."

"I don't want to leave with this mother of a storm barreling down on this place. I'm trying to help you if you'll let me."

"I'm *fine*," Mark said absently. "And you can help by getting yourself out of here so I have one less person to worry about."

Carter lowered his voice, appearing uncertain. "I don't want to leave until I'm sure *we're good*, too. Mark...I need you to understand that I wasn't deliberately trying to find something to ruin things for you. I thought I was doing the right thing by just checking out Sapphire. I ended up opening a portal to hell."

Mark felt the persistent ache he'd been carrying around inside him worsen.

"I understand," he assured him. "And you were right. I needed to know. But I don't want you telling anyone else what you found out about her."

"Like I told you before, it stays between us."

He nodded, believing that Carter would keep his silence. Neither of them wanted to expose Samantha. He'd relayed to Carter what she had told him, about getting involved with the wrong people when she was still basically a kid. That she had killed a violent man in self-defense and gone into hiding out of fear of reprisal or imprisonment. Carter had asked about the money she had supposedly taken, but Mark had no answer. At this point, he wasn't sure he wanted to know. The approaching storm had taken precedence over everything.

"You really want to help? I have something you can do. Escort the women to Augusta this morning."

Carter shook his head. "No way. I'm offering to stay here and help you take care of last-minute—"

"So you can keep an eye on me. But where I could really use you is in making sure they get there safely." Mark held his gaze. "The roads will be wet and overcrowded. There's no doubt going to be some road rage, and Mercer has her hands full with Mom and Emily. It would be a relief to me knowing you were driving them there."

"You're serious?"

"Dead serious."

After a few beats, Carter reluctantly bobbed his head. "If that's what you really want. But I expect you to meet up with us."

"I will. You should get packed," Mark advised. "Mercer's getting Emily's things together now."

Carter went off in the direction of the guest rooms.

Mark hadn't been lying. He did feel a small weight taken off him knowing that Carter would be making the trip, too. Although it was only a few hours to Augusta where their aunt lived, he was concerned about traffic congestion. He also hoped Carter might provide a distraction for Emily, who thought he hung the moon. Since finding out about the upcoming trip, she'd been asking repeatedly why Samantha couldn't come with them. When she discovered Mark wasn't in the car, either, he was worried about how she might react.

Going into his office, he noticed that housekeeping had been there but hadn't completed their job in light of the evacuation frenzy. A vacuum cleaner sat in the middle of the floor, still plugged into the electrical socket, and an abandoned bag of trash leaned limply against the wall. Mark sat down behind his desk, taking a short break from all the commotion. Closing his eyes, he rubbed his forehead, his weariness extending far beyond the storm preparations.

He'd done the right thing to call it off with Samantha. For Emily's sake and for the sake of the hotel, he reminded himself. But no matter what Samantha had done in her past or what she had been involved in, he *still* had feelings for her. He felt mixed up and painfully alone.

The things he'd said to her had damaged her, he knew.

Even if they were no longer together, Mark vowed he would do whatever he could to help her. But he had been wondering what *help* actually meant—whether it was simply keeping quiet about her true identity, or persuading her to go to the police and then paying for her legal defense. He recalled what Todd Hamilton had told him about the Leary brothers. What if Samantha was right that exposing herself would put a target on her back? The thought of her being placed at risk made cold pool in the pit of his stomach.

In that moment, Mark hated that he was having such a hard time dealing with the truth. He ran his hand over his face. Last night, Mercer had told him of Samantha's plans to sell the café and leave town once the hurricane was behind them. It hadn't completely surprised him, but the revelation had still left him shaken.

Was he really going to just let her go?

His throat felt tight. On impulse, he retrieved his cell phone from his pants pocket. More than anything, he just needed to hear Samantha's voice. He would give her a brief call, make sure she was all right and planning to go inland soon, if she hadn't left already.

His finger remained poised uncertainly over her number on the phone's screen for several seconds, until the quiet of his office was disrupted by the intercom console on his credenza.

"Mr. St Clair?"

He recognized the soft inflection as belonging to one of the women who worked the concierge service. "Yes, Peggy. What is it?"

"We have an emergency. The driver taking guests to the Charleston airport just called. The limousine has had a breakdown on I-526, and several passengers are going to miss their flights."

"I'll be right there." Sighing in resignation, Mark returned the cell phone to his pocket. His call to Samantha would have to wait awhile. Which might also give him some time to figure out exactly what he was going to say to the woman whose heart he had broken.

The noontime sky looked like gray velvet hanging low over the quaint beach town. From his seat in the passenger side of the Cadillac Escalade, Red Leary peered out at the boardwalk and dark plane of sea just beyond it. The weather had continued to deteriorate as they'd traveled along the coastline, the smell of rain adding an extra fecund note to the sea air. They had looped north and taken a back road south to Rarity Cove, avoiding the one-way evacuation route headed out of Charleston proper. Red sipped coffee from a local Gas 'n Go, scowling faintly at the bitter taste.

"It's not looking good. The wind's picking up," Cyril commented, keeping a white-knuckled grip on the leather steering wheel. "Figures that when Trina finally turns up, it's in someplace that's about to be underwater."

Red saw him give a nervous glance to the rough waves pounding the shore.

"What's the matter? You afraid of a little rain?"

Cyril shrugged his massive shoulders, returning his eyes to the road and slowing the vehicle as two teens on foot darted in front of them. "I'm not much of a swimmer, that's all. Like I said before, I don't know why we couldn't wait until this blows over—"

"Because I said so, that's why," Red snapped, tired of repeating himself. He had a cool half-mil to recoup, one way or another, and he wasn't taking a chance on the opportunity getting away. Sipping from the foam cup, he continued his watch along the beach as the vehicle moved forward. A few thrill-seekers still roamed the shore, strutting around with surfboards under their arms as if the impending hurricane might turn the Atlantic into the Pacific and make it the perfect place to hang ten. The idiots would deserve it if Mother Nature washed them away in the storm surge. He squinted at a police officer that had reached the surfers, his body movements indicating they were being told to leave.

"What if he was feedin' us a line of shit? You thought about that, boss?"

Red pressed his lips together. He knew in his gut the private investigator hadn't lied to them. Men being threatened with extreme violence rarely did, not if giving up the desired information could keep them breathing.

One of the girls at the Blue Iris had come to Red about the man who'd been asking around about Trina. He'd had a few drinks and a lap dance in the Champagne Room while talking to her, telling her enough about himself that it hadn't been all that hard to track him down. After Cyril had landed a few well-placed punches, the once-tough PI had blubbered like a bitch, abandoning all rules of client confidentiality. He had been hired by phone by a man named *Carter St. Clair*, he'd confessed. And while his client's number had a New York City area code, St. Clair had instructed him to send the invoice to him at a hotel outside Charleston, South Carolina.

The St. Clair.

Red thought of the photos he'd been sent and their beach-like locale, his radar tingling. The PI wouldn't be issuing anyone a warning. Once they had gotten the information they wanted, Cyril had snapped his neck, dropped him back into his desk chair and then set his office on fire.

"Been through what I've been through just to end up drowned," Cyril muttered under his breath.

"Take a right," Red instructed, having seen the street sign at nearly the same time the automated voice on the GPS sprang to life. Frowning, he lowered the window and tossed out the remainder of the foul-tasting coffee, including the cup. Cyril turned the vehicle onto a long stretch of peninsula, its road bordered by gnarled live oaks. Their massive limbs stretched across the road, garlands of Spanish moss swinging in the ominous breeze.

They rode in silence until the asphalt turned into cobblestone, leaving them idling in front of a black wrought-iron gate with a large brass plate across it. *The St. Clair* was engraved on the plate in elegant black script.

Cyril whistled. "Swanky place."

They passed through the entrance and got closer to the grand, antebellum-style hotel just as the drizzle kicked up a notch, blurring the windshield between each sweep of the wipers. Vacationers stood under the hotel's awning as bellmen loaded their luggage into the backs of waiting luxury cars.

Like rats leaving a sinking ship, Red thought, studying the oversize rear of a woman in a hot-pink jogging suit as she rummaged through her designer purse and tipped the bellman.

He'd never been much for the beach. His skin burned too easily, and he hated the sand that was everywhere—in the hotel carpet, the floorboards of cars, in his shoes. But Devin had been a real waterdog. He could almost see his little brother at the age of ten or so, waving at him from the plank of a diving board before disappearing headfirst into a pool. Red shoved away the image and the emotion it conjured inside him, reminding himself why he was here. Devin, idiot asshole that he was, had taken something that didn't belong to him. And his strongly held conviction was that his brother's girl had made off with the bounty. He planned to extract some sweet revenge for his troubles, too. The SUV passed through the parking lot, mostly empty except for a smattering of vehicles.

He dug out his cell phone and called the hotel.

"Carter St. Clair," he demanded when an operator finally answered, but he was told Mr. St. Clair had departed due to the impending storm. Red hung up, pissed. "He's not here."

"Smart man. We should go, too—"

"Slow down," Red ordered, annoyed by Cyril's perpetual whining. "And run the wipers faster. I can't see a goddamn thing."

At the edge of the lot, there were several covered parking spots in an open-front, bricked structure, all of them marked *Reserved*. But only one still held a car. Red sat up a little straighter, squinting at the convertible. Its top was up, but it still made his heart skip a beat in recognition. Reaching inside the glove box, he pulled out the photos, flipping through them. The *maybe* Trina stood next to a cherry-red Lexus convertible in the images. She'd been in conversation with the female driver, oblivious to the photos that were being snapped.

"Stop." Red unleashed his seat belt and climbed from the SUV. Shoulders hunched against the drizzle, he stalked to the car, then bent forward and peered through the driver's side window. A miniature disco ball hung from the rearview mirror. The same as the convertible in the photo. He loped back to the shelter of the SUV, brushing the rain from his hair as he got inside. "Go ahead and park so we can check the place out."

"You got it, boss."

They were so close. Red's mouth formed a grim line. If Trina wasn't here at the hotel, she was somewhere in this town—unless she had already hightailed it out. If so, they would find a place to hole up and wait for her to return.

Hurricane or not, he was going to find her.

CHAPTER THIRTY-FOUR

STANDING IN THE circular driveway in front of the Big House, Mark closed the trunk to Olivia's older-model, mint-condition Mercedes with a soft whump. They'd decided to use it for the trip to Augusta since Carter had only a rental—an open-air Hummer, of all things—and Mercer's convertible was too small for the four of them plus luggage.

Lifting his daughter into his arms, Mark kissed her cheek. Emily wore a yellow rain slicker over her T-shirt and shorts, as well as rubber boots designed to look like cheerful frogs. He felt his heart tug. "Be a good girl for Aunt Mercer and Nana, okay, Emily?"

"*You come*, Daddy," she begged, sounding fretful. Mark suspected she sensed the somber mood. A steady drizzle had set in over the town, and that would only increase throughout the day as the outer bands of the storm approached.

"I'll be there. Just as soon as all the hotel guests and workers are safe and out of the storm."

"*I* stay, too." Emily's small hands clung to his neck.

"You can't, sweetheart," he said, his chest tight.

Mercer stepped forward. "C'mon, Em. Let Daddy get his work done so he can hurry up and join us. Remember, we talked about this at home?" Taking her hand, she coaxed Emily away once Mark had gently disentangled himself and placed her back down.

Carter had just finished securing Emily's booster chair in the backseat of the Mercedes. Wiping his hands on his jeans, he straightened and trudged over to Mark while Mercer settled Emily into her seat.

"Drive safely," Mark advised.

"Precious cargo." Carter gave a serious nod. He regarded Mark from under the brim of his ball cap. "I'm calling your cell and making sure you're out of here before sundown. I might even want you to send me digital photos of interstate markers as proof."

"Don't count on it." The rain picked up a bit, and Mark pushed his damp hair back from his forehead. "I'm planning to take the back roads, head north and circle around."

The two men shared a brief embrace. A second later, Mercer came up, holding a rain poncho she'd found in the backseat over her head. Standing on tiptoe, she put her free arm around Mark's shoulder and hugged him, too.

"You need to remember the hotel can be replaced," she whispered against his ear. "You can't."

Wind caused the palm trees in front of the house to sway, their fronds fluttering and snapping.

"You should all get going," Mark pointed out.

As Carter and Mercer got into the car, Mark turned toward the house's columned front porch. Olivia appeared stoic as she held a black umbrella, her pale hair protected by a clear rain bonnet. Mark went over and escorted her to the front passenger seat. He started to open the door, but she placed her hand on his arm.

"Twenty-six years ago, I left this place with you children—Mercer just an infant—only to find a pile of rubble and your father standing in the middle of it when I returned," Olivia recounted softly, looking back toward her home. "What if it happens again?"

"It won't," Mark promised. "The hotel and your house will be here when you come back. What about Marisol?"

"She left yesterday with her daughter's family." She patted his cheek, her blue eyes worried. "Please be careful and join us as soon as you can. I love you, darling. And I want you to know...I'm sorry things didn't work out between you and the restaurateur."

"You're lying," Mark noted. "But I appreciate the effort."

Olivia blushed a bit. "What happened, exactly? No one tells me a thing anymore."

"It was like you said, Mom." Mark squinted at the ominous sky, not meeting her gaze. "She and I...just weren't right for each other."

"But at least you know now that you do have the potential for happiness again. That your life can go on without Shelley. That's a good thing, Mark."

Mark simply nodded, his heart heavy, unable to say more.

He opened the car door and helped Olivia inside. His clothing and hair soaked, he stood next to his station wagon and watched as the sedan pulled from the driveway and headed out.

≈

As it grew later in the day, the hotel still held a small handful of guests, most of whom were traveling inland by car, but for one reason or another still straggled behind despite repeated prodding. Mark worked at the front desk in the lobby, helping with the last checkouts since only one of his clerks remained. Outside, the rain preceding Hurricane Gina had set in, and it appeared hours later than it actually was due to the darkened skies. The cast-iron streetlamps around the hotel's exterior were already on, their lights emitting a fuzzy golden glow in the all-pervading grayness.

A chartered bus idled outside, awaiting the remainder of hotel employees who did not have their own transportation to evacuate. Mark had arranged for the bus to take them and their families to one of the hurricane shelters that had been set up inland.

Hopefully, in another hour he might be ready to leave, as well.

He had just finished fielding a complaint from a guest, upset that the bad weather had cut short his vacation, when his cell phone rang. Extracting it, Mark saw the name on the screen.

"Todd," he answered. "Hold on a minute, all right?"

He signaled his departure to the lone desk clerk, then walked to the rear of the lobby where it was quiet enough to hear.

"Have you headed for high ground yet?" Todd asked once Mark resumed the call. "I hear they're calling for a real gully washer."

Mark glanced at a family who hustled past him, hauling their own suitcases since bellmen had gotten scarce. "Not yet, but I'm working on it."

"Don't wait too long. None of that captain going down with his ship business." The attorney's tone grew serious. "Mark, I know you're probably knee-deep in this hurricane mess right now, but I've got some information for you. I thought you'd want to know, but if this isn't the right time..."

Mark felt the thud of his heart. Despite all that was going on around him, he said, "Now is good."

"I spoke with some people in the know around here. People I trust. There's some confusion, apparently. The police *do* want to talk to Trina Grissom. But she's wanted as a potential witness for the state, not as a murder suspect."

Confused himself, Mark squeezed the bridge of his nose. "I

don't understand. Samantha—Trina—she told me she killed the guy. She stabbed him to death."

"Well, I've got a copy of the autopsy report from the Shelby County Medical Examiner's Office right here in front of me." The airwaves crackled behind Todd's voice, and Mark hoped he wouldn't lose the connection. "Devin Leary died of a gunshot wound to the back of the head, execution-style. That's the official cause of death. According to my contact, the number one suspect is a Russian named Sergei Boklov. A real badass. He's an *entrepreneur* importer into the US, if you will—drugs, weapons, conflict diamonds, that kind of thing. He also leaves his signature on killings by taking an eye from the victim. Leary's corpse was missing one peeper. That's confidential information, by the way."

Mark realized he'd been holding his breath. Surprise threaded through him, as well as a flare of hope. "So you're telling me there was no stab wound?"

"The autopsy indicates Leary had a secondary wound to his throat, but it wasn't the fatal strike. It missed both the jugular and carotid. Probably bled like a son of a bitch, though. Maybe your friend *did* stab him, but this Boklov guy came in behind her and finished the job."

Trying to process all he'd just heard, Mark stared out through the rain-splattered window, a fluttering sensation in his belly. A few hundred feet out, rough waves crashed on the now-deserted beach, and it was hard to tell where the body of dark ocean stopped and the bruised sky began. Was it possible that Leary simply fainted, perhaps from seeing his own blood, and Samantha had mistakenly believed him dead?

"There's something else you should know," Todd said, hesitating. "This Trina Grissom…she has no criminal record, but her name comes up several times in a dossier the Feds' Organized

Crime Task Force maintains on the Leary brothers. Miss Grissom was brought into the hospital on more than one occasion after being beaten by the deceased."

A cold sickness washed over him. Samantha told him Devin Leary had been dangerous. She said she'd stabbed him in self-defense. But she hadn't gone into much detail, and Mark had been so distressed by her deception that he hadn't pushed for information. The confirmation that she had been physically, repeatedly abused hit him hard. He massaged his forehead, still keeping the phone to his ear.

"Apparently, the cops urged her to charge Leary with assault, but she refused every time. Insisted he didn't do it. Probably afraid to tell the truth—can't say I blame her," Todd continued. "The gist I got was that the Memphis PD, probably the FBI, too, would still like to talk to her. Even if she didn't witness the murder—and by your account, she didn't—as the live-in girlfriend, they figure she was in a position back then to know about illegal business dealings the Learys might have had with Boklov. They've been trying to put Boklov and Devin's brother, Red, away for years."

After a long silence, Todd asked, "You still there, Mark?"

He swallowed past the lump in his throat. "Yeah. I'm just trying to get my mind wrapped around this."

"The good news is your friend isn't a murderer. At least not according to the Memphis Police."

"And none of what you found out could lead anyone to her?"

"I was careful—my sources are airtight."

They talked a few more minutes, then Mark thanked him and disconnected the phone. He ran a hand over his face, his breath temporarily bottling up in his chest until he forced himself to exhale. He had to tell Samantha what he'd found out.

A call to her cell phone elicited no response. In fact, the device went straight to voice mail, as if it was turned off. Even if she'd already left town, she would have her cell with her. He left an urgent message, asking her to call him. The news was too big, too confidential, to leave in a voice mail.

Mark checked his wristwatch, noticing that time was running out. The lobby had grown quieter, but there were still a few people remaining. He would do what he could to clear the hotel and secure it quickly, and then he would go by Samantha's apartment and the café to check for her before he left town.

≋

The day had not gone according to plan. Samantha's intention had been to finish storm-proofing the café as best she could, load up her car with some of her belongings and food donations for the shelter, and be on her way out by early afternoon. What she hadn't counted on was an elderly neighbor falling on the rain-slicked sidewalk at her apartment building when Samantha had been there, packing her suitcase.

She had of course driven Mrs. Holtz to the urgent care center and waited while her ankle was X-rayed. Fortunately, it had turned out to be only a bad sprain. Then she'd taken the woman, slowly hobbling on crutches, back to her apartment that was two doors from her own. She'd sat with her until a nephew arrived to drive her and her two Siamese cats inland, since she wouldn't be able to manage the car's brakes and gas pedal with the injury.

By the time Samantha made it back to the café to pick up the food to deliver to the hurricane shelter, the streetlamps along the town square were already glowing. Rain smacked the Camry's roof, and a patrol car with its siren on moved past her on the otherwise mostly empty street. Pulling into the alleyway behind the Sea Breeze Centre, she saw Luther's old pickup parked next to the

Dumpster. Turning off the car, she opened the door and made a run for it.

"You should already be gone," Luther criticized as Samantha raced through the service entrance into the kitchen. He wore a rain poncho, although his shaved head was uncovered.

"Don't ask—something came up." She did the best she could to wring her long hair free of excess water and then tugged at the sodden tank top stuck to her abdomen. "You really didn't have to meet me here, Luther. You should be at home where it's dry, at least."

"I figure the faster we get this food into your car, the sooner you'll be on your way out. I can't believe Mr. St. Clair's lettin' you gallivant around by yourself with this storm rollin' in. He's supposed to be a gentleman—"

"Luther," Samantha said, interrupting his tirade. She couldn't stand to hear Mark being taken to task. She shook her head. "Mark and I...we're not seeing each other anymore. He isn't responsible for me."

"Oh," he muttered heavily, looking disappointed. "That's too bad. I thought you two were a real good match."

At his words, an emptiness settled inside her. She had deluded herself into thinking so, too, until her past had come calling.

"Well, I guess we better get you on the road, then."

Big muscles bulging, he hauled a box of perishables from the counter and shouldered his way out the door, headed to her car. Samantha picked up another box and followed him outside, the rain cold on her bare arms. They worked together until every last inch of available space in the Camry was loaded with food that wouldn't survive the absence of refrigeration. Then together they darted back inside. This time, Samantha grabbed a towel from the pantry and used it to try to dry herself off.

"You ready to go?"

"I'd like to have one last look around," she admitted. "Just to make sure everything's unplugged."

But in truth, she knew the café was ready to be locked up. She had been there all that morning, helping Luther get the equipment up on their makeshift risers. She just needed another chance to commit the place to memory, in case the storm destroyed the one thing that had ever really belonged to her.

Luther waited as Samantha took a brief tour around the storefront. It looked desolate, with chairs stacked on tabletops, the shelving empty and refrigerated display case bare.

"Okay," she murmured finally, throat tight. "It's time."

She shut off the lights. As they walked back toward the kitchen, Luther snapped his fingers. "Damn near forgot my rain hat. I hung it in the storeroom."

He took a right while Samantha continued on toward the kitchen. As she cleared the entryway, an icy chill curled around her spine, nearly stopping her heart. Two men stood just inside the service door, dripping with water. Both had guns. Samantha reeled backward.

"Greetings from Memphis," Red Leary said without cracking a smile.

CHAPTER THIRTY-FIVE

LIKE HIS BROTHER, lankiness emphasized the hard sinews of Red's body. But where Devin had been handsome, Red's features were rawboned, appearing overly sharp under a mop of cinnamon hair now streaked with gray. As he knocked the rain from his shoulders, his eyes narrowed on Samantha.

"So it really *is* you."

Doom tunneled through her. Samantha tried to find her voice—to scream for help, to call to Luther to warn him, but her vocal cords were paralyzed. Stumbling from the kitchen, she made a dash for the storefront, only to remember the entrance had been secured by the building's hurricane shutters. That knowledge didn't keep her from trying to wedge open the door.

"Nice place."

She whirled, her lungs flattening. Red had trailed her into the café. His companion, an oversize lout with thick shoulders and no neck, stood behind him. "I forgot how much you liked to cook. All those little cakes and pies you used to make for the girls. 'Course, Devin said it was a waste of your *talents* to put you in the kitchen."

Samantha's breath shallowed as he came closer, her heat beating wildly as panic rioted inside her. Lenny was dead—how had Red still found her? She wrapped her arms around her belly, her legs weak and threatening to give out.

"The police are patrolling the streets," she managed to get out. "An evacuation is underway. If I scream—"

His hand shot out, catching her by the throat and cutting off her breath. Her blood curdled as he dragged her to him. She could smell the spearmint scent of his chewing gum and the underlying nicotine as his face hovered inches from hers. "Make no mistake. You *will* scream before I'm done with you. Besides, that wind starting to pick up out there? No one's going to hear you."

He shoved her backward. Samantha fell against the wall, her bottom landing painfully on the floor. Her hand to her throat, she coughed, her eyes filling with tears. Her hope was that Luther had gotten out. In her peripheral vision, she could see the other man— was his name Cyril?—looming nearby. He was as solidly built as a refrigerator, with a blunt face and flat-eyed expression.

Red looked around the café. "How'd you pay for all this, Trina?"

Her voice shook. "I-I took out a loan from the bank—"

"Bullshit." He motioned to Cyril. A sob escaped her as the man yanked her upright.

"Try again. Tell me how you paid for this place."

Samantha blinked, unsure of what Red wanted to know. "I'm telling the truth! I worked at clubs in New York and paid my way through culinary school. But I-I took out a loan to open the—"

The hard slap across her face buckled her knees. Cyril grabbed her, keeping her standing.

"You better tell him the truth, sugar."

Red's eyes burned angrily. Taking his gum from his mouth, he wadded the mass into a ball, jamming it under one of the table-tops. Then he withdrew a pack of Marlboros and a lighter from his pocket. Firing up a cigarette, he took his time, making a show of drawing the stream of nicotine into his lungs. Samantha's blood roared in her ears.

"Make it easy on yourself and fess up about the diamonds. It *was* only fair, right? Devin siphoned them off Boklov, so you grabbed them from wherever he stashed them and got the hell out when the shit hit the fan."

Her stomach roiled with terror. Lenny had mentioned diamonds, too. And she *did* remember Boklov. A menacing brute with a Russian accent, he had been in Devin's company on multiple occasions. "Please believe me! I-I don't know what you're talking about! I don't have any diamonds!"

"My brother was a fucking idiot," Red ground out, jabbing his cigarette in front of her as smoke billowed from his nostrils in twin streams. "But you always had a brain, Trina. I could tell that about you."

She shook her head, cowering. "Red, I-I swear to you—"

"They weren't in Devin's apartment. Boklov turned the place upside down. They were missing, and so were you. In my book, two and two sure as *shit* makes four."

"I-I didn't take anything!"

Red shifted his gaze to Cyril and nodded. Cyril jerked Samantha back against the barrel wall of his chest, locking her in place with a meaty forearm across her sternum and trapping her arms. She cried out, struggling. Red moved forward until the hot embers of his cigarette were an inch from Samantha's face. Fear sawed through her, hollowing out her chest. Panting, she turned her head away and closed her eyes.

"Devin had good taste, at least. It'd be a shame to ruin that pretty face."

"Please," Samantha whispered, her throat clogging with tears.

"See, I *know* you're lying." He leaned even closer, voice lowering into a rasp as his breath blew the damp tendrils of her hair. "Devin *told* Boklov you had the diamonds. In fact, it was the last thing my brother said before Boklov blew his brains out. I hold *you* responsible for that, Trina. He couldn't give back what he didn't have."

Things were moving too quickly, her mind racing and none of this making sense. *She* had killed Devin, not Boklov. Confusion and fear clawed at her. "This…this is all wrong! Wait, please—"

"No more waiting."

Cyril roughly fisted his hand in her hair and snapped her head back, exposing Samantha's throat. Her heart lurched. Sobbing, she struggled but was able to move only an inch or two. The side of Cyril's gun lay against her temple as he kept her clamped in place.

"I want the diamonds or I want the money for them—a half-million dollars." Red moved the burning end of the cigarette until she could no longer see it. The butt was almost against her skin, in the hollow of her neck in the most tender of places, under her left ear. She knew because she felt its frightening heat. She moaned softly, tears slipping down her cheeks.

"What'll it be, Trina? A hot kiss on your neck to start with?"

But the excruciating burn never came. Instead, Samantha crumpled to the floor with Cyril, his weight taking her down as he fell. Breath knocked out of her, she saw Luther standing where the other man had been a second earlier. He wielded a broomstick from the storeroom like a baseball bat. He'd been hiding, apparently, waiting for what he hoped would be the right time. Samantha shoved at the unconscious man sprawled half on top of her, crushing the air from her lungs. His weapon lay on the floor out of reach. She cried out upon seeing Red's gun pointing at Luther.

"Move again, and you're dead."

"Luther!" Samantha cried. "Do what he says!"

But Luther glared fiercely at Red. "How 'bout it, Stretch? You want to put down that gun and take me on like a real man? Or are you just about beatin' on women—"

She screamed, her insides twisting as the gun went off, the sound more like an arrow shot from a bow than a booming firearm. A silencer. Luther stumbled. Samantha's world stopped as he fell. Red picked up Cyril's gun and tucked it into his pants as, sobbing, Samantha finally pulled her way free and crawled to where Luther lay. He writhed, his forehead wrinkled in pain. Blood leaked through the poncho at his left upper arm. The smell of blood and gunpowder burned like bile in her throat. Sorrow flooded through her.

"The next one'll be through his heart." Red stalked closer, standing over them and pointing the barrel at Luther's heaving chest. "You better start talking, Trina, or homeboy here's a dead man and you're next."

She had to pull herself out of her blind panic, knowing it was the only way Luther might survive. Body racked with tremors, she tried to think. "You...you said Devin told Boklov I had the diamonds. What exactly did he say?"

Red let out a growl. "What the fuck do I care?"

"I'm trying to figure this out!" Samantha snapped despite her fear. Her eyes slid to Cyril as he came to, moaning and clutching the back of his head. Now there were two of them again.

"Boklov said you took them. Devin was talking some nonsense about you and some goddamned toy..."

An image of Emily holding the worn teddy bear sprang to her mind, stealing away what little breath remained inside her. She recalled Devin going through her suitcase that night, how livid he'd been when he had pulled out her belongings, especially the bear. Had he hidden the stolen diamonds inside Walton, thinking no one would ever look there?

Then, if they'd been found, he could have blamed the theft on her.

"I'm running out of patience," Red warned.

"All right...wait!" On her knees, Samantha bent over Luther, doing her best to shield him. Swallowing hard, she turned her head and stared up into Red's hateful eyes.

"I know where the diamonds are. All of them."

CHAPTER THIRTY-SIX

"YOU SHOULD ALREADY be inland, Mr. St. Clair," the young police officer advised, handing Mark back his driver's license through the Volvo's window. His shoulders were hunched against the wind, and he wore a yellow vinyl raincoat with a clear elastic baggie protecting his uniform cap. Behind him, the sky appeared bruised, the last remaining daylight slowly fading away. "We're getting ready to hunker down ourselves. One of the local cell towers is already out, too. Things are going to start getting real ugly fast."

"I'm headed out now," he assured the officer.

"We'll get out to check on your property as soon as the storm's passed and the road's clear."

Mark thanked him. Once the man had taken a step back, he closed the window and pulled back onto the road, staring through the onslaught of rain hitting the windshield. But as soon as he was out of the patrolman's line of vision, he took a right toward Samantha's apartment instead of getting on the road that led out of town.

He had to check. She was probably long gone by now, but she hadn't returned his phone messages, even when he had said it was urgent. Maybe that was because of the cell phone outage, but it could also be that she just didn't want to talk to him. He couldn't blame her. Mark berated himself for the time he'd let pass without making contact, using the impending storm as an excuse to distance himself.

As he drove, he tried Samantha's number again. This time, the call failed to connect at all. A strong blast of wind nearly moved the car on the road just as the pink stucco of the Wayfarer Apartments appeared on his right. Its parking lot was nearly empty, and Samantha's car wasn't there.

Still, he pulled into the space in front of her apartment. Bracing himself against the downpour, he got out and ran to her stoop, knocking on the door and calling her name. No answer. That left one place to check before he got the hell out, too.

His jeans, sneakers and T-shirt soaked, he returned to his car. Wind blew and palm trees swayed as he swiped water from his face and pulled out of the lot.

Reaching the downtown square a few minutes later, he saw that it looked like a ghost town. There were no cars on the streets, and the few buildings that were without hurricane shutters had plywood boards nailed over the windows and doors. Traffic lights at the intersections swung on their cables like pendulums, flashing a cautionary yellow. Already, he saw that a telephone line was down and lay snakelike across the road in front of the pharmacy.

He felt a wave of foolishness for coming here, knowing he was probably wasting precious time when he should be on the road. That feeling remained as Mark passed the Sea Breeze Centre... until he rounded the corner and peered into the rear alley. Surprise made his skin tingle. Samantha's car sat next to Luther's ancient pickup.

Also disturbing, the service door to Café Bella stood open in the driving rain.

Mark parked behind Samantha's car and cut the engine. He got out, making a run for the yawning door.

"Samantha?" He clicked the light switch on the wall inside the entrance, but the interior remained dark.

"Samantha!" he called again, stamping water from his feet. Mark walked farther into the kitchen and then felt his way into the shadowed storefront. Only a thin film of light seeped in from the outside.

His heart began to beat harder at the pounding coming from somewhere down the back hallway that led to the restrooms and storeroom. He traveled in that direction, keeping a hand on the wall in the grainy darkness. His stomach quivered as the closet came into sight. An iron bar from one of the café shelves had been wedged underneath the door's latch. More pounding shook the door.

"Hang on!" he yelled. Had they been robbed? Mark tugged at the bar until it came free and opened the door. His scalp prickled at the sight of Luther leaning heavily against the wall. He wore a T-shirt, and even in the shadows Mark could see blood staining his left sleeve. A cloth of some kind had been tied around his arm to staunch the flow. Samantha wasn't with him.

"They took her, Mr. St. Clair."

Fear dug into Mark's gut. "Who did?"

"Two men." Luther grimaced in pain. "Pretty sure one of 'em was Red Leary."

His heart turned over at the name. How had Leary found her? And if Samantha hadn't been the one to kill Leary's brother, what did he want with her? The money she'd supposedly stolen? "Luther, *listen to me*. Do you know where they went? What kind of car they're driving?"

When Luther weakly shook his head, Mark pulled his phone from his pocket, hoping to alert the police, before remembering the outage. He tried anyway, but there was still no service. He found his way back to the darkened kitchen, trying the landline there, but it was dead. Mark thought of the wire he'd seen down in front of the pharmacy. He ran a hand over his face, tamping down panic and trying not to think about what might be happening to Samantha right now.

"Shoulda known I hadn't seen the last of 'em."

Luther's deep voice caused Mark to turn around. Blood leaked down the larger man's arm as he wobbled unsteadily into the kitchen.

"Last of who?"

"Took care of the first one. Oily little bastard with a comb-over. Came in here a couple of weeks ago, threatening Sam. She was so shook up she left his note in the storeroom, telling her where to meet him."

The Sea King.

"But *I* met up with him first." Luther's features had hardened, and for the first time Mark believed he saw a flash of the man who had indeed served time in a maximum-security penitentiary. "Followed him into Charleston. Cozied up to him at a bar and helped him get his drink on. Little by little, he gets drunker and starts tellin' me his business...about the Blue Iris and Leary...why he was here."

Mark went still. So Luther had learned Samantha's real identity, too.

"Sam's a kind, fair woman. Don't care what nobody says."

Luther's mouth twisted with disgust. "The way that perverted son of a bitch talked about her—the things he said he was gonna do to her before handing her over to Leary…"

Luther shrugged his big shoulders, his gaze meaningful. "Not my fault if the fool can't hold his liquor. *Or swim.*"

He swayed then, nearly crashing to the ground. Mark found a chair and pulled it out for him. "Sit down, Luther. You're bleeding pretty bad."

"It's a flesh wound, is all. Bullet grazed my arm pretty good. But the fat one hit me with somethin' before they threw me in the closet. I'm dizzy as hell." Gingerly, he touched his crown. His voice grew ragged as he looked up at Mark. "Sam's the only reason I'm breathin' right now. She told 'em she would take 'em to what they wanted, but only if they left me here alive. But I could tell by their eyes they're plannin' to come back to kill me, soon as they're done with her."

Mark swallowed, his throat dry. "They wanted something?"

"Diamonds."

He thought of what Todd Hamilton had told him about Boklov.

"Said she could take 'em to where they were. At first she swore she didn't know, then all the sudden she started talkin' about some stuffed animal."

Mark straightened, a heavy feeling inside him. The PI Carter hired had said Samantha had stolen a large amount of money. Was it possible the teddy bear she had given Emily contained not actual money but…diamonds? But why would Samantha have given Emily the toy if something so valuable was hidden inside it?

Regardless, adrenaline made his blood rush. Mark suddenly knew where they had gone. Samantha was taking them to his house to retrieve the bear.

The problem was that it was no longer there. Mark had it in the backseat of his car. Mercer had texted him earlier, asking him to bring it with him when he joined them in Augusta. Emily had forgotten it and wanted it with her.

"They're gonna hurt her. They already started."

Mark's stomach clenched. "How long have they been gone?"

"Maybe ten minutes."

He had to get back to the resort. Now.

Mark tried his cell once more, cursing under his breath when it registered no service. Then he handed it to Luther. Service would most likely come back in town before it did on the neck of land the hotel was on. "Keep trying to reach the police on this. If you get through, tell them I've gone back to my house at 22 Ocean Lane on the resort property. That's where they've taken Samantha."

"I'm coming, too."

He stood unsteadily. As much as Mark could use his help, the man was in no condition. He would only slow him down. "Stay here, Luther. Just keep dialing emergency services. If you think you can, go outside on the street and try to flag down a cop. Maybe one will pass by."

He took off through the service door, launching himself into his car and quickly backing out despite the rain gushing from the downspouts and the standing water on the asphalt. If he was lucky, the patrol car that had stopped him earlier would still be out on the road. Maybe it had even kept Leary's vehicle from venturing farther. If not, he could try driving to the police station for help, but it was on the other side of town—a ten-minute loss each way—and he had no guarantee anyone on the small force would be there. He knew what those men would do to Samantha when they got to his house and couldn't find what they wanted.

There wasn't time to waste.

Nor was there any guarantee the peninsula road would remain accessible for much longer. With the storm moving in, parts of it would no doubt begin to flood. All along the way, Mark kept his eyes open for blue lights cutting through the downpour that would signal assistance. But the roads were completely deserted now, with even the police holed up inside somewhere. There wasn't time to drive around searching for a stray squad car. Every second counted.

Passing the Rarity Cove town welcome sign, Mark squinted through the rain hitting the windshield. A line of lanky palm trees bent in the storm's outer bands like arthritic old men. His knuckles white on the steering wheel, he drove as fast as he could and hoped he wouldn't end up hydroplaning and spinning into a ditch. He had to get there.

He was unarmed, but he had what they wanted.

He was the only chance Samantha had.

The sky had turned completely black by the time the Cadillac Escalade roared into the bungalow's driveway. The oceanfront home appeared dark and deserted, its windows shuttered. The once picturesque trees surrounding it swayed wildly.

There had been no other choice. Samantha would never have brought them here if she hadn't been absolutely certain Mark and his family had left for Augusta hours ago. She sat rigidly beside Red in the backseat, listening to her rapid heartbeat in her ears and the hard drum of rain on the vehicle's top. Red's fingers cupped the back of her neck, his touch causing revulsion to pool in her stomach. His other hand held his gun, which lay across his thigh. The SUV rocked in a gust.

"We need to make this fast, boss. If it keeps raining like this, the road back's going to flood," Cyril pointed out nervously.

"We'll go when I get what I want," Red snapped. "I'm not leaving a half-mil worth of diamonds to be washed away in the storm tide."

Flinching with cold fear, Samantha closed her eyes as he put the tip of the gun's silencer against her temple. Her heart felt like it might explode. "And we *are* going to find them here, just like you said—right, babe?"

With a heavy sigh of resignation, Cyril cut the engine, their view of the bungalow blurring once the wipers stopped and the twin beams of headlights shut off. They had driven over several rows of flowering bushes when the gate cordoning off the private road failed to open, even with the passcode Samantha relayed. She tried to console herself with the knowledge that she had gotten the men away from Luther. Her hope was that he would find some way to escape—use something in the storeroom to break down the door, if he had enough strength—before they returned for him. And she knew they would.

She felt a terrible tension in her body. She had no illusions. Red would leave no one behind as a witness.

Rain battered the parked vehicle, darkness making it impossible to see the roiling sea that was only a short distance away. Red braced the SUV's door open against another fierce gust, gripping Samantha's arm and dragging her out roughly behind him. The hard rain stung her skin like needle pricks, blinding her as the three of them made their way onto the covered porch.

"Open the door."

Her insides twisted as the gun jabbed low in her back. Although the swing and rockers had been put away, the urn that sat on the stairs, where the key was usually hidden, had been placed against the home's exterior wall and under the relative safety of the porch eaves. Samantha checked beneath it, but the key was gone. "The key…it's not here."

With a curse, Cyril brushed her aside. He pulled away the plywood that covered the door's panes with his bare hands and shattered the glass using the butt of his gun. Then he reached a beefy arm inside and turned the lock.

"Shut off that noise," Red ordered as they entered, referring to the loud whine of the security system, which must have been running on a backup battery. Somehow, Samantha managed to remember that passcode, too. With trembling fingers, she obediently punched the numbers into the keypad as Cyril went around flipping light switches in vain.

"No electricity," he said.

"Of course not, moron. Look for a flashlight or some candles." Red shoved Samantha farther into the house. "Now get me what I came for."

He followed behind like the grim reaper as Samantha walked on weak legs down the shadowed hallway, her arms gripped over her clenched stomach. Like the rest of the house, hurricane shutters covered the windows in Emily's bedroom, making it dark as a cave without even the seashell nightlight giving out its pink glow. Samantha felt her way along the whitewashed shelves that held an expansive collection of dolls and stuffed animals, searching for Walton's familiar, worn fur.

He wasn't there.

Blood rushing in her ears, she moved to the bed, running her hands over the comforter in search of the bear. But there were only throw pillows piled against the headboard. Dropping to her knees, she felt frantically under the bed. The night she had made dinner here, Walton had been in this room.

"Well?" Red's voice was strained with impatience.

"I-I'm looking—"

She whimpered as he sank his hand into her hair and yanked her back to her feet. "You *said* they were here. What's your fucking scheme? To get us marooned out here?"

"No! I swear!" But her time was ebbing away. Samantha's chest hurt with the knowledge. All she could think about was that she didn't want Mark or Emily to find her body here. If she begged, maybe Red would discard her somewhere else, possibly on the beach for the rising waters to claim her.

She had a sudden, sickening realization. She'd made a horrible snap decision in bringing them here. Samantha had been trying to save Luther's life, but had she just exposed Mark and his family, too? She had counted on the teddy bear being here, on them taking the diamonds and leaving. But if Emily had it with her...

Samantha startled as a flash of light flooded the room, leaping in around the shutters' edges and exposing the hard, angry lines of Red's face. At the same second, a booming explosion jarred the walls. It must have been the transformer farther down on the resort property.

"Jesus, Mary and Joseph," Cyril intoned from the doorway, where he held a flashlight.

"Shut up!" Red warned, turning his head and pointing a finger in the larger man's direction. Then he returned his attention to Samantha.

"Like I said before, you're a smart girl." His voice lowered into a husky rasp as he ran the tip of his index finger down her cheek. "You know I'm going to kill you, right?"

Her body gave a hard shudder as heat burned behind her eyelids.

"But I promise you this. Give me those diamonds right now, and I'll make it easy on you."

She made a choking sound as the long barrel of the silencer caressed a point behind her ear. "One shot. You won't feel a thing."

But then he gripped Samantha's chin, his fingers digging into the soft flesh underneath. Her jaw felt as if it might snap, and tears ran down her cheeks at the sharp flare of pain.

"I want the diamonds. Now. Or I take you apart piece by piece, Trina. It's up to you."

He released her, shoving his gun into the waistband of his pants. Samantha held her aching jaw as Cyril moved the flashlight's beam around the room. Her intuition told her Walton wasn't anywhere in the house. She wouldn't be able to produce the diamonds.

"What's it going to be?"

"I-I don't have them," she managed to whisper.

His eyes narrowed as he regarded her. Red made a sweeping gesture with his arms and roared, "You *said* they were here!"

Samantha wrapped her arms around herself.

His nostrils flared. He cut his gaze to Cyril and began to roll up his shirtsleeves. "Give me that light. If the diamonds—any of them—are here, find them. Start tossing the place while I spend some time with my brother's whore."

Cyril disappeared from the doorway, a fat ghost.

The hard blow sent Samantha sprawling backward onto the bed. The room tilted, starbursts crowding her vision. She felt a tingling numbness in her cheekbone that quickly turned into screaming pain. Red set the flashlight on the dresser so that it bathed her in its harsh light. His deadly quiet voice felt like a razor scraping over her nerves.

"Where are they?"

Samantha's heartbeat galloped. Managing to sit up, she breathed shallowly through her mouth, trying not to hyperventilate. Fear shrouded her like a veil, but she would never, ever tell him they were with Mark's daughter or where the St. Clairs had gone. Outside, rain pummeled the house. The winds howled.

"This is a girl's room. Does the kid who lives here have that bear?"

"She only has the stuffed animal!" she lied. "I took out the diamonds and sold them! They're gone!"

He scowled hard. "Then where's the money?"

Samantha shrugged weakly. "I-I spent it, most of it, a long time ago. You were right all along—I used what was left of it to start the café."

He cracked his knuckles. The sound of it made her stomach roll. "You're jerking me around, *bitch*. First you say you know where they are, you drag me all the way out here in the middle of a goddamn hurricane and now you're telling me they're *gone?*"

"I had to get you away from Luther..." She lifted her chin and forced herself to look him in the eye with defiance. She had to make him believe her. "And I *was* hoping the storm would trap you here."

Electricity charged the air around them. In the flashlight's swath, Samantha could see him evaluating her claim. Then his lips curled into a thin smile that belied the glittering rage in his eyes.

"We've got some time to kill while Cyril looks around. Devin always said you were a tight little ride. Maybe I'll give you a go."

Her skin tightened with revulsion and terror. She searched the shadowy room for something, anything, she could use as a weapon against him. If she killed him, he wouldn't be able to hurt anyone else. Red advanced, but Samantha scrambled backward and kicked him, missing her mark but hitting him hard enough in the thigh to make him release a blistering curse. She attempted to crawl off the bed, but brutal hands were on her, twisting her body and flipping her onto her back despite her struggling. She strained, reaching for a pink pencil on the nightstand and jabbing hard at his eye with the pointed end. Red partially dodged the blow, the lead sinking deep into the skin over his cheekbone. He howled in pain and fury. Catching her hand, he wrested the makeshift weapon from her fingers as she screamed. Flinging it away, he drove his fist hard into her stomach. Samantha fought for breath, stunned. It hurt to fill her lungs. Reaching over, he ripped the tieback from the window's frilly curtains.

She kicked and scratched wildly at him, trying to keep him from winding the cord around her throat. But she was no match for his size or strength. She wheezed, her body arching off the bed and her hands clawing frantically as the cord cut off her breath. He straddled her, his face flushed and eyes fevered. He yanked it tauter, the veins in his arms bulging with the effort. Samantha dug her fingernails into his skin.

A horrible déjà vu fell over her.

"I know about Devin's breath games. He accidentally *killed* one of our girls with that shit. You say you sold the diamonds and spent all the money? I don't believe you! Either way, *I'm* going to get my money's worth—from you, or whoever's with that little girl."

Samantha's pulse pounded in her skull, her lungs cramping and begging for air. She reached up, trying again to scratch at his face. But deprived of oxygen, her movements had grown uncoordinated and clumsy. A panicked sweat broke out on her body. As she began to lose consciousness, he eased up a bit, allowing her to cough and take in a few feeble breaths.

"The diamonds or the money, Trina. Where's the kid with that stuffed animal? Tell me, and I might let her live."

When she only dragged air into her lungs, he drew the cord

taut. Drops of blood from where she'd wounded him with the pencil fell onto her face.

He took her to the edge of asphyxiation before relenting again, allowing only a weak gasp for air before continuing her torture. Her brain grew fuzzy, and her heart skittered in shallow, erratic beats. Red licked his lips. Dazed, Samantha was aware of his arousal straining against his pants as he watched her face. Fingers fluttering weakly at the cord around her throat, she felt helpless tears slide from the corners of her eyes.

In his own way, Red *was* raping her. His ultimate turn-on was violence, and Samantha had become his playmate. He eased and tightened the cord again and again, his smile cold.

CHAPTER THIRTY-SEVEN

"HOW MUCH MORE can you take, babe? Tell me the truth, and I'll make it all stop. Just tell me where that family went."

He loosened the cord once again as her vision began to grow dark. Lightheaded, trembling from the slow, painful bouts of suffocation, Samantha felt her throat working, but no sound emerged except ragged little gasps for air. Her fingertips were sticky with blood—her blood, she realized vaguely—from where she'd clawed at the makeshift garrote. He was killing her slowly, relentlessly. This is how it would end. And all she could do was hope that God would keep Mark and his family safe. That she hadn't doomed them, too.

"Have it your way." Red snapped the cord taut with a grunt. She convulsed, fresh pain searing her throat. But just as suddenly, it went slack, leaving her coughing. Red's head whipped around at the crashing sound that had come from the front of the house. "What the fuck? Cyril!"

The other man didn't answer.

Getting off the bed, Red hauled Samantha with him. When her legs failed to support her, he wrapped an arm around her waist and pulled her against his chest, moving to the doorway and down the hall, leading with his gun. "Cyril!"

Rain hammered the house as candles set up around the living room emitted weak, flickering light. Samantha expected to see the large bay window broken out, its shutters ripped away by the winds, or a tree poking through the roof. Instead, Cyril lay facedown on the floor, moaning. Samantha's chest squeezed. The heavy bookcase had toppled over on him, pinning the lower half of his body. Books, framed photos and shards of glass were scattered everywhere.

"I have what you want, Leary."

At the unexpected sound of Mark's voice, Samantha's damaged throat clogged with tears. Terror sluiced through her, a thousand times worse than before. *No, God, please. Don't let him be here.*

Red whirled, keeping her against his chest, his gun pointed.

Her heart turned sideways as she saw Mark standing in the shadow of the grandfather clock, also holding a gun. Confusion welled inside her. Why hadn't he gone to Augusta? He must've slipped inside and managed to push over the bookcase, taking Cyril by surprise, then confiscating his firearm. His concerned gaze met hers for a bare second before focusing on Red.

"Do you want the diamonds or not?"

He'll die, too, and it will be my fault.

Red hugged Samantha to his body, a human shield. "Where are they?"

Keeping the weapon in his right hand carefully trained, Mark reached into his pocket and pulled out a small cloth bag. He tossed it onto the area rug halfway to where Red and Samantha stood. "Leave her here and go. You can take the diamonds. Your friend's

legs are probably broken, but you can still get him out of here
before the road's completely—"

Samantha startled as Red fired into Cyril with a muted *thwap*.
A wounded accomplice was nothing but dead weight to him. A
spasm went through Cyril's big body, and then he lay still. Blood
bloomed on his back. Shocked, Samantha opened her mouth to
cry out, but only a pitiful croak emerged.

Mark appeared stunned at Red's atrocity, too, but kept calm.
"*You can have what you came for,* Leary. The road's still passable for
now—get out while you can."

"That's generous of you." Samantha's blood iced as Red placed
the tip of the silencer under her jaw. It felt hot, the acrid smell
of gunpowder strong. "But you're going to put down that gun,
asshole. Now. Unless you want to see me do to her what I just did
to him."

"You kill her, and I'm going to kill you," Mark warned.

"You really want to test that theory?"

Samantha's voice emerged hoarsely. "Don't do it, Mark, don't
put down the gun—"

"Shut up!" Red pressed the tip harder into her flesh. She shook
her head, her breath coming in cramped waves as Mark's eyes
slowly filled with fear.

"Don't," she rasped again. "No matter what. He'll kill you!"

"She won't be so pretty without her face. Shame." Red kissed
the top of her head, and her body shuddered as she felt his grip on
the trigger shifting. "Bye, babe…"

Mark's voice split the air. "No!"

Hesitantly, he lowered his weapon, his shoulders sagging in
defeat. Anguish and apology were written on his features as he
looked at Samantha. She'd known in her heart he wouldn't be able

to watch her die. Tears slipped down her face. He was as good as dead now, too.

"Put the gun on the floor and kick it over. Now."

Mark did as he was told. Only then did Red lower the gun, although he still kept a tight hold on Samantha, his fingers biting into her wrist as he scooped up the other weapon and shoved it into the back of his pants, then moved to snatch up the bag. He jerked Samantha around, jabbing the gun in Mark's direction although his eyes locked on hers. Blood trickled down his cheek from where she'd stabbed him with the pencil. "Who's this cowboy? Is this his house?"

"Don't hurt her," Mark entreated. "My name's Mark St. Clair. Look, I have money. We can work something out."

Red chuckled darkly. "Another pretty boy, huh, Trina? *The St. Clair.* Looks like you traded up real good. Living in the lap of luxury while my brother's rotted in the ground, thanks to you."

"I-I didn't know where Devin hid the diamonds! Please! He doesn't have anything to do with this—" Samantha gasped in pain as Red twisted her wrist hard to silence her. Mark took a step forward.

"Don't you fucking move!" Red pointed the gun at Mark's face. Samantha knew in that instant he would die first. Red would want her to watch.

With a hoarse cry, she tried to wrench herself free, lunging for the gun with her other hand. Samantha shoved wildly at Red's arm to unsteady his aim, to give Mark a chance to take cover. She felt her wrist snap with another vicious twist, the pain nearly making her faint. With a growl, Red threw her off, knocking her into the coffee table. Samantha fell hard, shattering the glass top. When she looked up, both men were struggling for control of the gun. It fired somewhere into the house with another nerve-searing *thwap* and flash of light. Red swung out, striking Mark with his fist and sending him stumbling a step back. He never had a chance to recover. The gun caught him viciously on the temple next.

He crumpled.

A strangled cry escaped her. Bleeding from the broken glass, wrist throbbing, Samantha began crawling like a wounded dog to where Mark lay, but Red already stood over him. Mark appeared conscious but dazed.

Red pointed the silencer's long barrel at Mark's heaving chest, and Samantha felt herself sinking. She would die with him. They would be together. "Hope a piece of ass was worth it, son. You don't mess with anything that belongs to the Learys."

"You don't have the diamonds," Mark panted. "Look…"

Red dug the small bag from his pocket, cursing as his fingers pried at the tight drawstring opening. At the same time, Samantha heard a rising buzz in her ears as she saw the shift of shadows on the other side of the room. From her spot on the floor, she tried not to give away with her eyes that they were no longer the only people in the room. Luther must have come through the service door that led in from the rear courtyard, his entrance masked by the storm's rising force.

Something glimmered dully in the darkness. He gripped a large kitchen knife.

Red's features contorted with rage. "Gravel?"

"I have them, just like I said. The diamonds are here on the property. But you kill either of us, and you'll never—"

Mark flinched, trying to protect himself with his forearm as the bag flew at his face. Red's boot struck him hard in the ribs, then struck him again in a second brutal attack. She wanted to scream at Luther to help him, but Samantha clapped a hand over her mouth, her eyes tearing as he gasped and writhed on the floor.

All the while, Luther crept steadily closer. Red pointed the gun at Mark again.

"Two seconds," he warned, breathing hard. "You're going to tell me where those fucking diamonds are, or I'm going to start with your kneecaps and work my way up to—"

Red whirled, apparently becoming aware of Luther's presence. But before he could fire, Luther threw the knife hard. It sailed through the air, its blade plunging into the center of Red's chest.

Shock passed over Red's face. A second later, his fingers released the gun. He dropped to his knees and then to the floor face-first, the fall shoving the blade more deeply into him with a wet, sickening sound. Samantha's stomach lurched. Luther gripped the wall for support. Sinking down beside Red's body, he landed with a heavy, sodden thud.

The house shuddered in a frenzied gust. Around them the winds roared.

Gina had made landfall.

"Mark," she whispered, panicked when he didn't respond. He lay in a protective position on his side, breathing shallowly but unmoving. He'd passed out. A trickle of blood leaked from his hairline. Gently, she shook his shoulder and brushed his rain-damp hair from his forehead, uncaring of the pain that shot through her wrist, her throat. "Please, Mark. Please wake up!"

He groaned as his eyes slowly fluttered open a few seconds later. Relief flooded through her. "Mark…"

With some effort, he rolled onto his back, grimacing as he held his ribs.

"Don't try to get up, all right?"

"I'm okay," he said, although he sounded weak. He squinted at Red's sprawled form on the floor a few feet away and then at Luther, who gave him a halfhearted smile before leaning his head back against the wall and tiredly closing his eyes. Despite the makeshift bandage, blood trickled down Luther's arm.

"Thank you," Mark uttered to him.

"Couldn't find any police," Luther said. "Town's only got a half-dozen of 'em anyway."

The hurricane shutters rattled like a death knell.

Despite her objections, Mark eased himself up with a painful grunt to sit against the wall, too. His features reflected his own upset as he studied Samantha's face so close to his in the shadows. She shook visibly as his fingers gently touched the swelling on her cheekbone. Looking at her throat, the bloody scratches and deep bruising she knew were there, he cursed softly.

"I'm so sorry, Mark," she murmured, burying her head against his shoulder.

He hushed her, his own voice low and filled with self-recrimination. "I'm the one who's sorry. No one's *ever* going to hurt you again." He swallowed heavily. "Including me."

Samantha pressed into him as much as his injuries would allow, trying to find his warmth as her tears mingled with the wet shirt molded to his solid body. His heart beat under her palm, and she said a prayer of gratitude for it even as, overhead, hard rock-like sounds replaced the driving rain. It had begun to hail, unusual in a hurricane.

"Why are you here, Mark?" She raised her head and said hoarsely, "You're supposed to be in Augusta."

She saw his eyes go to Luther again.

"I called you and never heard back. I couldn't leave without making sure you'd made it out of town. That you were safe." Mark frowned, his fingers covering hers that lay on his chest. "Something kept telling me to check on you. Thank God I did. I found Luther in the storeroom."

When Samantha had taken Mrs. Holtz to the urgent care center, the sign in the exam room had instructed that all cell phones be turned off. She'd forgotten to turn hers back on.

"Road's underwater by now for sure," Luther said. "It was startin' to flood when I came through. We won't make it if we try to get back out tonight."

"Then we'll have to ride it out here," Mark said with determination. Samantha felt his flinch as something large hit the roof. A tree limb? He tightened his hold on her, trying to keep her safe. "But we need to get into the center of the house where there aren't any windows and it's more structurally sound. We'll go to the attic if the waters rise this far."

"Can you stand, Mr. St. Clair?" Luther asked.

Mark wiped at the blood trickling down his temple. "I think so. You?"

"Yeah. Sure could go for some of the hard stuff to take the edge off, though."

"There's a liquor cabinet in my study. Help yourself." Squeezing his eyes briefly closed, he appeared pale in the candlelight. "Bring a couple of bottles back. We could all use a drink."

Unsteadily, Mark eased himself up, using the wall with Samantha helping as best she could, her left wrist stiff and throbbing. His wince as he straightened, his hand pressed to his side, cut through her. They all needed medical attention, but he could be bleeding internally.

She owed both these men her life. Samantha stood beside Mark, a coldness filling her as they looked around the carnage. She had been prepared to die tonight. Instead, Cyril lay dead under the overturned bookcase, Red nearby. His gun was still on the floor by his splayed hand.

"He's dead," Mark assured her. Still, Samantha bent and

timidly took the gun, as well as the one tucked inside the back of his pants.

Fresh tears slipped down her cheeks.

"Hey." Mark gently caught her face in his hands as she returned to him. "We're going to get through this. The storm, too."

She was only able to nod mutely in response.

"And then we're going to get back to our lives. *Together.*"

"I didn't kill Devin," she said through her tears. "Red said—"

"A man named Sergei Boklov did. The Memphis Police know that. That's one of the reasons I've been trying to reach you."

She shook her head, still confused and needing him to believe her. "I didn't steal any diamonds, Mark. I wouldn't—"

He hushed her again as the winds screamed. A sob escaped her that was a mixture of anguish and relief as he pressed his lips to her forehead. She trembled harder, hearing his soft curse as the roof moaned. An odd, greenish light was visible around the shutters' edges that raised the hair on her nape.

"We need to go," Mark said.

Her stomach rancid with fear but her heart grabbing on to hope, Samantha tried not to think about the high winds and rising waters. Instead, she concentrated on the man who cared enough for her to go on a fool's mission to try to save her.

Taking up candles, they followed Luther's path down the hallway, seeking some shelter within the house that might protect them from the storm raging outside.

CHAPTER THIRTY-EIGHT

SAMANTHA AWOKE WITH her head on Mark's chest. Her back was cramped, and she shifted slightly in the tub in the hall bathroom where they'd taken refuge last night. Then she lifted her head completely.

There was no noise, she realized. No pummeling rain or howling winds. The bathroom door remained closed, but a shallow light was visible beneath it. *Morning.* Had the worst of the storm passed? The roof hadn't caved in on them, nor had the waters gotten high enough to flood the house.

Mark.

The candles had melted down to nubs, but in their flickering light, she could see the sable brush of his lashes, his closed eyes. She recalled him holding her through the night, promising her over and over that she was safe as she dealt with the aftershock of Red's violence. Her heart twisted at the ugly bruise marring his temple. Gently, she shook his shoulder, suddenly fearing he hadn't just fallen asleep from exhaustion as she had, but had slipped into unconsciousness. Her worry eased as he roused, appearing disconcerted to be lying in a bathtub with Samantha curled against him.

He rubbed a hand over his face. "God. I must've drifted off."

"We both did." Voice hoarse, she swallowed painfully.

"I don't hear anything outside."

Samantha smoothed his rumpled hair back from his forehead. "How do you feel?"

"It hurts a little to breathe," he admitted, grimacing as he pushed himself up straighter. He frowned, his eyes worried as his fingers traced over her injuries. She was certain they both looked as though they had been through hell and back, but somehow they'd survived.

After all these years, Red was no longer a threat. But dread knotted inside her as she thought of the two dead bodies lying in another room of the house. What they would tell the authorities, she wasn't sure.

Samantha climbed carefully from the tub, her abused body protesting. It took a little longer for Mark to get himself out, and she helped as best she could with her swollen wrist. She'd lifted his shirt last night and examined the mottled bruising on his upper abdomen in the candlelight. He very possibly had a broken rib. As she opened the bathroom door, gray morning light illuminated the paleness of his features.

Samantha followed him down the hall, her breath catching as they reached the entrance to the living room.

"Oh, Mark," she murmured, looking up in dismay at the low, dreary sky overhead. A large section of roof was gone. Drizzle fell into the home's interior as larger droplets clung to loosened shingles before plopping onto sodden furniture. The bay window, including its hurricane shutters, had been ripped away. But the bodies Samantha had feared seeing again were no longer there. Her stomach quivered in surprise.

"The area rug's gone, too. Where's Luther?" Mark asked.

"I don't know," she said uneasily.

Luther had been with them at first, hunkered down on the bathroom floor with a bottle of aged whiskey, his back against the tub as they listened to the mayhem outside. But complaining that he felt caged in and claustrophobic, he'd eventually left to pace the house and keep watch over the encroaching waters.

Going to the front door, Samantha noticed Luther's pickup was missing. She turned as Mark stepped around the overturned bookcase, one hand pressed against his side. Forehead creased with the effort, he bent to retrieve a framed photograph that lay amid household items and tree branches. Samantha went to him and placed a hand sympathetically on his back. The frame's glass was broken, but Shelley's photo remained mostly intact.

His face was still as he held the photo and looked around at the damage to his once-beautiful home. "We made it through. That's all that matters."

After they'd located bottled water and some edible dry goods in the pantry, Samantha spotted Luther walking onto the property. She wondered what had happened to his truck. Mark kept her close as they stepped carefully onto the debris-covered porch to meet him. As he approached, Luther's shaved head glistened, his clothing soaked. At least the fresh gauze Samantha had wrapped around his arm last night appeared relatively clean, with only a small amount of blood leaking through its white.

"Been down the road a piece," he said as they took the steps down to the front lawn. "There's downed limbs and the like, but the water's recedin'. It'll be passable soon enough, unless there's trees over it farther down."

"Luther, where're the bodies?" Mark asked.

"I took care of 'em, Mr. St. Clair. They won't be found."

Samantha stared at him in the slackening mist. He flexed his large, corded biceps, scowling slightly as he tested his wound.

"Luther." She shook her head softly. "You can't do that."

His eyes were gentle as they held hers. "You've been real good to me, Sam. Truth be told, a lot better than most folks 'round here. You deserve to have a good life. Bringing the police in because of those two thugs won't do anything but open up a whole other world of hurt for you."

They had filled in the rest of the story for Luther while they'd ridden out the storm. Samantha felt Mark's hand move against the small of her back.

"He's right," Mark conceded tensely. "If you come clean with the police about who you really are and what happened here last night, they're going to want you to testify against Boklov."

Samantha felt a hard chill, as if Red himself had reanimated in front of her. She didn't know anything about Boklov killing Devin, but she *would* be able to place him in Devin's company on multiple occasions. They had done business dealings together— she'd witnessed the exchanges of money and suspected it was being laundered through the Blue Iris. She still couldn't believe Devin had dared cross Boklov, even if he had set her up as a scapegoat in the event he needed one. Samantha sighed with anxiety, knowing Boklov would put a price on her head if he believed she was any threat to him at all. She'd be in just as much danger as before.

She squinted against the sunlight, trying valiantly to break through the iron-gray morning. Just beyond where they stood, the ocean still tossed roughly, its depths sullen and remarkable in its violent beauty. The sandy beach was a mess, eroded and littered with whatever the waters had pushed onto shore.

"I'm wondering if I want to know what you did with them," Mark said to Luther.

"Probably not." Luther stared off toward the northern side of the peninsula. The St. Clair family owned the south portion of land, but the rest of it was a government-protected wildlife and salt marsh preserve. Luther had once told Samantha that he knew the swamps there like the back of his hand.

"Remember what we talked about yesterday, Mr. St. Clair?" Luther used a muscular forearm to swipe at his perspiring forehead. "About some fools not knowin' how to swim? Must be a commonality—Memphis boys sinkin' like they got an anchor attached to 'em." He raised his big shoulders in a shrug, although the hard glint in his eyes was telling. "Who knows? Maybe one was."

Samantha's skin prickled with the realization of what had really happened to Lenny Cook. "You *knew* about Lenny?"

"Knew what he was trying to do to you," Luther said, a bitter edge to his voice.

Shocked, Samantha stared at him, trying to keep her heart still. "But how...what about the Sea King—"

"Did I ever tell you about my old buddy, Zeke? One of the few friends I've got around here. Two of us were practically raised together. The Sea King might be a run-down rattrap, but it's all his. Zeke took care of the Crown Vic, too—sold it for parts three counties over." Luther looked at Mark. "You don't need to worry about that bloodied rug, either. Soaked it in gasoline from my truck and burned it to ash—the stuff inside their wallets, too. Ain't nobody going to track any of it back here. I also burned the photos they had of Samantha with your sister. They were in the SUV's glove box. Must be the ones Cook sent."

"You've been a busy man," Mark observed without levity.

Luther merely grunted. "Worst of the storm's been gone for

hours now. Idle hands and all that. It's only about a two-mile walk back from the marsh."

Samantha's fingers had tangled with Mark's. She squeezed them, thrown by just how far Luther had gone to protect her. As if Luther could sense her disquiet, he said, "Lenny Cook was a *bad man*, Sam. He was going to hurt you and then, once he had his fill of you, turn you over to Red. I couldn't let that happen." Reaching into his pants pocket, he extracted Mark's cell phone and gave it to him.

"Service is still out, but I'm sure they're workin' on it. Help's gonna be here before too long, especially if your family alerted the police here that you never reached Augusta. You're the prince of this town, Mr. St. Clair. They'll be on their way out to you." Luther paused briefly, surveying the damage to the house. "I'm fig-urin' it's best if I'm not with y'all when the authorities show up. They and me ain't never got along."

"Where're you going?" Mark asked.

Luther nodded to Red and Cyril's Cadillac Escalade. Several branches lay across its dented hood. "Reckon it's drivable. I'm going to take it down the road a bit—at least as far as I can get with the flooding. Thought I might park it behind the Big House, lie low until I see the police pass through. Then I'll head out."

He looked off again toward the marshland. "If anyone finds my truck out there, they'll think the storm got me, and that's fine by me."

Samantha's lips parted in surprise. "You're leaving Rarity Cove?"

"I've been able to save a little money working at the café. It'll maybe get me that plane ticket to Haiti. My aunt's gettin' on in years. I want to meet her before it's too late."

She nodded in understanding, aware of Luther's wanderlust and desire to connect with family.

"That SUV will take me to the Atlanta airport. If the police end up tracking it down, it'll be far from here," Luther said. "I'll take their guns with me and get rid of 'em, too. Already put 'em in the SUV."

Features serious, he focused again on Mark. "If any of this ever comes to light, if someone *does* find the bodies—which I doubt since I made sure the fish would take a likin' to 'em—you put it all on ol' Luther. You tell 'em it was me."

He made a move to the SUV, but Samantha stepped forward, touching his arm and halting him. "Please wait, all right? I...have something for you."

She disappeared inside the house. Samantha returned carrying a cellophane bag containing what looked like dull quartz. Mark had shown it to her earlier. He'd hidden it as a final bargaining chip in the event the confrontation with Red went poorly. She handed it to Luther. "I was hoping you might have some use for these."

His jaw dropped as he peered down at the bag.

"They're uncut and unpolished, but they're worth a lot of money. You can use them to go to some of those places you've talked about."

"Sam, I can't. Like my momma would've said, they got *bad juju* on 'em."

"Then do something *good* with them. Break the spell," she urged quietly.

Luther looked at Mark uncertainly.

"You're going to need some money," Mark reasoned. "Do you know anyone who can sell them, under the radar?"

"I've got some contacts from my time in prison. I suppose they'll know how to handle this. Probably get me a quick passport for a price, too." Luther put the diamonds in his pocket and looked at Samantha with sad eyes. "Well...I guess this is good-bye, then."

She hugged him hard. Then the two men shook hands. With

Mark's arm around her, Samantha watched as Luther cleared the limbs from the SUV's hood and got inside. Starting the engine, he waved once, then backed over the downed branches and rubble in the driveway as he headed out.

Throat tight, Samantha turned to Mark. "How did Luther know about me? Who I really am?"

"Who you *were*." Tucking several strands of wind-whipped dark hair behind her ear, Mark gazed at her with solemn conviction. "You aren't Trina Grissom anymore. You're Samantha Marsh, if that's who you want to be."

She shifted uneasily. "But how'd he know, Mark?"

"Lenny Cook told him. You left his blackmail note in the storeroom at Café Bella. Luther found it and took matters into his own hands."

"I can't believe what he did for me," she murmured, still disconcerted by what she'd learned. But regardless of his hand in Lenny Cook's demise, Luther had most certainly saved her life and Mark's last night. Samantha looked down the road once more, but the SUV was gone now, its rumble a distant echo in her ears. It had taken the same bouncing path through the bushes that she had forged with Red and Cyril in the storm. She'd been so certain then that her life was over. Samantha couldn't help it—she felt a shadow of fear fall over her again. The mist on her skin made her shiver.

"Hey." Mark pressed his lips to her forehead. "It's *over*. You're safe now."

"All these years I thought I killed Devin. I *stabbed* him, Mark. I checked his pulse and couldn't find it—"

"You were scared out of your mind and made a mistake. I had a friend I trust implicitly make some inquiries. The medical examiner's report lists the cause of death as a gunshot wound to the back of the head. You injured him, but you didn't take his life.

Boklov did." Mark swallowed heavily, deep regret visible on his face. "I...made mistakes, too. I should have trusted you instead of condemning you." His voice frayed. "I couldn't handle the truth and I almost lost you because of it."

Samantha touched his face. "You risked *your life* to save me."

"I don't care if it's the right thing or not. I don't want you to reveal yourself to the police." Anger and desperation crept into Mark's expression. "The way Devin Leary abused and exploited you for years. What his brother did to you last night. You've suffered enough. I don't want you risking yourself ever again."

Lungs constricting, Samantha didn't respond. They stared at one another for several charged moments before turning to view the exterior destruction to the bungalow. In addition to the damaged roof, a tree had fallen onto the house. Farther along the shoreline, the roofs of other bungalows that were part of the resort appeared to have sustained similar destruction.

"Let's hope the hotel fared better." Mark released a breath. He looked at his car and the massive tree limb that lay across the shattered windshield, then startled slightly as his phone rang. "Cell coverage is back."

She stood by as he tried to calm down whoever was on the other end of the line.

"I'm still here at the resort," he admitted, running a hand through his hair as he listened to the caller. "I know...I know what I promised, Carter. Look, I got stuck here. It was unavoidable. I couldn't get out last night, but I'm fine."

His blue eyes met Samantha's as he spoke. She could tell by what he *didn't* say that he was letting his family think he'd merely been foolish.

"If you can stop lecturing me for a second, can I ask how my daughter is? Yeah, go get her and put her on."

Samantha moved closer, placing her hand on his forearm as Mark spoke with Emily. It sounded as if the child had remained peacefully oblivious to the worry that had no doubt held Mark's family captive ever since he'd failed to show up in Augusta.

"Samantha's fine, baby," Mark said. "Guess what? She's right here with me. We'll both see you soon."

Mark talked to Olivia and Mercer next, repeating his apologies, then disconnected the phone.

"How bad was it?" Samantha asked carefully.

"Carter's fuming. He had the Augusta authorities alert the local police by radio last night when I didn't show up, but by then the peninsula road was washed out." Mark absently pressed his hand against his side as he spoke. His paleness still concerned her. "To be honest, now that he knows I'm okay, I think he's enjoying being the responsible male in the family for once. He doesn't get much opportunity to rake me over the coals. I'll let him own it for a while."

A sudden thought sent anxiety flickering through her. "Mark, what about Carter? If we decide not to go to the authorities..."

His handsome face grew serious as the breeze lifted his short hair. "He won't expose you."

She wrapped her arms around herself, aware of the return of sea gulls high in the air above them. "Your family must've been terrified when you didn't arrive last night."

"Olivia was pretty upset," he conceded.

"I'm so sorry, Mark."

"She'll be fine. The St. Clairs are a resilient bunch." He stared again at his home. "We're going to have to go through the mess in there and try to find a needle and some thread, though. You probably heard Emily asking about Walton. I don't want her to find out I disemboweled her favorite bear."

Despite his attempt to lighten the mood, Samantha knew the

St. Clair was much more than property to him. She understood what its legacy meant. Mark had invested his time and his heart in it, so much of himself. The hotel was somewhat visible in the distance—still clearly standing—although any damage was indeterminable in the grayness.

He drew her to him, his hands smoothing the wild tangles in her hair. They heard the faint sound of sirens, which stopped altogether eventually. Assistance didn't seem to be moving any closer, but they were on the road, trying to get through.

"We're both pretty beat-up, but we're going to have to make up something to explain the injuries to your throat," Mark told her. "Some freak accident in the storm."

Biting her lip, Samantha bowed her head, overwhelmed. Luther had cleared away any sign of what had really occurred here last night, leaving open the unexpected possibility of their simply having peace.

Mark must have sensed her uncertainty, because he tilted her face up to his with gentle fingers and regarded her with a searching gravity.

"*I love you*," he uttered fiercely. "And I want to spend the rest of my life proving it to you if you'll let me. We deserve a *chance*, Samantha. Give us that."

The breeze that whipped in from the ocean was salty and strong, and a fine mist continued to fall around them. Samantha put her arms around his neck and buried her face against his shoulder.

They were both safe. Tears of thankfulness stung her eyes.

EPILOGUE

Seven Months Later

EACH SPRING BROUGHT with it the first influx of vacationers into the Rarity Cove community. But this year, the season also marked the grand reopening of the St. Clair. While the hurricane damage had been only moderate, Mark had made the decision to close the resort over the fall and winter months so renovations could be fully completed prior to the next tourist spike.

It had also given him time to spend with his new wife.

From his vantage point inside the hotel, he admired the work of master carpenters who had repaired the flood and wind damage and rebuilt the rear veranda. They had also replaced the shattered windows and domed, stained-glass skylight that was the focal point of the lobby. Things seemed to have almost returned to normal as staff worked to check in the inaugural wave of guests. Mark looked out through the tall, arched windows onto the Atlantic, his attention briefly captured by a schooner gliding gracefully past with sails whipping in the ocean breeze. His gaze returned to the lobby, however, as excitement rippled through the crowd.

Carter had apparently arrived.

Mark approached the throng surrounding his brother, waiting on the periphery as he autographed materials thrust at him and patiently posed for photos taken by media that had traveled over from Charleston. There would also be interviews that afternoon. Carter had gotten his wish. He'd left the soap after the network pilot he had shot was picked up, after all, as a midseason replacement. The drama about an urban hospital and its surgeons had become an overnight hit. Carter had recently been on the cover of both *TV Guide* and *Entertainment Weekly*, and there was buzz about a possible Emmy nomination. Mark had asked him to come down for the reopening. He'd counted on his presence, in fact, to help generate publicity.

Carter's return home last summer and the events that followed had finally begun a healing process between them. Mark felt closer to him than he had in a very long time, although discounting television, he'd seen him only once since then, when he had flown in to serve as best man at his and Samantha's private, family-only wedding ceremony on the beach, which had taken place on a mild fall afternoon in mid-October.

Despite his rising fame, Carter appeared low-key, dressed in slacks and a long-sleeved shirt.

"Mark," Carter called when he saw him. He signed one last autograph before excusing himself, then walked over and embraced Mark with a warm backslap.

"Thanks for coming. I know you're in the middle of filming."

"I wouldn't miss it." Carter looked airbrushed handsome as usual, but also tired. Mark could only imagine how insane his life had been for the last several months, between shooting on location and flying around the country for promotional junkets for the show. The part had also required him to relocate to California.

Carter clipped his sunglasses onto his shirt pocket. "I have to head back Sunday afternoon. I'm on set early Monday, but you've got me until then."

In conjunction with the reopening, the hotel was hosting a fundraiser for a Charleston non-profit that night. A trip to LA that included dinner with Carter was being offered as the silent auction's headlining item.

Mark clasped his brother's shoulder, directing him toward his office, where they would have privacy to talk. Once the door had closed behind them, Carter dropped into one of the wing chairs, stretching his long legs out in front of him.

"How's Samantha?" he asked.

"She's starting to get tired." Even now, Mark felt his heart lift, thinking of the surprise pregnancy that had led to their quickly planned nuptials. He blamed the outdated condoms from his nightstand, but the truth was, he wouldn't change a thing. "She's had to slow down, and it's driving her crazy. She's also gotten the impression that she's starting to look like she swallowed a beach ball."

Carter smiled at the image. "Does she?"

"A little," Mark admitted. "But she's still beautiful."

"I can't wait to see her."

Like Mark, Carter had kept Samantha's troubled past a secret. He knew almost everything, with the exception of the events the night of the hurricane that had resulted in the deaths of Cyril O'Keefe and Red Leary. That was a burden Mark and Samantha shared alone, along with Luther, wherever he was.

"The place looks great with the updates—better than ever," Carter said.

Mark nodded his thanks. He'd taken a seat on the edge of his desk. "So how's *your* life, little brother?"

"Hectic." He lifted his broad shoulders in a shrug. "But I can't complain, so I won't."

Still, there was something subdued about him, something that had changed. Mark wondered if stardom had panned out as Carter had hoped. Regardless, Mark felt pride. Carter played the role of Dr. Gabriel Hammond on *The Healers* with a mix of compassion, intelligence and smartassed humor that was endearing. The critical reviews for the show had been positive, and Carter had been hailed as the standout new star among the cast.

"I've been offered a movie role," Carter confided. Restless, he got up and went to look out the large window at the pool area and beyond it, the ocean. "I'm on contract with the network, but the producers are willing to shoot while I'm on hiatus. They loved my screen test. My agent says if I want the part, it's mine."

He named the director and other actors—two Academy Award winners among them—who were attached to the film. Mark was impressed.

"Just stay grounded, Carter."

He turned and gave his trademark dazzling smile. "If I don't, I'm sure you'll be happy to bring me back down to earth."

Mark walked to him. Nostalgia filtered through him as he recalled the two of them as children, playing along the shore, sailing, trying to one-up each other during endless summer days. There had always been an air of competition between them, but Mark believed that was over. "I'm proud of you, Carter. I want you to know that. You deserve every success."

Carter met his gaze, his midnight-blue eyes showing his appreciation. Then they grew somber. "Is she safe, Mark?"

No one had shown up asking questions—no police or federal

agents, no other members of Memphis's underworld. Months ago, the news reported that Lenny Cook *had* been identified as the accidental drowning victim from the Charleston canal. The Memphis Police had traced his credit card transactions to the area after his ex-wife reported him missing. But nothing more had come of it. The matter seemed closed.

With regard to Leary and O'Keefe, Mark had learned online that the Cadillac Escalade had indeed been discovered at the airport in Atlanta. Speculation was that Leary had fled the country due to a pending indictment for racketeering. Mark had finally begun to breathe easier now that Samantha's nightmare might really be over. Even his attorney friend Todd Hamilton had advised against her voluntarily coming forward. *Let sleeping dogs lie*, he'd counseled, off the record. The unplanned pregnancy had finalized their decision. Samantha had Mark's child growing inside her. That put another innocent life at stake.

"As long as the FBI and Memphis Police don't know about her, she's safe," he said. "She can't be compelled to testify. Which means Sergei Boklov won't come after her."

"And if that ever changes?"

Mark's stomach hardened. "Then we'll deal with it."

Carter nodded thoughtfully before shifting their conversation to lighter fare. "You know, as best man, I still owe you a party."

"Forget it."

"C'mon. Mercer's in town throwing the baby shower," Carter persisted. "Jonathan's here with her, and he and I are going to take you out for a few drinks after the whole auction to-do tonight. Nothing extreme—just to celebrate the hotel's reopening and *other things*, like the baby. New beginnings. Think of it as a bonding ritual between the men in the family."

Mark raised a stern eyebrow. "The cradle-robbing professor's part of the family now?"

"He might as well be."

He sighed in agreement. The truth was, Mark *did* like Jonathan, despite the substantial age difference between him and Mercer. He seemed like a good man. Once the drama surrounding the hurricane had settled, Mercer had moved back to Atlanta. She and Jonathan were living together in his rambling old Victorian just off the college campus—over Olivia's staunch objections. Mercer had taken a job handling public relations for a downtown artists' collective.

"Charleston, baby—be ready at ten sharp." Carter headed toward the office door. "And we're using the limo service so none of us is driving."

Once he was gone, Mark sat behind his desk, smiling faintly even as he shook his head in resignation. Fighting Carter was like battling a force of nature, and he knew from experience it was better to just give in and go along for the ride. A photo of Samantha, her arm around Emily's shoulders, sat in a silver frame across from him. He picked it up, regarding it with the eyes of a husband and father.

He felt genuinely blessed for the second time in his life.

≋

"I felt it!" Emily let out a squeal of laughter, her hands planted on Samantha's round belly. "Do it again!"

"She can't just do it on command, Em." Mercer sat cross-legged on the floor, working on the posh gift bags for the women invited to the baby shower. "Besides, Sam's not doing it. That's your baby brother kicking in there."

Samantha slipped her fingers through Emily's blond hair, marveling at the way her curls danced when she let them go. Her other hand rested on top of her stomach, and her swollen ankles were propped on the ottoman in the newly renovated seaside bungalow. She smiled as Emily put her ear next to her belly, listening.

"They say you can hear the ocean in there," Mercer commented glibly.

"I really don't know about this shower, Mercer. It's not like I know that many people."

"Well, I do, and so does Mom. And believe me, everyone knows who *you* are. You're the wife of Mark St. Clair and owner of the very successful Café Bella. The women around here are thrilled you're married now and knocked up, to boot. It makes it less likely their husbands will be ogling you."

"What's *ogling*?" Emily asked, her lisp only barely detectible now. Although she hadn't started kindergarten with her friends, her sessions with the psychiatrist had been expanded to include a speech therapist, and her diction and vocabulary were improving daily. With home tutoring, the plan was for her to start first grade in the fall.

"Staring, sweet pea," Samantha told her. She rolled her eyes at Mercer. "And no one is staring at me right now."

"Daddy stares at you." Emily grinned, revealing a missing front tooth. Samantha tweaked her nose, making her giggle.

A knock sounded at the door. Olivia entered, dressed to the nines in a straight linen skirt and white blouse, her ever-present double strand of pearls around her neck. Although Samantha and Mark's mother had been living in a relatively neutral peace, there still seemed to be *things unsaid* between them. Samantha knew Olivia had bristled at Mark's announcement that they were getting married. But she also suspected he'd made it clear that she would have to accept her new daughter-in-law or risk losing her son.

Admittedly, however, Olivia had seemed pleased at the news

of her pregnancy, something Samantha and Mark had kept quiet until she was several months along. She had been surprised as well as touched to learn that Olivia had insisted on co-hosting the baby shower. But between her and Mercer, the shower had grown to nearly ballroom-sized proportions and was taking place just prior to the silent auction.

"I came by to have a word with you," Olivia said to Samantha. "Just the two of us."

Mercer appeared to have gone a little pale. She looked worriedly at Samantha, then got to her feet. "Come on, Emily. Let's go outside for a while. You can help me water the azaleas. Then maybe we'll take a walk on the beach."

Olivia patted her granddaughter's head as she skipped past. "Mercer, put a hat on that child. She's got my fair complexion, and she's going to turn out as freckled as a turkey's egg."

She waited like an imperial queen while Mercer located a floppy beach hat from the foyer closet and plunked it on Emily's head. Samantha felt her heartbeat quicken as the door closed behind them, leaving her alone with Olivia.

"How are you feeling, dear?"

"A little tired."

Olivia sighed. "I remember being pregnant with Mark. I was as big as a house and didn't want to do a thing but sleep. With Carter, that wasn't possible since I already had a toddler to chase around."

"Thank you for giving me the shower, Olivia," Samantha said sincerely. "I'll be rested up by its start, I promise. I left the café at noon to get off my feet."

"You need to stop working."

"I *have* cut back. And I've hired a manager who starts next week." If Luther had been here, the position would have gone to him. Thinking of him, Samantha felt her heart tug, recalling what

she'd received in the mail a few months ago. There had been no
return address on the envelope, but inside it had been a newspaper
clipping written in French. Mark had been able to translate it for
her. It had been about a very large, anonymous donation made to
a Haitian orphanage. The envelope's postmark was Port-Au-Prince.

"It's nice your business is doing so well. But normally, I'd say
something old-fashioned like St. Clair women don't work." Olivia
frowned as she repositioned her Louis Vuitton purse in her lap.
"Of course, Mercer's already disproved that, but *she* doesn't have
children yet. She's not even married…"

Samantha expected another complaint about Mercer *shack-
ing up* or *living in sin*, but Olivia let the opportunity drift away.
Samantha decided to face the speeding train head on.

"You wanted to talk to me?" she asked.

With manicured fingernails, Olivia unlatched the clasp on
her purse. She pulled out a small, elegantly wrapped box and presented it to Samantha. "I wanted to give you this."

"The shower's in just a few hours—"

"This isn't for the baby. It's for you."

Hesitantly, Samantha accepted the box. Eyeing Olivia curiously, she unwrapped the gift. Seeing what was inside, she felt a
lump form in her throat. Her lips parted, her heart beating dully
as she stared at the cameo that had belonged to her mother. The
hairline crack in the conch shell had been repaired, its tarnished
frame replaced with gleaming white gold. It now hung from a delicate, expensive-looking chain.

"I hope you don't mind." Olivia sounded a little nervous.
"Mark gave it to me. I wanted to do something special to make up
for my, as he put it, snobbish behavior toward you. I took it to my
estate jeweler. I understand it has sentimental value. Mark told me
you lost your mother when you were very young. Like Emily did."

Samantha simply nodded, unable to speak. The cameo blurred a bit in front of her eyes, and she silently cursed her raging pregnancy hormones.

Olivia's hands twisted in her lap. "You should know...I had quite a hissy fit when Mark told me he intended to marry you. He took me to task for my behavior."

"Olivia..."

"My son's right. I am a snob," she acknowledged, her clear-blue gaze unwavering. "And it's true that you're not the woman I would've picked for him. But you *are* the woman he chose, Samantha. And I can see that you've made him happier than I ever thought he could be again. Emily's happy, too, and doing so well. I thank you for that."

Her hand moved tentatively to touch Samantha's stomach. She smiled softly. "You're also the mother to my very first grandson."

"Thank you, Olivia," Samantha whispered, a tremor in her voice.

Just then, the door opened, and Mark appeared on its threshold. He frowned as his gaze moved between his tearful wife and his mother.

"Oh, just calm down, Mark," Olivia said. "Despite how this must look to you, I'm not here to terrorize anyone. I just came by for a chat and to see if Mercer got around to finishing the gift bags. She insisted on doing them herself."

She looked at Samantha once more and then got up to kiss Mark's cheek. "Have fun tonight, darling. I hear Carter and Jonathan are taking you out."

"Are you okay?" Mark asked once Olivia had made her way out of the house.

Samantha nodded mutely. He looked at the box she held. "I

see she gave you her gift. I hope you're not upset that I let her restore it."

"It's beautiful," Samantha said, wiping at a tear that had escaped down her cheek. She began to push herself up from the couch, and Mark came over to assist her.

"Would you help me put it on?"

Mark took the chain and stood behind Samantha to fasten it. When he was done, she turned to him.

"What's wrong?" he asked, seeing her face.

"What Olivia did was incredibly thoughtful and kind." Worriedly, she shook her head. "Mark, if the truth about me ever comes out—"

He laid a finger against her lips, hushing her.

"It won't," he said quietly. "And even if it does, she'll handle it. *Just like we will.* I've told her you've had a rough life. I just didn't go into unnecessary details. Mom isn't as obstinate as she acts, especially where family's concerned. And that's what you are now. *Family.*"

His words soothed her, as did his hands stroking over her hair. "Besides," he added, "She's over the moon about the baby. You could knock over a package store and kick two puppies on your way out, and she'd probably look the other way."

"You can't keep me pregnant for the rest of my life."

"Is that a challenge?" Mark smiled softly and slipped his arms around her. Laying her palms against his chest, she gazed up at him, her heart filling.

"I love you more than I ever imagined possible," he murmured, his expression fading into seriousness. "And I thank God for you every day."

Each day, it seemed her love deepened for him, as well.

Samantha felt her pulse beat hard at the base of her throat. "You gave me a new life. You *are* my life, Mark."

His kiss was slow and gentle, the touch of his lips sweet against hers.

In Mark's arms she had found her safe harbor. And she was Samantha *St. Clair* now, something that still seemed like some kind of impossible daydream. She had a caring, handsome husband and a wonderful family that would soon expand to include a precious new baby. Samantha wanted Mark's child more than life itself.

As he held her, her head on his shoulder, she thought of her tattoo, the last physical evidence of Trina's existence. One day she might finally have it removed. But Mark had suggested the butterfly was proof something beautiful could emerge from a dark and difficult passage. She wanted to believe her life *before* had been her chrysalis, and she had broken free.

Even if by some twist of fate the truth of her past ever did come to light, she also knew that she and Mark would face it together. Whatever it meant. They had each other now. There were no more secrets between them. Samantha steeled herself in his strength, his protection and abiding love.

I belong.

Those words meant everything to her. With Mark, here in this small coastal town, she had finally found home.

ACKNOWLEDGMENTS

Thank you sincerely for taking the time to read BEFORE THE STORM. As always, my readers are the reason I write and I'm so appreciative of your ongoing enthusiasm and support.

I am also grateful for the work of Joyce Lamb, who edited this book, and for critique partners Michelle Muto and Kelly Stone. Thanks also to my agent, Stephany Evans of FinePrint Literary Management.

Finally, thank you to my husband, Robert, for your unending patience, love and companionship.

Other Works by Leslie Tentler

Midnight Caller
Midnight Fear
Edge of Midnight
Fallen

ABOUT THE AUTHOR

Leslie Tentler is also the author of FALLEN as well as the Chasing Evil Trilogy (MIDNIGHT CALLER, MIDNIGHT FEAR and EDGE OF MIDNIGHT). She was a finalist for Best First Novel at ThrillerFest 2012, and is a two-time finalist for the Daphne du Maurier Award for Excellence in Mystery and Suspense. She is also the recipient of the prestigious Maggie Award of Excellence.

Leslie is a member of Romance Writers of America, International Thriller Writers, and Novelists, Inc. A native of East Tennessee, she currently resides in Atlanta.

If you enjoyed reading Leslie's work, please consider leaving a review, however short. Of course, simply telling others you enjoyed this book is also sincerely appreciated. Word of mouth is the best promotion.

Visit Leslie and sign up for her newsletter at

www.LeslieTentler.com.

CPSIA information can be obtained at www.ICGtesting.com
Printed in the USA
LVOW10s1815220616

493670LV00007B/651/P